CONNIE MASON

WINNER OF THE *ROMANTIC TIMES* STORYTELLER OF THE YEAR AWARD!

"Connie Mason writes the stuff fantasies are made of!"
—*Romantic Times*

VOW OF HATE— PLEDGE OF LOVE

Without volition, Tony drew the quaking girl into his arms, at first wishing only to soothe and quiet her so he could go to sleep. Instinctively Amanda cuddled into his warmth, finding a semblance of relief in the low sounds of comfort he was making deep in his throat. Little by little she began to relax, forgetting for the moment that this was the man she vowed to hate, savoring the only tenderness she had known since her mother's death.

If Amanda was comforted by their intimate contact, Tony was intensely aroused. The small, warm body curled so trustingly into his was creating a riot of emotion in his hardening body. With a life of their own his hands sought and found her....

CONNIE MASON

Caress and Conquer

LEISURE BOOKS ▙ NEW YORK CITY

To Frank and Francis Roti,
the greatest parents in the world.

To Jerry,
husband, friend, lover,
the best possible.

To Jeri Ann, Michelle, Mark, Beth, Paula, Joey,
Matthew and James,
my children and grandchildren who give my life
meaning.

A LEISURE BOOK®

November 1993

Published by

Dorchester Publishing Co., Inc.
276 Fifth Avenue
New York, NY 10001

PROLOGUE

LONDON
1759

Amanda pulled her servicable brown wool cloak tighter about her slender shoulders and shivered uncontrollably as thick clouds of dense, gray fog swirled specter-like about landmarks she was totally unfamiliar with. It seemed like hours since she had left the cozy warmth of the kitchen hearth to purchase a length of lace that her mother needed to complete a ballgown for Lady Linley, whose patronage would keep them from starvation's door and debtor's prison. Amanda's mother, Nora Prescott, provided their only source of livelihood by plying her needle diligently with dexterity and imagination. If Lady Linley's gown was ready on the morrow as promised and she was well-pleased wih Nora's efforts, she would likely spread the word to her influential and rich friends. Better paying customers meant an easier life for Nora and Amanda.

Amanda, nearly sixteen, daughter of Jonathon Prescott, professor, dead these four long years, and Nora, a lady of poor but gentle birth, lately turned seamstress, realized the importance of the length of lace she clutched in her frozen fingers. Seamstresses were plentiful in London in the year 1759 and it was a continual struggle to provide their meager fare and keep a fire in their hearth on cold nights. Ever since Amanda's father died unexpectedly, she and her mother were forced by reduced circumstances to move from their cozy cottage on the outskirts of London to a mean two room dwelling at the edge of London's slums where Nora earned their keep by sewing for the middle class matrons.

Lady Linley was the first really important customer to come Nora's way in the four years since she had been obliged to provide for herself and her daughter. Due to a slight miscalculation Nora found herself a length short of a particular beige lace found only in a certain shop on Theadneedle Street. At first Nora was reluctant to allow Amanda to venture out at a time when most decent young women were safely behind closed doors and only street walkers and pickpockets roamed the dark lanes and alleyways.

But Amanda, always a little too adventuresome and spirited to suit her mother, would not hear of her mother going for the lace when she was perfectly capable of performing the errand herself. Besides, Nora still had a few hours labor left on the dress before morning.

Amanda had little difficulty in locating the lace merchant's shop or in procuring the lace she required, but when she left the shop to return home she found herself surrounded by a thick, chilling fog that rolled in unexpectedly from the waterfront covering the city like a silent, gray shroud. Although fairly familiar with the streets in this section of the city, Amanda had become disoriented and taken a wrong turn along the way, and was now hopelessly lost. That she was near the waterfront was evident by the tangy, saltwater spray that clung to her cloak and chilled her bones. And now she was frightened. Not only for herself but also for her mother, who without the lace would be unable to complete Lady Linley's gown within the prescribed time.

Suddenly a break in the mists ahead enabled Amanda to focus on a faint light shimmering in the darkness, heralding either an inn or a shop still open, where she could ask directions. Luckily for her she had not been molested by drunken seamen nor accosted by pickpockets. She supposed none but the most hardy would venture out on a night such as this. Gathering her courage, Amanda headed resolutely in the direction of the light, praying desperately to find a kindly soul willing to help a poor girl in distress.

As Amanda made her way toward the distant light and her hoped-for safety, three well-dressed young men of quality stood before the entrance of the *Gull and Swan*, a better than average waterfront inn and common house; the light from the window a welcoming beacon in the encompassing gloom.

Francis Landry, son and heir of the Duke of Attabury; James Driscoll, second son of the Earl of Winchester and Harry Windom, heir to the dukedom of Herefordshire, calmly surveyed the patrons of the crowded inn through the none-too-clean window.

"Do you see him, Harry?" asked James, who was somewhat nearsighted and had trouble focusing on the subject in question.

"Over there, by the fireplace," nodded Harry, pointing out the direction with his tousled head of blond curls. Immediately three pair of eyes swung toward the sprawling figure of a tall, rawboned young aristocrat whose slightly disheveled raiment and ruddy coloring suggested one well into his cups.

"Zounds!" remarked Francis, smiling indulgently, for at thirty he was the older of the four friends inseparable since boyhood. "Looks like old Tony is making the most of his last night in London. Did you note the way that barmaid is ogling our young friend?"

"Leave it to Tony," laughed James wryly. "He has a knack of attracting fair maidens without even trying. He can't help it with those rakish good looks and devil-may-care manner."

"I'll wager that barmaid is no maiden," grinned Francis wolfishly.

"No wager there," answered James in a droll voice.

"Well, chaps, shall we go in and give Tony a rousing send-off he's not likely to forget for a long time to come?" asked Francis. "It's a nasty night and that fire looks too inviting to ignore."

"Let's really make this a memorable night for old Tony," piped Harry, his handsome face alight with devilment as a grand adventure began to form in his fertile mind.

"What do you have in mind?" asked James skeptically. "From the looks of our friend I doubt he'll be on his feet much longer. Remember, his ship sails for the colonies on the morning tide. He'd never forgive us if it sailed without him."

"I propose we find the youngest, most

beautiful prostitute in all of London Town this night and present her to Tony with our compliments," suggested Harry mischievously. "After all, it will be a long time, if ever, that we see him again and we owe him that much for all his years of loyalty."

"And just where do you propose to find such a paragon of youth and beauty on a night such as this?" scoffed the more practical Francis.

"We can do it," chimed in Harry, caught up in the excitement of James' spur of the moment venture. "One of us can go inside and entertain Tony and try to keep him from becoming any more drunk while the other two scour the vicinity for just the right woman. He's spending the night at the *Gull and Swan* and we can sneak her up the back stairs and tuck her in Tony's bed. Imagine his surprise when he finds his bed warmed by a beautiful, experienced whore."

"Won't be the first woman of experience or otherwise our friend Tony has had in his bed," reminded Francis, his tone suggesting countless nights spent in whoring and debauchery.

"True," grinned James, nodding vigorously, calling to mind some of their more amorous escapades, "but we intend to find Tony a woman to surpass all women."

"Well, have at it friends," intoned Francis dryly. "I'll attempt to keep Tony reasonably sober so he can enjoy the fruits of your labor." Without another word he turned from the window and entered the warmth of the inn leaving his two friends to carry out their deviltry.

As fate would have it, it was at that precise moment that Amanda happened onto the two high-spirited young men. In fact, they could not have missed her passing if they tried, for she blindly stumbled into them out of the fog, clutching at Harry's coat to keep herself from falling. In so doing, her hood fell away and a riot of rich auburn curls spilled about a delicate heart shaped face from which large green eyes, thickly fringed with dark, feathery lashes blinked at the two men with something akin to shock.

"My God!" breathed Harry reverently as he caught the young girl's slim shoulders to keep her from falling. "Call it fate, call it a gift from the Gods, but I believe this little angel is meant for Tony. What say you, James?"

James could only stare at the apparition before him. She had materialized from out of the fog as if on cue and seemed fashioned for but one purpose. "I've never encountered a street walker of her caliber before," he whispered, awestruck. He gazed longingly at the wide, green eyes, small, slightly upturned nose, full, trembling lower lip and skin as smooth as satin. "It's a shame to waste her on Tony who is likely to be too drunk to appreciate this delicious morsel."

"Where is your sense of loyalty," remonstrated Harry. "Tonight we pay back Tony for all he's done for us during our long friendship. This little filly will sober him up quick enough once she has him in bed."

Amanda listened to their verbal exchange with a growing sense of horror. Instinctively she sensed no malice in their treatment of her but it was obvious they mistook her for something she was not. She was certain that once she identified herself and explained her circumstances they would not only apologize but see her safely home for they were obviously men of breeding.

But before she could open her mouth the man called Harry who held her alarmingly close, spoke, "How much, Mistress?" he asked bluntly, arching his fine, blond eyebrows.

"Oh, no sir!" began Amanda vehemently, "you are mistaken. I am not . . ."

"Come now, Mistress," interrupted James, seeing her feeble protests as a means of securing the highest price possible for her favors, "you are not dealing with untried boys. We are well aware of what you earn and are willing to pay generously for your services this night. Not for ourselves, you understand," he added magnanimously, "but for our friend who is leaving on the morning tide for the wilds of the new world."

"Please, sirs," begged Amanda, wide-eyed with fright, "if you'd only listen."

Suddenly the door to the inn swung open and Francis stepped out, breathing a sigh of relief when he spied his fellow conspirators with one of the loveliest women he had ever seen, despite the fact that she had yet to reach full-blown womanhood.

"Zounds!" he exclaimed appreciatively as his eyes roamed freely over the girl struggling in Harry's arms. "I don't know where you found her on such short notice but it is none too soon. Get her upstairs to Tony's room before he's too far gone to enjoy her." He thrust a key into James' hand, ventured a covetous glance at Amanda's unspoiled beauty and made his way back inside the inn.

Before Amanda could react she found herself being bodily dragged through a narrow alley toward the back of the *Gull and Swan*. A scream of protest rose in her throat but was quickly stifled by a gentle but firm hand across her mouth.

"Quiet, Mistress," warned Harry, oblivious to Amanda's distress as he chuckled over Tony's surprise and gratitude when he discovered their parting gift in his bed. "If someone finds out what we're about there are bound to be others in line to share your favors and Tony would not like that at all."

Amanda shuddered, rapidly losing heart as she realized how slim were her chances for escape. It seemed that her entire fate rested with a man named Tony who intended to use her as he would a paid prostitute!

All too soon Amanda found herself alone in a sparsely furnished room with the two men named Harry and James. She fervently prayed that they, too, didn't intend to use her vilely as she shrank away from their hands, which were clutching and tearing at her clothing.

"Undress, Mistress, and slide between the covers," ordered James, happily anticipating the sight of the girl's lush charms revealed in all their nudity.

"No!" protested Amanda violently, still bent upon explaining their obvious mistake. "My name is Amanda Prescott and I'm . . ."

Once more she was forestalled by a hand upon her mouth. "I'm sorry, Amanda, but I thought I heard Tony coming up the stairs and I don't want him to find us here."

Once more his hands were upon the fastenings of her dress. "Let me help you with these," he said by way of explanation. And then there were four fumbling hands divesting her of every stitch of clothing until she stood blushingly nude before the two gaping young men unaccustomed to gazing upon such a multitude of beauty and charm.

Finally finding her voice, Amanda, thoroughly outraged, screamed. But as luck would have it the sound did not carry to the noisy common room where boisterous revelry was in progress.

"Why did you do that?" queried a puzzled Harry. "I told you we would pay you well. There's no cause for you to raise a ruckus." So saying he pulled a gold coin from the pocket of his lemon-yellow, satin waistcoat and tossed it carelessly at Amanda's feet.

As if mesmerized by the glittering coin, Amanda watched it arch high in the air and hit the floor, rolling to a stop at her bare feet. She lifted her eyes just as the door to the room closed firmly behind the two departing figures. The loud click of the key turning in the lock sent chills of apprehension up and down her spine. Frantically she searched the small room for her clothing and cried aloud when she found them gone, along with Harry and James, she supposed unhappily.

Nothing in Amanda's sheltered life had prepared her for such a situation. To be found naked in a man's room would brand her a whore. But to submit willingly was abhorrent to her. Was there no honorable way out of this predicament? she silently lamented. Her first thought was to cover her nudity as she pulled the counterpane from the bed and wrapped it mummy-like around her slim form. Decently covered, she gathered her courage and began to beat and kick upon the locked door, calling loudly for help . . . to no avail. If anyone at all heard, they chose to ignore her. Finally, discouraged and hoarse from yelling, Amanda threw herself upon the bed and gave in to the hysteria that had been slowly building within her small body. Her last conscious thought before exhaustion claimed her was for her poor mother, by now sick with worry over her only child who failed to return home with the bit of lace so vital to their livelihood.

Tony Brandt, second son of the Duke of Briarwood, slowly and carefully picked his way up the dimly lit stairway to his room. Thanks to his friends his last night on his native soil had not been as lonely as he had originally anticipated. Not only had the evening been a gay, carefree farewell to all he had ever known and loved, it also proved to him how right his decision was to leave.

Here in England he had nothing to look forward to but living off the largesse of his wealthy family. His older brother would inherit the title and nearly all of the riches, including the family estate outside London. Of course, Richard would never turn him out and his life would not change from what it now was. In time he would take an eminently suitable bride and continue in much the same manner, supported by a generous legacy from his mother. But Tony, too proud to subsist in such a manner, wanted more, much more out of life.

Continuing along the hallway to his room, Tony's lean, handsome face clouded in anguish at the thought of all he was giving up for honor and pride, for he could not in all honesty continue living on the bounty of his generous family. At twenty-six Tony was off to the colonies, to Charles Town to be exact, where he owned a large tract of land purchased from the crown with the bulk of his legacy. A loan from his father would enable him to build his house and purchase slaves necessary to work his land. It was a challenge, but one which Tony eagerly anticipated.

Tony paused at his door, his befuddled mind puzzled over the fact that his key was fitted firmly into the lock instead of in his pocket. He couldn't even hazard a guess as to how it had gotten there. His head was too fuzzy to think, in any event. He knew he had imbibed far more freely than was his custom, but the voyage to the colonies would be a long one and somehow he was far gone in his cups before he realized what was happening.

The room was pitch black when he entered and Tony fumbled about clumsily until he found and lit the candle on the night table, its dim glow casting dancing shadows upon the walls. Reeling slightly, he quickly undressed, lifted the counterpane and crawled into bed. Almost immediately he came into contact with a fragrant softness that both startled and entranced him at the same time.

Moving his hand cautiously he encountered a small but well-formed mound that could only be a woman's breast. He lingered a moment, fingering the nipple until it stiffened against his palm. Reluctantly abandoning his new-found treasure Tony moved his hand downward over a taut, slightly concave stomach and gently swelling hips before finally coming to rest at a soft, warm place nestled between satiny thighs. Despite his inebriated state Tony instinctively knew his enchanting bedmate was not the pretty barmaid whose slightly overblown charms he had been ogling all evening. His body reacted violently to the sweetly curved body sleeping so trustingly in his bed.

Eager to cast his eyes upon the luscious body he had been exploring, Tony gently turned the sleeping girl toward him. As he did so, Amanda awoke with a start to find herself being handled intimately by a strange man whose face she could barely make out in the flickering candlelight. It took her a moment to remember where she was and when she did, she was seized by an uncontrollable urge to scream and run unclothed from the room before something too horrible to contemplate happened to her. Hiding her face in embarrassment, Amanda called out the names of the two men who had abducted her; for they were on the tip of her tongue when she could think of no other.

A low chuckle answered her soft cries, followed by a slightly slurred voice saying, "Ah, I should have guessed what my friends were up to. Well, my lovely, no sense wasting a gift well meant." So saying, he drew the quaking girl into the circle of his strong arms, savoring the satiny smoothness of her young flesh against his own nude body. "But where did they find such a delectable lass?" he asked wonderingly.

Before Amanda could blurt out the truth and explain her presence in his bed, Tony's mouth crashed down on hers in a savage kiss that left her struggling for breath. Completely innocent in the ways of men, Amanda panicked when Tony's tongue forced her mouth open to feed upon the sweetness within. With his muscular body pinning her to the matress, Amanda had little or no hope of escape. Not only was his mouth ravaging hers but his hands invaded the very core of her womanhood, turning her insides into the consistency of jelly despite her fear and disgust. Never had she been subjected to such intimate abuse! Never had she thought such feelings possible; base feelings that this man whom she surmised to be the mysterious Tony was forcing from her tortured body. She was being plunged into sensations she wasn't prepared for.

Suddenly she stiffened as a sharp pain rent her body and only Tony's mouth covering hers kept her from screaming aloud. His body began thrusting in and out of her tight warmth, and just when Amanda thought she could bear no more the pain eased, to be replaced by a tingling sensation that soon gave way to a burst of fire that spread from her loins through every part of her body as Tony's rhythm increased and his breath became ragged. But before the beginnings of passion could blossom into full-blown ecstasy, Tony quickened his pace until his body grew tense, shuddered, and exploded with the force of his climax.

When he rolled off her, Amanda felt strangely let down, as if there should be something more to compensate for all that pain. His even breathing told her that her ravisher had fallen asleep almost immediately after slaking his lust on her unwilling flesh, his sinewy arm holding her prisoner.

It was nearly dawn when Amanda again awoke. The candle still flickered on the night stand enabling her to study the features of the man sleeping beside her at will. His dark, hawk-like features reminded her of the pirates she had once read about in one of her father's books. Hair dark as a raven's wing, worn long, unpowdered and clubbed in the back framed a face harboring a generous mouth and thickly lashed eyes now closed in slumber, under black eyebrows that nearly met in the center of his brow. Despite the boyish look in slumber, his face had a ruthless quality to it that made Amanda shudder. It was a face she was not likely to forget. Suddenly the candle extinguished with a sputter, putting an end to her scrutiny.

Tony opened his eyes just as the candle died out but the light had been enough to catch a glimpse of rich, auburn hair and smooth, creamy skin. Although fleeting, it had been enough to rekindle and inflame his senses once again, sending a burning brand through his loins. Tony never thought he could desire a whore as he did the one he had possessed only a few short hours ago. She was either very new at the profession or very experienced. Her timid response to his love-making was reminiscent of one newly awakened to the game of love. If he didn't know better he could have sworn his entry had been impeded by her maidenhead, but then everyone knew whores possessed ways and means to feign innocence, and this one was obviously one of the best.

Unable to deny his urgent need, Tony reached for the warm flesh at his fingertips and pulled the girl's resisting body atop his hardening maleness. His mouth searched for and found an erect nipple as his hands plundered the curves and crevices of her body. Amanda moaned, scarcely aware of the sound as a sweet lassitude filled her senses and thickened her blood.

"Don't do this to me," Amanda pleaded, her voice sounding strangely hoarse in her ears. "I'm not what you think."

"I think you are exquisite," came Tony's langorous reply. "You surpass my most fervent expectations, my love. Now relax and let me take you on an ecstatic journey where only the two of us may travel."

Before she could answer Amanda found herself caught once more in the silver web of Tony's hands and lips. No part of her body was left unscathed from his violent onslaught. Her nipples became a shrine upon which to mouth his adoration, her belly an altar to worship, her velvet sheath the vessel to offer his homage. And in the end it was Amanda who cried out in wild abandon, wishing for it never to end. Afterwards she slept in her lover's arms, strangely at peace with herself. Tomorrow would be soon enough to think about her mother's lace and what she would do when she awoke and found herself alone and abandoned in a strange room with nothing but a gold piece to keep her company and the memory of a man who had ruined her life.

Pale streaks of crimson lightened the eastern sky when Tony awoke. His head felt fuzzy and he attempted a smile, recalling the rousing send-off his friends had arranged the night before. He knew he had imbibed too freely of strong liquor but forgave himself the indiscretion this one time. Leaving his homeland for good certainly called for some kind of celebration.

Turning his head slowly he studied the woman, who looked more like an untried girl than an experienced prostitute, sleeping at his side. Last night it had all seemed like a beautiful dream; where he had imagined the soft-skinned temptress who had given him long hours of rapture. Tony's experience with the opposite sex was considerable and he had been told by numerous lovers that his technique was above reproach, so he couldn't help but wonder why this particular woman fought him at first, acting like a young virgin about to be raped. But he had soon tamed her, he smiled, vividly recalling the way her sweet body responded to the touch of his hands and lips. Unconsciously he ran a hand possessively along the smooth curve of Amanda's hip and was disappointed when she did no more than sigh and snuggle deeper into the soft mattress.

Amanda was sprawled on her side facing the wall, one slim arm curved over her head partially obscuring her lovely features, her coppery hair tumbling about her face in a profusion of tangled curls which further obstructed Tony's view of pert nose, full red lips and the curve of a downy cheek. But at the moment Amanda's face was the last thing Tony was interested in.

Even in her slumberous state Amanda felt the warmth of Tony's palm as it slid around her body to cup and mold her breast. "No, please, not again," she pleaded in a muffled voice as she hid her face in the pillow. Ignoring her plea that same hand dipped to find her stomach before going on to tease the tiny bud of her feminity.

"Just once more," Tony breathed raggedly, bending down to nip and nibble at a shell-like ear. When his tongue slowly, maddeningly worked its way in and around the sensitive organ, Amanda tensed, losing complete control of her senses as a liquid fire invaded her limbs.

Keeping her face purposely averted, Amanda was determined that this strange man who had stolen her virginity should not see how he affected her. Never would she allow him to recognize passion on her expressive face. Tony attempted to turn Amanda on her back in order to mount her but she resisted with such force he merely shrugged and entered from behind while Amanda lay on her side. He chuckled when he felt her stiffen.

"Had I known you preferred it this way I would have tried it sooner," he goaded, amused.

Amanda's resistance was short lived as Tony buried himself deeply inside her, taunting, teasing, driving her mad with his bold manhood and brave fingers as they massaged the pink nub he had discovered at the juncture of her thighs. Against her will, the feeling of intense pleasure, of wanting, began to build and Amanda felt her body responding, moving against Tony with consuming vigor, heated flesh slapping against heated flesh until the erotic friction left her gasping.

"You're wonderful," Tony panted, pacing himself until her pleasure peaked before seeking his own. "Where did my friends find you? Whatever they paid you is worth every cent."

Amanda was beyond answering as she sighed in tormented ecstasy, her body a savage blending of fire and ice. When Tony grasped her buttocks, pulling her against his driving flanks, she exploded in a blaze of feeling so intense she nearly fainted, Tony's hoarse cries echoing in her ear.

Thoroughly disgusted with her performance, Amanda sobbing softly, refused to look at the man who brought her traitorous body such joy. Lost in an eddy of quiet content, Tony did not seem to notice as he arose and began dressing.

"I'd like nothing better than to romp in bed with you all day but my ship sails with the morning tide," he said, fumbling in the half light for his clothing. Amanda did not answer nor did Tony seem to expect one.

When he was dressed and ready to leave he could not stop himself from turning back to the delectable body gracing his bed. "Do I get a kiss goodbye, sweetheart?" he teased lightly.

When no answer was forthcoming he lifted a slim hand that lay limply at the edge of the bed and pressed a kiss to her tender palm that was insolently sensuous. Then he was gone, leaving Amanda sobbing until she fell into a troubled sleep, her pillow wet with tears.

1

Charles Town, South Carolina 1760

Amanda stood at the railing of the ship along with her fellow passengers staring with bleak despair toward shore. In fact, given her mood, she cared little what became of her. Life as she knew it had ended that day nearly a year ago when she awoke in a strange room in an inn near the waterfront, alone, robbed of her virginity by a man she had never seen before, and paid like a whore with a gold coin.

At least she hadn't been forced to leave the room naked for when she awoke she found her clothing neatly folded on a chair next to the bed. But to her acute embarrassment she wasn't even allowed the dignity of sneaking out of the room unseen because the innkeeper presented himself at her door with a breakfast tray before she could escape, a knowing smirk pasted across his coarse features. When she finally departed the scene of her shame she meant to leave the gold coin on the floor as an act of defiance, but at the last minute, prudence prevailed and she slipped it into her pocket.

As it turned out that coin kept Amanda and her mother from starvation for a long time. When finally Amanda had arrived home it was to find her mother nearly prostrate with grief, thinking her poor daughter lay injured or dead in some deserted alleyway. All because she had sent the young girl out on the streets when she should have been safe behind locked doors.

What made matters worse was that Lady Linley had arrived early that morning expecting to find her gown finished. She had left in a huff determined that Nora Prescott would never gain the patronage of any of her influencial friends. After that things went from bad to worse. Nora's health had deteriorated to the point where she could no longer ply her needle. She spent most of her time huddled in bed coughing her life away. Amanda had been forced to reveal what had happened to her that shameful night and Nora found it difficult to live with her own guilt. She could not help but hold herself responsible for her dear daughter's rape. If she hadn't miscalculated on the amount of lace needed for Lady Linley's gown Amanda would not have been accosted on the street and violated.

When Nora became too weak to leave her bed, Amanda used the last of their money to pay for a doctor who told her there was nothing more to do but make her mother's last days comfortable. Then, when the last of their meager supply of food ran out, Amanda trudged the streets looking for work of any kind. But who would hire a young girl who looked too frail to survive a full day's work when there was an overabundance of buxom, ruddy-faced farm girls willing to labor from sun-up to sundown for a pittance?

In desperation Amanda turned to stealing from food vendors, not much, but enough to keep them alive. It was on one such foray that she was caught in the act by a sharp-eyed baker. Nothing Amanda could do or say would divert the vindictive man from calling a constable and charging the terrified girl with theft, a crime often punishable by death in eighteenth century England.

When Amanda was brought before the magistrate she pleaded for her life, explaining tearfully about her mother, too ill to leave her bed. But the law was explicit. In short order Amanda was sentenced to death by hanging. But the magistrate was not completely heartless. Due to her youth and first time offense, her sentence had been commuted to life in prison. Amanda, looking back on that period in her life, would have preferred death to Newgate Prison where the dregs of humanity existed in a kind of living Hell.

In one way Amanda had been lucky, if you could call selling your body for a promise of protection luck. Amanda's innocent beauty and youth had immediately attracted the constable who had arrested her. When she begged him to be allowed to visit her sick mother before being incarcerated he worked the situation to his own advantage by promising to see to her mother himself as well as protect Amanda from sexual abuse by prison guards if she would willingly lie with him whenever he came to her. Without a moment's hesitation Amanda readily agreed, for even her inexperienced mind could imagine the horror of being used and abused by countless men. And he did promise to take care of her mother, she thought dismally in an effort to assuage her guilt for giving in so easily.

Once Amanda acquiesced to the constable's demands he wasted no time in extracting his payment, taking her roughly for the first time in the coach carrying her to prison. No sooner had they begun moving than the constable calmly began removing her clothing until she was completely nude. He spent a few moments lapping greedily at her soft, pink-tipped breasts, one hand rudely insinuated between her thighs, then thrust into her, pushing her back against the cushions as he assaulted her shrinking body. For her mother's sake as well as her own Amanda did not protest but lay like a frozen statue, enduring the ordeal through sheer force of will. As the constable pumped and groaned out his ecstasy, Amanda could not help but think back to that night a year ago in the inn when a raven-haired stranger had brought her body to a peak of passion she never knew existed. How could one man cause her such joy while another brought only revulsion? she wondered desperately. Both had been strangers to her. To his credit, Amanda admitted grudgingly, the constable had not been totally ungentle, nor hurting. He merely satisfied himself then allowed her to dress.

Amanda's life in Newgate had been far worse than she imagined. The shock of being housed with hardened criminals, seasoned prostitutes and sadistic guards had at first nearly driven her to the brink of insanity. But, true to his word, the constable saw to it that Amanda was neither molested by guards nor sent upon by her fellow prisoners. And once a week he returned, led

Amanda to a small cubicle, bare except for a narrow cot, stripped her nude, played a few minutes with her breasts and collected his due from her young body. Afterwards he reported on her mother's welfare while she dressed, then led her back to her cell where she suffered the jibes and lewd remarks of her fellow cellmates in silent dignity. Though she was treated with contempt, and often referred to as "Princess," she was not abused by the other women prisoners who at times could be more sadistic and abusive than the guards.

More than once Amanda had reason to be thankful for the constable and his protection. Each night she looked on in abject horror as the guards chose one or another of the women and took them on the floor right before her eyes. After a few such nights Amanda felt that she had never been innocent. Youth had fled in a few short months leaving her old beyond her eighteen years and a shell of her former self. All because three men thought her a whore while the fourth used her like one! If nothing else, hate kept her alive.

Peony was one of the young girls who was chosen most often by the sadistic guards. She was younger than Amanda, even, and well versed in the art of sensual pleasure. They became friends of a sort although at times Peony seemed barely able to endure Amanda's company. Amanda supposed it was because she received preferential treatment.

One night a new guard, one Amanda had never seen before, entered the crowded cell to pick over and choose his pleasure for the night. His discerning eye passed swiftly over and discarded most of the women, falling finally on Peony and

Amanda. After what seemed like hours but was in truth only minutes, the guard pointed a stubby finger sporting a blackened nail at Amanda and said coarsely, "On your back, slut!"

"No!" spat Amanda with more courage than she felt. "You can't! You're not to have me!"

The guard smiled nastily, revealing a line of rotted teeth. "Who's to stop me? You are all either whores or thieves or you wouldn't be here. No one cares how often or in what manner the likes of you are used." So saying he shoved her down on the damp stone floor, flinging her dress over her head. Her cellmates, happy to see Amanda suffer the same treatment they experienced almost nightly, laughed and jeered, calling out coarse encouragement to the would-be rapist.

But at the last minute Amanda was saved when the constable arrived. Apprising himself of the situation in one glance and barking out a terse order that stopped the guard in his tracks. The guard promptly fell upon Peony when his first choice had been denied him and after that Amanda's position as the constable's private property was never again challenged.

Toward the end of her first month in prison the constable, on one of his weekly visits, informed Amanda of her mother's death. He had paid for her burial and she expressed her gratitude in the only way she knew how. After that the days and nights ran into one another with nothing to relieve the horror, the monotony, except the constable's sexual assaults, which in itself was another kind of horror. Amanda existed in a void as dark and chilling as the grave. She was living, yet dead, able to communicate, yet mute, capable of feeling, yet emotionless. Even now, out of prison and on the way to the Colonies, if she could believe the magistrate, she was unable to be thankful about her future. Eighteen years old, and she already had broken the law, been thrown into prison, used her body to gain favor, and was now about to be sold body and soul to another human being for a period of seven years. How much more could she endure? she wondered despairingly.

"What's the matter, Princess, ain't there nothin' out there what pleases you?"

Startled back to her surroundings Amanda turned to face the brash-faced girl at her elbow, identifying her immediately as Peony. Though Peony couldn't have been more than fifteen years old she was already street-wise and hardened beyond her years. The product of a prostitute mother and one of her many customers, Peony had been abandoned to the streets at the age of eight and used her wiles to exist, mostly by stealing and begging, until she reached eleven and turned her talents in another direction. Accused of theft by one of the men she serviced who hadn't the coin to pay her, she was thrown into Newgate where she languished along with Amanda until the magistrate, remembering their youth, had included them in a passel of women being shipped to the Colonies as indentured servants.

"What is there to be pleased about?" answered Amanda tonelessly. "One of those people standing on the dock as we arrive will soon own us. We are trading one form of degradation for another—slavery!"

"Well, you're alive ain't you?" scolded Peony, brown eyes snapping. "There's blue sky above you, ain't there? You're not in a dark hole being

31

used by sadistic guards. Things could be worse. Why, just think, in seven years you'll only be twenty-five years old and free to live your own life. Me, I'm grateful to that bloody magistrate for sending me here." So saying she flounced off seeking more congenial company amidst the ragged group of women huddled further on down the deck.

Flushing at Peony's well-meant rebuke, Amanda turned her eyes toward the shore; her green eyes were bright with unshed tears in her pinched face. Always slim, she was now gaunt and pale. She had been sick during much of the tedious crossing and the meager, unappetizing fare served to prisoners refused to remain long in her shrunken stomach. At least she hadn't been molested by any of the seamen. The captain, a humane, God-fearing man, would allow none of his crew access to the women without their consent. Even so, there had been plenty of willing women, Peony among them, who regularly serviced the seamen for extra rations or a coin now and again.

Amanda thought back to the day she heard the magistrate sentence her to seven years of servitude. At the time she had been so grateful to escape the horrors of prison life that she wept unrestrainedly, certain that anything was preferable to playing whore to the constable who extracted his due from her unwilling flesh time and again.

But the long journey had provided her ample time to seriously contemplate her future. Seven years might not sound like a long time, but to Amanda it stretched out endlessly before her. Talk was rampant aboard the ship and stories of cruel and abusive masters or mistresses were told and retold, often embellished with the tales of whippings and other forms of punishment equally reprehensible. Amanda even heard that the younger, more attractive women were often purchased by houses of prostitution and forced to remain in bondage far longer than the seven years specified in their indenture papers.

There is no justice, thought Amanda sadly, who was guilty of no more than stealing a loaf of bread to feed her dying mother. To Amanda's way of thinking, the only crime she was guilty of was being caught. The real crime had been committed against her by a rogue named Tony and his high-born friends who mistook her for a prostitute and robbed her of her innocence on a foggy night in London Town.

Casting her eyes over the landscape, Amanda thought how different Charles Town was from crowded London which teemed with humanity from all walks of life. From her vantage point she could see narrow streets radiating in all directions from the harbor and lined with wooden structures she assumed were businesses and dwellings, all appearing much alike in design. The whole of it, in comparison with some of the great stone estates of England, seemed small and mean. Beyond the city itself stretched dense birch and pine forests rising to lofty heights. Here and there a sparkling stream meandered haphazardly amid the trees and fields.

Though the sun kissed her sallow cheeks and warmed her shriveled flesh, Amanda's emotions remained frozen; all feeling had long since fled.

Suddenly there was a movement on shore as the gangplank was lowered and a dozen or more people surged forward, anxious to purchase the Articles of Indenture of the unfortunate convicts who would be forced to work long hours for masters bent on obtaining the most from their investments. Among them, a tall, raven-haired man who stood out head and shoulders above all others strode forward with grim purpose.

Tony Brandt had need of a housekeeper. Some stern-faced, imposing woman with the will and stamina to keep his house servants in order and put in a full days work in the fields when needed. His neighbor, Stanley Carter, had suggested purchasing the Articles of Indenture of a convict, many of whom had committed nothing more serious than stealing a bit of bread to feed their families. It wouldn't be too hard to identify such a woman, Tony surmised as he carefully scrutinized the prisoners mustered on deck for inspection.

Though pale and gaunt from their prison confinement and weeks at sea, there appeared to be several good prospects among the women assembled. Tony listened intently as the Captain of the ship paused before each, stated their name and charges against them.

Half-way down the line Tony spied the type of servant he had in mind. Tall, buxom, raw-boned, the woman reminded him of a country wife born to raise children and toil alongside her man in the fields. Slightly past middle age she seemed the perfect choice and Tony approached the Captain to make his intention known when a slight movement to his left caught his eye.

A frightened, auburn-haired girl of tender years was being forcibly dragged forward by a fat woman dressed in somber clothing and accompanied by a thin man wearing a parson's collar. Something about the girl struck a responsive chord in Tony. Perhaps it was her terror-stricken green eyes; or maybe the riot of auburn curls framing a thin little face whose beauty refused to be dimmed by deprivation. Though her tattered, dirty dress hung on her spare frame, Tony instinctively knew a nourishing diet would soon fill out the hollows. But it was not the girl's obvious attributes that attracted Tony. It was a strange feeling of deja vu. It was as if somewhere, somehow, he had encountered the young felon, although he knew it was an impossibility. In all his years in England he had little contact with women of her class. Sidling nearer, Tony listened to the exchange between the fat woman and the Captain.

"Stealing, you say, Captain? Whoring, too, most likely. One evil harbors another, I always say," sniffed the fat woman, wiping perspiration from her florid face. "Only God knows what obscenitites she has committed. The innocent looking ones are the worst offenders."

"Stealing is the only crime Mistress Prescott is accused of," replied the Captain scornfully. "As Christians it behooves us all to give charity to those less fortunate."

"Quite right, Captain," rejoined her sparrow-like husband, leering openly at Amanda. "Left to my tender mercies the girl will soon repent of her evil ways."

Although he fooled his wife, both Tony and the Captain well knew what the young girl could look forward to if left to the parsons' "tender mercies."

The captain cleared his throat loudly and said, "The law is quite explicit in such matters. The women you see before you are all subjects of the king whose orders state they are to be indentured as servants for a period of seven years, and not used for . . . er . . . other purposes."

"What purpose do you think we have in mind, Captain?" huffed the woman with hot indignation. "We have need for a scullery maid. The last one we purchased up and died on us. My husband" she explained, slanting the parson a fond look, "Godly man that he is, doesn't hold with slavery so we are forced to contend with these criminals the King sends to us."

"My dear," clucked the parson consolingly, "where is your compassion for these poor, misguided creatures? Under my tutorage this child will soon repent of her sins. Her sweet body shall become a vessel of the Lord."

As the parson spoke his beady eyes took on an unholy glow, reflecting the very devil himself. Amanda shrank within herself, thinking death preferable to living with the sanctimonious parson and his mean-tempered wife. In her mind she was trading one hell for another. And worse, she had no choice in the matter.

Tony had heard enough to set his teeth on edge and his blood to boiling. He had no idea why the fate of a half-starved urchin should cause him such anguish, but he realized he could not just sit back and allow the lecherous parson to put his hands on that poor young girl's frail body no matter what kind of life she had led in the past.

Forgetting the purpose for his being there; completely ignoring the elderly woman considerably more suited for the job of housekeeper, Tony stepped forward and addressed the captain whom he knew slightly through their mutual friend, Stanley Carter.

"Captain Blakewell," he began with cool deliberation, "if you will recall, sir, I have prior claim on this particular girl. You have already agreed to my request to purchase the Articles of Indenture of Mistress Prescott." He nodded carelessly toward Amanda. "I am desperately in need of a housekeeper."

"Housekeeper! Bah!" scoffed the parson's wife derisively. "Bed warmer would be more like it. Pick another, sir, there are plenty more to choose from."

"I have already made my choice, Madam!" interjected Tony forcefully.

"And I repeat, pick another," glowered the furious matron.

"What say you, Captain Blakewell?" asked Tony, looking directly at the bemused captain. "Who has prior claim to this girl?"

Captain Blakewell studied Tony through shrewd eyes, weighing carefully his statement of prior claim upon the prisoner. He was slightly acquainted with the young man, having encountered him on several occasions at the home of Stanley Carter and his lovely daughter, Letty. He knew that Carter highly valued the young nobleman and hoped for a match between his daughter and Tony. Though nothing was mentioned so far about an engagement the young people were good friends and often together.

Captain Blakewell couldn't help but wonder over Tony's motives in thwarting the parson's bid for the girl. It was obvious even to him that with a little rest and care Amanda would blossom into a raving beauty. Could he in all honesty allow a young, unattached male free access to a girl like Amanda Prescott? Yet, wouldn't it be far worse to allow her to fall into the unscrupulous hands of an aging lecher like the parson who was likely to use her vilely? Whatever the young man's intention, it took little time for the captain to consider both claims and decide in Tony's favor. Nothing Tony could do, he contended, could compare with what the parson had in mind.

"Sir Tony does indeed have prior claim upon Mistress Prescott," he acquiesced, using Tony's title to reinforce his lie as well as to intimidate the other couple. "We have already completed arrangements."

"Why didn't you say so in the first place," sputtered the parson's wife, reluctantly releasing Amanda's bruised arm.

"My fault," muttered the captain vaguely. "No matter, there are plenty of others to choose from. Make your choice and see me later." With a wave of his hand he dismissed the odious couple.

For the first time since the fat woman had grasped her arm Amanda felt able to breathe again, drawing in deep, shuddering gulps of air.

"Are you all right, Mistress Prescott?" asked the captain solicitously, alarmed by Amanda's sudden pallor.

"Thank you, Captain, but I'm. . . I'm fine," lied Amanda, feeling far from well.

Not until that moment did she look directly at the man who was to be her master for the next seven years. The shock of recognition sent her reeling. Before her stood the one man in all the world she had vowed to hate until her dying day. He and his companions were the cause of all her troubles. Everything bad that had happened to her began on that day she had found herself in this man's bed, the brunt of a cruel joke.

Tony was stunned by the hatred and revulsion blazing from Amanda's emerald eyes. He had expected gratitude, perhaps fear, but never out and out hatred. But what could he expect from a convicted felon who associated with the dregs of humanity? he asked himself, disgusted by his obsession with a frail waif who undoubtedly had sold her body countless times to nameless men despite her tender years. The streets of London were filled with homeless young girls such as Amanda Prescott, he thought, but he had the misfortune to fall for her innocent face and wide, frightened, green eyes. There was not much he could do about it now. He had acted precipitously and purchased the papers of a girl who looked too sickly to become more than a liability in his household. With this in mind, he spoke more harshly than he intended.

"Get your belongings, girl. You'll be leaving with me as soon as I finish negotiations with the captain."

Amanda glared belligerently at Tony. The thought of finally accusing the man she deemed responsible for all her suffering flooded her slender form with a vindictive will to live and see him punished. It seemed there was a God after all. For the next seven years Amanda would be in a position to make Tony pay over and over for his callous treatment of her. It was obvious he didn't recognize her as the girl he had deflowered a year ago in a mean waterfront inn. But there was no mistaking him with his satanic good looks and air of command. Even drunk he had been in complete control of the situation. For the moment Amanda chose to obey his command, yearning for the day she would reap her revenge. She had no idea of how or when, only that the day would come.

While Amanda disappeared below to gather her meager belongings, Tony accompanied

Captain Blakewell to his cabin to complete their verbal transaction. He had no idea what had compelled him to purchase a servant who obviously was too frail to serve in the capacity for which she was intended and could only hope she would at least earn her keep.

"Are you certain the Prescott girl is what you want?" the captain asked shrewdly, fully aware of the suddenness of Tony's decision to have Amanda.

Though his precipitous action had caught him unawares, Tony knew that he would not back down. For some strange, unexplained reason he could not allow the parson to have Amanda. "I think, given the proper training, of course, the girl will make an adequate housekeeper," Tony said with more conviction than he felt.

Captain Blakewell shrugged eloquently, then began to fill out the necessary papers. "I'd hate to be in your shoes when Letty gets a look at the young miss whose services you've just purchased," he added offhandedly.

Though Tony did not appreciate the captain's left-handed advice, he was well aware of Letty Carter's temper and knew she counted on being his wife one day. Perhaps she would be, Tony mused, but he had no intention of marrying any time soon no matter what Letty expected.

2

The sun was still a red ball high in the sky when Tony helped Amanda secure her small bundle in the back of his wagon loaded with sundry supplies and then settled her none too gently on the seat beside him. Amanda sensed his antagonism but had no idea as to its cause. Did he finally recognize her? she wondered, slanting hooded eyes in his direction. If so, how long would he keep up the pretense of not knowing her? For what purpose had he purchased her indenture papers? Did he really need a housekeeper or had he acted out of compassion to her plight? Whatever his reason he was obviously sorry he had acted so hastily.

For some distance they travelled along in silence, each bent upon their own thoughts, until Amanda's frail body began to slump with exhaustion. It had grown dark and hunger pangs gnawed at her stomach. Besides, she had not relieved herself in hours and stubbornly refused to admit to Tony that she was at the end of her endurance. Finally, as if sensing her distress, Tony pulled the wagon into a stand of tall pines and stopped. Amanda nearly fainted with joy. Her bladder nigh to bursting she jumped unaided from her perch and headed toward a growth of dense bushes, her face red from embarrassment.

Tony cursed himself roundly for allowing his resentment toward the girl to gain the upper hand causing him to disregard her needs. No matter what she had done, she was still a young girl in a strange land far from family and friends. Immediately his attitude softened and he vowed silently to make amends for his shoddy treatment.

A cheery fire was blazing when Amanda returned and she moved wordlessly toward its warmth. Tony was hard pressed to stifle the surge of desire contracting his loins painfully at the sight of her fragile beauty limned against the dancing flames. Amanda was startled to hear a low, vibrant voice addressing her from across the fire. It was his first attempt at communication since they lad left the convict ship.

"Mistress Prescott," Tony began hesitantly, "I appreciate your show of stamina but hereafter if you feel a need to relieve yourself along the trail you have only to ask. I am not as heartless as you make me out to be."

Amanda flushed to the roots of her hair to hear him speak so openly of bodily functions. Evidently customs differed in this crude, new world.

"I didn't know if I was allowed to speak," she answered in a show of spirit that left no doubt as to the low opinion she held for him.

Tony shook his head angrily. How dare she treat him like a cruel slave driver! he fumed, his glowering features darkening with rage. Irrationally, he decided to put her in her place, to leave no doubt as to who was slave and who was master.

"Make yourself useful," he ordered harshly, pointing vaguely in the distant darkness, "and fetch a bucket of water from the stream."

Immediately Amanda realized she had spoken out of turn, incurring Tony's wrath. She had yet to learn what he intended for her once they reached his home. She bit back an angry retort. Perhaps he had a wife who would treat her kindly, she thought hopefully. Sighing wearily, Amanda looked around for the bucket intending to meekly follow her master's orders even if it killed her. And it nearly did.

Several yards from their makeshift camp the ground sloped unevenly and sharply downward toward the streambed Tony had pointed out. Faint and weary from exhaustion and hunger, Amanda became careless and lost her footing on some loose gravel, tumbling head over heels down the embankment until she came to rest at water's edge, her body half submerged in the frigid stream.

She was still unconscious when Tony found her after becoming alarmed by her long absence. Gathering her in his arms with more gentleness than necessary, Tony carried her slight weight back to the fire where he placed her tenderly on a pile of blankets. Noting that her clothes were sodden and she was shuddering uncontrollably, he decided to undress her lest she catch a chill and become ill. Methodically he began removing her wet, clinging clothes, noting as he did her protruding ribs, concave stomach and slim limbs. She had a body, Tony thought unbiddingly, that would challenge the best when filled out. Even as thin as she was her breasts were shapely with firm, rose-tipped nipples. He watched entranced as the cooling air hardened them into erect buds. Experimentally he ran his hands over her body searching for broken bones, and found none. But in the process his own body reacted violently to the stimulation. Made guilty by the direction of his thoughts, Tony hastily drew a blanket over the nude girl and turned his mind reluctantly toward finding them a meal.

Amanda awoke a short time later to a delicious aroma permeating the crisp air. She attempted to arise but immediately fell back, groaning in pain. Her head hurt and she was dizzy. Only then did she remember what had happened to her. Once again hatred for Tony welled up in her with renewed vigor.

Alerted by her moans, Tony left off his chores and approached the crude pallet upon which he had placed Amanda. "Do you hurt?" he asked solicitiously. "I could detect no broken bones when I examined you."

"You. . . examined me?" asked Amanda, horrified. The thought of his hands on her body made her decidedly uncomfortable.

"Of course," Tony answered blandly. "If you had any broken bones who do you think would have set them?"

It wasn't until that moment that Amanda realized she was completely nude beneath the blanket. "My clothes!" she gasped accusingly, "you have removed my clothes!"

"Only to dry them," he assured her quickly, pointing to where they were drying on long poles staked around the fire. "You were shivering and I was afraid you'd catch your death."

"How do I know you didn't. . . didn't. . ."

"Take advantage of you?" Round eyed, Amanda nodded her burnished head. "Hardly," he intoned disdainfully. "I'm not in the habit of seducing unconscious women, especially one likely to give me the pox."

The extent of his cruelty stunned Amanda into muteness. Never in her life did she expect to be referred to in such a manner. It only served to reinforce her resolution to punish Tony one day for bringing her to such a pass.

"I am not a whore!" she blurted out, incensed by his unprovoked attack upon her reputation.

"It makes little difference to me, Mistress Prescott," Tony pointed out. "You are to be my housekeeper if you can be taught such skills. If not, you will earn your keep in the fields as soon as you are physically able. I have no need of a bed partner, so if you harbor any thoughts along that line, forget them."

"Pompass ass," Amanda spat, forgetting herself. "You weren't always so particular, if I recall. I never have nor will I ever willingly share your bed! Now, if you intend to work me to death you'd do well to feed me."

Tony could not help but smile at Amanda's show of courage though he deplored her lack of respect. The meaning of her angry words puzzled him somewhat but he realized she was at the end of her tether and spoke out of desperation and anger. What else could he expect from a convict? He would soon teach her her place, he resolved, but until that time he had best heed her words and feed her.

A rabbit roasting on a spit sputtered and hissed making Amanda's mouth water. Tony unspitted it, divided it in half and handed Amanda her portion. Both ate greedily, savoring the gamy taste of the done-to-a-turn carcass.

"Delicious," sighed Amanda, contentedly licking the grease from her fingers. She was sitting up with the blanket wrapped mummy-like around her body. "Is there anything else to eat?" she asked, accepting a cup of strong, hot tea brewed in a battered, copper kettle.

"Didn't they feed you on the ship?" Tony asked as he rummaged around in a bag of supplies he had purchased in Charles Town.

"Most of the time I was too sick to eat," admitted Amanda. "Not that the food was plentiful, or good, for that matter."

Tony was silent for a moment, well aware of the hardships endured by a young girl left to the mercies of hardened convicts and seamen deprived of women during the long crossing. Once more compassion softened his heart.

"Here," he said, offering Amanda a stick of jerky and piece of hardtack, "try this."

"What is it?" she asked, eyeing the dried meat suspiciously.

"Dried venison pressed into sticks. It's very nourishing," Tony explained. "It's highly concentrated and surprisingly tasty once you get used to it. Bite off a piece and soften it in your mouth."

Amanda did as she was told and was soon gnawing happily on the jerky, alternating it with hunks of hardtack and washing the whole down with tea.

"My God, you were hungry!" exclaimed Tony wonderingly as he watched the food disappear. Amanda finally finished and sighed in obvious contentment. "How is your head? Does it still hurt?"

"Feels much better."

"Then you'd best get some sleep. I'd like to get an early start in the morning."

Made bold by his sudden show of friendliness, Amanda decided to ask about his home; her home also for the next seven years. "How much farther to your estate?" she asked, eager for any kind of information.

"In South Carolina they are called plantations," Tony informed her. "By tomorrow afternoon we will be on my holdings which lie parallel to the Santee River."

"Your holdings. Are they extensive?"

"You might call them that. It is prime land and I was fortunate to be able to purchase such a valuable tract from the crown."

"What do you grow? This land looks so different from England. Many of the plants and trees are unfamiliar to me."

"This new land *is* different," concurred Tony, warming to his subject. "It's vast and intriguing. Pristine white sands form the coastline dotted with low growing palmetto. Further inland, wooded foothills give way to pine covered mountains. Every contrast imaginable is seen in this fertile country. After a while you'll grow to love it as I do. Rice and indigo are the chief money crops. River's Edge produces both."

"River's Edge?"

"Yes, I've named my plantation, River's Edge. That name seemed appropriate."

"Then you never plan to return to England?"

"Perhaps to visit, one day, but never again to live. I've made my own life here in the Carolinas, and it's a good one."

"Your. . . your wife, is she a Colonial?" asked

Amanda timorously.

"I'm not married," stated Tony emphatically. "But I suppose sometime in the future I must if I want an heir."

For some reason his answer brought a flush of pleasure to Amanda. Chagrined by her wayward thoughts, she stared moodily into the dying fire, trying to imagine what the future held for her. Soon she was yawning hugely, catching Tony's attention.

"Off to sleep with you, Amanda. I suppose it's all right if I call you by your first name, isn't it?" he asked, suddenly aware that he had addressed her familiarly. Somehow it sounded right rolling off his tongue.

Wordlessly Amanda nodded and hunkered down into the blanket while Tony made up his own pallet across the fire from her. Because he had given Amanda most of the blankets, his own seemed woefully meager, but he made the best of it, carefully building up the fire before he went to sleep.

Amanda woke up shivering, her chattering teeth the only sound in the still, moonless night. The fire had extinguished itself to embers and a raw, early April wind whistled through the tall pines. As so often happens that time of year, the warm days of early spring were deceptive in that the nights could be chilled by cold, wet rains while the days were bright and sunny. Such was the case when Amanda awoke. A fine, light rain was just beginning to fall and the temperature had dropped dramatically. Thinking her clothes would help ward off the chill, Amanda arose from her pallet, wrapped herself in a blanket and stumbled about in the dark searching for her dress and petticoats.

Suddenly a loud click rent the stillness and Amanda froze in her tracks, recognizing immediately the sound of a cocked pistol.

"Who goes there?" came Tony's tense voice.

"It's me, Amanda," shot back Amanda quickly.

"What the devil are you doing roaming around in the dark at this time of night?" he asked angrily. "Don't you realize I could have shot you? There is much you have to learn if you expect to survive in this wild country."

"I'm c...c...cold," chattered Amanda. "I wa...want my clothes."

Suddenly Tony became aware of the dramatic change in temperature. Swearing softly he dashed cold, wet raindrops from his face and hair and arose swiftly, gathering up his blankets and tossing them beneath the wagon. Then he rescued Amanda's damp clothing and added them to the heap under the wagon. Lastly, he collected Amanda's pallet tossing it after the rest of their belongings before turning his attentions to Amanda herself.

"Come here, Amanda," he ordered brusquely, clutching her small, chilled hand as he roughly pushed her beneath the crude shelter. Spreading out half the blankets to form a ground covering, Tony gently pushed her down, intending to cover her with the remaining blankets. Amanda reached for her clothing.

"No," Tony admonished, divining her purpose. "They are still damp from the rain."

"But I'm freezing," wailed Amanda in real distress.

"These wet rags won't help you," countered Tony. "Probably do you more harm than good. Lie down and I'll cover you with the rest of these blankets."

She did as she was told and in a few minutes she stopped shivering as her body slowly began to warm. But it wasn't long before Tony, lying atop the blankets beside her began shaking with cold much as Amanda had done only moments before.

"Damn! If I'm going to freeze out here while you're all cozy and warm," he swore, seizing an end of the blanket and scooting underneath, determined to soak up some of the warmth Amanda was jealously hoarding.

Amanda gasped in shock as she came in contact with his chilled flesh; before he had joined her he had hastily removed his drenched shirt and pants. "What do you think you're doing?" she sputtered angrily.

"Keeping us both from freezing to death," Tony growled disgustedly. "Now lie still and go to sleep. We have a long day tomorrow."

Trying hard to ignore the firm, muscled body pressed close against her back, Amanda, realized the truth of Tony's words and, already made drowsy by the combined body heat, closed her eyes and fought desperately to still her wildly beating heart.

Suddenly it was a year ago and Amanda was in bed with a stranger determined to force her to his will. All the horror, the terror of that night as well as everything that followed pressed down upon her with crushing impact. Hot, scalding tears spilled unbidden from her green eyes followed by heart-rending sobs as grief gave way to despair.

"What's the matter now?" asked Tony, exasperated as he rose up on his elbow. "Are you still cold?"

"N. . . no," choked Amanda between sobs.

"Are you sick?"

"N. . . no. At least I don't think so. Anyway, you wouldn't understand."

"You're right," ground out Tony. "I wouldn't understand." His words brought on a fresh torrent of tears.

Without volition, Tony drew the quaking girl into his arms, at first wishing only to soothe and quiet her so he could go to sleep. Instinctively Amanda cuddled into his warmth, finding a semblance of relief in the low sounds of comfort he was making deep in his throat. Little by little she began to relax, forgetting for the moment that this was the man she vowed to hate, savoring the only tenderness she had known since her mother's death.

If Amanda was comforted by their intimate contact, Tony was intensely aroused. The small, warm body curled so trustingly into his was creating a riot of emotion in his hardening body. With a life of their own his hands sought and found the twin mounds of her small breasts. Experimentally he rubbed his thumb back and forth across a nipple until it became firm and erect against his palm.

Amanda's sharp intake of breath caused Tony a moment's distress at what he was about to do to a girl hardly out of childhood. Especially to one as lost and forlorn as Amanda appeared to be. But it was too late to stop now. Already his body was aflame with desire, his blood pounding through his veins. The smooth, cool skin beneath his hands quivered as his passionate onslaught became more intimate, moving resolutely toward a soft, moist goal.

"Please. . ." Amanda began. But her words were cut off as his lips and tongue took her by storm, penetrating her defenses, assaulting her brutally.

Abandoning her mouth, Tony slid his lips along the smooth plane of her cheek to the pulsating hollow at the base of her throat. When his mouth finally closed on a tender, swollen nipple, sucking gently, Amanda came to her senses and began struggling, pushing him away with her hands, thrashing her legs wildly.

Shifting his weight, Tony came to rest on top of Amanda, immediately stilling her bucking body. With one hand he grasped both wrists, pinning them above her head. Amanda loudly voiced her protest but once more was silenced by Tony's bruising mouth. Again and again he kissed her until she hadn't the will nor the power to resist. Sensing her submission, Tony released her hands and immediately found them twined about his neck. Amanda moaned softly as his hands worked their way along the curves and hollows of her body until he found the sweet dampness between her thighs.

Gently he worked his fingers in a rotating motion, dipping within her honeyed warmth. "Amanda," he whispered huskily into her ear, "you are like a sweet, unspoiled child even though I know you are probably a whore. Dear God, how I want you! Open your legs and let me in."

Amanda was too caught up in the throes of ecstasy to make any sense out of his words. Her body was aflame, her blood boiling as thoughts of the passion he had brought her to long ago leaped to her mind. Tony's expert caresses carried her to the brink, her body tensed, every nerve ending was tingling with vibrant feeling. Instinctively she spread her legs allowing Tony to slide easily inside. He filled her completely, and she gasped in delight.

At first he moved so slowly Amanda thought she would die from wanting. When he finally increased his tempo she matched his strokes, clutching at his shoulders in an attempt to draw him closer. Somewhere in her brain a brilliant burst of light was building, building, until it exploded and she went hurtling into space, crying out at the joy and pain. Tony's cry of completion followed hers by seconds.

Feeling strangely at peace as she descended slowly from her high pinnacle, Amanda could not believe that she had acted so wantonly, that she had responded so dramatically to Tony's lust, for that was the only name for it. How could she allow herself to be seduced by him again when she knew he cared little for her as a woman, she wondered dismally. She was a handy vessel for his passion, nothing more.

Lying beside her, Tony was enmeshed in thoughts of his own. He was thoroughly confused by his conflicting emotions concerning the skinny, undernourished convict he had just made love to as if she were someone precious and rare instead of a thief and whore. Of course he had no proof that she was a whore but she hadn't been a virgin, of that he was positive. Even her token resistance had been half-hearted and easily overcome. If her response to his lovemaking was any indication she was a hot little piece who used her body to her own advantage. It was obvious she was not without experience, although he had only himself to blame for falling under her spell. He must steel himself against her wiles, he decided grimly, lest she forget who was master and who was servant. Nowhere in his ordered life was there room for a convicted felon no matter what he felt for her. Pity, maybe? Realizing that at this point his emotions were too confused to function, Tony embraced sleep, hoping for a clearer mind on the morrow.

Beside him, Amanda, also, had given up her musings and was lost in a world of dreams.

3

Amanda awoke slowly, coming out of sleep like one drugged. The place beside her, recently occupied by Tony, had grown cold and so had she. Reaching for her clothes she hurriedly dressed beneath the blankets and crawled out from under the wagon, wondering how Tony would react to her after their intimacy the night before.

She didn't have long to wonder. Tony had already hitched the horses to the wagon and seemed anxious to depart. The skies were gray and forbidding, a light rain still fell. Tony scowled, giving Amanda the impression that his mood matched the lowering weather.

"Make yourself useful," he growled. "It's about time you learned your place and began earning your keep. Fold up those blankets and pack them in the back of the wagon. Be sure to cover them with the canvas to keep them dry." His curt, impersonal tone caused her a moment's apprehension.

"Yes, sir," obeyed Amanda in a tone suggesting anything but obedience. Tony slanted her a scathing look but for reasons of his own chose not to rebuke her at this time even though her insolent manner raised his ire.

In fact, he was undecided how to treat Amanda. Seeing her this morning in the full light he was struck anew by her fragile beauty and youth. She appeared like a pale flower on a slim stem, capable of being blown away by a strong wind.

"Do you have a cloak?" he asked, suddenly, compellingly aware of her tattered, damp dress plastered to her slim curves. The sight caused an unwelcome moment of discomfort as Tony's body reacted violently to the sight of firm, upthrust breasts outlined dramatically by the thin material of Amanda's worn dress. It was beyond his ken how such a bedraggled creature could arouse his passion to the extent that he wanted her again, recalling to mind her ardent response of the night before.

"I have a cloak in my bundle," answered Amanda as she drew out the threadbare garment and clasped it around her thin body.

"Can't make a fire," Tony muttered distractedly as he handed her a strip of jerky and piece of hardtack. "If it stops raining later I'll stop and build a fire. Maybe make us some tea. Meanwhile we make do."

Nodding mutely Amanda gnawed hungrily on the jerky, glad of the full feeling it created in her empty stomach. Soon they were back on the trail, the springless wagon bumping along the rutted roadbed until she felt as if every bone in her body had been bruised.

The morning progressed much as the day before except that Tony was careful to stop periodically and ask her if she needed to go into the woods. Around mid-day they pulled into a grassy place not far from the river and Tony attempted to start a fire. While Amanda fetched water, Tony shot a squirrel and had it dressed and spitted before she returned. To Amanda the hot, strong tea was as welcome as the food. Nevertheless she ate her share with gusto then cleaned up afterwards under Tony's watchful eyes, which she noticed were a strange silver gray. The first time she had really seen them up close.

The sun finally broke through the heavy blanket of clouds turning the air warm and humid. On a sudden whim Amanda wandered off toward the river while Tony fussed with the wagon, repairing a wheel that had become loose. To Amanda's inexperienced eye the water looked placid and inviting. It had been ages since she had had a bath and the sparkling water was too inviting to resist. Impulsively she began removing her clothes, eager to have her bath before Tony finished with his chores. Gingerly she tipped a foot into the water, and finding it surprisingly warm, waded in up to her waist. What she wouldn't give for a sliver of soap, she sighed wistfully. Making do with what she had on hand, Amanda scooped up fistfull of sand and rubbed herself until her skin was nearly raw. She decided to wait and wash her hair later when she had some soap. Just then a movement in the bushes along the river's edge caught her eye.

Tony stood only a few yards away holding a piece of soap before him. "This might help," he called. Before she could respond he had shed his clothes and waded toward her. Immediately Amanda crouched down in the water until only her head was visible. Gingerly accepting the soap from his outstretched hand, she watched warily while he swam several yards away and proceeded with his own bath. Satisfied that he did not mean to instigate a repeat of last night Amanda quickly lathered herself, rinsed, then washed her hair. It felt heavenly to be clean and sweet smelling again.

Tony finished bathing first and stood on the sloping bank wrapped in one blanket and holding another as he waited for Amanda to emerge. Her cheeks turned crimson when she realized he intended to stand there until she joined him.

"There's no need to wait for me," called Amanda hopefully. "I'm perfectly capable of finding my own way back."

"Nevertheless, I'll wait," insisted Tony devilishly. "Most Indians around here are friendly but I've recently heard that the Cherokee have been stealing livestock and raiding small farms."

"Indians!" cried Amanda in alarm. "There are Red Indians here?"

"Of course," laughed Tony. "If you recall, this land belonged to the Indians once. Most of it still does."

That's all Amanda had to hear, immediately picturing a red-skinned savage spying on her from behind every bush. With a squeak of terror she started toward shore. But her exit wasn't as uneventful as her entrance. Unknowingly she stepped off into a deep hole and with a surprised sputter disappeared beneath the surface. Desperately she fought for footing, only to find herself being dragged deeper down by an undertow she failed to notice before. In that instant Amanda realized she was about to die and thought with gratitude on those few moments of ecstasy she had experienced in Tony's strong arms. Just before she blacked out she felt a powerful tug on her waist-length hair that floated about her like a radiant shroud.

Amanda came to, sputtering and coughing while Tony sat with her limp body draped across his lap, slapping her back. "I nearly died!" she choked, shaken by her harrowing experience.

"Nonsense," scoffed Tony indulgently. "I'm an excellent swimmer and you never were in any danger of drowning. Now aren't you glad I waited for you?" His eyes crinkled with amusement and Amanda couldn't help but smile at his sudden light-hearted mood.

"I. . . I think I'm recovered now, so if you'll let me up. . ."

Only then did Tony realize he still held her protectively in his arms. He was amazed at how right and good it felt. "No thanks for saving your life?" he asked, his silver gaze suddenly kindled with a strange light that made Amanda shiver.

"Thank you," she answered demurely, shifting uncomfortably in his arms, experienced enough to realize that he was becoming aroused.

"Your hair is beautiful," he whispered huskily, burying his face in the soft, fragrant curls. "And so are you."

"Sir Tony, please. You don't know what you are saying. Let me go."

Instinctively Tony's arms tightened, feeling her wildly beating heart against his strong chest. He wanted desperately to kiss her and he did, thoroughly, passionately, abandoning all his well-meant resolutions of the night before. Breathing deeply of the clean, sweet smell of her hair and skin, Tony's lips began making forays into the warm hollows of her neck and irresistible allure of rose-tipped breasts. Bold fingers located the altar of her womanhood.

For a few ecstatic moments Amanda abandoned herself to the warm, pleasurable lassitude that slowed her blood to the consistency of thick honey. Then common sense took over and she twisted from Tony's grasp, surprising him by her strength and determination. Once on her feet she grabbed up her dress, holding it before her in an effort to shield her nudity, green eyes hard and cold as emeralds.

"Is this your way of proving your mastery over me? Or have you already forgotten your own words?" she taunted boldly.

"I am the master and don't ever forget it," warned Tony ominously, angry at being thwarted from his passionate pursuit. "I own you!"

"You own my labor for seven years, not my body, and certainly not my soul. Contrary to your belief I am not a whore to be used at will."

"Don't act the innocent with me, Amanda," Tony shot back insultingly. "You weren't a virgin when I took you. You were never married. What other explanation can you give me?"

Red dots of rage exploded in Amanda's brain. "I owe you no explanation. What do you know of my past? Or how difficult it was to survive in Newgate? Would you even care if I told you how I was imprisoned for stealing a stale loaf of bread to feed my dying mother? How dare you brand me a whore with one breath and make love to me with another! Leave me alone, Sir Tony. Oh, never fear, you'll get your money's worth out of me. I'll work my fingers to the bone if necessary but I'll not be used as a sexual convenience!"

Amanda was so incensed that Tony could only stare at her in amazement. Most of what she said was true but it rankled to be put down by a mere slip of a girl who for some obscure reason he wanted to love and protect one minute and punish the next. Speechless, he watched as she turned on her heel and fled. Thoughtfully he pulled on his clothes and returned to the wagon where Amanda, fully dressed, awaited. Scowling fiercely, he took his place beside her and, clucking to the horses, resumed their journey. For hours on end silence reigned. There was a monotony about the road that lulled them into a kind of stupor. Besides, it seemed they had said all there was to be said.

But Amanda could not still the thoughts that ran rampant through her fertile brain. Was she to be tormented by Tony's nearness for the next seven years? she asked herself grimly. Would he continue to use her whenever it pleased him despite her brave words refusing to become a sexual convenience? Hadn't she suffered enough already without being tortured by the nearness of the man who had raped her and had no memory of the deed? For months she had been obliged to perform sexually for the constable in order to survive and when she left England she promised herself she would never be used against her will again.

Amanda could not help but think of the way her body reacted the moment Tony put his hands on her. From the moment he touched her she was lost. Lost in a world of sensual pleasure she never knew existed, responding with an eagerness that stunned her. She vowed to remain vigilant lest his masculine wiles ensnare her in a trap from which there was no honorable escape.

Tony's thoughts went less deep. Were more concerned, in fact, with feelings and senses. He had no idea why he desired Amanda, a cunning waif who had obviously seen and experienced much despite her tender years. But desire her he did, and with an intensity that shocked him. Nothing good would ever come of his desiring a convict, Tony realized, and he would do well to curb his misdirected passion and turn his desire to Letty who was more deserving. As for Amanda, Tony determined he would do well to teach her her place in his household early on and save them both a lot of grief and unpleasantness.

The sun was a pale orange sphere low in the western sky when the slate-gray rooftop of River's Edge came into view. Excitement was a hard lump in Amanda's throat. It was such a long time since she had lived in a real home that even the thought of long years of servitude could not dim her spirits which had perked up considerably at the sight of the imposing structure that was Tony's home.

It wasn't a massive English estate, but to Amanda it seemed a mansion, its fresh coat of white paint bright and welcoming. The house was over two stories high with another half-story beneath a steeply pitched roof. Tall windows were evenly spaced along the front framing two high columns holding up a railed balcony, affording a magnificent view of forests and rivers beyond.

"It's so big," breathed Amanda reverently. "And so beautiful."

"I'm glad you approve," intoned Tony dryly.

Tony stopped before the impressive door between the two columns and helped Amanda down from the wagon. Almost immediately the door flung open and a fat black woman of undetermined age, wearing a crisp, white apron and bright red bandana covering tightly kinked hair, waddled through the portal.

"My, my, Massa Tony, we was expecting you yesterday," clucked the slave. "I was ready to send Linus out looking for you. What done kept you so long?"

"I'm sorry, Jemma," laughed Tony, hugging the rotund form, "but the trip from Charles Town took longer than usual. The blasted rain delayed us."

While they were talking Amanda shrank behind Tony until she was barely visible. But the slave's sharp, black eyes spied her immediately. "Is that the housekeeper you done went to Charles Town for?" She eyed Amanda warily, prepared to dislike the woman brought in to usurp duties that heretofore had been hers alone. In fact, she had almost decided to be as uncooperative as possible, considering herself far superior to a lowly convict.

Grasping Amanda's arm. Tony hauled her forward. Jemma's eyes widened in disbelief. "This is Amanda, Jemma. She is the new housekeeper."

"Why, that's no housekeeper, Massa Tony," Jemma scoffed, rolling her black eyes heavenward until only the whites showed. "That's just a chile. A pitiful, skinny chile. What got into you, Massa Tony? How come you brought home a girl what ain't fit for any kind of work lessen she's fattened up? Why, jest look at her! She couldn't stand up in a good wind. You done lost your mind, Massa Tony?"

"That's enough, Jemma," admonished Tony

63

sternly. "My reasons are my own. As soon as Amanda is able, she will assume her duties. Until then she is in your care. See to it that she is fed well. Keep her in bed a few days if necessary. She's no good to me the way she is. Once her health improves she will do well enough."

"Yas suh!" nodded Jemma, grinning widely. "You jest leave this chile to me. I'll have her fat and sassy in no time."

"Not too sassy," laughed Tony indulgently. "Put her in that little attic room on the third floor."

"No suh! I shorely won't do that, Massa Tony," contradicted Jemma, scandalized. "You put this here chile in my care and I aim to take care of her good. No hot, airless attic room for her. No suh!" she reiterated. This chile is gonna have the room next to yours with all them windows where she can get plenty of fresh air and sunshine. Ain't gonna put her in no attic."

Shrugging his shoulders in good-natured acquiescence Tony allowed Jemma to lead a surprisingly meek Amanda inside while he followed close behind. Amanda was stunned by the opulence of the stately plantation. The soaring doorway gave way to an enormous hallway. From the left of the front door a magnificent mahogany staircase swept up to the second floor, an ornately carved balustrade closing in the second floor hall. Aubusson carpets graced the floors, and tapestries and paintings from nearly every master decorated the walls.

"First thing I's gonna do is feed you both," declared Jemma leading the way to the back of the house then through a narrow breezeway separating the kitchen from the main house.

Amanda was immediately impressed by the huge, spotless kitchen sporting both an open fireplace and gigantic cookstove. It was obvious that this warm, friendly room was Jemma's domain as she seated both Tony and Amanda at the round oak table bleached white from constant scrubbing and proceeded to dish out a savory stew kept warm on a back burner. Next came tall, beaten bisquits and cool glasses of cider. Without being urged Amanda ate hungrily, savoring every mouthful of the delicious fare. Only when she was repleat did she sit back and notice that both Tony and Jemma were staring at her with something akin to awe.

"My, my, that chile shore can eat," chuckled Jemma. "She won't stay skinny long with an appetite like that. Who been starving you, girl?"

"I . . . after my mother became ill, there was never enough to eat. And in prison there was rarely enough food to go around. The fare aboard ship was so . . . so . . . disagreeable I was able to keep down little of it." Both Tony and Jemma were aware of the tremor that passed through her body and the look of something akin to pain that darkened her green eyes.

"Never you mind," soothed Jemma, "you got nothing to worry about here. Massa Tony's a good man, a kind master. And old Jemma ain't gonna let no one hurt you." Jemma's maternal instincts had been so aroused by Amanda's words as well as her pitiful condition that she became thoroughly convinced that Tony had brought the young girl to River's Edge for no other purpose than to allow Jemma to mother and cosset her.

Correctly reading her thoughts, Tony chose not to contradict Jemma for the time being. At least not until Amanda was able to assume her duties. He had purchased a housekeeper and he was damn well going to have one. "Take your charge to her room and see if you can find her something decent to wear," he motioned carelessly in Amanda's direction. "She looks like a ragamuffin."

Fuming in silent offense, Amanda opened her mouth to shoot back an angry retort but Jemma forestalled her. The wily slave had immediately sensed the antagonism between her master and the indentured servant and sought to diffuse the volatile atmosphere. At first she had been amused to find that Amanda wasn't as meek as she appeared. But now she thought that the explosive situation would bear watching.

"Don't you worry none, Massa Tony. Old Jemma will fix up this chile with some proper clothes and brush all that shiny hair until it sparkles like a new penny." So saying she took Amanda by the hand and led her out of the kitchen.

"What you do to Massa Tony to make him talk to you like that?" she asked when they were out of earshot. "Did you sass him? Ain't nothing makes him madder than being sassed."

"Ask him what he did to deserve being sassed, as you call it," answered Amanda. "I didn't beg him to buy my papers. He did it of his own free will and then acted like I forced him into doing something against his better judgment."

"Hmmm," was Jemma's only response. Best wait and see what develops, she thought sagely. Could be more here than meets the eye.

The bedchamber that Jemma proudly assigned to Amanda was like something out of a dream. Tall windows pierced the walls which were situated to receive the morning sunshine shimmering across the broad east lawn. It was definitely a woman's room, decorated to please a woman. Amanda couldn't help but wonder who the room was intended for. It was done mostly in a sunny yellow with blue accents and it suited her perfectly. Even the dainty white Provincial French furniture seemed designed especially for her. The large canopied bed, deeply flounced with yellow ruffles and set on a pedestal looked too elegant to sleep in. Never had Amanda beheld such luxury.

Surely Tony didn't mean for her to occupy this room, she thought irrationally. In this day and age an indentured servant was considered on the same level as a slave. And in some instances, even lower. Amanda thought it better to refuse the room now rather than be turned out by Tony after Jemma left. She had no desire to give him the satisfaction of turning her out and degrading her in such a manner.

"This is too fine for me, Jemma," she began. I'm certain Sir Tony would rather I occupy the attic room. Perhaps you'd better take me there. I wouldn't want to get you in any kind of trouble. This room is obviously meant for a guest. . . or a wife."

"Lordy, chile, how you do go on. I knows what I's doing. Now git undressed and climb into bed. I'll wait and carry away them rags you're wearing." Still Amanda hesitated. "Do like I say, chile, afore I undress you myself."

Amanda needed no further urging. In a few short minutes she stood nude before a frowning Jemma.

"Jest like I thought," Jemma said disapprovingly. "All skin and bone underneath them rags. But you got possibilities, chile, you shore do. Now, into bed with you."

While Amanda pulled back the counterpane and crawled beneath the covers, Jemma gathered up her clothes, holding them gingerly between two fat fingers and headed out the door.

"Jemma," Amanda called before the slave was out of sight. "Thank you." Her only answer was a wide, toothy grin and a grunt.

Amanda was nearly asleep when she was startled by someone knocking on her door. "Who is it?" she called, instinctively pulling the blanket closer about her nude body.

"It's Sir Tony, Amanda, may I come in for a moment?"

Amanda hesitated, realizing she had no right to forbid him entry. He had probably come to escort her to the attic room where she undoubtedly belonged, she thought ruefully. "Come in," she finally answered.

Tony entered the room, pausing in the doorway. For some reason the sight of Amanda's slender form, hardly more than a slight bulge beneath the covers strangely moved him. "Are you comfortable?" he asked, his voice harsh in the stillness. "Given her way, Jemma would be dressing you in silks and satins."

Amanda gulped, a bud of panic flowering in her breast. It was just as she had suspected. Tony meant to banish her to the attic room. "If you'll leave the room, Sir Tony, I'll find something with which to cover myself and leave immediately. I never intended to impose myself where I don't belong."

Tony assimilated her words slowly, her

meaning at first escaping him. He scowled darkly when finally he understood. "I didn't come here to evict you," he said indignantly.

"Then why did you come?" snapped back Amanda, gritting her teeth in exasperation.

"I'll be damned if I know!" he retorted, stung by her animosity. Turning on his heel he stormed from the room, slamming the door behind him.

Amanda breathed deeply, a bright flush staining her pale cheeks. Once again she had allowed her wayward tongue free reign and in the process had earned nothing but reproach and harsh words. Besides, she had no business angering a man who would be her master and in charge of her life for seven long years. Sighing regretfully, Amanda sank back into the comfortable bed dreaming of the night she and Tony had surmounted the stigma of master and slave; a night spent in Tony's arms, a night when time stood still.

4

Amanda spent nearly a week in the beautiful, sunny room, doing little else but eating and sleeping. Somehow during those lazy days Jemma managed to fashion two servicable but attractive dresses for her from material she salvaged from some dark corner of the house. She also presented Amanda with two nightgowns, a soft, frilly robe and various undergarments.

For the first time in months Amanda's green eyes sparkled with a new vitality and her figure gave hint of the shapely woman she was capable of becoming. Until today she had taken all her meals in her room, carried to her by Tess, a vivacious house servant about her own age, or by Cory, another of the slaves, even younger than Tess. Both girls were like friendly, eager puppies, not quite certain how to treat the white girl installed in the best guest room in the house. When they would treat her as a superior, Amanda soon put them straight, explaining that she was only a servant herself and would soon be working alongside them.

Tess was shocked. "But you'se a white girl. It ain't right."

It was only after Amanda explained that her servitude would last but seven years that Tess understood. But Amanda had insisted that both girls use her given name.

Amanda dressed carefully in an attractive light green dress of sprigged muslin with short puffed sleeves and low, square neckline. The bodice accentuated her young, firm breasts and tiny waist, flaring out over narrow hips accentuating their slimness. She had brushed her hair one hundred strokes and tied it back with a velvet ribbon. She felt and looked better than she had in months.

In a mood of eager anticipation Amanda left the room that had been her refuge for one week, able and willing to take up her duties as house-keeper. As she started down the wide, curved staircase her critical eye spotted a thin layer of dust coating the mahogany steps as well as the balustrade, marring their gleaming elegance. The carpets she had so admired in the dim, evening light a week ago were caked with dirt; windows were dingy with grime, the thick, velvet draperies festooned with cobwebs. Though Jemma was an excellent cook it was obvious that her talents stopped short of housekeeping skills. Amanda could hardly wait to organize the house servants into some semblance of order and prove to Tony that she was capable of performing the duties he had assigned to her.

First she decided to explore the rest of the house. To the right of the staircase were two closed doors leading from the large hallway. Peeping into one revealed a sunny, pleasant parlor whose beige walls complimented the gold brocade draperies. The furniture looked elegant as well as comfortable. A formal dining room lay behind the second closed door. Above the long mahogany table hung an Austrian chandelier whose prisms were badly in need of cleaning.

Turning her attention to the other side of the hall, Amanda discovered a large ballroom whose tall French doors led out onto a verandah, and next to it a book-lined office that she supposed was Tony's private domain. Then she decided to inspect the outside of the house in the full light of day. One could almost describe it as an English country estate. White clapboard with black shutters and two red brick chimneys rising from its three stories. Colonnaded breezeways connected the main house to outbuildings which housed the kitchen and storehouse. Everything about the plantation pleased Amanda.

Some distance from the back of the house she could see two neat rows of newly painted slave quarters lined up facing each other. Beyond that lay the fields, now green with crops she supposed were indigo and rice. Completing the picture was the sparkling ribbon of the Santee River flowing gently through the acres.

Her inspection tour at an end Amanda returned to the front of the house just as two people on horseback were in the process of dismounting. The man, whom she immediately identified as Tony, helped his attractive companion from her perch. With an air of familiarity she slid effortlessly into his arms, her own arms twining about his neck as if they belonged there. So engrossed were they in one another that neither noticed Amanda, rooted to the spot, wide-eyed, as Tony's mouth came down hungrily on the woman's full, red lips. From where she stood it looked as if their bodies were pasted together, hip to hip, thigh to thigh.

Embarrassed, Amanda started to move off but evidently she wasn't fast enough or quiet enough for Tony spied her out of the corner of his eye and motioned her forward. Hesitantly she approached the attractive couple. From a distance the woman in Tony's arms looked merely beautiful but on closer observation Amanda thought her the most ravishing creature she had ever seen. Never could she hope to compete with such a sophisticated woman, she thought despairingly. Tall, nearly as tall as Tony, definitely voluptuous, with pale blond hair, nearly silver, and bold blue eyes. Her skin was smooth and flawless as white alabaster. She was dressed in stark black velvet with a jaunty hat perched at a rakish angle atop her glorious hair. Beside her Amanda felt as awkward and self-conscious as a new born puppy.

"Amanda," Tony began as the woman stepped out of his arms and regarded Amanda through narrowed, suspicious eyes, "you look wonderful. I knew Jemma would have you on your feet in no time. Why, I do believe you've gained some weight." There was a teasing twist to his mouth and his silver eyes sparkled.

Amanda flushed with pleasure. It was nice to be thought attractive again, even by Tony.

"Who is this creature, Tony?" demanded his companion haughtily.

"This is Amanda, Letty. Remember? I spoke to you before about the indentured servant whose papers I purchased. On the advice of your father, I might add." Then he turned to Amanda. "Amanda, this is Letty Carter, a good friend and neighbor."

Amanda curtsied respectfully but instinctively knew Letty Carter would never be her friend. Her eyes were cold and contemptuous, raking Amanda as if she were a bug that had just crawled out of the woodwork.

"Housekeeper!" exploded Letty derisively. "Your bed warmer, more likely!" Her fair complexion became mottled and red with rage; her lips were drawn into a snarl making her appear almost ugly. "Tony, you are either very stupid or very naive. This... this... slut is no more qualified to be a housekeeper than... than a baboon. What kind of persuasion did she use to get you to buy her papers? Anyone with half a mind can see she's a prostitute besides a... what did you say she was, a thief? Get rid of her, Tony. Sell her papers to someone else. She'd do well in a brothel."

Throughout Letty's venomous attack Tony stood by flabbergasted at the hatred and abuse coming from her beautiful red lips and aimed at Amanda who had greeted her quite respectfully, given Amanda's volatile disposition. He saw Amanda's delicate features turn vivid red, then dead white. At that moment his compassion for her seemed boundless; he wanted only to comfort and protect her from cruel, unfeeling people like Letty who had no conception of the suffering and indignities forced upon a young girl confined in Newgate and transported on a prison ship.

"Letty," snapped Tony angrily, "I think you've said enough. You are embarrassing Amanda."

"Embarrassing Amanda! How dare you

rebuke me. Have you been beguiled by her innocent airs and youth? Have you already had her, Tony?" Suddenly Letty's eyes widened, mindful of what she had just said. "My God! It's true! She's sharing your bed! No wonder you took your time coming to me when you returned from Charles Town. Isn't one woman enough for you?" Letty's reptilian gaze came to rest on Amanda's shocked face.

Acting with a swiftness born of jealousy Letty lashed out cruelly with her riding crop, raising a long, angry welt across Amanda's pale cheek. Amanda cried out in pain and fell back under Letty's unprovoked attack. But Letty's next stroke never fell, for Tony, galvanized into action, seized the instrument of torture from Letty's hand and tossed it on the ground, gray eyes dark with disgust.

"Letty, what has gotten into you? Amanda is my servant. If she needs punishing I'll be the one to do it! I think you are making too much of this. There is nothing between Amanda and myself. In fact, this is the first time I have set eyes on her since she arrived a week ago. She is nothing but my housekeeper, an indentured servant, bound to me for seven years. The least you could do is show a little compassion for her plight."

"Her plight, as you choose to call it, is of her own making and no concern of mine," snapped Letty maliciously.

"Letty, I think you had better leave. I'll see you tomorrow."

"Dismissing me, Tony? That's a first."

Tony sighed heavily, slanting Letty a quelling look. "I have work to do, Letty. I enjoyed our ride but I do have a planation to run."

Immediately Letty was contrite, pouting prettily as she pushed her lush body against Tony. "You promise you'll call on me tomorrow, darling? Father would love to see you. It's been ages and ages since you've had supper with us. I know!" she clapped, her face lighting up. "Spend the night with us! Say you will, darling, please!"

Anxious to be rid of Letty and see to Amanda's hurt face, Tony was ready to agree to anything, "Yes, yes," he agreed instantly. "I'll come to supper, and spend the night if it's all right with your father."

"Oh, Tony, you won't be sorry," Letty cooed seductively. "You know how happy I can make you." Her last words were spoken with a mysterious smile aimed directly at Amanda who stood stifly erect and stone-like throughout the whole degrading episode.

Was she always to be reviled and vilified for a single crime she was forced to commit? she wondered dejectedly, hardly aware that Letty had mounted her horse and ridden off with a self-satisfied smirk on her lips. The day that had begun on a note of pleasure now turned to ashes in her mouth. What did the beautiful Letty mean to Tony? If Letty's broadfaced hint could be believed they were lovers, not merely good friends as Tony suggested. It was evident to Amanda that Letty intended more than friendship. But what of Tony? Was Letty the woman he meant to marry one day?

"Amanda," It seemed as if Tony's voice was coming from far away. "Are you hurt badly?"

Amanda blinked rapidly, bringing everything that had just transpired sharply into focus. She was still cupping her swollen cheek, and though the pain was great, she doubted that she was badly injured. "No," she answered dully, meeting Tony's concerned gaze. "I'm sure it will heal in a few days."

"Damn, Amanda, I'm sorry this had to happen. I know Letty has a vile temper and has been spoiled rotten by her father, but that doesn't give her the right to treat you so shabbily. To strike you was reprehensible. You belong to me, Amanda, I won't have anyone mistreating you."

Amanda's heart soared. Did he mean what he said? she wondered. He must care for her a little to rescue her from Letty's acid tongue and sharp riding crop.

"Let me see," said Tony, gently removing Amanda's hand from her injured cheek. Swearing under his breath he traced a finger along the jagged ridge marring her otherwise flawless skin. When he reached her chin he tilted her face upward, at the same time lowering his own. Amanda, bowing to the inevitable, closed her eyes and allowed him to possess her lips. From his first feather-light touch tiny buds of sensation burst softly into bloom. His mouth moved in unhurried, sensuous exploration. The taste, the essence of him filled her being. After what seemed like ages, he broke off the kiss murmuring, "I'm sorry, Amanda, I didn't mean to take advantage of you but you looked so unhappy I couldn't help myself. Come, let's see what Jemma can give you for that nasty welt. It looks painful."

"Sir Tony," Amanda ventured as he led her by the hand into the house, "is Mistress Carter your betrothed?"

"What makes you ask that?"

"She's very possessive. . . and jealous."

"There's been no announcement," shrugged

Tony even though he knew her father as well as Letty expected them to marry soon.

"If she were to become mistress here," Amanda persisted doggedly, "I'm sure she would not want me to remain at River's Edge."

"Do you like it here, Amanda?"

"It's. . . very nice."

"That's all? Just nice?"

"It's a beautiful plantation. I'm afraid Jemma spoils me and I'm beginning to like it too well. It's almost the same as when my father. . ." Biting her lip she fought hard to control the flood of tears threatening to inundate her as memories, both good and bad, loomed before her.

Jemma was horrified when she saw Amanda's face. "What you do to that chile, Massa Tony?" she asked accusingly, thick fists resting on ample hips. "I never knowed you to be so mean before. You never even beat one of the field hands so why you go and pick on this poor chile?"

"Relax, Jemma," laughed Tony, likening the fat slave to a mother hen protecting her chick. "I didn't touch Amanda."

"Well someone did, that's for shore. Who done it, Amanda? Who hurt you?"

Amanda remained mute, unwilling to involve Letty lest she anger Tony.

"You might as well tell me, Massa Tony. You knows I'll find out sooner or later."

"If you must know, Jemma, Mistress Carter allowed her temper to surface and struck Amanda with her riding crop," said Tony.

"What you do to that witch, chile, to make her so mad?"

Tony was quick to defend Amanda. "She did nothing, Jemma. And don't talk of Mistress Carter that way. Now, are you going to put something on Amanda's face or not?"

"Yas, sah, I fix her up. You go on with your chores. I'll see to Amanda."

At that moment Tony wanted nothing more than to sit back and absorb Amanda's fresh beauty but he sensed he was being dismissed and, shrugging good naturedly, left after a long, lingering look that left Amanda shaken. His graphic eyes spoke eloquently of his desire.

Jemma set to work immediately, smoothing a cooling salve on Amanda's bruised cheek. "Why did that Mistress Carter attack you, chile?" she asked.

"I truly don't know, Jemma. She took an instant dislike to me. She even accused me of sharing Sir Tony's bed."

A low chuckle burst forth from Jemma's throat. "Well, chile, would that be so bad?"

Shocked, Amanda sputtered, "But it's not true!"

"From the look Massa Tom jest gave you he shore do wish it was true, honey."

Blushing furiously Amanda lowered her long lashes. Jemma was too close to the truth for comfort. She was certain that the slave could read her mind, and if she could then she would know she had lain that one night in Tony's arms, matching him kiss for kiss, thrust for thrust. That was something even she did not want to think about.

Amanda's days were filled with activity. Her first priority had been to acquaint herself with the rest of the house servants. In addition to Jemma, who occupied a small room off the kitchen, and Tess and Cory, who stayed sometimes in the house on the third floor, there was Linus, the butler, Jemma's elderly husband who shared her room, and six girls who came to the big house daily to perform various tasks but returned nightly to their own living quarters. With a skill she didn't know she possessed, Amanda soon had every available pair of hands, with the exception of Jemma and Linus whose duties were well defined, cleaning, scrubbing, shaking and beating from sunup to sundown. After being worked so diligently most slaves would have become sullen and resentful, but because Amanda worked nearly as hard as they did, never demanding more from them than she was willing to give herself, she earned their respect as well as their willingness to work. Most of the people on the plantation were aware of her pecular place in the household, slave, yet not a slave, free, but not free. Every one of them were as sympathetic to her plight as she was to theirs.

Of Tony, Amanda saw very little. It seemed to her that he went out of his way to avoid her. But that was perfectly all right with her for whenever she saw or spoke with him her nerves were a quivering mass of conflicting emotions. At times he could be kind and gentle, his eyes akindle with a strange light whenever he encountered her in passing. At other times he appeared grim and disapproving, barely acknowledging her presence with a curt nod of his head. Amanda knew that Tony was seeing Letty regularly for she often stopped by early in the morning for their daily ride together, only to return flushed and exhilarated, her cheeks aglow with color, her clothing disheveled. Some nights Tony did not return home at all after calling on Letty and her father and Amanda instinctively knew he had spent them in Letty's bed. Not that it made any difference to her, she tried to convince herself.

Amanda paused at the top of the gleaming staircase and ran her hands lovingly along the balustrade, remembering the first time she had done that weeks ago and her hand had come away grimy. Now, everything that met her eye shone and sparkled. The brilliant June sunshine filtered through gleaming windows, splintering, then coming to rest on the jewel-like colors woven into the Aubusson carpets below. A smile of satisfaction curved her full lips, her green eyes mirroring the pride and joy she felt at what she had accomplished in a few short weeks.

Tony walked out of his study and immediately spied Amanda, a secret smile curving her shapely lips, a picture of symetric beauty and feminine grace. The slim lines of her body had filled out and rounded in all the right places, high, full breasts, tiny, indented waist, gently curved hips. What a contrast from the bedraggled waif he had brought to River's Edge, he thought, amazed. Her thick, auburn tresses glinted more red than brown in the bright sunlight and Tony thought it indecent for anyone to have such long, feathery eyelashes. She was clad, attractively, thanks to Jemma's ingenuity, in a pale yellow voile that if anything accentuated her youth and vulnerability.

Tony's heart beat furiously in his chest and a warm, intense pleasure flooded his loins as he recalled the night he had taken her beneath the wagon, a lost, forlorn child who had responded to and delighted in his lovemaking. As if suddenly aware that she was being watched, Amanda glanced down, meeting Tony's rapt gaze. It seemed like hours that they stood there, neither willing nor able to break eye contact, each aware of the other as they had never been before. Tony was the first to look away.

Clearing his throat, he said, "Amanda, would you come into the study? I'd like to speak with you."

"Of course," answered Amanda crisply as she started down the staircase. She silently prayed that she would do or say nothing to anger him during this interview. She had been treated well and had grown to love River's Edge and it's people. She would do anything to remain here. . . well, almost anything, she reconsidered.

Tony stood in the doorway waiting for Amanda to precede him into the study, and when she did he closed the door behind them, carelessly motioning her into a chair. For some reason his mouth felt like cotton and he cleared his throat, deliberately avoiding looking directly at Amanda lest he become distracted by those guileless, emerald eyes.

"How long have you been here, Amanda?" he asked, knowing full well the exact month, day and hour she set foot on River's Edge.

"About eight weeks," she answered, puzzled by his line of questioning.

"Have you been well treated? Do you like it here?"

"I've. . . been happy here, Sir Tony. Happier than I ever expected or have a right to be," she answered honestly.

Somehow her answer pleased Tony. "You have the same right to be happy as anyone, Amanda."

"Even the slaves?" she asked innocently.

Tony scowled darkly. "They are happy in their

own way," came his stiff reply.

Immediately Amanda knew she had once again overstepped her bounds and made him angry. Seeking to make amends, she quickly added, "Jemma has been so good to me. She is like a second mother. I swear she is trying to make me as fat as she is."

Despite himself, Tony smiled, and his mood lightened perceptibly. "You've done a splendid job in whipping the house into shape. I've never seen it look better. I'm too much in the fields to supervise the house slaves and Jemma is too busy with the cooking to oversee the cleaning."

"That's why I'm here," reminded Amanda in a low voice. "I'm your housekeeper. I'm only doing my duty."

"So you are," conceded Tony, slanting her a sideways glance to see if she was mocking him. Satisfied that her expression was innocent of any double meanings, he continued, "We haven't had many guests here since your arrival at River's Edge but tomorrow night will change all that. I've asked Letty and her father to dine with us as well as Nathan Grover, my overseer. You've seen Nathan but I don't believe you've met him. A nice young man and a damned good overseer."

Amanda's attention sharpened, wondering what he wanted of her. The menu planning and cooking rested solely with Jemma. She clearly intended to keep to her room the moment Letty showed her face at River's Edge. She had seen Nathan Grover in Tony's company often enough but never had the occasion to meet him. She wondered what prompted Tony to have a dinner party at this time and asked him.

Tony hesitated only a moment, then, shrugging his shoulders, said, "It's Letty's birthday. Her father asked me to host a small party in her honor as a favor to him. His cook is ill and unable to cope with guests."

Amanda nodded, wondering what all this had to do with her. "I'll see that the house is in order and the best china and silver laid out. Is there anything else?"

"Just have plenty of fresh flowers around, Letty loves flowers. Oh, yes, have two guest rooms prepared. Letty and her father are to spend the night."

Amanda's whole body tensed. How could she hope to avoid Letty if she was an overnight guest, she wondered despairingly. "Which rooms would you like prepared, Sir Tony?"

"The one across the hall from mine should do nicely for Letty," Tony said after a moments thought. "Give her father any one of the others at the end of the hall."

Amanda flushed, knowing exactly Tony's reasons for placing Letty across the hall from him and her father as far away as possible. He wanted easy access to his mistress.. "I'll see to it," she acquiesced, nodding curtly. Thinking the interview at an end she turned to leave.

"Amanda, I haven't dismissed you," Tony said sharply, stopping her in her tracks. "There is one more thing."

Amanda swung around to face Tony, finely arched eyebrows peaked, waiting somewhat impatiently for him to continue. Tony took a deep, steadying breath and Amanda instinctively knew she would not like what she was about to hear.

"I want you to serve us at table tomorrow night."

Amanda gasped. "Sir Tony, you can't mean it!" She was horrified to think that she should be paraded before Letty and her father, open to ridicule and treated with contempt. Why would Tony insist on such a thing? He knew how much Letty hated her, didn't he?

"Amanda, I do mean it. You have no choice in the matter. Letty specifically asked for you to serve the meal. It is her birthday and I don't have the heart to refuse her." He paused, his voice softening, "I want you to be on your best behavior." Amanda scowled darkly, but before she could retort, Tony blithely continued. "I'm afraid I'm partly to blame for putting you in this position, but Letty can be very persuasive. What harm can it do?"

Amanda exploded. "What harm! What about my pride and self-respect? Does that mean nothing to you? You know Mistress Letty hates me and would stop at nothing to embarrass me. I have done nothing to her! Nothing!"

"Amanda," Tony said consolingly, "Letty can do nothing to harm you. You are accountable to no one but me. I know Letty isn't perfect but basically she is a good person."

Amanda was openly skeptical. Either Tony was blind to Letty's faults or so in love with her he chose to ignore them. And for some reason she hoped it wasn't the latter.

"I won't do it, Sir Tony," she insisted stubbornly. "I won't be ridiculed by your mistress and her father."

Storm clouds gathered in Tony's dark visage and Amanda immediately realized what she had said. "How dare you speak to me in such an insolent manner!" Tony raged. "My private affairs are none of your concern. Perhaps Letty is correct in insisting that you need disciplining. I'm sure you wouldn't have been treated so well if you had gone to live with that lecherous parson and his odious wife."

Amanda shuddered, banishing such a terrifying thought from her mind. She tried to think of something to say to placate Tony, but realized with a sinking heart that his temper was beyond that point. Consequently, she remained silent, succeeding only in adding to his anger.

"Don't just stand there glaring at me with those innocent, green eyes, Amanda," stormed Tony. "Answer me! Would you have preferred the parson to me?"

Somehow his words triggered a violent reaction in Amanda, causing her to lose all self-control as she faced him. Thrusting out her small chin defiantly, "I would!" she shouted belligerently, immediately regretting her rash words as a cruel, wolfish smile curved Tony's mouth.

"Then I shall treat you as he would have done!" With that he closed the space between them in two angry strides, seizing her roughly by the shoulders, pinning her against his hardening body so that she was aware of his arousal.

"No!" Amanda cried in growing alarm, his arms like two steel bands squeezing the breath from her slender form.

Before another word could pass her lips Tony's punishing mouth smashed down on hers with cruel savagery, bruising her lips against her teeth. His flaming tongue parted her lips, sucking the very soul from her body as he probed, tasted, withdrew, then thrust again until she moaned, helpless to resist his violent passion. A bud of panic flowered in her breast as she felt his burgeoning manhood prod her stomach. Did he mean to rape her? Why, oh why did she insist on angering him so when she knew the position she was in, realized that he was perfectly within his rights to punish her in any way he saw fit? But she was determined to keep Tony from heaping indignities upon her. After submitting to the constable she swore that no man would take her again without love. With considerable strength, Amanda twisted violently in Tony's arms catching him off guard. When his arms dropped away she swung one hand upward catching him a glancing blow across the cheek. Reflexively, Tony struck back with his open palm, sending Amanda reeling against the wall with the force of the blow. Surprised more than hurt, Amanda stared at Tony with wounded eyes, unable to believe he could be so cruel. The beginnings of tears glistened on her long lashes, her left cheekbone bearing the full imprint of his palm.

"Oh my God!" Tony moaned, the sight of Amanda's crumpled form shocking the anger from him. "What have I done? I've never struck a woman before in my life!"

Immediately he was kneeling at Amanda's side, helping her rise, stunned by the surge of anger and lust she had aroused in him. How could one defenseless girl defy him so brazenly? Amanda shrank away from his helping hands, determined to show no weakness in his presence.

"I don't need your help, Sir Tony," she ground out defiantly.

Tony flushed. Never before had he allowed his emotions to rule his head so completely. Why now? he wondered. And why toward a girl who could not defend herself? "I'm sorry, Amanda," he began, "but you. . ."

"You owe me no explanation, Sir Tony," Amanda interrupted coldly. "It's within your right to punish me as you see fit. More than anything it's made me aware of my lowly position in your household. I'm no better than one of your slaves and from now on will endeavor to remember my place. I will serve the meal to you and your guests tomorrow night. It was foolish of me to protest in the first place. "After all, why should my feelings mean anything to you? I am merely an indentured servant with no rights, no feelings." With those words she turned on her heel and stalked from the room, head held high, small shoulders erect.

For several minutes afterwards Tony did not move, staring thoughtfully after the proud figure he had held in his arms only moments before. Lord knows he hadn't meant to strike her. Hadn't meant to kiss her, either. But he couldn't help himself. What's more, he would have taken her right there on the study floor if she hadn't deflected him from his purpose at the last minute. He would have torn off her clothes without a moment's hesitation and possessed her body until she screamed with ecstasy and responded with the passion he knew her capable of. God, what was wrong with him? he wondered guiltily. Wasn't Letty woman enough for him? Perhaps he ought to marry Letty to end his obsession once and for all for the auburn-tressed enchantress he had taken under his roof.

Amanda surveyed the diningroom with satisfaction. The long table set with gleaming china, chrystal and silver reflected the soft, glowing candlelight. The whole house had never looked better and Amanda was proud of her accomplishments. Though exhausted from her labors she knew her ordeal was just beginning. She had the whole evening ahead of her in which to bow and humble herself before Tony and his mistress. She hadn't spoken to Tony since he had struck her but she often caught him following her with dark, brooding eyes as she performed her duties. She quivered inwardly when she considered how she had almost let him take her the previous day in his study. She had succumbed once to his seduction but she had been weak and unable to withstand his passionate onslaught. Things were different now, she owed her body to no man. All she was required to do was to work and serve her sentence of seven years. And if she was to survive intact she must avoid Tony and Letty at all costs, even if it meant to hold her tongue in check.

Amanda wandered out into the dusk, breathing deeply of the cool evening air. The day had been hot and stifling and the breeze felt good on her flushed skin. If only the day was over, she sighed, scuffing her foot into the soft grass as she walked. Suddenly she met with an immovable object and she stumbled. Immediately she felt herself caught up by a pair of muscular arms. Looking up she encountered two merry brown eyes in a broad, friendly face smiling at her.

"I'm s—sorry," stammered Amanda. "I didn't look where I was going."

"It's my pleasure to be of assistance. It's not every day that a lovely woman falls into my arms."

Amanda flushed with pleasure. She recognized the pleasant, openly friendly face immediately as belonging to Nathan Grover, Tony's overseer as well as trusted friend. He often came to the house in the evenings to chat and relax with Tony over a cigar and brandy. Sometimes their voices carried to her room, raised in amicable debate.

"Are you on your way up to the house, Master Grover?" Amanda asked to cover her embarrassment.

Nathan laughed. "Please, Amanda, call me Nathan. And, yes, I'm on my way to join Tony's dinner party. You don't mind if I call you Amanda, do you? I know we've never met and it's presumptuous of me, but I've caught glimpses of you often enough and hoped to meet you."

Amanda found it easy to like Nathan Grover. Touched by his obvious sincerity she couldn't help but smile and nod. "If I call you Nathan it's no more than right that you should call me Amanda. After all," her eyes darkened perceptively, "I'm just an indentured servant, you have a right to address me any way you please."

"Amanda, I meant no slight," came Nathan's agonized reply.

"No offense taken," assured Amanda hastily. She had no wish to antagonize this man who treated her with such kindness and respect.

They walked in silence toward the house for a few moments while Amanda studied him through lowered lids. He appeared older than Tony by a few years. Though not so tall, his massive torso gave him the appearance of great height. Beneath his shirt his chest and arm muscles rippled with implied power, his legs like two sturdy oaks encased in knee-high boots. Sun-streaked, sandy hair, worn collar length framed a strong-featured, darkly tanned face.

When they reached the house Amanda turned toward the kitchen. "I've work to do, Nathan, I hope you enjoy the party."

"Not so fast, Amanda," smiled Nathan, grasping her hand. "When can I see you again? It's been pleasant talking with you like this. I'd like to spend more time with you."

Amanda was speechless. Was it possible for a man to court an indentured servant? she wondered. No matter what Nathan thought, she was positive Tony would not allow it. Aloud she said, "I don't know. I've just met you. Give me time to think about it."

"Of course. I didn't mean to rush you. You must realize what a beautiful, desirable woman you are. No man in his right mind would not enjoy just being in your company."

"Nathan!" Amanda exclaimed, embarrassed by his sincere words.

"It's all right, Amanda," laughed Nathan, brown eyes teasing, "sometimes my bluntness is my undoing. Go back to your duties, my dear. Somehow I'll contrive a way to see you again."

Later, as she prepared to serve dinner to the guests in the dining room, Amanda thought about her meeting with Nathan. She had thoroughly enjoyed talking with him and was grateful for his kind words. It did much to boost her morale. Something she desperately needed if she was to get through this night. Despite her misgivings she hoped to be allowed to see him again. With him she knew exactly where she stood, his open, friendly nature in direct contrast with Tony's dark moods and high-handed treatment.

"Chile," reminded Jemma gently, "Massa Tony done wrung the bell for the first course. Don't fret, you'll do jest fine."

Amanda drew a long, steadying breath, Jemma's words hardly registering on her benumbed brain. She had heard the bell and knew she could not delay a moment longer. Squaring her small shoulders, she nodded absently to Jemma, grasped the enormous soup tureen by the handles and started for the dining room.

Tony watched with wary eyes as Amanda stopped first before a wickedly smiling Letty. Compassion evident on his wrinkled features, Linus stepped forward from his place behind Tony to serve the soup to Letty. Tony visibly relaxed as they moved on to the next person until each was served and the tureen rested safely on the sideboard. Platters of meat, fowl, savory vegetables, rich sauces and steaming rice followed one upon the other until the very sight of food sickened Amanda.

While Tony and his guests were engaged in eating and trading light table talk, she had a few minutes to silently appraise Letty and her father. She thought she had never seen Letty looking more beautiful with her pale, silvery hair piled high atop her well-shaped head in a mass of curls held in place by a diamond tiara. Two springy sausage-like spirals hung down her swan-like throat, resting on each bare, white shoulder. The tops of two pearly breasts, bared to the nipples, rose and fell enticingly above the deep decolatage of a vivid red gown liberally sprinkled with diamonds. Amanda had never seen the like. She had heard Letty tell Tony the gown had come all the way from Paris. A gift from her father.

Stanley Carter was a complete surprise to Amanda. She had expected an older version of Letty but was pleasantly shocked to find his eyes resting on her with kindness and understanding as she served him. It was almost as if he was aware of what his daughter was up to but was powerless to interfere.

Thus far nothing had gone amiss and Nathan's low murmur of encouragement when no one was looking did much to bolster her courage. Only Letty's cold, relentless glare and Tony's watchful gaze stopped her from relaxing as she performed her duties. Amanda knew Letty would act. What form her perversity would take Amanda couldn't even guess at, but that Letty would strike, she had no doubt. That knowledge was firmly entrenched in her bones, as well as in Stanley Carter's sympathetic eyes.

It was nearly time for Amanda to return to the kitchen for the elaborate birthday cake Jemma had worked on all day. The spectacular three-tiered confection was iced with mounds of fluffy white frosting, delicate pink rosebuds and pale green leaves. It was a masterpiece worthy of an artist, which Jemma surely was. Suddenly all eyes swung toward Tony as he arose and placed a small, square box before Letty who was seated across the table from him. Letty's blue eyes glitted as brightly as the gems encircling her head and festooning her gown as she greedily reached for the box. Privately, she had expected Tony to present her with an engagement ring on her birthday to formalize their relationship and had told her father as much. It had taken some doing to arrange to have the party at Tony's home, and more coercing to convince Tony that none but Amanda could serve them, gleefully picturing in her mind the expression on Amanda's face when Tony announced their engagement. No matter how hard Letty tried in the past to pin Tony down to a commitment he had thus far managed to evade her, becoming more and more remote since Amanda had entered his household.

"Oh, Tony," gushed Letty releasing the lid to the velvet box, "I've waited so long for..." Stopping in mid-sentence, her eyes raised slowly from the box and came to rest on Amanda, two blue-white chips of ice that sent chills of apprehension along her spine. But before Tony had a chance to recognize her disappointment, Letty turned back to her gift, drawing out a gold chain from which dangled an exquisite pearl. "It's lovely," she intoned without enthusiasm.

Stanley felt keenly his daughter's disappointment, aware that she had expected to come away from her birthday party betrothed. He had hoped for the same thing himself. Letty needed a forceful man like Tony to tame and subdue her violent nature. After tonight he could only think that Tony had no intention of marrying Letty and they had best look elsewhere for a husband. Letty was twenty-five and much too beautiful and passionate to remain a spinster. He had long considered returning to England. With his money it would not be difficult to buy Letty a titled husband. Now, a trip was definitely in the offing.

Amanda could not take her eyes off the pearl necklace. It looked expensive but she knew by Letty's reaction that she had expected much more. And being a woman Amanda instinctively knew what Letty wanted. An engagement ring. But for some reason Tony had withheld her heart's desire. Did that mean Tony didn't love his mistress? she wondered hopefully. That he had no intention of proposing marriage?

"Put it on me, Tony, darling," purred Letty,

determined not to show her disappointment.

Tony clasped the necklace around her neck. The creamy pearl nestled between her ripe breasts, absorbing the warmth of her heated flesh. Then he kissed her lightly on the lips wishing her a happy birthday. Returning to his place he nodded curtly to Amanda indicating that it was time to bring in the cake.

5

Tense and nervous Amanda hastened to the kitchen where Jemma was putting the finishing touches on the birthday cake. The slave's sharp eyes immediately noted Amanda's state, likening her to a tightly wound spring ready to uncoil at the slightest provocation.

"What's wrong, chile?" she asked, clucking sympathetically. "Is that witch pestering you again?"

"Not exactly, Jemma, but she hates me. I just know she's waiting for the right moment to spring on me."

"You jest imagining things, honey. Everythin's been going along jest fine so far. Don't fret, Massa Tony ain't gonna let no harm come to you." Jemma turned back to the cake, hefted it's weight in her arms and eyed Amanda skeptically. "You shore you can manage this? Maybe I'd better call Linus."

"No, I'm strong, I can do it," assured Amanda,

gingerly accepting the large platter from Jemma. She was nearly dwarfed by the huge cake but found that she could indeed manage the weight without too much difficulty.

A round of applause greeted Amanda's entrance. Even Letty was impressed by Jemma's handiwork.

"Set it before Letty," Tony ordered, "the first cut belongs to her."

Amanda slowly made her way to Letty, her arms shaking under the burden. Heaving an inward sigh of relief she bent to settle the platter carefully on the cleared off place before the guest of honor. But before she could accomplish the final act that would mark the end of her duties for the evening, Letty, her malicious act concealed by the long tablecloth, viciously stabbed the sharp point of her knife into the soft flesh of Amanda's upper thigh, piercing through dress, petticoat and chemise with one deft stroke. Pain followed astonishment across Amanda's expressive face as she cried out, desperately trying to balance the cake in her quaking arms as her injured leg gave way beneath her. What transpired next happened so fast that before the others realized anything was wrong, the cake plopped onto Letty's lap.

Uttering a cry of outrage, Letty jumped to her feet, knocking her chair backwards. All eyes were focused on the beautiful Parisian gown now ruined beyond redemption. "You clumsy ox!" screamed Letty, brushing ineffectually at the gooey mess sliding down the front of her gown. "You did this deliberately! You were jealous of my gown and my place in Tony's life!" Eyes shooting blue flames, she turned to Tony, shouting angrily, "You refused to have this slut punished when I said she was in need of discipline, now look what happened. This time I insist you have her whipped. Better yet, let me show that little thief her place!"

Tony was stunned. It all happened so quickly that he had noticed nothing until Letty jumped up from the table, brushing frantically at her ruined gown, the remains of her birthday cake at her dainty slippers. His gaze slid to Amanda who stood nearby, white-faced, eyes wide with terror, one hand clutching the upper part of her thigh as if in pain.

He was certain Amanda hadn't done it on purpose but he had to sympathize with Letty who surely had a right to be angry. But to beat Amanda was unthinkable. After that one time he had struck her, his guilt had been awesome and he never intended to hurt or allow her to be hurt again.

"Now, Letty," he soothed, "Amanda didn't purposely drop that cake in your lap. I know how upset you. . ."

"No, Tony, you don't know how upset I am!" shot back Letty, unwilling to allow Amanda to escape so easily. "If you did you would punish her this instant. I am your guest of honor! Why do you insist on coddling and protecting that. . . that. . . convict?"

Her vicious attack prompted her father to speak up, embarrassed by his daughter's violent behavior. "Control yourself, daughter. Give Amanda the benefit of the doubt. Show your breeding, girl!" Letty slanted him a quelling glance.

Amanda rubbed her wounded thigh, listening intently to the exchange. She prayed that either

Stanley or Tony would succeed in calming Letty. She saw Nathan's compassionate look and sensed that even Tony did not blame her, and was grateful. But there was no placating Letty who grew angrier by the minute. Amanda looked at Tony beseechingly, green eyes huge in her white face. More than anything she wanted to turn and flee, but stood her ground, for to run would be to admit her guilt. And she was guilty of nothing.

Slowly Letty came to the realization that Tony had no intention of punishing Amanda, that all her contriving had gone for naught, destroying the most beautiful gown she had ever owned in the process. Her rage knew no bounds as she lunged for Amanda, an animal-like snarl curling her lips.

Amanda reeled under the sudden attack, falling beneath Letty's flailing arms and legs. Huddling in a ball on the floor she fought to protect her face and head. Acting almost in unison, Tony and Nathan sprang forward. Tony placed restraining hands on Letty while Nathan knelt to protect Amanda. Finally Letty let herself be quieted, and then realizing her close proximity to Tony, fell into his arms weeping and bemoaning the disastrous end to her birthday party.

"You'd better leave, Amanda," Tony ordered sternly once she was on her feet. "Go to your room. You've caused enough damage for one night."

"But, Sir Tony, I didn't mean. . ."

"I don't want to discuss it now," replied Tony roughly. Tony's harsh words to his indentured servant cheered Letty immensely even though her sobbing grew more frenzied.

"You'd better do as he says," whispered Nathan in a low voice as he turned Amanda toward the stairs. Amanda had no recourse but to limp from the room, Letty's loud wails ringing in her ears long after she reached the sanctuary of her bedroom.

The moment Amanda disappeared from sight Letty's sobs abated. "Take me to my room, Tony," she pleaded, "my party is ruined and I've developed a terrible headache."

With an apologetic smile aimed at the two men remaining at the table, Tony put an arm around Letty's slim waist and led her from the room murmuring soothing words into her ear as they mounted the curving staircase. When they reached the room Tony had assigned to Letty, he released her waist to open the door but was stopped in his tracks by Letty's sharp intake of breath, her agitation ill-concealed.

"What is this, Tony?" her shrill voice demanded. "This isn't the room I usually occupy. You know I prefer the large room next to yours. The one with all those lovely windows overlooking the lawns."

Tony frowned, forseeing another scene like the one he had just witnessed in the dining room once Letty learned that the bedroom she considered hers was now being occupied by Amanda. "The room is being redecorated, Letty," he lied smoothly, "and I thought you'd prefer. . ."

"You're hiding something, Tony. What is it?" she asked, eyes narrowing suspiciously. The words no sooner left her lips than she swiftly crossed the hall and flung open the door to Amanda's room. Cursing softly, Tony followed.

Amanda had immediately gone to her room just as Tony ordered where she flung off her dress and petticoats to better examine the throbbing gash in her thigh. That's how Tony and Letty found her, bent over a candle, every curve of her slim, shapely form, thinly clad in a filmy chemise, clearly outlined by the soft, glowing light. The hem of her chemise was drawn up to reveal one long leg where a small, but ugly wound, oozing blood down a shapely thigh was clearly visible. Tony's breath left his chest, mesmerized by the enchanting creature whose nearly nude body was bared to his hot gaze. Amanda immediately smoothed down the raised chemise to cover her exposed limbs.

Letty's shocked features hardened into grim lines. No matter which way she turned she was thwarted by a nobody, a non-person who had not even the right to exist. "You've given my room to this. . . this. . . slut?" demanded Letty, turning accusing eyes on Tony. "I cannot believe that you could stoop so low. I thought the house slaves reside on the third floor."

Tony flushed, recognizing that Letty's resentment was not completely without justification. He had no business allowing a servant to remain in a guest room, even if it did seem to suit Amanda so well.

"Sir Tony," cut in Amanda, who by this time had overcome the shock of having her privacy so rudely invaded and hastily donned a robe lying nearby, "I think Mistress Letty is right. I don't belong in this room. I'll move my things immediately."

Tony stiffened, silver eyes smoky with anger. Although he was uncertain at whom his anger should be directed, at Letty for turning the embarrassing situation to her advantage, or at Amanda for suggesting she vacate the room thus challenging his judgment as master.

Turning to a fuming Letty, he explained patiently, "When Amanda arrived she was weak and ill. She needed immediate care if she was to fulfill her duties. Jemma suggested we put her in this room where she could enjoy the fresh air and sunshine. Putting her in the attic room would have hindered her recovery and rendered her useless to the household."

Letty's icy eyes were openly skeptical. "She looks well enough to me," she sneered derisively. "Why have you allowed her to remain in a room she's obviously not fit to occupy? Any fool can see she'd be more comfortable in a cell, or in a hut along with the other slaves."

Tony had reached the end of his patience. The entire evening had been a fiasco. Whether or not Amanda had deliberately dumped the cake in Letty's lap was debatable, but for the first time he had become aware of Letty's vindictive and cruel nature. Drawing himself up to his impressive six-foot three he was determined to put a stop to the whole deplorable affair.

"I owe no one an explanation for my actions, Letty. If I choose to house a servant in a guest room it's my business. I suggest you retire to the room assigned to you. I'm sure you'll feel better in the morning." Then he turned steely eyes on Amanda, his stern visage causing her to quake inwardly. "I'll deal with you in the morning. Your 'accident' deserves some kind of punishment which I will administer in my own good time."

Tony had no intention of doling out any type of punishment to Amanda but he hoped his words would go a long way in placating Letty. Evidently they did. With a self-satisfied smirk she swept grandly out of the room, her ruined gown swirling about her slim legs.

"Tony, darling," purred a gratified Letty as she paused before the door to her room, "I'm sure you realize that when we are married Amanda will have to go. I don't consider a convict trustworthy enough to be allowed free reign in a house filled with so many valuables. Perhaps she would do well in the fields," she hinted maliciously.

Tony gritted his teeth in exasperation. "Letty," he reminded her gently, "I have never proposed marriage to you."

Letty's volatile temper nearly was her undoing. Struggling to control the rage Tony's callous declaration evoked, she retorted, "Not in so many words, Tony, but I assumed our. . . intimate relationship spoke for itself. I gave everything to you, darling, and you took."

"I took only what you offered, Letty, and gave in return. We enjoyed each other's body. You loved what I did for you, but I don't love you. Fond, yes, but I had always hoped for more in a marriage. I won't blame you if you look elsewhere for a husband."

"Tony," Letty cajoled, "I don't want to look elsewhere, darling. I love you enough for both of us. I know you could learn to love me in the same way."

Tony sighed heavily. "Let it go, Letty. You're upset and tired and I'm not in the mood right now to continue with this conversation. I'm sorry your birthday party ended on such a discordant note. I'll see you in the morning. Goodnight, my dear."

But before Tony could depart he found his arms filled with a soft, warm bundle of curves pressing urgently against his hard frame. "You're not getting away from me that easily, lover," Letty whispered, her warm, seductive breath prickling his ear. "I'll come to you later."

In her room Letty stalked angrily back and forth, re-examining Tony's words over and over again in her mind. She had devoted too much time and energy fostering their relationship to let it falter and die. Everything had been fine up until Amanda arrived at River's Edge. If only there was some way to rid herself of the threat to her happiness once and for all. Contrary to Tony's denial she was positive that Amanda had become Tony's mistress. What other explanation could there be for the way he defended her. Finding Amanda in the room next to Tony's only served to reinforce her belief. Blessed by fortitude as well as determination, Letty was not about to give up on Tony. She would not rest until Amanda was banished once and for all from River's Edge and Tony's life. Until that could be accomplished she would use all her seductive wiles to entice Tony back into her arms. Suddenly Letty's smile was like a bright ray of sunshine in the darkened room. Tonight, she vowed, she would use her body as she never had before, dazzling Tony with her passion and prowess in bed. She would use her passion to bind him to her forever.

The house was quiet when Letty slipped wraith-like into Tony's room, wearing nothing but a thin nightgown fashioned of the sheerest material available. She had planned this night for weeks and meant to make the most of it. She and Tony were completely compatible when it came to sex and tonight she meant to demonstrate just how much he needed her, how good it was between them.

Tony was still awake. He knew Letty would join him and lay waiting, half in anticipation, half in dread. Letty always managed to bring out the animal in him and their matings were usually wild clashes of strength and passion in which he ended up feeling more used than satisfied. But perhaps an erotic session in bed was just what he needed to purge his mind and body of the copper-haired minx sleeping in the next room, he reflected thoughtfully.

Of late it seemed that thoughts of Amanda were his constant companions. Not a day or night went by without a painful reminder of her sweet surrender, the clean, fresh lines of her young, supple body intruding at times when he least expected it. But Amanda was not the woman for him, Tony scolded himself sternly. She was a convict, and was possibly a prostitute, not the type of woman he was likely to share his life with. Tony decided that if anyone had the power to erase thoughts of Amanda from his wayward mind and body it was Letty whose fierce ardor and heated loins nearly consumed him whenever they came together.

Tony sensed her presence immediately and turned his head toward the door where Letty stood poised on the balls of her bare feet. Tall and stately, her voluptuous figure beneath the filmy nightgown was fully revealed in the light that Tony had left purposely burning. Her long silver hair caressing bare shoulders and ample hips mesmerized him as she moved gracefully to his side.

"I told you I'd come to you, Tony," she whispered huskily.

"Didn't you hear me say I was tired, Letty?" Tony asked grumpily as he fought a losing battle to suppress his rising ardor.

"You can't fool me, darling," Letty smiled smugly, shrugging her white shoulders to release the straps of her nightgown. With no means of support remaining, the bodice of her nightgown slid down around her waist to reveal two perfectly formed mounds with prominent pink nipples already erect with desire. "You want me as much as I want you."

Executing a provocative twist the wisp of material fell to her feet and Letty slid into bed beside Tony, her flesh warm and inviting. "My God, Letty," Tony groaned as if in pain, "you're shameless."

"And you love it, admit it."

"What you need is a husband. Someone to cool those fires racing through your veins."

Letty laughed seductively, running her hands along the planes and angles of Tony's hardening flesh. "I want no man but you, darling. No one can please me as well as you."

Tony sighed wearily. He had been over this same ground time and again with Letty. "Marriage between the two of us wouldn't work, Letty."

"But we are so good together, Tony."

"Only in bed," contended Tony dryly. "Strange as that may seem it isn't enough to build a marriage on, Letty. In all our times together you have never conceived and I want children. Had you become pregnant from our encounters I would have married you despite the fact that we are not suited to one another."

Letty remained silent. She dare not tell Tony that she was no longer capable of producing a child. When she was very young, no older than Amanda is now, she had become pregnant by one of the slaves who worked in the stables, a handsome boy whose impressive size thoroughly intrigued Letty from the moment she laid eyes on him. In the end she had her way but it had cost her dearly. The black midwife who performed the abortion botched the job so badly that the doctor she was forced to consult secretly told her she was no longer capable of conceiving and bearing a child. But if Letty had her way that information would never reach Tony's ears.

Instead of responding Letty slid her lips wetly along Tony's lightly furred chest, licking, teasing with her tongue as she paused at his taut stomach before moving boldly downward.

"Damn you, Letty, you're a witch," Tony rasped between clenched teeth as he wound his fingers in Letty's silken locks to draw her closer as her greedy lips opened to devour him.

6

After Tony and Letty departed, Amanda slumped dejectedly down on the bed. Vaguely she wondered what manner of punishment Tony had in mind for her. Would he whip her? Starve her for a time? Lock her in the cellar? Amanda shuddered, already picturing herself being stripped and whipped, her tender flesh flayed bloody. Tony's edict had been so forceful that Amanda was certain not even Jemma could save her. Weary from hours of hard work, exhausted by strain and tension, Amanda sank back against the pillows, welcoming oblivion with open arms as she drifted off to sleep.

Hours later Amanda was awakened by strange sounds emanating through the thin walls from Tony's room. Fully awake, she listened intently trying to distinguish the sounds. After only a few minutes she knew exactly the nature of the murmurings and groans of the male and female voices coming to her from the other side of the wall. Tony and Letty were pleasurably engaged in passionate lovemaking! From the joyous burst issuing forth it was obvious that both were thoroughly enjoying their encounter. Amanda covered her ears but the impassioned moanings and grunts became like thunder in her ears, nearly driving her mad. Finally, she could stand it no longer. Without a coherent thought in her head except to escape from the sounds of Letty's and Tony's lust for one another, Amanda ran from the room, down the curved staircase and out the door into the warm June night, stopping only when she was far enough away to muffle any sound coming from the second floor bedroom.

Leaning against the bole of a live oak tree Amanda surrendered to her despair, her slim body trembling with heart-rending sobs. Never had she felt so alone, so abandoned. Engrossed as she was in her own misery she failed to hear the soft crunch of approaching footsteps.

"Amanda, what is the matter?"

Amanda started violently, nearly scared out of her wits until she recognized Nathan Grover's massive torso and shoulders. "Oh, Nathan," she gasped, fighting to control her wildly beating heart. "You frightened me so."

"I wouldn't harm you, Amanda, you know that. Tell me what's wrong. Has someone. . . has Tony punished you for tonight?"

"I'm not frightened of you, Nathan. You're the only person besides the slaves who has been kind to me." Once again bright tears flowed copiously down Amanda's pale cheeks.

Nathan's soft heart immediately went out to the young girl whose sorry state of affairs gave mute evidence that she had been sorely abused during her short life. "Let me help you," he pleaded as he drew her into his arms in order to comfort her.

The feel of Nathan's strong arms about her was immensely comforting. Amanda could not help but lay her head against his shoulder as he smoothed copper curls away from her damp face.

"My dear, my dear," crooned Nathan, "you are such a tiny, little innocent. Who would want to hurt you?"

"I'm to be punished by Sir Tony tomorrow for something that was none of my doing," sobbed Amanda, hiding her face against Nathan's broad chest.

"Come now, Amanda," scoffed Nathan. "I find that hard to believe. I've known Tony a long time and he has always been unfailing kind to his servants. Perhaps a tongue-lashing but. . . "

"You don't know him, Nathan," interrupted Amanda, shaking from a new eruption of tears, "he's already struck me once and this time I'm afraid it will be much worse. I've. . . I've humilated his lover!"

"He struck you?" repeated Nathan in disgust. "My God, Amanda, I had no idea he could be so cruel. You are such a little thing he could have hurt you badly."

"I'm afraid that's what he intends to do tomorrow, or today, I should say."

"Don't cry, Amanda, I won't let him hurt you. I'll speak with him before he has a chance to do you any harm."

"Oh, Nathan, I wouldn't have you jeopardize your job for me. I'll survive. I don't think he means to hurt me badly, just punish me."

"What did you do to Letty to make her hate you so?"

"I wish I knew," sighed Amanda dejectedly.

Nathan's warm brown eyes studied her lovely features by moonlight, seeing for himself the slightly trembling, full red lips, wide green eyes, bright with tears, flawless skin and shapely form clearly visible beneath her thin night garb, and in his heart he knew the answer to his own question.

"I won't let Letty harm you, Amanda. You now have me to protect you. Trust me, my dear. I'll speak to Tony first thing in the morning. He'll listen to me. We've been friends since he first arrived in South Carolina."

"Thank you, Nathan," murmured a gratified Amanda, lifting her tear-streaked face to gaze into his eyes.

Nathan was too much a man to resist for long the lure of those ruby lips. Gently, so as not to frighten her, he captured her mouth with his own, savoring the salty taste of her tears upon her flesh. Experimentally he outlined the tender shape of her lips with his tongue until they opened under his gentle probing. His kiss deepened and held, until he could feel Amanda quiver in his arms.

Tony and Letty had just concluded their passionate interlude to their mutual satisfaction and Letty sprawled, sated and drowsy in Tony's bed, her nude body glistening with a thin sheen of perspiration. Tony, still feeling restless and strangely incomplete, had arisen and strolled to the balcony overlooking the wide expanse of lawn bathed in brilliant moonlight. God, but he was confused. Though he had enjoyed Letty's lush body immensely and thrilled to her experienced caresses, he somehow felt letdown now that it was over. Try as he might he could not turn his thoughts from the young girl fast asleep in the next room, so close, yet so far away. There was no denying that he wanted her. She had to be some kind of sorceress, he reasoned, to prevent him from enjoying completely Letty's lush charms.

As Tony stared out into the night he became aware of the shadowy movements of two people standing beneath a live oak tree, clasped in a passionate embrace, the man's mouth nearly devouring the woman's. With growing alarm he had no trouble recognizing the slim, auburn-tressed form being so thoroughly kissed. Amanda! His discovery was like a scream in his brain. His hands balled into fists when he realized that Amanda's soft, pliant body was molded firmly and without resistance to Nathan's brawny form. His expelled breath echoed loudly into the stillness of the night, alerting the nude woman lolling in the bed.

"What is it, Tony?" asked Letty in a languid voice.

No answer was forthcoming. Tony was too preoccupied examining his conflicting emotions where Amanda was concerned to reply. Why should the knowledge that another man found Amanda desirable bother him as it obviously did? It took considerable self-control on his part to keep from rushing headlong down the stairs into the yard and yanking Amanda from Nathan's arms. Unconsciously a low growl of anger formed in his throat as he refused to acknowledge what he felt in his heart.

Curious, Letty roused out of her stupor to join Tony on the balcony, sighing as the warm breeze caressed her nude flesh. Following the direction of Tony's intense gaze Letty instantly spotted the source of his preoccupation. A low, mirthless chuckle rumbled from her throat. "Now will you believe me, darling? I told you she was a slut who will stop at nothing to lure a man into her bed, any man. She must be a witch to ensnare Nathan so easily. She probably made an assignation with him right under our noses. Why, I'm surprised she didn't proposition my father. He's certainly a better catch than Nathan."

Letty's words cut into Tony like a double-edged blade, leaving a wound that would be a long time healing. Reluctantly his dark, smoky gaze left the lovers beneath the tree and turned back to Letty, suddenly aware that the sharp points of her naked breasts were stabbing, hot and demanding, into his back. Why did he waste so much time thinking of Amanda, he wondered dully, when he had a warm, passionate woman at his fingertips?

Letty thrilled to Tony's unexpected attention as he let his hands trail lingeringly over her abundant curves. She cupped her breasts, offering them to his mouth, uttering a muted yelp as his teeth came down on an engorged nipple with more force than she liked.

"Softly, lover, softly," she murmured, excitement turning her voice silky as Tony's tongue outlined an aureole in ever widening circles and his hand drifted to the moistness between her legs.

Finding her ready for him, Tony lifted her off the floor and, wrapping her long legs about his waist, thrust upwards, impaling her on his engorged manhood. Letty's scream of ecstasy alerted the couple below and both turned in unison to locate the source of the disturbance. Amanda's shocked gasp joined Nathan's as, unable to turn their eyes from the scene of unbridled passion being enacted before their eyes, limned in the pale moonlight, they watched until both participants shuddered and cried out with the force of their climax. Only then did Amanda abruptly turn away from Nathan, eager to seek the privacy of her own room where she could drown her heartache in tears.

Sleep eluded Amanda. She arose at dawn, pale and blurry-eyed, purple smudges marring the transluscent skin beneath her eyes. The picture of Tony and Letty passionately engaged on the balcony was etched forever onto her brain, turning the night into one long nightmare.

Confronting Jemma in the kitchen the next day had been an ordeal Amanda dreaded for she was forced to reveal everything that had transpired the night before. Baring her thigh she exhibited the wound that Letty had so cruelly inflicted with the knife and now was festering and filled with pus. Hesitantly, she described her meeting with Nathan beneath the live oak tree but could not bring herself to tell about the sexual encounter between Tony and Letty that she and Nathan had witnessed.

Clucking and shaking her brightly turbanned head, Jemma set about applying a healing poultice to Amanda's thigh to draw out the infection, binding the whole with a piece of linen.

Limping slightly Amanda set about putting the house in order after last night's abortive birthday party. The moment she heard Tony and Letty descending the stairs she withdrew to the kitchen and remained there until they had finished breakfast and Letty and her father departed for Tidewater, their plantation.

With trepidation Amanda waited for Tony's summons, although Jemma had scoffed at the idea that he would beat her. When he finally approached her later that morning she was a mass of quivering flesh, anticipation nearly as devastating as the punishment itself. When finally she faced Tony across his desk she found she could not look him in the face without hearing once again Letty's hoarse cry of completion as she writhed in Tony's arms, impaled by his manhood.

"I'm gratified to see you are shamed by your behavior last night," Tony intoned dryly, eyebrows peaking when he saw her bent head and downcast eyes, mistaking it for remorse.

Bristling, Amanda raised her head to glare belligerently at Tony. How dare he blame her for something that Letty had so cleverly mastermided, she fumed silently. Certain that she would be punished no matter what, she unwisely decided to speak her mind.

"I have no reason to hang my head with shame," she bit out angrily. "Look to your precious Letty for the cause of all that transpired last night."

"What the hell are you talking about, Amanda? How could you blame Letty for your own carelessness?" Tony demanded. "I've never known you to be so clumsy. You ruined Letty's lovely gown, and even if by the remotest chance it was an accident, Letty had every right to be angry."

In all honesty Tony did not believe for a minute that Amanda had deliberately set out to humiliate Letty but her moonlight tryst with Nathan the previous evening had angered and upset him more than he cared to admit. Lashing out at her seemed the right thing to do in view of her wanton behavior with his overseer.

With a flash of indignation Amanda threw all

caution to the wind as she lashed out bitterly. "Is my word not good enough for you? Does being a convict make me a liar? You're an arrogant bastard, Sir Tony! If you give me half a chance I'll show you what your precious Letty did to me!" Immediately Amanda realized her error.

Thunder clouds gathered in Tony's glowering face; his eyes shot gray smoke and there was a grimness to his mouth that set her teeth to chattering. "You have one minute, Amanda, to have your say before I punish you. By God, I had no intention of beating you but you give me no choice. Never have I been faced with such complete insolence in a servant and I won't stand for it now, not even from you!"

Petrified with fear Amanda could neither move nor speak. She had fully intended to show Tony the deep gash on her thigh but his anger and threats of a beating had completely immobilized her. Never in her whole life had she been physically abused, not even in prison, thanks to the constable, until she came to River's Edge. Now, faced with the possibility of bodily hurt, she could only stare at Tony, mouth agape, green eyes wide with terror, her face pale.

"Your minute is up, Amanda," Tony announced grimly, "and I have heard nothing to vindicate you or sway me from my course. If I allow you to remain unpunished after your abysmal behavior every slave on River's Edge will lose respect for me as their master. My word will mean nothing." With cool deliberation he picked up his riding crop resting on the desk.

Astonishment followed disbelief across Amanda's face. She never believed Tony meant to beat her until this minute. With a courage born of resolve she squared her thin shoulders, thrust out her small chin, and focused blazing, green eyes on smoldering gray. No matter what it cost she would not give him the satisfaction of beating her, she vowed as she decided that now was the time to show Tony the full extent of Letty's cruelty and watch his face register shock and guilt at his unjust accusation.

Still staring into Tony's eyes she slowly began raising the hemline of her gown until it was knee high, baring her shapely calves and ankles. But to Tony's shock and bewilderment she didn't stop there. The hemline began inching up even further.

"My God, Amanda," he choked, his voice strangely strangled, "have you no shame? Do you think to stay my hand by seducing me? Another time, perhaps. I'm not at all averse to a tumble with a servant, as you well know, but. . ."

Tony's vicious words were cut off in midsentence as Amanda sprung at him, lips drawn into a snarl, claws bared. Somehow the insults delivered by him were far more humiliating than if they came from another. That he thought her a slut was obvious. Letty had certainly done her job well.

But Amanda's attack was easily thwarted given Tony's superior strength. Capturing her wrists in one large hand, Tony wrestled Amanda to the floor, holding her face down. Releasing her wrists, he put one booted foot against her neck, using just enough force to pin her effectively to the floor but not enough to hurt her. Amanda screamed her outrage as Tony carelessly flipped her skirt and petticoats above her head baring the two quivering mounds of her smooth, white buttocks.

The enticing sight was nearly his undoing. He didn't really want to hurt her, just give her one or two good whacks with his riding crop to teach her a lesson in obedience. And now, with Amanda laying bared and vulnerable before him feelings of guilt and disgust at what he was about to do assailed him. Distractedly he noted the bandage Jemma had wrapped around her thigh and wondered how she had injured herself. Gone completely still beneath the pressure of Tony's foot, eyes tightly shut, Amanda waited stoically for the first blow to fall, determined not to cry out or beg no matter how much pain he inflicted on her innocent body.

Arm upraised, riding crop at the ready, Tony cursed loudly, unable to summon the will to bruise the tender flesh cringing at his feet. No matter what her crime, whipping was not the answer.

Suddenly the door burst open admitting an outraged Nathan, eyes bulging from their sockets, disbelief mirrored in their shocked depths. "My God, Tony, I can't believe you could be so despicable!" he cried, staring at Tony as if he were the devil himself.

Tony flushed, well aware of how the damning scene looked to Nathan. "I have done nothing, yet, Nathan," he said calmly. "But Amanda deserves to be punished."

"Amanda is innocent!" blasted Nathan. "Even I could see how much Letty hates her. She would do anything to see Amanda abused and ridiculed."

"How gullible you are, Nathan. Has Amanda tried to seduce you, also? Evidently she has succeeded all too well and gained a protector in the process. Just remember, Nathan, Amanda is

119

my property to punish as I see fit," he informed
Nathan coldly, although he had no intention of
confessing his reluctance to hurt Amanda in any
way.

"If you persist with your efforts to harm
Amanda I will be forced to fight you. And believe
me, Tony, it won't be a pretty fight for I'll use
every dirty trick at my disposal to protect Amanda
from your lash. Better yet, sell me her papers, I'll
make sure she is never mistreated again."

Tony was flabbergasted. First, because
Nathan had dared to interfere, and second, that he
evidently held such strong feelings for the little
hellion. Tony could not fight in the face of such
righteous indignation. He needed Nathan and
since he really didn't want to beat Amanda anyway he removed his foot from her neck and non-
chalantly flicked her skirt back in place with his
riding crop.

"Amanda is my servant and shall remain
mine," he answered blithely. "Now take her out of
here, Nathan. She is free to go this time but if she
continues to defy me at every turn, as well as
humiliate my guests, she won't escape so easily
next time. It would be wise if you concern yourself
with your duties and leave the disciplining to me."
So saying, he turned on his heel and strode from
the room, passing a distraught Jemma hovering in
the hallway, nervously wringing her hands.

Seeing the black woman's reproachful glare,
Tony shouted, "I didn't lay a hand on her! You all
seem to be ignorant of the fact that I am master
here!"

Nathan wasted no time in going to Amanda's
aid as he knelt beside her prostrate form and
gently raised her to her feet, holding her upright

against his massive chest. With compassionate eyes he took in her tearstained face and disheveled clothing, cursing Tony under his breath.

"Did he hurt you badly?" he asked, fighting to control the emotion threatening to engulf him. Never had anyone affected him so strongly as did this small, beautiful girl who had done nothing to earn the abuse heaped upon her slim shoulders. In his eyes she could never do anything wrong no matter what anyone said. It was incomprehensible that she could be a convict and an indentured slave to anyone, especially Tony.

"No. . . no," stammered Amanda truthfully, realizing that she was shaken but unhurt. "He didn't touch me, but if you hadn't burst in when you did. . ." Shudders wracked her body at the thought of how close she had come to being marred for life. "I think I was humiliated more than hurt. In fact, I'm sure Sir Tony planned it that way to put me in my place."

"I still find it difficult to believe Tony could be so cruel. I've never known him to act so. . . so. . ." He shrugged eloquently, unable to voice the right word.

"I know what you mean, Nathan, and until he actually had me beneath his whip I didn't believe it either."

"I won't let this matter drop, my dear. I intend to continue with my suit to buy your papers. And when I succeed I'll burn them and free you."

Tears of gratitude glistened at the corners of Amanda's eyes, a tremulous smile creased her sad little face. "You'd do that for me, Nathan?" she breathed wonderingly.

"For you, I'd brave anything. Anything at all. Haven't you guessed how I feel about you?"

Amanda's long lashes lowered until they were feathery smudges against her pale cheeks. As kind and gentle as Nathan was she doubted she could ever feel about him in the same way. When she raised her eyes she was startled to find Nathan staring at her curiously, as if he wanted to kiss her. Finally, he did, a very gentle kiss, a mere brushing of lips. How she wished she could love this unique man who desired nothing more than to protect and love her.

The next day Tony's eyes did not quite meet Amanda's whenever they chanced to meet. It was not as if he was guilty of any wrongdoing, Tony told himself as he watched Amanda's supple form go about her duties. He would never have been able to hurt her no matter how angry she made him.

Not only did Tony have Amanda's willfulness to contend with, but Letty's incessant demands that Amanda be punished. "She needs to be put in her place," Letty had said indignantly. And in a way Letty's argument that Amanda needed disciplining was valid.

Letty was a convincing minx when she wanted to be with her satiny flesh eager and ready to respond at the slightest touch and her hungry mouth ever willing to tease and devour. Perhaps he would do well to marry the witch and put Amanda out of his thoughts forever.

Suddenly Amanda came into view and all his musings came to an end at the sight of her willowy form moving gracefully through the room. Then, unbidden came the thought of her in Nathan's embrace, her sweet body clasped tightly in his arms. It made him want to lash out at her, to chastise her for the seduction scene she enacted with Nathan the night before.

"Amanda," he said harshly, stopping her in her tracks, "I would like to speak to you about last night."

Amanda became attentive, not wishing to arouse Tony's anger as she had done the day before. But try as she might she could not look at him without picturing him on the balcony with Letty, driving her to ecstasy while she and Nathan looked on.

"I want you to keep away from Nathan," he continued when Amanda made no response. "I don't appreciate what you are doing to him, seducing him with your feminine wiles. He is unaccustomed to dealing with women of your ilk."

Amanda's head snapped up sharply, green eyes blazing as she impaled him with her brittle gaze. "I like Nathan. He. . . he is kind to me, but I have not attempted to seduce him."

"I saw you, Amanda. You were in Nathan's arms. He was kissing you and you neither protested nor made any effort to stop him. What is that if it isn't seduction? Nathan has never been one to chase after just any woman and you have him panting after you like a hound after a bitch. He wants to buy your papers. It's obvious that you've bewitched him with your innocent ways, but we both know you are not an innocent, don't we Amanda?" smirked Tony nastily.

Amanda wanted to slap the silly smirk from Tony's face so badly she had to clench her fist to keep from striking out. "Is that all?" she asked icily, determined to leave his odious presence unscathed.

"No!" stormed Tony, strangely unsettled by

her cool reserve. "By God, I'll make you pay attention to me!"

His hands were not gentle as they grasped her slim shoulders, pulling her into his hard embrace. His lips, more punishing than tender, took hers in a burst of passion that sent her senses reeling. Twisting the fingers of one hand into her tangle of curls he held her head prisoner while his mouth continued to plunder and ravage, his tongue forcing itself rudely into her sweet, warm depths. His other hand found the curve of her breast and he followed the contour until he discovered a nipple, his thumb and forefinger working it into a hard nub.

With a will of their own Amanda's arms found Tony's neck and tightened, bringing him even closer. Feeling her response, Tony's mouth softened, his kiss deepened, becoming gentle. Cursing the weakness that caused him to always fall victim of her seductive wiles, Tony suddenly flung her aside.

"See what I mean, Amanda?" he spat contemptuously, completely dismissing his own desire. "You practice seduction without even trying. Your look, your manner, the way you move your body. You are a born temptress, but I'll not allow you to beguile me as you have Nathan."

Then he abruptly turned on his heel and stormed from the room leaving Amanda so bewildered and upset she could gladly have killed Tony had she a weapon.

7

June was drawing to an end, the hot, humid days and nights a reflection of Amanda's temperament. Though she had only little verbal contact with Tony in the weeks following Letty's fateful birthday party, she felt herself in the midst of a boiling cauldron. Something was wrong but she could not define it. Her temper flared dramatically at the slightest provocation, and she often felt Jemma's narrowed, speculative gaze upon her. Nothing seemed to go right, adding to Amanda's agitation. Tess and Cory took to avoiding her as did the other slaves under her supervision. To make matters worse, Tony seemed always to be hovering at her elbow, a strange, hungry glint in his silver eyes. She was certain he was just waiting for the opportunity to take up where he left off the day Nathan rescued her from his whip.

Nathan had been a frequent visitor to the big house; not just to confer with Tony but to satisfy himself that Amanda was not being mistreated. He often came for her in the evenings, walking with her along the river, holding her small hand, kissing her gently when she allowed it. True to his word, Nathan continually badgered Tony to sell him Amanda's papers until the issue nearly ended their long association, becoming a bone of contention between them.

Tony had no intention of giving up Amanda. No matter how hard he tried to convince himself otherwise. He would greatly miss her presence if he could not gaze upon her small, curvaceous figure and beautiful face daily. Of late, it seemed he found all manner of excuses to remain nearby while she performed her duties around the house. He cursed himself for his weakness but only God knew how much he desired her. Even Letty, with her hot passion and ardent kisses, could not dim that desire. Each day he fought a battle within himself and had thus far managed to come out victorious. But if he couldn't possess her, neither would Nathan, he vowed with grim determination. He knew Nathan often called on Amanda but he had made it a point to observe them carefully and to his knowledge they had never been intimate. In his heart he felt he would have known if Amanda and Nathan were lovers.

Though Nathan had been unsuccessful in his quest to purchase Amanda's indenture papers, he had gained one concession from Tony. Tony had promised never to lay a hand on Amanda or inflict any other kind of cruel punishment. Tony agreed to this grudgingly, for even though he could never bring himself to hurt Amanda again, he sought to keep his true feelings from Nathan; feelings he had difficulty sorting out in his own mind.

Arising one morning in the early dawn, Amanda realized with a start that she had been at River's Edge exactly two months. Stretching luxuriously she savored the cool, pre-dawn breeze, dreading the moment that the sun would make its brazen appearance, a relentless, golden ball in a clear, blue sky. The daytime heat was nearly unbearable to Amanda, born and bred in damp, foggy England where the sun rarely penetrated the chill of the London mist. Today, for some obscure reason the simple act of getting out of bed became a difficult chore, her sluggish body felt clumsy, her limbs leaden.

Turning her wistful gaze toward the river Amanda was struck with a compelling urge to submerge her fevered flesh in the clear, cool water, washing away her lethargy along with the sweat. Brightening perceptively, Amanda drew on a light-weight dress, ignoring completely her petticoat and chemise. She gathered up her towel, a bar of soap and a comb and started for the beckoning river, humming a sprightly tune under her breath.

Wisps of gray mist hovered at ground level and the grass felt damp and cool beneath her bare feet. Pale streaks of dawn crept with rose-hued fingers across the gray-blue sky. The world at this hour was serene and Amanda enjoyed the sheer exhilaration of being alive.

It took her no time at all to shed her single garment and wade into the soothing water. She often came to the river to bathe but never had it felt so refreshing. By the time she finished bathing and washing her hair the sun was a pale globe rising in the east whose brilliant beams lent a breathtaking radiance to Amanda's burnished tresses, rivaling the sun itself. Standing in waist deep water Amanda seemed unaware of the beguiling picture she presented. The pearly beads of moisture glistening on alabaster skin, dripping from the tips of perfect twin mounds peaked with pink rosebuds; the enticing outline of hips and limbs barely visible below the surface. But standing a few yards away, concealed by thick bushes growing along the riverbank, a pair of smoldering eyes were totally and compellingly cognizant of the captivating creature cavorting in the water like a beautiful sea nymph found only in fairy tales. At that moment nothing in the world could have torn the interloper's eyes from the shimmering figure.

A familiar tightening stirred Tony's loins. A feeling he experienced too often of late whenever his eyes fell on Amanda. Why did he want this girl so badly? he wondered dismally. What was there about her that caused him such anguish and confused his emotions to the extent that she brought out the worst in him? True, she was lovely, but so was Letty, who never denied him her body. But strangely, it wasn't Letty he wanted, it was Amanda. That one night she had yielded so sweetly to him, her innocent ardor reminiscent of a long forgotten encounter, illusive, yet intensely vivid, was never far from his thoughts. So scrawny and obviously ill Amanda had been that night, that Tony had often chided himself for taking her so callously.

How different Amanda's body looked now, he thought, his hot gaze devouring the new fullness to her taut breasts, the outward flare of slim hips, the soft, attractive curve of her stomach. Reflecting the sunlight beneath the water, Tony was mesmerized by the shimmering copper of a perfectly outlined triangle nestled at the juncture of long, tapering limbs.

A loud noise startled Tony and he was surprised to disover it was the sound of his own ragged breathing, harsh and rasping even to his own ears. His heart was beating wildly as his fists clenched wetly until his knuckles were white. Beads of sweat were prickling his forehead. At that moment nothing could have turned Tony from his course. It was pre-ordained, written in the annals of time, masterminded by the prophets.

Tony moved from his concealment, driven by a need he no longer could control. Dropping his new rifle in stocked curly maple and a brace of rabbits bagged on his early morning hunting foray, Tony began stripping off his clothes, never taking his passion-glazed eyes from the girl in the river. Her back was to him, as she submerged one last time beneath the sparkling surface, before reluctantly starting back to perform her duties for the day.

Tony's entrance into the river was quiet and unheralded, his smooth passage barely causing a ripple on the placid waters. Shaking her glorious mane of hair Amanda emerged, eyes closed, face tipped toward the sun. Suddenly she felt rather than saw a shadow block off the warmth and opened her eyes, sensing immediately she was not alone. Tony stood inches away, his glazed eyes fastened on the wildly beating pulse at the base of her throat, sliding downward to quivering breasts, nipples hardening as if from a sudden chill. Instinctively her arms crossed protectively across her chest.

"Sir Tony," she stammered, the shock of seeing him before her nearly rendering her speechless. "What are you doing here?"

Tony smiled sardonically. "This is my land," he said imperiously.

Amanda took a step backward, fearing yet knowing the answer to her next question. "What do you want?"

"Very simple, Amanda, I want you."

Amanda took another step backward. Resolutely, Tony followed, disregarding her gasp of dismay.

"Why are you tormenting me like this?"

"I'm not tormenting you, I want to love you."

"I've tasted your brand of love, Sir Tony," Amanda bit out angrily. "You took me once, branded me a whore, called me a liar, struck me, nearly succeeded in beating me; my God, how can you treat me so cruelly? Go back to your mistress!"

Tony flushed darkly, his black-winged brows a horizontal line across his forehead. Much of what she said was true, he realized with a start of guilt, but she had undermined his authority until he had no choice but act as he did. If he had seemed harsh and unyielding she had driven him to it with her willful disobedience and tart tongue.

Suddenly contrite, Tony replied, "Forget what's gone before, Amanda. I could never hurt you. I. . . I want you to believe that. For some reason you've gotten under my skin. The sight of you drives me crazy. I want to touch you, to love you. The taste, the feel of you are etched forever on my brain. Let me love you again, Amanda!"

"You're mad!" countered Amanda extending her arms in front of her in an effort to thwart his intention.

"Yes, I'm convinced I am," admitted Tony, his breath quickening, his body already hard and demanding as he openly admired the pale swell of her breasts rising and falling rapidly in anger. All his thoughts were focused on her body and the ache in his loins.

Against her will Amanda was slowly being seduced by Tony's soft, confusing words and compelling eyes. With one hand he reached out and stroked the tender flesh of throat, breasts, gently curving stomach, hips, naked desire evident in his dark visage. Then, in a motion so swift it startled her she was in Tony's arms, his mouth moving brutally against hers, tasting, taking, savage in his desire. Drained of all will, Amanda slumped against him in obvious surrender and would have fallen if he hadn't lifted her easily in his arms and started back toward shore, mouths still clinging wetly. Gently he laid her down on the sweet-smelling, grassy bank, gazing at her rapturously for a few moments before stretching out beside her.

Finally coming out of her trance Amanda spoke, her voice weak and ineffectual. "Don't do this, Sir Tony. You care nothing for me. You might want me and are determined to have me. But I don't want you!"

"I don't believe that, my love," he whispered silkily into her ear, startling her with the endearment. "And I give you leave to call me Tony."

"Please, Sir Tony," she began, squirming under his hands as they ruthlessly plundered her satiny flesh. She tingled everywhere he touched and he touched everywhere.

"Tony. Call me Tony. I want to hear you say it."

"Please, Tony. . ." Abruptly her words were cut off as he captured her lips once more, his tongue swirling, teasing, taunting in the deep velvet recess of her mouth.

Amanda felt his passion, was overpowered by it, and then felt her own passion answering. To her horror she found that her body was responding to his skill while her mind rejected him. Feeling the beginnings of her response, Tony smiled, smug in his knowledge that she was now his for the taking.

Though Amanda realized she would hate herself when it was over she was helpless to resist as his seeking mouth left her bruised lips to rove freely from breast to breast, sucking gently on one erect nipple, flipping the other relentlessly with a hard tongue, then moving lower, lapping droplets of water from smooth stomach and creamy thighs. With a gasp of shock Amanda arched sharply upward, her body a trembling mass of raw, tingling sensation.

In one smooth motion Tony rolled her beneath him, body poised, manhood a throbbing, palpatating extension of himself eager to enter the gates of Paradise.

"Let me have you, Amanda. To touch you, hold you like this drives me crazy with wanting. I need to love you."

To her utter horror Amanda's legs separated easily, her hips rising in eagerness to accept his offering. In the moment before he claimed her completely Tony's silver eyes sparkled as they raked her, sweeping the length of her nakedness, savoring this instant of her surrender.

As if reading his thoughts, Amanda was assailed by waves of despair when she realized how easily she surrendered to Tony's smooth words and expert caresses. With a strength born of resolve she began hammering her small fists against his steely chest. Caught off guard Tony nearly became unseated by the distraught girl but he was not to be denied.

"Let me love you, my love," he begged, undaunted by her sudden reluctance. With a swift, clean thrust his penetration was so smooth it made her gasp aloud. Down, down, down into the heated honey of her he plunged.

Against her will Amanda began to move in abandon beneath him in a wanting so intense she ached with the need. Her body arched and yielded, every pore, every nerve ending alive and throbbing; her blood boiling as rivers of molten lava flowed into her limbs, concentrating at the place of his penetration.

Never had the act of love so affected Tony. His passion grew wings and soared to heights he never before had experienced. What was it about Amanda, a convict, a small bundle of contradictions, to inspire such emotion? he wondered as he watched her passion-glazed eyes grow luminous in her flushed face. Then all coherent thought fled as he felt a spasm of erotic quivers splinter through Amanda's slight form. Her soft moan crecendoed into a high-pitched wail as she exploded into a million tiny fragments, echoing Tony's hoarse cries, his own climax nearly ripping him apart.

Breath rasping in her chest, heart beating erratically, Amanda slowly returned from her ecstactic journey to find Tony leaning over her on one elbow, his eyes akindle with a strange light. What was it? she wondered. Awe? Disbelief? Love? No, surely not love. But what?

"Why are you staring at me?" she asked curiously. "You've gotten what you wanted, now leave me alone." Shamed by her total abandonment tears sprang to her eyes and spiked her long lashes with shimmering drops of water.

Tony was thoughtful for a moment, and then his grin flashed big and white in his tanned face, making him appear almost boyish. "After what we just experienced I don't believe I could ever leave you alone again. My God, Amanda, I know you were affected in the same way!"

"Listen to me, Tony," replied Amanda, dropping the sir as if she had never used it. "You've taken unfair advantage of my position, my inexperience, forcing a response from my untutored body with your skillful caresses. You are my master, I dare not resist."

"My love, you wanted me, don't deny it."

With downcast eyes Amanda reluctantly admitted the truth of his words. "What do you want from me, Tony? What am I supposed to say?"

"Say that you care for me a little," he prodded.

"Why, so you can mock me? No, thank you. I wanted you, let it go at that." Once more her rebellious nature was taking over.

"Amanda, we have to talk," Tony said, helping her to a sitting position where she would be less likely to inflame his passion again so soon.

Amanda stared at him warily. "What is there to discuss?"

"Us."

"There is no us."

"How can you say that after what we just experienced?"

"Was what we experienced any different from what you feel with Letty?"

The jibe hit home but Tony remained undaunted. He knew Amanda was something special and he didn't want to lose her. He owned her, true, but he wanted more from her than mere service. He wanted her trust, her fidelity, and, yes, damn it, her love. He wanted no other man to taste her sweet surrender, possess her passionate body. He wanted her for himself. How he would accomplish this feat was not yet clear in his mind, or even where she fit into his life, for that matter. But have her he would.

"My love, Letty has never been more than a convenience to me. Granted, she'd like to be more, but it can never be."

Things were going too fast for Amanda. Her brain turned fuzzy, her head hurt. She still wasn't sure what Tony wanted from her, or expected her to say. For the moment silence seemed the wisest course to follow.

Sensing her withdrawal, Tony drew her close until she nestled comfortably in the curve of his arm. "Tell me about yourself, Amanda. I want to know everything. What kind of life did you lead in England? I find it hard to believe you were a common thief."

"I wasn't a thief!" denied Amanda hotly, slanting him a quelling look.

"You forget, my love, I have your papers. They state you were convicted of thievery."

"What was I to do, Tony? My mother was dying. She needed medicine. We had no money. I couldn't get work. I was desperate. I. . . I stole a loaf of bread and was so inept at it I was caught. Have you ever been to Newgate, Tony?" she sobbed hysterically, the telling dredged up the whole degrading episode as if it was yesterday.

With a pang of pity Tony watched her soft

shoulders shake. Could anything be more horrifying to a sixteen-year old child than finding herself in a prison amidst the lowest scum and degenerates? he wondered compassionately.

"Where was your father when all this happened?" he asked gently.

"Dead. He died when I was twelve. After that, life as I knew it was never the same. Mother tried, but her health failed finally. I was raised so gently that I was woefully unprepared to make a living for us. We. . . we were forced to move to the slums and when our food and money gave out I. . . I. . ." a fresh torrent of tears streamed down her lovely features.

Tony clasped her more tightly, wanting only to protect her from further hurt. "Was it so terrible, Amanda, your time in Newgate?"

Amanda went still. Should she tell him about the constable? Or let him guess at the manner in which she was forced to survive. Was now the time to bring up that night in the inn when Tony had stolen her virginity?

"Don't tell me if it is too painful, Amanda," Tony said quickly, her sudden pallor and silence alarming him. How could he be so thoughtless as to ask her questions that were so obviously difficult as well as embarrassing to relate? But he had an overwhelming desire to know every detail of her life before coming to River's Edge. Perhaps there was a clue in her past that linked them together for he couldn't quite dispel the feeling that sometime, somewhere, they had met.

Suddenly, in a jumble of words long suppressed Amanda's story burst forth, hesitantly at first, then with growing courage when she read understanding and compassion in Tony's silver eyes. She described her horror and despair at finding herself locked in a cell with a group of depraved and half-mad women. Memory swept back with frightening clarity, recalling to mind the cruelty of the guards as they raped the women prisoners night after night.

"Stop! My God, stop!" cried Tony, aghast, totally unprepared to hear the true extent of Amanda's suffering. "I'd like to strangle every one of those jailers who raped you, a poor, helpless child unjustly jailed and cruelly abused."

"I... was luckier than most, Tony. The... guards didn't molest me."

"But, you said..."

"I know what I said and everything I told you is true. I... had a protector. A constable, a man who offered to keep the guards from raping me if I... if I..." Unable to continue Amanda buried her face in her hands, dreading the revilement Tony was sure to heap upon her.

"It's all right, my love," Tony consoled gently. "Who could blame you for choosing the lesser of two evils? But if I ever meet him face to face I'll kill him for taking your viginity in such a heartless manner."

Startled, Amanda raised her eyes to meet Tony's sympathetic gaze. Of course he would think the constable had been the first with her, she reasoned, Tony was too drunk to remember the frightened girl in the inn in London. She bit her lip and resisted the impulse to reveal her secret. It's all in the past, she thought, the present is what counts. And the future. She had already told him more than she intended.

"I gave myself to him, Tony, yet I can't bring myself to hate him. Especially after I saw with my own eyes what my fate would have been if left to the tender mercies of the guards. I would have killed myself rather than be passed from man to man, so in a way he saved my life."

"Was he so kind to you that even now he moves you to compassion?" asked Tony, jealousy turning his voice harsh and unforgiving.

"You don't understand, insisted Amanda stubbornly. "He promised to care for my mother and when she died he paid for her burial. By then I was dead inside. When he took me I felt nothing. Whatever he did to me was done to a lifeless body, a shell that held no resemblance to the woman I was in your arms a while ago. In all fairness I cannot say he was unkind, or hurt me in any way. I. . . I repaid him by submitting to him."

Pain clouded Tony's eyes as his anger melted in remorseful apology. Dare he listen to more? What she endured in prison probably was nothing compared to her treatment by sex-starved sailors aboard the prison ship on the long crossing from England. Stories were rampant about what happened to comely women aboard such ships.

But once Amanda began there was no stopping her as she spoke in low tones of the terrible confinement in the hold of the ship, berthed with women who spat abuse and often mistreated her, stealing all the best food for themselves while she wasted away, often too sick to defend herself.

Cursing himself for putting her through such anguish, Tony could not help but ask, "Did. . . did the sailors. . . were they. . . oh God, Amanda, don't make me say it."

"If I had to face being raped by countless men I wouldn't be here to tell about it. I would have thrown myself overboard. I am too cowardly to live with that kind of degradation. If I were ever faced with multiple acts of rape I would surely have found some way to end my life."

Tony exhaled, his breath ragged. How had she escaped? he puzzled. He did not have long to wonder as Amanda continued.

"The prison ship was blessed with a kind and compassionate captain. Under threat of dire punishment no man was allowed to take a woman against her will. I was not willing although there were plenty who were. Enough, in fact, that I was not molested." Amanda's voice faltered, then died altogether as she stared pensively at the gently flowing river.

"It's over, Amanda. No harm can come to you at River's Edge. I want us to start over. I. . . I find I care for you more than I wanted to admit. I was jealous of Nathan. I even thought you had become lovers. I wanted to punish you for it."

Amanda could hardly credit his words. Was this the same man who had struck her, insulted her, paraded his mistress before her shamelessly?

"Tony, I don't understand. What does all this mean?"

"It means," laughed Tony delightedly, "that I want us to be happy together. We are no longer servant and master. Oh, I may still hold your papers," he admitted, "but they no longer mean anything. I just want to love you, starting with right now."

With Tony's surprising words came Amanda's decision to finally reveal the secret she had held within her heart from the first moment she had seen him aboard the prison ship, appearing like a spectre from out of a bad dream.

"Tony, there is something I. . ."

"Shh, no more confessions," he cautioned, placing a restraining finger against her soft lips. "You've already told me more than I deserve to know."

"But, Tony, this is. . ."

"No, love, nothing is more important than my loving you again. And suddenly nothing was as he gently laid her back against the warm earth claiming her lips hungrily, passionately, his hands drifting languidly over her smooth, satiny flesh. She trembled, but this time not from fear. She was neither hot nor cold, yet somehow both. In a rapturous trance of sensuous heat she moved pliantly beneath him, arching closer to his hard maleness, all thought driven from her mind at his first intimate touch. Her low, constricted moan was muffled as his lips sought the tender shape of her mouth, molding it to his.

Lowering his head to her breast, Amanda felt and thrilled to the warm flicker of his tongue. "Tony, please," she groaned raggedly, realizing that she was begging like a wanton, yet uncaring.

"Yes, love, I know," Tony gasped, equally aroused. "I want you just as badly. Open your legs, love. Let me have you."

Obeying instantly, Amanda felt him slide in effortlessly, filling her, thrilling her, prodding her higher and higher with his hard, throbbing manhood. They rode the crest together, scaling the summit of ecstasy, both crying out in unison, clinging, writhing, their bodies slippery with sweat. Amanda knew that if she lived to be one hundred nothing would ever equal what she and Tony had just experienced.

Afterwards they bathed together, laughing

like children while they washed then rinsed each other in the clear water until the sun reminded them of the hour and they reluctantly dressed and made their way back to the house holding hands for all the world to see.

The next two weeks were as blissful as any Amanda had ever known. During the day her duties took up much of her time but the evenings and nights were devoted to Tony. At his insistence she joined him at the dinner table while a giggling Tess and Cory served them, obviously pleased by Amanda's raised status in the household. Afterward Tony joined her in her bed where they repeated over and over the joyous act of love.

It didn't take long for it to become common knowledge among the slaves that Amanda had become Tony's mistress. At first it took every bit of Amanda's courage to face Jemma until the wise slave put Amanda's mind at ease.

"Don't be shamed, chile," Jemma said, touching Amanda's hair in a friendly gesture. "Massa Tony, he can be mighty persuasive. And if he makes you happy, then take what happiness you can git. Not one of us thinks any less of you. We's jest glad that nasty Miz Letty don't come 'round much anymore."

"Oh, Jemma, you make me feel so much better. I couldn't stand it if all of you hated me."

"We all loves you, chile. Maybe," she hinted shyly, "jest maybe we's gonna have us a new mistress. One we's gonna love."

Amanda could not control the color staining her cheeks. Not once had Tony mentioned marriage. No, she thought ruefully, mistress is all she could ever hope for. Tony would never link his fine name to that of an ex-convict. God, but it hurt.

So badly that waves of vertigo suddenly turned her knees to rubber and she tottered from side to side, catching at the edge of the table to keep from falling. As if from a great distance she could hear Jemma calling her name. And then she heard no more as blackness claimed her.

Amanda surfaced into consciousness in fits and starts between intermittent flickers of awareness and spans of darkness, Jemma's worried face floating above her. She was surprised to find herself stretched out on the scrubbed floor with a pillow under her head and a cool cloth on her forehead. She felt foolish and told Jemma so. She had never fainted before and was puzzled as well as troubled by the sudden onset of her strange malaise, having exhibited no other symptoms of illness in the past few days.

Blushing under Jemma's shrewd scrutiny Amanda remained still while the old slave's fathomless eyes missed nothing, neither the new fullness to Amanda's breasts nor the barely discernable curve to her taut stomach. "Is there something you ain't telling me, chile?" she asked finally.

"I. . . I don't know what you mean," replied Amanda, embarrassed by Jemma's relentless probing.

"Think back, Amanda. Think carefully and then tell me if you ain't breeding."

"A. . . baby?" It was obvious by Amanda's wide, incredulous eyes and shocked expression that the thought had never entered her mind.

"That's what I said, chile," repeated Jemma calmly. "When did you last bleed?"

Counting back Amanda determined that her last menses had been on board the prison ship. In an awed voice she related this information to Jemma.

"Well, I knowed you only been sleeping with Massa Tony these past two weeks," said Jemma matter-of-factly. "So this chile gots to belong to someone else."

"Oh, no, Jemma, you don't know what you're saying!"

Jemma was openly skeptical. "You mean that you and Massa Tony been pleasuring each other all these weeks right under my nose without me knowing? Uh, uh, chile," she scoffed, wagging her wooly head from side to side. "There ain't nothing going on in this house that I don't know about."

"It. . . didn't happen in this house, Jemma."

"Supposing you tell me about it, honey. Maybe old Jemma kin help you."

"It happened that first night right after Tony took me from the prison ship."

"You mean to say Massa Tony raped you when you nothing but a poor, scrawny chile, alone and helpless, and sick besides?" she asked indignantly, her black eyes snapping with fury. "I thought I knowed Massa Tony but it turns out he's no better than an animal!"

"No, Jemma," Amanda quickly offered, "it really wasn't like that. It was more like I was seduced, and. . . I wasn't all that unwilling. It just happened. Never once did I think I could get pregnant from that one time."

"Humph," snorted Jemma derisively, "all it takes to make a baby is one hard jab and a good connection and it ain't no secret that Massa Tony got lots of experience in both them things. You got caught, chile, good and proper," she chortled gleefully.

"My God, Jemma, how can you laugh? This is serious. What am I to do?"

"Do? Why, tell Massa Tony, of course." It seemed so simple that Jemma was truly amazed Amanda should even ask.

"I suppose," Amanda agreed reluctantly, "but I don't know what good it will do. I can never hope to be more than I am. Tony would never marry a convict. His family would disown him."

"You just won't know, honey, until you tells him, now will you?"

Amanda realized that pregnancy wasn't something that remained a secret for very long and that sooner or later Tony would find out anyway. But their relationship was so fragile, so late in blossoming that she was loathe to disturb their newfound happiness until she felt more secure with her place in Tony's life. Surely a few more weeks wouldn't make any difference, she reasoned. According to her calculations she must be nearly three months pregnant and her figure, though curvacious, showed little evidence of her condition.

"I'll tell Tony, Jemma, when I think it's time," Amanda finally declared. "Until then, please don't tell anyone."

Jemma sighed. Personally she thought Amanda wrong in keeping that sort of information from Tony. "If that's what you want, chile," she acquiesced reluctantly, "but I think you making a big mistake." How little either of them realized what dreadful consequences that error of omission would bring!

Shortly after that conversation with Jemma, Amanda encountered Nathan who came to the house on some pretense or other in order to see and talk with her. "Amanda," he said, his perceptive brown eyes missing nothing of her happiness or glowing state of health. "Have you been avoiding me?"

Amanda flushed becomingly, knowing that she had indeed been avoiding Nathan. She was embarrassed enough having the servants aware of her shameful relationship with Tony but it would hurt greatly for Nathan to learn that she had become Tony's mistress. Especially since there was virtually no hope of bettering her circumstances. Besides, the knowledge would only succeed in driving another wedge between Nathan and Tony as well as lose her his friendship and respect.

"I've been busy, Nathan," she hedged, lowering her eyes. "There is always so much to be done in this big house."

"Is. . . is Tony treating you well? You certainly look happy enough."

"Things couldn't be better," smiled Amanda, thinking about her secret resting beneath her ribcage. "I'm very happy here. I'm well treated. I don't believe any convict could expect more."

"I would give you more, my dear, if Tony would allow it," lamented Nathan. "I would have you as my wife and mother of my children."

"You are very kind, Nathan, but I have seven years of servitude ahead of me before I can think of marriage," she temporized.

"Damn it, Amanda!" exploded Nathan, surprising her by his uncharacteristic outburst. "I don't mean to be kind! I love you and want your love in return, not your gratitude."

"You are a dear man, Nathan, and deserve someone better than myself. You don't know, you can't know, all I have been and done."

Was she deliberately trying to discourage him? Nathan wondered abjectly. "Do you think me completely stupid?" he retorted. "I am painfully aware of what happens to young beautiful girls in English prisons as well as what takes place aboard prison ships. Whatever you did or were forced to do matters little to me. I know what you are and I want you."

By the time Nathan finished his long speech, bright tears spiked Amanda's long lashes. How could she bear to hurt such a dear man? she chided herself. But as long as Tony wanted her she could not consider Nathan's proposal. Besides, she carried Tony's child and hoped desperately that he would marry her when she told him.

"Nathan," she informed him gently, "I am in no position to think about my future. For the next seven years my life belongs to Tony."

"I'll wait, Amanda."

Later that same day Tony had a visitor. Letty, feeling quite neglected of late, rode to River's Edge where she found Tony in the stables saddling his horse prior to joining Nathan for an inspection of the indigo fields. When she called out his name softly, he whirled to face her, wishing himself anywhere but confronting Letty.

"Good morning, Letty," he greeted, bristling with impatience. "What brings you to River's Edge?"

"Damn you, Tony!" Letty stormed, slapping her riding crop against a shapely thigh in annoyance. "Where have you been these past weeks? I've seen little of you since my birthday party."

Tony sighed wearily, suddenly tired of Letty's possessiveness. It was like a sickness with her and he cared little for her mistaken assumption that they would marry one day. "I've been busy, Letty."

"Too busy to make love, Tony?" she asked archly. "Unless you've changed drastically these past weeks you're never too busy for that. Or is Amanda satisfying all your needs?"

"Leave Amanda out of this, Letty," Tony demanded angrily.

"When are you going to wake up to the fact that Amanda is using you as a means of gaining her freedom?" Letty hinted nastily. "Amanda doesn't want you, she's a user. She's deliberately pitting you against Nathan in order to hold your interest. You must remember that Amanda is no innocent miss, nor is she in the same class as you or I. She has lived with criminals, committed crimes, used her body to gain favor. When are you going to realize she is making a fool of you?"

"You know nothing about Amanda or her circumstances," contended Tony hotly. "Have you no compassion, Letty? I don't condemn Amanda for doing what was necessary to survive and neither should you."

"Surely you don't mean to. . . to marry that woman?" Letty asked, shock following disbelief across her features.

"I have no plans for marriage, Letty, as you well know."

"Am I out of the running, darling?" Letty asked coyly.

Tony's only thought was getting rid of Letty as he carelessly replied, "You will be the first person I consider when I make my choice."

To Letty's way of thinking Tony's casual

answer constituted a declaration of sorts which satisfied her for the time being even though she was positive that Tony and Amanda had become lovers. Somehow, someway, she vowed, the opportunity would arrive for her to regain her former position in Tony's life. Until that time came she would continue to poison his mind against his indentured servant until he wanted nothing more to do with her.

8

"Why so pensive tonight, my love?" Tony asked, a lazy smile curving his sensuous lips. "Does my lovemaking bore you already?"

"You know better than that, Tony," Amanda sighed, snuggling closer to the warm, vibrant body beside her. "It's just that I find it hard to believe this is happening to me. To be loved by you, it's... it's... like something out of a dream. I'm terrified that I'll wake up and find myself back in prison, or worse."

Tony laughed indulgently, surprised himself by the strong feelings he held for the passionate young woman in his arms. "Do you believe this?" he asked hoarsely as his mouth claimed hers. Immediately Amanda's lips parted to experience the full ecstasy of his forceful kiss, stirring, sighing, his exploring fingers leaving fiery tracks over her heated flesh.

Amanda let her mouth curve itself to his, welcoming the invasion of her senses with soft, melting sweetness. A tightening low in her stomach twisted into a hard knot of need, and Tony, recognizing that need, reacting to a need of his own, thrust into the white hot center of her. With a cry of abandon Amanda arose to meet his hard, throbbing body with a strange, clamoring hunger. Totally consumed by his quest for completion Tony accelerated his strokes, faster and faster, fanning the embers of her feelings into leaping flames. Shameless in her demands, Amanda urged him on with soft words and incoherent sounds until, caught up in a violently spinning whirlwind, her passion exploded. Triggered by Amanda's volatile climax Tony allowed his own passion free reign, riding the crest of sensation as he would a tumultuous sea, uttering hoarse cries of joy along his ecstatic journey.

Noticing her expression Tony couldn't help but chuckle. Brushing a burnished coppery strand of hair from her dewy face he wondered if her heart was beating as wildly as his. He could spend the rest of his life making love to her. Suddenly he went still, the thought exploding in his brain. Why not? he wondered, amazed that he hadn't thought of it sooner. What's to keep him from marrying Amanda if he so desired? His neighbors might not think much of his taking a convict to wife but he owed no one an explanation. He wanted nothing more than to protect her and hold her in his arms forever. On that happy note Tony allowed sleep to claim him.

As usual Tony was up at first light. Thinking to let Amanda sleep late he crept noiselessly from her room and, calling to Lionel, a new boy brought into the house to be groomed as valet, sought his own room to shave and dress. Charged with nervous anticipation, Tony cursed Lionel's slow, clumsy hands in his eagerness to begin his duties. He had decided to ask Amanda to marry him and wished his long day in the fields over so he could tell her of his decision. After downing a hearty breakfast served by Linus he rushed out of the house, missing Amanda's entrance by a mere ten minutes.

Finding Tony gone Amanda went into the kitchen to eat with Jemma, humming tunelessly under her breath, her heart full of love. Only recently had she been able to admit to herself that she loved Tony. Before, she had willed her thoughts into safer channels, thinking he despised her. But now that fate had seen fit to bring them together she could dwell openly on her love. It was the future that she dare not delve into more deeply. For buried in the compartments of her heart was the knowledge that there could be no future for her and Tony.

Tony returned from the fields at the hour between light and dark when the last dying rays of the sun turned the landscape into shadowy images. Though tired and dirty the jaunty step had not left his gait nor had the eager anticipation faded from his handsome face. Amanda, watching for his approach, ran out to meet him. Catching her up in his arms he swung her high, laughing gaily at her giggle of delight as he planted a resounding kiss on her pliant mouth before setting her on her feet once more.

"Lord, I missed you, Amanda," he groaned, devouring her face and form with hungry eyes.

"Tony," chided Amanda gently, "you've only left my bed this morning."

"And wish I were there with you this minute, you little minx, so I could show you just how much I missed you."

A delighted smile rippled Amanda's soft lips, her face alight with incredulous joy. The look of love shining from her eyes spurred Tony to tell her immediately of his wish to marry her instead of waiting until later to do it. Cradling her beaming face between two large hands he opened his mouth to form the words but the insistent tattoo of hoofbeats reverberating into the encroaching darkness drew his attention. Reluctantly pulling his eyes from Amanda's poised face he turned to await the arrival of their visitor.

Stanley Carter reined in his stallion, his quizzical gaze wavering between Tony and Amanda, certain that he had just interrupted something both private and intimate.

"What brings you to River's Edge at this time of the evening, Stanley?" Tony asked, conscious of the older man's censurous gaze upon him and Amanda.

"I've just returned from Charles Town where I found a letter from England waiting for you when I called at the shipping office. Thought I'd drop it off on my way home." He handed Tony a thick missive fastened with a clump of wax emblazoned with an impressive seal.

Tony accepted the letter, studying it curiously for several seconds before remembering his manners. "Thank you, Stanley, I appreciate your thoughtfulness."

"What are friends for, son?" replied Stanley heartily.

"If you're in no hurry join us for dinner. Amanda can entertain you while I read my letter and bathe," smiled Tony placing a protective arm about Amanda's slim waist.

"If you're sure I'm not intruding," replied Stanley slanting a meaningful glance at Amanda.

"Not at all, Stanley, glad to have you," countered Tony a bit too quickly.

Stanley dismounted, flexed his stiff muscles then followed Tony and Amanda into the house. Tony immediately disappeared upstairs and Amanda went into the kitchen to see about setting an extra place at the table, leaving Stanley sucking reflectively at a glass filled with amber liquid.

Finding Tony and Amanda together earlier had come as somewhat of a shock. There was no denying their intimacy. It was obvious to Stanley that Tony had made Amanda his mistress. And not unwillingly by the looks of it. Where it all would lead to he had no idea, but of one thing he was positive. No matter how badly Letty wanted Tony he doubted an alliance between them would ever materialize. Tony had been given sufficient opportunity to declare his feelings for Letty and in his heart Stanley knew Letty was reaching for something she could never possess. Riding home from Charles Town he had been a bit remorseful at what he had done. Now, after seeing for himself the direction of Tony's affection, his doubts dissipated into thin air. In three days he would leave for England as planned. Letty needed a husband and he was certain England held the best possible prospects for his headstrong daughter.

Amanda soon returned to the parlor where she and the older man spent several uncomfortable minutes waiting for Tony to appear. When finally he strode into the room Amanda thought him the handsomest man she had ever seen. Dressed casually in tan trousers thrust into tall black boots that molded his muscular legs, a buckskin coat cut to emphasize the width of his broad shoulders, his immaculate stock open carelessly at the neck. His lean, deeply bronzed features, hawk-like and predatory, seemed better fitted to a pirate than a gentleman planter. His thick black hair above those strange silver eyes sent an involuntary ripple of excitement down Amanda's spine.

It was the faraway look in those silvery eyes that immediately drew Amanda's attention. It was as though a shadow had dimmed their luster. Alarmed, she quickly asked, "Tony, what is it? You look so strange. Did you receive bad news from home?"

Stanley, too, noted Tony's anguished look. "My boy, I hope I'm not the bearer of grim tidings," he said.

"I'm afraid it is bad news," Tony admitted, his voice choked. "The worst possible. My entire family has been wiped out by the plague sweeping through England. The letter is from the family solicitor urging me to return at once to see to the estates that are now mine."

His eyes rested on Amanda as he spoke. A pang of pain and remorse knifed through his vitals at her soft gasp. To be separated now, just when they had found each other, was unbearable. All his plans, his hopes for their future would have to wait until he returned.

Stanley's voice broke into his glum thoughts. "I know how you hate to leave your plantation just before harvest but you are fortunate to have a trustworthy man like Nathan to manage your estate in your absence. Or do you plan to sell out here and settle in England permanently? After all, you are an earl now."

"I have no intention of living in England. I like South Carolina and my life here. Perhaps I'll sell the lands, title and all. Of what use is a title in the colonies?"

Stanley cleared his throat. "Delivering your letter was not my only reason for stopping by this evening. I have long considered taking Letty and returning to England. I've plenty of money to live comfortably the rest of my days and provide generously for my daughter. It's time I found a husband for her."

Embarrassed by Stanley's broadfaced hint, Tony dropped his eyes, studying the tips of his fingers with feigned interest. Nor could Amanda stop the color from staining her cheeks and neck. Blithely Stanley continued. "The Columbia sails from Charles Town in three days and I've booked passage on her for myself. I have only to return home and pack my bags. Tomorrow should find me on my way back to Charles Town."

"You said you booked passage for yourself. Does that mean you are leaving Letty behind?" Tony asked.

"Letty refuses to accompany me at this time," Stanley informed Tony, sliding him a reproachful glance. "I have given her complete authority in all matters regarding the plantation. Ben Barker, my overseer, is quite capable of running things. More capable than myself, I might add. I was never cut out to be a planter. Letty has promised me she will sell my lands and join me in England the moment she receives word that I have found a suitable home for us." He didn't need to add, "and a suitable husband."

"You say the *Columbia* sails in three days?" asked Tony sharply.

"Yes, I believe that's her departure day."

Taking a deep, steadying breath, Tony stated resolutely, "Then you shall have a fellow passenger for I intend to book passage on the *Columbia*, also."

While Tony and Stanley discussed their plans to travel together to Charles Town Amanda stood helplessly by, plunged into despair more profound than any she had ever known at the thought of months of separation from Tony. She was already counting the days stretching out endlessly before her. It wasn't fair, she silently mourned, to be parted at a time when they had just discovered their love. And what of her baby? It was imperative that Tony be informed of her condition before he left. She should have listened to Jemma and told him immediately, she realized, a sudden twinge of awful premonition prickling the back of her neck.

The remainder of the evening until Stanley left shortly after dinner passed in a haze for Amanda. She felt uncomfortable sitting at the table with Stanley present but Tony had gallantly seated her as if she were anything but an indentured servant and she had no choice but to make half-hearted attempts at conversation. She could barely wait to excuse herself and leave the men alone to their cigars and brandy, which she did a little too soon for convention, and hurried directly to her room to await Tony.

Amanda had undressed, donned a nightgown and was sitting before the dressing table brushing her hair by candlelight when Tony finally joined her. He paused for a moment in the doorway, the sight of his lover's delicate features nearly taking his breath away. Glossy auburn hair with its underlying streaks of flame that even the darkness of the room couldn't dim, the sensuous mouth, the heart-shaped face, pointed, determined chin, now aquiver with barely suppressed tears. He spoke her name and she turned, the impact of long, dark eyelashes spiked with tears and sad, green eyes twisted his gut into a tight knot of pain.

Without realizing that she had even moved, Amanda found herself in Tony's arms, held against his heart by two steel bands while she sobbed against his immaculate stock.

"My love," he choked, unable to hold back his own grief, "it won't be forever. I'll be back before you know it."

"When, Tony, when?" asked Amanda, her lower lip trembling.

"It is July now," he answered, struggling to marshall his thoughts away from the soft body pressed so intimately against his. "I should be back after the first of the new year, barring storms and ice closing the harbor."

"So long?" wailed Amanda in a fresh torrent of tears.

"Please, Amanda, we have only this night. Don't let's waste it," Tony pleaded, lifting her face with one finger and kissing away the tears streaming down her pale cheeks. "I want to love you all night long. Don't let anything blight our happiness. I want to remember this night in the lonely months ahead."

His lips caught hers fiercely then, and she hung limp in his arms, surrendering to the magic fire that swept through her as his mouth softened over hers, devouring its curves, as his hand traveled down her back and moved caressingly over her hips and buttocks. A shudder went through her as his tongue pressed its way gently into her mouth. His hands were everywhere, now grasping her waist tightly, now smoothing her hair, as his warm tongue touched the tip of her own, stroking it urgently.

Slowly, reverently, he lifted the hem of her nightgown, drawing it over her head and dropping it on the floor. Hungrily his eyes ran over her softly, like summer rain. Then her arms went around his neck and desire flamed between them. Lifting her up easily, Tony strode the few steps to the bed, releasing his delicious burden reluctantly while he shed his own clothing.

Amanda could not help but admire the sculptured planes and hollows of his body, aware of the strength and beauty of his masculine form, his proud, jutting manhood claiming her eyes. Tony chuckled softly then stretched out beside her, his arms hungry for the feel of her softness. She strained against the hard length of him while his mouth enveloped the throbbing mound of her breast and his tongue flicked over her nipple like little touches of flame. Greedily he dragged his lips from the crest of one breast to let it scale the peak of the other. She lay gasping, twisting her fingers through the crisp waves of his hair while his lips and tongue teased and titillated. Amanda moaned softly, unable to bear the heart-stopping ecstasy sweeping over her in a sensuous mist.

The frenzy that possessed him mounted, and she reveled in it, blind with desire, until the moment when the consuming fire in her loins blotted out everything but his face above her as he moved from the pink, erect nipples to the pale goblet of her belly, until his tongue touched the hard, pulsating bud at the core of her femininity. It was a moment that had its own eternity.

Amanda's body spasmed in spontaneous reaction, his tongue seeking, stabbing, causing her to clutch frantically at Tony's shoulders, finding his skin burning to her touch.

"So sweet, Amanda," Tony whispered hoarsely, his voice a raw parody of itself. "You taste so sweet."

And then he was looming above her, moving fiercely inside her and she met his every thrust with wild abandon as her passion peaked into an eruption that welded his body to hers as he surged into her, filling her with sweet, liquid warmth. She lay gasping, consumed by waves of diminishing heat. His face was buried in the warm place between her breasts and Amanda could feel his own passion draining into her, his cries muffled by her heated flesh, his breath warm on her skin.

Breathing raggedly Amanda floated in the drifting, weightless descent of Tony's arms, his erratic heartbeat like thunder in her ears. She wanted nothing more from life than to love and be loved by this man. But with a pang of despair she realized that in a few short hours he would be gone and she still hadn't told him about the baby.

"Tony," she began, absently caressing his taut stomach.

"Um," Tony murmured, floating in an eddy of contentment.

"There is something I must tell you."

"Not now, darling, I don't want anything to interfere with our last hours together."

"But, Tony," Amanda insisted doggedly, "this is important."

"No, my love, nothing is more important than making love to you again. Besides, there is nothing you could tell me that would change my feelings for you." Suddenly he caught her hand and moved it downward to where his renewed desire throbbed strong and vigorous against her palm while his own hand stroked the smoothness of her abdomen, down and over the fiery triangle and inner reaches of her thighs. Amazed at his virility so soon after they had just made love, Amanda gave herself up to sweet sensation and the sudden fierce rise of ardor carrying them off once again.

Much later, with a resolve born of desperation, Amanda blurted out the secret she had kept to herself. "Tony," she began, gathering her courage, "I'm going to have a baby." Silence. "Our baby." Silence. "Darling, did you hear me? In six months I will give birth to your child." This time the silence was broken by a soft gurgling sound.

Asleep! Tony was asleep and hadn't heard a word she said. With a sigh of disappointment, Amanda snuggled into the warm curve of his arm deciding there would be time to tell him before he left in the morning. Twice more during the night Tony awakened her and made love to her, ravenously, tenderly, as if each time would be their last, allowing Amanda not one brief moment to tell him about the baby. In the morning, she told herself, exhaustion making coherent thought impossible.

Hot fingers of brilliant sunshine stabbed relentlessly at Amanda's prone form. Perspiration beaded her flesh and she had tossed aside the sheet Tony had thrown over her when he left at dawn. Gingerly she opened her eyes, squinting against the sun, stretching languorously, aware of a pleasant ache suffusing her body. A contented smile curved her passion-swollen lips as memories of the previous night and early morning washed over her. Still smiling she turned to Tony only to find the place beside her empty, the faint lingering male odor of him the only evidence that he had been there at all.

"No!" shrieked Amanda, jumping from the bed and rushing to the window. It was evident by the position of the sun that the day was well advanced and that Tony had risen quietly and left for Charles Town without saying goodbye. Frantically searching the room for she knew not what Amanda's eyes fell on a sheet of paper propped up on her nightstand. Snatching it up she read Tony's parting words to her, her eyes streaming tears.

Darling,
    You were sleeping so peacefully I didn't have the heart to awaken you. I'm afraid I wore you out last night, and besides, it's better this way. I want to remember you as you were in my arms during the height of your passion, not as a sad-eyed wraith waving goodby to me.
    I've left the plantation in Nathan's capable hands. He will take care of you. Don't despair, my love, I will be back to ask you something I wanted to ask before I learned I must return to England. I love you, Amanda.
Yours forever,
Tony

By the time Amanda had finished reading Tony's note tears of joy as well as despair were blurring her vision. To know that Tony truly loved her gave her indescribable happiness, but at the same time the thought that he was leaving without being told that he would soon be a father left her with a cold lump in the pit of her stomach. What would Tony think when he returned and found her with a newborn babe? she wondered. Would he be angry because she hadn't told him about her impending motherhood? Soon everyone would know that she was pregnant and the thought of facing that ordeal without Tony's protection was not pleasant.

Confronting Nathan's accusing eyes when he learned of her pregnancy would be extremely painful. What would he think when he learned that she had become Tony's mistress? Would he hate her? Or blame Tony for seducing her? Either way Nathan would be hurt. With a deep sigh Amanda prepared to face the first day of many, many more to come without Tony beside her, loving her, making her complete.

9

Amanda descended the long curving staircase, her hand trailing absently along the gleaming balustrade. One month, she thought disconsolately. Thirty days without Tony's comforting presence beside her. Those empty days and nights stretched out endlessly. Loneliness was her biggest enemy. Of course there was Jemma and Linus still in the big house. Since Tony left, Tess and Cory had moved back to the quarters with their families, their work having been drastically reduced by Tony's absence. Besides, the third floor bedrooms were uninhabitable in the heat of summer. Lionel had gone along with Tony to act as valet so the house was nearly deserted on that hot, humid August morning.

When Amanda reached the bottom of the stairs the sound of hoofbeats alerted her to the possibility of having guests call upon her, although that seemed unlikely since most of their closest neighbors knew by now that Tony had departed for England. It couldn't be Nathan, she reasoned, because he had called last evening to check on her to make certain all was going well at the house.

Knowing of only one way to satisfy her curiosity Amanda walked out onto the front porch to await her visitors beneath the huge white pillars. A sudden spurt of fear followed dismay across her mobile features when she spied Letty approaching on horseback accompanied by her overseer.

Amanda took an involuntary step backwards when the duo had dismounted and casually walked to within only a foot or two from where she stood.

"What do you want?" she asked, choking out the words despite the forboding that something evil was about to take place.

"Just listen to the little slut, Ben," Letty said to her foreman, her eyes bright with malice. "You'd think she was mistress here. We'll see how uppity she acts once Tony and I are married."

"That will never happen!" bit out Amanda angrily.

"I suppose you think he will marry you, a convict, a prostitute, a nobody? Be assured that will never take place."

Amanda bit her lip, aware that Letty probably spoke the truth but was too proud to admit it. But Tony loved her, didn't he? Even if he didn't marry her he would never marry Letty, would he?

"I see you have nothing to say to that," crowed Letty spitefully. "Just so you remember your place I came to teach you a lesson. I haven't forgotten the humiliation you caused me, nor the beautiful gown you ruined."

"You know well enough that accident was of your own doing," Amanda shot back scathingly. The cold, implacable rage in Letty's blue eyes made her almost sorry she had spoken out so hastily, even if it was in her own defense.

Letty's jealousy and hate for Amanda was alive, palpable, potent enough to destroy her. Amanda's eyes darted fearfully between Letty and her overseer, wondering what direction the beautiful blond's jealousy would take. Standing beside Letty, a wide, leering grin never leaving her ferret-like face, beady eyes moist with anticipation, Ben Barker licked his thin lips, awaiting his orders.

Ben, a man who did his job well and knew how to manage the slaves so as to get the most from their labors had a mean streak in him that had been heretofore tempered under the gentle guidance of Stanley Carter. But Letty was another matter altogether. She had deliberately allowed the overseer's perverse nature free reign in order to gain his confidence and trust. When the time came she wanted him willing to do her bidding without protest or judgment. She realized she could not carry out her vile plan without his help. Seeing him now, his lascivious gaze raking Amanda with barely concealed lust, Letty knew her first impression of the overseer had been correct. Given license to inflict and carry out his own brand of punishment upon the slaves had made him her ally.

"You've said enough," Letty cried, jealousy contorting her beautiful features. "After today Tony will never look twice at you. He won't even recognize you once Ben finishes with you."

"What are you going to do?" whispered

Amanda, fear stealing into her voice and turning her legs rubbery.

"First I intend to flay the skin off your back and after that mar that pretty little face so no man will look at you again," Letty snarled maliciously. "And once Tony and I are married I will sell you to the lowest whorehouse in Charles Town."

"You wouldn't dare!" gasped Amanda, drawing her breath in sharply, more frightened than she had ever been in her life. "Do you think Tony would countenance such brutality?"

"Tony isn't here nor likely to be for many months. By that time it will be history."

Panicstricken, Amanda took one step backward, then another, thinking to turn and run into the house and up the stairs to the safety of her room where she could throw the bolt before Letty realized what she was about.

A satanic sneer twisting her lips, Letty nodded to Ben who acted instantaneously. Rough hands seized Amanda's slim shoulders, forcing her quaking form hard against his wiry body. One hand plundered a soft breast and the unaccustomed handling of that tender mound brought a moan of pain to Amanda's lips.

Letty laughed. "Bring her out in the yard, Ben," she ordered imperiously. Ben half-dragged, half-carried Amanda to the hitching post in the front of the house. "Hoist her up and secure her arms over her head to the ring in the post."

Ben pulled out a rope dangling from a loop in his belt and did as he was told, thoroughly enjoying himself as he allowed his hands free access to Amanda's cringing flesh.

Calmly, deliberately, Letty inserted both hands in the neckline of Amanda's dress and ripped downward with a strength born of hatred, baring Amanda's back to the waist. Moving around to face Amanda she repeated the motion until both the young girl's breasts fell free, the full, creamy globes swaying like ripe fruits before Ben's lust-filled eyes.

"Are you sure you want to do this, Mistress Letty?" Ben asked, unable to turn his gaze from Amanda's flesh. "Why not give her to me? I'll see that she learns her rightful place. After I finish with her she'll be meek as can be, that I promise. After all, she is no better than a slave and I am accustomed to using them as I see fit."

"No!" cried Amanda. "Don't do this, Letty. You know it's wrong. I don't belong to you. Think of what Tony will do to you when he returns." Amanda's mind worked furiously, searching for the right words to release her from this nightmare. If she failed she knew that nothing could save her. Certainly not Jemma and Linus, slaves themselves who had little or no rights. Nathan was in the fields at this time of day and could not be counted on to save her even if he knew what was happening. And her baby! What would happen to her baby if she were beaten unmercifully? Amanda wondered wretchedly, this new fear more terrifying than any pain could ever be.

"Beg all you like," Letty goaded, sparing Amanda a venomous glance. "But it will do you no good. I've waited for this opportunity too long to let myself be dissuaded. I might even let Ben have you afterwards if you are in any condition to accommodate him. You are more suited to him than to someone like Tony."

Amanda blanched. Her stomach roiled dangerously and she nearly spewed out her breakfast.

All hope fled as she watched Letty walk to her horse and remove a long, wicked looking riding crop from the saddle. Letty handed the whip to Ben and stepped aside, her eyes gleaming with a strange light.

"How many?" Ben asked, flexing his arm to get the feel of the whip.

"Twenty," replied Letty without a moment's hesitation. "Ten on her back first, then turn her around for another ten. Don't spare her face."

"My God!" screamed Amanda, fruitlessly straining against her bonds. "Have you no mercy?"

"Probably will kill her," muttered Ben sliding Letty a skeptical glance.

It mattered little to Letty if Amanda died from the result of the whipping but at the last minute prudence intervened and she countermanded her first order. "Ten, then. Five front and five back."

Shrugging, neither condemning nor condoning Letty's decision, Ben drew back his arm. Amanda screamed even before the first lash cut cruelly into her tender flesh.

Amanda's first cry brought Linus rushing from the house with Jemma not far behind, her fat legs pumping furiously. "Lord! Lord!" cried Jemma the moment she comprehended what was taking place. "What you doing, Miz Letty? What you doing to that poor chile?"

"Beating her, what does it look like?" flung back Letty, annoyed at the unwanted interference.

"You cain't do that, Miz Letty. Amanda belongs to Massa Tony. He ain't gonna like this one bit, no suh, he ain't."

"Tony is much too lenient with that baggage," proclaimed Letty imperiously. "I feel it my duty to punish the slut in Tony's absence."

"But what's Amanda done?"

Growing angrier by the minute Letty lashed out at the slave who now stood protectively before Amanda, arms outstretched, daring Ben to strike. "Get out of the way, Jemma. If you don't move immediately you will be the next to feel the sting of the whip."

"I don't care what you do to me. You ain't gonna hurt this here chile."

Incensed by the slave's disobedience, Letty grabbed the whip from Ben's hands and let loose a vicious blow to Jemma's face, causing an immediate welt to raise on the wrinkled flesh.

Jemma cried out in agony and Linus immediately sprang to her defense. "Get her out of here!" Letty shouted at the old butler."

"No, I ain't going," replied Jemma stubbornly, her cheek streaming blood. "You don't know what you doing. Massa Tony, he be mighty angry if you hurt Amanda. Don't you know Amanda's gonna have a. . ."

"No!" shrieked Amanda. "Don't say anymore, Jemma. Just leave, please. I couldn't stand to see you beaten because of me. I'll survive. Just leave. It's best for all."

Never would she give Letty the satisfaction of learning she carried Tony's child. Armed with that knowledge she knew Letty would not hesitate to kill her.

"Listen to Amanda and get out of here, old woman," warned Letty. "You won't be hurt if you don't interfere."

Hanging her head, the picture of total dejection, Jemma allowed Linus to lead her into the house, her heart-rending sobs renting the morning calm. Satisfied that nothing more would disrupt her morning's pleasure Letty handed the whip back to Ben.

The sound of Amanda's second scream galvanized Linus into action, his old legs moving faster than they ever had in his life. Through the kitchen and out the back door he ran, praying that Nathan would be where he was supposed to be, his heart pumping blood at a furious rate, his lungs near to bursting.

Amanda's back was on fire. The second lash had drawn blood and she could feel the wetness seeping into the waist of her torn bodice. Never in her wildest imaginings did she dream anything could hurt so badly. When the third lash fell she began seriously considering her death and what Tony would do when he returned and found her dead at Letty's hands. Silently she mourned the baby she would never bear and wondered vaguely if it would have been a boy or girl.

With the fourth lash the terrible screaming began, shrill, mindless, over and over. She was unaware that the animal-like sounds came from her own throat. Delirious with pain, her body a mass of raw nerve endings, Amanda welcomed with open arms the blackness claiming her, thinking that she would probably never awaken as the last sound she heard was the whip whistling forward for the fifth blow to her torn and bloody back. Thank God she would never feel the other five delivered to her face and breasts.

But the fifth blow never fell. Nathan, having been alerted by a nearly incoherent Linus rode at breakneck speed to the house, leaving the butler weak and vomiting from his unaccustomed exertion. When he saw Amanda sagging limply against the hitching post looking more dead than alive his rage knew no bounds. One look at that slender back, criss-crossed with angry welts oozing blood was enough to spur him into action. Before the fifth lash landed Nathan flung himself at Ben, wrestling him to the ground where he methodically and brutally began pounding him senseless in an amazingly short time with his huge, ham-like fists. Letty stood impotently by, seething with rage, shouting invectives at Nathan for thwarting her well-laid plans.

Suddenly Letty's wild eyes fell on the whip that had fallen from Ben's hand when Nathan attacked him. Smiling deviously she picked it up and advanced menacingly on Amanda, caring little that the unconscious girl was beyond feeling. But Nathan was too quick for her. Leaving Ben's battered body lying in the dust he leaped for Letty, stopping her in her tracks.

"How dare you put your filthy hands on me!" Letty spat. "I'm only doing what Tony was too tender-hearted to do."

"Tony has never whipped a slave in his life and Amanda is no slave. Furthermore, she certainly has done nothing to warrant such punishment."

"Who are you to order me about?" demanded Letty.

"I am in charge here in Tony's absence and I am ordering you to collect that scum you call an overseer and leave. If either of you step foot on this property again you will be forcibly ejected. You can both be brought before the court for your actions today."

So saying he moved to release Amanda's battered body from the hitching post, glaring malevolently at Letty all the while. The moment Jemma saw that Nathan had emerged victorious in Letty's private vendetta against Amanda she came rushing from the house, kneeling above the prone form Nathan held so protectively in his massive arms.

"She done killed Amanda," Jemma wailed, her huge bulk shaking with grief. "She done killed my chile."

"She's not dead, Jemma. Look closely, you can see her breathing," Nathan assured the distraught slave. "She's badly hurt but she'll heal in time."

Leaving Amanda to Jemma's care for a few moments he turned back to Letty. "I thought I told you to leave."

"I'll see that Tony learns of your insolence," Letty protested weakly, backing down under Nathan's cold rage. On the ground Ben began to stir fitfully and Letty watched dispassionately as he rose unsteadily to his feet. How could she have thought her overseer a match for Nathan's superior strength? she wondered disgustedly.

For the moment Letty had no choice but to leave even though she had no intention of giving up. One day, one way or another, she would see Amanda suffer for this effrontery to her pride. She had set her sights on Tony and in the end she would have him. She would retreat for now but she would allow nothing or no one to stand in the way of getting her heart's desire. Marshalling all her dignity Letty strode to her horse, mounted, and rode off regally without a backward glance, her disgruntled and bruised overseer trailing behind.

Once more Amanda commanded all of Nathan's attention as he gently and carefully gathered her in his arms, paying special attention to her bloodied back, and carried her into the house and up the stairs to her bedroom where he placed her gently on the bed on her stomach. Wincing at the sight of the pitifully torn and flayed flesh he set about helping Jemma remove pieces of cloth and dirt from Amanda's back. Jemma, despite her own injury called upon all the healing powers she possessed as she tended to the slim form lying lifeless and unconscious on the bed.

"Lordy, Lordy, I shore hopes she don't lose her baby," wailed Jemma, turning wide, black eyes on Nathan. "Whatever will I tell Massa Tony?"

Nathan went still, completely and totally flabbergasted by Jemma's surprising disclosure. No wonder Tony refused to sell Amanda's indenture papers, he surmised in a flash of insight. And then in a rush of anger he became enraged with Tony for leaving Amanda alone when she carried his child, especially with someone as vindictive as Letty lurking nearby ready to do her worst. How could Tony do such a thing? How could he take advantage of a child like Amanda and then callously disappear for months on end. If Amanda lost his child he would have no one to blame but himself, and, of course, his former mistress, Nathan seethed. Nor would he blame Amanda if she turned against Tony for leaving her alone and unprotected at a time when she was most vulnerable.

"Amanda is pregnant?" he asked, looking down on her with compassion.

"Oh, Lordy," moaned Jemma, "I thought Amanda done tole you."

"No, she said nothing," admitted Nathan dryly. "But I haven't seen much of her lately. With Tony gone I have little time to spare."

"Don't blame Amanda, Massa Nathan," Jemma pleaded.

"I don't blame her, Jemma. How can I? It's Tony who's to blame. He doesn't deserve Amanda. I'm certain he forced this on her. He doesn't love her like I do. He's only using her. There are times when I'd like to kill the bastard."

Then he turned on his heel and stormed out to leave Jemma to her tender ministrations.

10

Amanda slowly awoke feeling as if she were swimming her way upwards through layers of cotton. She was laying on her stomach, face pressed into the pillow, her entire body awash in a river of burning, searing pain. Any kind of movement set off a chain of agony so severe it rendered her completely helpless. In fits and starts she remembered the source of her terrible suffering and an involuntary cry escaped her clenched teeth.

"You awake, chile?" asked a solicitous voice near her ear.

Groaning from the effort Amanda carefully turned her aching head and saw Jemma standing beside her, her inky eyes full of concern. "Does it hurt bad, honey?"

"Bad enough," answered Amanda weakly, gritting her teeth against the pain. Amanda was surprised to find herself still alive and her thoughts went immediately to the tiny being growing inside her. Had she lost her child? she wondered, fearing to ask the question burning on the tip of her tongue.

"Your baby be jest fine," grinned Jemma, immediately sensing Amanda's concern. "Ain't nothing gonna make him give up his warm home."

Jemma's comforting words laid Amanda's worst fears to rest as wearily her purple-rimmed eyes closed once again.

The next time she awoke the sun was making deep inroads into the shadows in her room and though her back felt like it had been skinned with a sharp knife her head was clear. Moving her hand gingerly she touched her face feeling for the tell-tale welts Letty had promised her, heaving a sigh of relief when she encountered nothing but smooth, firm flesh. Vaguely she wondered what had happened after she blacked out that dissuaded Letty from scarring her face? It seemed unlikely that Tony's ex-mistress grew soft-hearted at the last minute. If anything Amanda's suffering heightened Letty's perverse pleasure.

At that moment Jemma entered the room carrying a tray which she sat down on the nighttable next to the bed. " 'Bout time you had something in that stomach of yours," the black woman announced cheerfully, which immediately lifted Amanda's spirits. "If you gonna keep that babe healthy you gots to eat." So saying she carefully arranged her considerable bulk at the edge of the bed and calmly proceeded to spoon porridge into Amanda's mouth, clucking disapprovingly when the young girl signalled that she could eat no more. "Ain't had nothing in your belly for two days," she chided gently, "now open your mouth and eat."

Meekly Amanda obeyed until the bowl was

empty, which pleased Jemma to no end. "How long have I been like this, Jemma?" Amanda asked as the slave began smoothing a cooling salve on her ravaged back.

"Two days, chile. Massa Nathan, he worried you ain't never gonna wake up. But I tole him you strong and soon be well again."

"Nathan?" asked Amanda puzzled. "How does he fit in? I can't remember anything after that fourth lash. I must have fainted. What kept Letty from marking my face with the whip?"

"Massa Nathan, that's what," chortled Jemma gleefully. "You shoulda seen that man. Swooped down on that ole Ben like a madman, he did. Then he sent that ole witch Letty packing. Won't be pestered by her or her overseer no more."

"How did Nathan get here so quickly? I had given up hope. I never expected to come out of the ordeal alive."

"My ole man, that's how," answered Jemma, her huge breasts swelling with pride. "That man ain't never moved so fast in his whole life. He found Massa Nathan and Massa Nathan lit out on his horse like the devil hisself was after him."

"I'm grateful to Linus, Jemma. And to you for caring for me."

"We only protecting what belongs to Massa Tony," Jemma beamed.

Amanda's next visitor was Nathan. By that time she was able to sit up in bed propped up by several soft pillows. Tess and Cory had been in that morning and bathed her and brushed her hair until it fell in gleaming ripples against the pillow, a perfect foil for her pale skin and vibrant green eyes.

"If anything had happened to you I would

have never forgiven myself," were Nathan's first words as his eyes moved warmly over Amanda in an effort to convince himself that she was really recovering from her many hurts.

"Thanks to your timely intervention I will be fine in no time at all," she reassured him. "I can't believe that Letty really meant to. . . to hurt me so badly." Her slight body quivered beneath the covers, alarming Nathan.

"Am I tiring you?" he asked, noticing her sudden pallor. "If you want me to leave. . ."

"No, please stay, Nathan. Tell me what happened after I fainted."

"Not much," Nathan laughed wryly. "It was pretty much one-sided." Then he went on to describe his entrance upon the scene of Letty's cruelty and his immediate reaction. Even Amanda had to smile as she pictured Ben's slender form being pounded senseless by Nathan's massive fists.

"Jemma said your baby wasn't harmed by your ordeal. I'm. . . I'm glad, Amanda, even if I am jealous that the baby you carry belongs to Tony."

Embarrassed, Amanda's downcast lashes rested like two dark wings against pale cheeks. "I know what you must think of me, Nathan," she said in a low voice, "but. . ."

"No, Amanda, it's not what you think. I don't blame you. If anyone is to blame it's Tony. You had no choice but to give in to him. As an indentured servant you have virtually no rights, no protection from his lust. God, I'd like to kill him! How could he leave you knowing you are to bear his child? Didn't he realize that Letty would find some way to hurt you?"

"Tony had no choice, Nathan, he had to

leave," replied Amanda in an effort to sooth any bad feeling Nathan might hold for Tony. "And he didn't know about the baby. He still doesn't."

Nathan was astounded. "You didn't tell him before he left?"

"I had only just realized it myself, and somehow I never got around to telling him. I guess I. . . I was afraid he would be angry with me."

"Angry? My God, Amanda, how could he be angry? I would sell my soul to have you bear my child!"

Amanda flushed, thinking she had no right to be loved by a man as good and kind as Nathan. If only she could love him in return. But it could never be. Tony was the only man she would ever love.

"When will your baby be born?" asked Nathan, rousing her from her reverie.

"In about five months."

"Why, you've only been here four months. That means. . ." Nathan drew in his breath sharply, his eyes grew hard and cold and Amanda quivered, wrongly assuming his anger to be directed at her. "My God, he raped you! He raped you the minute he took you off the ship and got you alone!"

"No, Nathan, it wasn't like that, really," insisted Amanda. "He took me, yes, that first night on the trail. But it wasn't rape. It just happened."

"Stop trying to defend him, Amanda. You were half-starved and helpless against him and Tony took advantage of your weakness. It was rape pure and simple. I could never respect a man like that. When he returns I intend to tell him just what I think of him and then leave River's Edge. Let him find another overseer. And when I leave,

Amanda," he said, gentling his voice to a warm caress, "I want you to come with me."

"But my papers. . ."

"Forget the papers. I'll find some way. We'll be married and Tony can do nothing about it."

"You don't understand, Nathan. I. . . I love Tony. And there's the baby."

"Did you think I wouldn't love your child? What do you take me for? I'll cherish it, just as I will you." Amanda opened her mouth to speak but Nathan continued before she could form the words. "You only think you love Tony. All women are half in love with the first man who takes them. But I promise you I'll make you forget him. I don't mean to hurt you, darling, but do you really think he'd marry you? He's an earl now. He owes it to his family as well as himself to marry someone of the same class, someone with a large dowry."

Nathan's brown eyes softened at Amanda's bleak expression and he was immediately contrite. "I'm sorry, dear, I know the truth is hard to bear but it's best you don't yearn for something that can never be."

"But the baby will. . ."

"Be well provided for, I'm sure. Illegitimate, of course, but Tony will see that he or she wants for nothing. How many more will you bear him if you remain as his mistress? What will happen when he marries?"

"Please, Nathan, stop! I don't want to hear anymore. Right now I can't think beyond the birth of my child. I will do nothing hasty before Tony returns. I owe him that much."

"You owe him nothing but I will abide by your decision. But no matter what, I still intend on leaving River's Edge when he returns."

Amanda sighed wearily. Her head began to ache again and she needed to turn over on her stomach to relieve the pain in her back. Recognizing her discomfort, Nathan stood. "I'd better leave, I'm tiring you. But I'll be back again. Soon. I'm placing guards around the house as a precaution. I don't trust Letty, and I won't be caught offguard again."

"Thank you, Nathan. I don't deserve someone like you."

"I love you, Amanda. You deserve much, much more. More than even I can give you."

Before she realized what he was about, Nathan bent forward, his mouth slowly descending on hers, his gently caressing lips tender, the scent of her fragrant body filling his senses. "Get well, darling," he whispered lovingly before he left.

Amanda did get well quickly. Once her lacerated back began to heal, thanks to Jemma's mysterious salve, her natural vitality and zest for life returned. In a week she was moving stiffly and carefully about the house. And in two weeks only tenderness and slight twinges remained to remind her of her terrifying experience.

Nathan came to the big house regularly, often taking the evening meal with Amanda so she would not be so much alone. After dinner, concerned that she wasn't getting enough exercise, he walked with her along the river in the moonlight until the nights grew too cool for strolling.

Time held no meaning for Amanda. If it wasn't for her burgeoning figure she would have thought time stood still. She existed in a void, as dark and forbidding as the prison that once held her. In early November Nathan brought back a letter for her on one of his trips to Charles Town for supplies. With shaking hands, fighting back a deep forboding she could not name, Amanda read Tony's words.

According to Tony he was having problems with settling the estate and selling his title. Things were bad in England. Plague had decimated the population and funds were scarce. There was no hope of his returning to South Carolina before March. He hoped she was well and that Nathan was managing without him. There were a few personal words at the end but they did little to dispel the feeling that things were not as they should be. Had Tony met someone he cared about? she wondered frantically. What would happen to her if he returned with an aristocratic wife? Over and over she scanned the letter, trying to read between the lines but each reading left her more bereft than the last.

Later, she read the letter to Nathan, including the personal words at the end meant for her ears alone. "He might come home with a bride, you know," said Nathan, preparing her for the worst.

"I've thought of that," responded Amanda dismally. "But you heard what he said to me at the end of the letter. I refuse to believe he doesn't care for me."

"Of course he cares for you. Who wouldn't?" replied Nathan feeling her pain as if it were his own. Just the thought of Tony leading Amanda to believe he loved her was enough to make Nathan furious. He agonized over how to convince the woman he loved that the man she loves is only toying with her affections, using her for his own enjoyment.

After that communication from Tony Amanda

heard nothing more. She had no alternative but to bide her time until March in order to prove to Nathan that Tony really did love her. Perhaps he might even marry her after he saw his child and held him in his arms. She decided it was better to cling to her fragile dreams than to give in to despair.

By early November Amanda felt and looked as clumsy as an ox, or so she thought. Nathan insisted that approaching motherhood only enhanced her beauty. Jemma was inclined to agree. But Amanda could only look at her distended stomach and grimace, praying for the next weeks to pass quickly before she burst, for she looked large enough to deliver momentarily. Warily, Jemma watched Amanda grow, shaking her head in wonder, proclaiming the child to be a strapping boy with Tony's powerful frame. Privately, Jemma feared that the baby grew too large for Amanda's small body and she anticipated a difficult delivery should the child go full term. She was wise enough to keep her fears to herself.

One day in mid-November Amanda awoke to find a light snow had fallen, transforming the landscape into a white fairyland. Long, thin icicles decorated the overhang as well as the live oaks in the yard. The spectacular show staged by mother nature pleased Amanda and she clapped her hands in delight, moved by the sudden whim to taste one of those icy treats.

Descending the stairs, her step lighter than it had been in weeks, Amanda felt strangely serene. And she knew she would feel even better once she popped one of those cold, icy delights into her mouth.

Disregarding her shawl hanging on the hall

tree, Amanda stepped out onto the porch not realizing that beneath that deceptive frosting of snow lay a treacherous coating of ice. When she felt her feet slide she tried desperately to check her fall by catching onto the handrail, but she succeeded only in further unbalancing herself as the porch came up to meet her ungainly body with bone-jarring force. Feeling nothing at first, thinking herself only shaken, Amanda attempted to rise. Grunting with the effort, she paused to catch her breath. And then came the pain, searing, tearing, ripping across her gut, grinding the breath from her lungs in a whoosh of agony. Amanda screamed, cradling her stomach protectively as she fought against the contractions threatening to expel her precious burden.

Jemma heard Amanda scream and flew from the kitchen as fast as her plump legs would carry her. Amanda's cries led her out the front door where her frightened eyes saw the pregnant girl writhing in agony on the snow-covered porch. Her first thought was to get Amanda inside out of the cold but she soon realized she was incapable of lifting the girl despite her own ample girth. Nor was Amanda capable of moving herself. Jemma needn't have worried for Amanda's cries had also brought Linus who immediately sized up the situation and went for Nathan.

In the meantime Jemma snatched an afghan from the sofa, covered Amanda's shivering form and knelt beside her, attempting to comfort her with soothing words. "It's gonna be jest fine, chile," she consoled gently. "We's gonna have us a fine baby afore the day is done."

"It's too soon, Jemma," gasped Amanda, biting her lip against the pain. "Nothing must happen to Tony's child."

"Nothing will, honey," assured Jemma, patting her hand confidently. "Yore chile's big enough to survive. Jest hold on, honey, ole Jemma's gonna take care of you."

Within minutes Nathan came running up, coatless and out of breath. "My God!" he exclaimed, his face paling. "What happened? Is Amanda hurt?"

"She's gonna be jest fine, Massa Nathan, jest as soon as you get her up to bed. We's gonna have us a baby," Jemma grinned, attempting to tease away Nathan's anxiety. "It weren't a bad fall and nothing seems to be broken, but you'd best get her inside afore she freezes."

Nathan needed no further urging as he carefully gathered Amanda in his brawny arms and carried her to her room. "I'm sorry to be so much bother," Amanda panted between contractions.

"I'm glad I am here for you, dear," Nathan said fondly. He would have said much more but Jemma shooed him from the room so that she might prepare Amanda for the birth of her child.

Jonathan Anthony Brandt made his unexpected appearance ten hours later, crying lustily from the moment of birth until he was put to Amanda's breast where he sucked greedily, giving no indication of being premature, or of being fragile. Jemma had no trouble with the birth which had progressed normally. But when she saw the size of the child she gave a silent prayer of thanks to whatever God who saw fit to allow Amanda to deliver early. If the birth had taken place six weeks later she was certain that not even her tremendous skill would have been sufficient to save mother and child.

Throughout the long day Nathan paced the length of the upstairs hallway assuming the role of expectant father as if he were born to it. At the baby's first cry he had burst unheralded into Amanda's room to assure himself that she was still alive. Immediately his eyes were drawn to her exhausted, radiant face, damp with perspiration, yet shining with a love he felt privileged to witness. No matter that the child belonged to another man. At that moment Nathan felt more the father than Tony could ever hope to be.

Gazing in awe at the tiny bundle held lovingly in Jemma's arms, Nathan was amazed at the coal black hair surrounding a small reddish face. With one huge finger he traced the sweet curve along a soft, downy cheek and suffered a pang of longing so intense that his breath caught in his throat, threatening to choke him. Under Jemma's wise old eyes he pressed a kiss on Amanda's forehead and tiptoed out of the room to go get roaring drunk.

From the moment of Jon's birth Nathan relentlessly pursued Amanda, begging her to go off with him so they could marry. In his heart he knew Tony would never make Amanda his wife and he tried every excuse imaginable to convince her to leave Tony.

"Please, Amanda," Nathan urged one day when he came to visit her and the baby, "let me take you and Jon away from here. I want to give your child a name. Do you want him to be labeled a bastard all his life?" He hated to use such blunt language but he hoped to shock Amanda into facing the truth.

"I know you mean well, Nathan, and in my own way I love you for it," Amanda said lightly. "But I can't leave Tony without giving him a chance to see his child and. . . and. . ."

"He'll never marry you, dear," Nathan insisted gently before she had time to finish her sentence. "If he doesn't marry Letty it will be to someone who will bring money or property into the marriage."

"What about love?" asked Amanda softly. "I know Tony loves me. He's told me so many times."

"Love is the least of reasons to marry in this day and age. I don't mean to hurt you, dear, only open your eyes to the inevitable. If you leave with me now, before Tony returns, I'm certain he won't bother to search for you. I'll make a good life for us, I promise."

Amanda shook her head sadly, knowing in her heart that Nathan could not know just how strongly Tony felt about her. Tony loved her and would love his child. When he returned from England they would be a family. Tony would not want another man raising his son, Amanda told herself with a conviction born of her own deep love for the man.

To Nathan, she said, "I won't let you convince me Tony does not want me or our son. He really does love me, Nathan, and I will wait for him. Besides, you would get into trouble, running away without owner's papers for me. Be sensible."

After that Nathan did not press her again to go away with him, but neither did he discontinue his almost daily visits.

Only Jon's tiny presence made Christmas bearable for Amanda. Jemma prepared a feast fit for a king which Amanda and Nathan could not begin to do justice to and there was even an exchange of gifts. But Amanda's heart wasn't in it. She wanted Tony, desperately. She had hoped for a letter or greeting of some sort, but no loving words came from across the sea.

All manner of thoughts confused Amanda's mind at Tony's apparent lack of concern for her. Perhaps Nathan was right, she reflected painfully, and Tony came back with a highborn wife. If only she had been able to tell Tony about the baby before he left. If she had listened to Jemma he might already have returned to her by now, she sadly lamented. Yet, despite her despondency, the long days and nights passed, as did the dreary winter months. And suddenly it was spring, a time for hope.

11

Amanda smiled lovingly down on baby Jon's burnished head as he nursed greedily at her pale, milk-swollen breast. She never ceased to be amazed at how he had grown and changed since his birth. Hair, once black, now resembled burnished oak while the newborn blue of his eyes hovered between blue-gray and silver. To Amanda he had the look of his father, strong featured with a fine, high forehead. She loved him more than she loved any other human, and that included his father whom she had never ceased to love despite an absence of seven months. Would Tony ever return to see his son? she wondered. And would he be as pleased as she to have a child such as Jon?

Looking at little Jon it was increasingly difficult for Amanda to believe he had been born prematurely. He was a large baby, healthy and happy who would obviously equal or surpass his own father's height and build. He seemed to thrive on Amanda's abundant supply of milk and all the attention showered upon him by the small household, including Nathan who was a frequent visitor.

Buttoning her dress Amanda lay Jon down in his cradle, one that had been lovingly crafted by Nathan, and went downstairs to begin her day. It was unusually warm that last day of March and the windows had been thrown open to receive the full benefit of the balmy air after a long, wet winter. Amanda hoped to begin spring cleaning today so the house would be sparkling when Tony returned. Both Tess and Cory were already waiting for her in the kitchen. She soon had the two willing girls armed with mops and buckets and disapatched upstairs to begin on the guest bedrooms; she intended to do her room and Tony's bedroom herself, determining that she had about four hours left to work uninterrupted before her son awakened and demanded his dinner.

Three and a half hours later Amanda heard voices in the downstairs hall and stopped her labors to listen, her heart thumping wildly in her breast at the familiarity of the resonant tones echoing through the house. With a cry of indescribable joy Amanda flew into the upstairs hall and froze at the top of the stairs when she saw Tony exhuberantly greeting an unusually animated Linus and a tearful Jemma.

He looked thinner, there were shadows under his cheekbones, but he was tremendously handsome in doeskin trousers pushed into shiny black boots and a brown velvet coat festooned with limp but immaculate stock. Amanda wasn't even aware that she spoke his name until he looked up at her, his eyes akindle with incredulous happiness. Then she was floating down the stairs and into his arms, laughing, crying, shaking with emotion.

"You're even more beautiful than I remembered," whispered Tony, covering her face and neck with fervent kisses. "God, how I missed you!"

"You're beautiful, too," Amanda managed to choke out, hardly aware of what she was saying.

Tony laughed, his warm gaze devouring her tearful face as if he had never seen her before. Holding her at arm's length he hungrily raked the voluptuous form which had grown even more so in the months he was away. Even her perfect breasts were fuller, more enticing than he remembered. It took every once of control he possessed to keep from catching her in his arms and carrying her up to bed. When he did it would be a night neither of them would soon forget.

"I thought you would never return," sighed Amanda, content to just stand there in the circle of his strong arms.

"You can't imagine all the difficulty I encountered, my love. When I arrived the whole country was just recovering from the plague. To further complicate matters my father's solicitor, the one who wrote me, died shortly before I reached London. It took months to wade through all the legal matter pertaining to the estate, especially since I had to employ new lawyers unfamiliar with my affairs," Tony explained. "Selling my title and estate took a considerable length of time."

"I was worried. The one letter you sent me was so... uninformative, so... so... cold."

"My love, forgive me. I was harrassed and weary. Besides, I never was a very good correspondent."

"It doesn't matter, Tony, you've come back to me, that's all that counts."

"Did you ever doubt it?"

"Not really. But. . ."

"But, what?"

"You could have married?"

"Married? Not when it's you I. . ." Suddenly Tony paused, cocking his ear to an unfamiliar sound echoing down through the deserted halls. Arching an eyebrow he looked at Amanda as the angry wail continued.

Smiling, Amanda was about to tell Tony about his son when Tess appeared at the top of the stairs holding a red-faced, arm waving Jon in her arms.

"He shore is hungry, Amanda," Tess giggled. "Seems like every time this boy opens his mouth he 'specks to find it filled with a nice soft. . ." Her voice froze in mid-sentence, her eyes round as saucers when she saw Tony standing in the hallway. "My, oh my," was all she could say, turning on her heel and scurrying out of sight with an indignant Jon who was almost never kept waiting for his meal.

Still smiling, Amanda turned back to Tony expecting to see surprise registered on his face, or, hopefully, even pleasure, but never disbelief, disgust, anger. "Tony, what's wrong?" she asked worriedly.

"Am I to believe that that baby is yours?" he asked coldly.

"Why. . . yes, of course. But you don't. . ."

"When was he born?"

"Born? Mid-November, does it matter?"

"Maybe not to you but it does to me."

"What do you mean?"

"Your. . . child. . . was born much too early to be mine. If you remember I took you from the prison ship in early April. Were you expecting to foist it off on me?'' he asked cruelly.

"Tony, how could you think otherwise? Of course the baby is yours. Who do you think fathered him?''

"You had plenty of time to tell me I was to become a father before I left for England. Why didn't you?'' He didn't wait for her answer. "I'll tell you why. Because you deliberately lied to me! You told me no one took you against your will on the prison ship. If that's the truth, then it's obvious you had a lover among the sailors, or maybe more than one for all I know. You were already pregnant when I made love to you that first time!'' Pride made Tony's voice harsh and unforgiving.

"That's not true!'' denied Amanda, her world suddenly crumbling beneath her feet.

"Why did you lie to me, Amanda? I loved you. Enough to ask you to become my wife.'' At Amanda's surprised gasp, he said scathingly. "Oh, yes, I wanted to marry you, to love and protect you forever.''

"Please listen to me, Tony!'' pleaded Amanda, growing more frantic by the minute. "I wanted to tell you before you left that I was expecting your child but somehow every time I tried something prevented me from speaking. And Jon was born prematurely. Just ask Jemma, she'll tell you how it was.'' Quickly scanning the hall Amanda saw that it was empty except for her and Tony, the two slaves having tactfuly withdrawn the moment she had flown into Tony's waiting arms.

"Do you take me for a fool, Amanda? Of course Jemma and everyone else here will agree with whatever you say. I'm well aware of their feelings for you. If you had just seen fit to tell me the truth I might not be so bitter. I could even have learned to live with your child. I truly loved you, Amanda."

"Please believe me, Tony, Jon is your son."

Tony surveyed her with slow deliberation, his silver eyes so forbidding that she recoiled, unable to accept the aspects of the situation she now faced. It was like a nightmare in which she was trapped. Imploringly she lifted her eyes to the dark, handsome planes of his face, saw the fine white lines splaying out from his narrowed, hard eyes. Then her own anger was building. Let Tony think what he wanted! she fumed in silent fury. She had her son and that was enough for her. When her indenture was served she would leave and make a life for her and Jon without Tony. The arrogant, untrusting bastard didn't deserve her and he sure as hell didn't deserve Jon!

"I'm sorry, Amanda, I find that hard to believe," Tony finally answered, his voice flat, devoid of all emotion. A hard rock rolled down to shut out his expression.

"Why, you say you loved me! You don't know the meaning..." But that's as far as Amanda got as she stood, mouth agape, staring over Tony's shoulders at an apparition from out of her past.

Tony, seeing her stricken look, turned to follow her gaze. "Francis, come in," he said to the man who had just walked through the door. "I wondered what had kept you."

If the young man heard Tony's greeting he gave no indication of it. He seemed as shocked at seeing Amanda as she was of seeing him. "Tony, do you know who this woman is?" Francis asked, immediately recognizing the auburn haired beauty, older and more mature, yet unmistakenly the young prostitute his two friends had procured to service Tony on the eve of his departure for America nearly two years ago.

"Of course I know who this woman is," replied Tony, annoyed. "If you remember I spoke of Amanda constantly on the crossing." His last words were spat out contemptuously, causing Francis to raise his eyebrows.

"Yes, Amanda, that's her name," Francis said, nodding vigorously.

"What's wrong with you, Francis? Have you suddenly lost your senses?" asked Tony in a fit of pique. He was puzzled by his friend's obtuseness.

"But this is the young woman who..." Francis paused, the wary, trapped look in Amanda's green eyes causing him to stop in mid-sentence. There is more here than meets the eye, he thought, flicking his gaze between Tony and Amanda. He wisely decided to find out what was going on before he blurted out things that were better left unsaid.

"Young woman who what?" questioned Tony suspiciously.

"Why, the young woman whom you told me about is what I started to say. She is all you said, and more. You're a lucky dog, old chap."

"So I thought myself," replied Tony bitterly, fixing accusing eyes on Amanda. "But certain... things... have changed in my absence. It's too involved to explain right now."

"Tony," began Amanda.

"Later, Amanda," Tony commanded sharply. "We'll talk later, after I've gotten over the initial shock of... of... finding what I found." Amanda felt a flush heat her cheeks, embarrassed that Tony's friend should be a witness to her degradation.

Sensing Amanda's discomfort, Francis said,

"Where are your manners, Tony? Aren't you going to introduce me to this lovely young lady?"

"Forgive me, Francis. This is my indentured servant, Amanda." Then turning to Amanda. "Amanda, this is my boyhood friend, Sir Francis." Amanda flinched at the emphasis Tony placed on the words "indentured servant."

Francis was thoroughly confused and more than a little puzzled. For months on end Tony had spoken lovingly and glowingly of his Amanda whom he planned on wedding the moment he was home in South Carolina. But it was increasingly obvious that something unexpected as well as disastrous had taken place in the short time that Tony had first walked through the front door until now. If he hadn't decided to see that all his luggage was unloaded and intact he might have been privy to what had actually transpired between the two. Equally baffling was the fact that Tony never once mentioned that Amanda was the very same girl whose favors he had enjoyed in that waterfront inn in London. Sighing heavily, Francis acknowledged his introduction to Amanda, feeling sorry for her as she choked out a proper response.

Suddenly baby Jon's demanding cries rent the air. White lines of anger formed around Tony's mouth and his gray eyes went murky. Scowling darkly, he said, "I'm sure Francis is tired, Amanda, show him to the room at the end of the hall. And see to... your child. Try to keep him quiet. I don't wish my guests to be disturbed by a squalling brat."

Stunned by his cruel indifference, Amanda could only stare, mouth agape. Only when Francis touched her arm gently did she square her small shoulders, direct a look of pure hatred in Tony's direction and turn on her heel, leading Francis toward the staircase.

Francis' mind worked furiously as he followed Amanda, thoroughly beguiled by the seductive sway of shapely hips. So Amanda had a child in Tony's absence, he surmised. But why should that upset and anger Tony? Surely a child by so lovely a woman he planned on marrying anyway wouldn't be so hard to accept. Unless. Careful, Francis, he told himself. You are a guest in Tony's house. Best not to jump to conclusions. Far better to wait until he learned more about the situation at hand.

Amanda remained in her room to feed Jon so was unaware of the dramatic scene unfolding in Tony's office. Nathan had arrived from the fields and for over an hour the two discussed all that had transpired during Tony's long absence. Finally, their business concluded, Tony was startled when Nathan asked, "What are you going to do about Amanda?"

"What do you mean?" asked Tony sharply.

"Don't be obtuse, Tony. Are you going to marry Amanda and give your son a name?" Jon is a son any man would be proud to acknowledge."

"I am not 'any' man," rejoined Tony sarcastically. "Did she tell you I was the baby's father?"

"Of course," shot back Nathan angrily. "Why would she lie?"

"Why indeed? The child was born much too early to be mine. I've always been good at sums and these just don't add up. And don't give me that line about the baby being born prematurely. Even at a distance I was well aware of the size of him.

Do you take me for a fool?"

"Yes, a damn fool, Tony. I refuse to work for a man I cannot respect. I'm leaving River's Edge. And I intend taking Amanda and Jon with me." Tony raised his eyebrows, surprised by the venom in Nathan's voice. He and Nathan had been friends since his arrival in South Carolina and now a little strumpet was breaking up an alliance that had been profitable to both of them.

"I refuse to sell Amanda's papers and there is no other way she would be free to leave. If you take her against my wishes I will see that you are hunted down no matter where you go." Why didn't he just sell her to Nathan and get rid of the problem once and for all? Tony asked himself. But the thought of her leaving River's Edge was abhorrent to him. While in England he had missed her dreadfully. Thoughts of her filled his every waking hour and he dreamed of her each night. The feel of her fragrant skin against his mouth, the way she gasped aloud as her passion ignited, the tightness of her sheath as she caressed him inwardly. He had returned full of hope and happiness, only to be hurt and disillusioned. Why then couldn't he bring himself to let her go?

"You are a bastard, Tony," Nathan bit out from between clenched teeth. "You don't want Amanda, but won't allow anyone else to have her, either. We'll see about that. If Amanda agrees to leave with me we'll go west where even you can't find us." Whirling on his heel he slammed out of the room and, taking the stairs two at a time, stood before Amanda's door calling her name.

Startled, Amanda opened the door, wondering at the circumstances that brought an intensely agitated Nathan to her bedroom. "Nathan, what is wrong?" she asked, frightened by the strange look muddying his warm, brown eyes.

"I'm leaving, Amanda! Now! Tonight!" he proclaimed adamantly. "Get your things together, you and Jon are coming with me."

Amanda was thoroughly confused. Did this mean that Tony didn't want her under his roof and had sold her to Nathan? When she asked Nathan that question he shook his head negatively from side to side.

"I tried, Amanda, God knows I tried. But he refused. So I told him I was taking you and Jon without his consent."

"What did he say to that?" asked Amanda fearfully.

A dark flush stained Nathan's tanned cheeks and his scowl grew fierce. "It doesn't matter, darling. We'll be married immediately."

"The law is on Tony's side," reminded Amanda gently. "He'll hunt us down and you'll be jailed. And I'll still end up back here."

Nathan realized the wisdom of her words but couldn't bear the thought of leaving her behind to Tony's tender mercies. "Please come with me, Amanda. We'll go far away. Someplace where Tony will never find us."

"I can't do that, Nathan. We'd be hunted down, living in fear from day to day. In a little over five years my life will be my own. I can survive that long."

"You'd do well to listen to her, Nathan," came an authorative voice from behind. Tony had come up to his room to find Nathan and Amanda engaged in animated conversation outside her door. He couldn't help but hear Amanda's last words.

"If I can't take Amanda with me now I'll find someway to do it legally," promised Nathan, bringing a huge, clenched fist under Tony's nose to better emphasize his words. "Until I do if I find you've hurt her or your. . . her son in any way I'll kill you with my bare hands."

"Contrary to your belief, I am no child abuser," protested Tony in a fit of indignation. "Nor am I one to be lied to by a slut!"

Amanda was devastated by Tony's thoughtless words but she could not stand by and listen to the two men arguing over her without speaking up. At any moment she expected them to break out in fisticuffs. "Nathan, I think you should leave. Really, I'll be alright. Tony would never harm an innocent child, and I don't think he'd hurt me, either."

"Thank you for your vote of confidence," mocked Tony, a sardonic smile twisting his lips. "Amanda is right, you know. Why should I want to hurt her? I can think of far more pleasant things to do with her. But, I forget, you are probably well aware of her special talents."

Even before the words left his mouth Tony found himself flat on his back with Nathan's massive hands around his throat. Fighting for breath Tony broke Nathan's stranglehold only to find himself being squeezed to death by two muscular arms clamped about his chest like a pair of steel bands. The narrow hallway seemed no longer able to contain the thrashing bodies rolling around on the carpeted floor. Horrorstricken, Amanda could only stand aside and watch; she certainly wasn't strong enough to separate the two.

Suddenly a third body entered into the foray.

Francis, who had been resting in his room, was disturbed by the fracas in the hallway and rushed headlong into the welter of flailing arms and legs.

Heartened by Francis' appearance, Amanda cried, "Help me, Sir Francis! We have to stop them before they kill each other!"

Together they managed to pull Nathan from Tony and restrain him long enough for Amanda to plead with him to leave.

"All right, Amanda, I'll leave," conceded Nathan grudgingly. "But only because I'm afraid it will go harder on you if I don't. But I'll be in Charles Town should you need me. I won't desert you."

Through narrowed, glazed eyes Tony watched resentfully, or was it jealously? as Amanda smiled fondly at Nathan, then touched his cheek gently in farewell. A low growl rising deep in Tony's throat gave vent to his feelings, but through Herculean effort he managed to control the unexpected surge of emotion coursing through his body. But it still did not prevent him from glaring murderously after Nathan's departing figure.

"It's obvious you've been distributing your favors in my absence," Tony accused scathingly the moment Nathan disappeared from sight. "Who else besides my overseer has been enjoying you?"

Amanda froze, unable to believe her ears when she heard Tony's unjust accusations. How could he be so hateful to her after their joyful reunion? Only moments ago he had wanted her to be his wife and now he was reviling her in a most despicable manner.

"What happened to you, Tony?" she asked, her voice edged with tears. "I love you and I thought you loved me. Why won't you believe me?"

Tony studied her face intently. How could she look so innocent and still have done and experienced so much? he asked himself impatiently. "I was prepared to forget your sordid past, Amanda, and marry you, until you duped me, presenting me with a child that could not possibly be mine."

"Tony, I. . ."

"No, Amanda, let me finish. When I was in London I called on the magistrate who sentenced you, intending to learn the name of the constable who defiled you and make him pay for what he did." Amanda paled, shaking visibly as she imagined what Tony had learned from the man.

"I did eventually find the man, Amanda, but I did not like what he told me. Do you know what he said?" Amanda merely shook her head from side to side. "He told me you weren't a virgin when he took you. That you were a prostitute who plied her trade on the streets of London."

"No Tony! It's not true! Why would he lie?"

"He had no reason to lie. Part of your story is true enough. About your sick mother and stealing food, but there is obviously much you omitted. Like selling your body, for instance. How old were you? Fifteen? Sixteen? And already an accomplished whore."

Amanda was stunned. It was obvious to her that the constable had lied to save his own skin. Why couldn't Tony see that? "But. . . you said you wanted to marry me? Why would you say that if you believed the lies the constable wove for you?"

"I told you I was ready to forgive you for your earlier transgressions. You were a child forced to live by any means available. I thought you had changed and. . . and I loved you."

"And I love you, Tony," Amanda replied unhappily. How could things have come to such a sad ending? she wondered dismally.

"When I saw you just now standing at the top of the stairs looking so lovely, so innocent, it didn't matter what you had been or what you had done. I still wanted you."

"You are wrong about me, Tony."

After a long pause that seemed to go on forever, Tony replied, "I truly wish I were wrong. You lied to me about the child. You led me to believe you remained chaste aboard the prison ship and less than eight months after I take you from the ship you present me with a child you say is mine. I can't swallow it, Amanda. I'm sorry."

"If you feel that way why did you refuse to allow me to go off with Nathan?" Amanda challenged wrathfully.

Tony had no answer. He only knew it was painful for him to think of letting her leave. Perhaps he merely wanted to punish her for making him love her, for being a slut instead of the abused young girl he had been led to believe. But that damned constable had soon disabused him of that notion. What hurt the most was the fact that had Amanda bothered to tell the truth things might have been different.

Amanda did not push for an answer. She had already been shamed and slandered enough by Tony for one day. He would only be goaded by anger should she continue to defend herself and she was well aware of the violence he was capable of when aroused to anger. She also knew her own temper and wisely decided to leave matters where they stood for the time being. Though she and Tony were finished she still had Jon to fill her life. But was that enough? she wondered sadly as she watched Tony's stiff back disappear down the stairs.

Amanda was grateful that Francis had not remained to hear their conversation. She knew he probably thought her to be a prostitute and Tony's incriminating words would only serve to reinforce that mistaken belief, at least until she was presented with the opportunity to explain the circumstances of that night in London so long ago. She could only hope that Francis believed her when that day came.

12

The ensuing days were intensely painful for Amanda as she strived mightily to carry out Tony's tersely barked orders, yet never seeming to please him. It was just as well she saw very little of him during those heart-breaking days. Nathan's resignation left a void that only Tony could fill until such a time that he was able to engage a new overseer. It was time to sow the rice seeds in specially prepared beds or frames. Then, in about twenty-five days the seedlings would be transplanted into paddies. The most difficult work followed; standing ankle deep in water planting three or four seedlings in each hill. A back-breaking task that usually took every available pair of hands.

Each morning Francis joined Tony in the fields, lending a hand wherever it was needed. He was so impressed with River's Edge that he had almost decided to buy property and settle down in South Carolina, and everything about planting

rice was absorbed for future use. Amanda saw
Tony only twice each day, once before he left for
the fields and again when he returned, and then
only long enough to receive curt instructions or
criticisms concerning her duties. Francis was
usually with him, remaining silent but watchful.
He had yet to discover what had happened to
drastically change Tony's attitude toward
Amanda, and so far Tony had offered no plausible
explanation. But he did not intend to let the
matter rest. When the opportunity arose he was
determined to solve the mystery for himself.

One of the worst moments of Amanda's young
life came with Letty's entrance once more into
Tony's life. Seven days after Tony's return Letty
showed up at the front door, having heard through
the slave grapevine that Tony was back from
England and that Nathan was no longer overseer
at River's Edge. As luck would have it Tony and
Francis had returned early from the fields that
day since the last of the rice beds had been seeded.
Both men were in an excellent frame of mind.
Amanda was in the hallway when they entered the
house, awaiting orders from Tony concerning
dinner, when Letty arrived. Dressed in a deep
purple velvet riding habit that emphasized her
tall, shapely figure Letty was the perfect picture
of elegant femininity. The long, jaunty feather
decorating the perky hat perched atop her bright
head lent her a rakish air. Her innocent-seeming
beauty and quiet demeanor gave no hint of her
true nature and Amanda shuddered, remembering
all too well the lashing she had received at the
hands of that cold, cruel woman. Willing herself to
remain expressionless, Amanda watched in perverse admiration as Letty worked her wiles upon

an unsuspecting and gullible Tony.

"Tony, darling," Letty gushed, flinging herself into Tony's arms, "how could you be so naughty?" Ignoring Tony's raised eyebrows she continued blithely, a pout pursing her full, red lips. "You've been home seven whole days and I just now learned you had returned. Does my friendship mean so little to you that you forgot all about me? I thought surely you'd have a message for me from my father."

Letty looked so adorable that Tony could not help but plant an exuberant kiss on her enticing lips, forgetting that he had once thought her cruel and vindictive. Francis could only look from Letty to Amanda in complete bewilderment.

Finding his manners, Tony reluctantly, or so it seemed to Amanda, parted from Letty to introduce her to Francis. Letty made the proper response, batted her long eyelashes seductively and seemed duly impressed, but it was obvious she had eyes only for Tony.

"I do have a letter from your father, Letty, and I had intended to deliver it personally but unforeseen circumstances necessitated a delay I hadn't planned on," explained Tony.

"I forgive you, darling, but only if you invite me for dinner so you can tell me all about father."

"You don't need an invitation, Letty, you are always welcome at River's Edge," smiled Tony, drinking in her beauty like a man parched after a hike through a desert. For a week he had surreptitiously watched Amanda as she moved silently about, wanting her, yet denying himself, hating her for making him want her still. Letty's arrival had been providential. What better way to slake his hunger for one woman than in the arms of another, especially one such as Letty who was all a man could want.

"Why don't you spend the night?" Tony asked, suddenly, warmed by the thought of spending the night in her bed.

"Darling, I'd love to," accepted Letty jubilantly.

"See to the guest room, Amanda," Tony ordered brusquely, turning to the silently fuming indentured servant who heretofore had been completely ignored by Tony and Letty.

As if seeing her for the first time, Letty focused glittering eyes on Amanda, stunning Francis by the look of pure animosity emanating from their icy depths.

"Put me in the room next to Tony's," Letty commanded imperiously. "It's always been my favorite."

"Prepare the room across the hall," Tony countermanded smoothly, "I'm sure Letty will be more comfortable there."

A wooden smile froze on Letty's face, but her eyes flashed blue flames as she watched Amanda silently react to Tony's orders. She had hoped that Tony's feelings for Amanda had altered in the months he was gone but obviously he was still obsessed with the baggage, she thought sullenly. But one thing was certain, which Letty was grateful for: Amanda had not told Tony about the flogging she had received. Evidently Nathan hadn't mentioned the incident, either.

Before Letty's father left for England he had imparted all of the details to his daughter concerning the intimacy he observed between Tony and his indentured servant. Yet, that closeness was not now evident to Letty as she listened to

Tony issue orders in a cold, emotionless voice. Whatever had happened to change things involved Nathan, she wrongly assumed. Perhaps Nathan and Amanda had become lovers in Tony's absence. Yes, she decided, Tony definitely showed very little warmth or affection toward Amanda. For the first time in a long while Letty felt as if everything she had ever desired was about to fall into her hands.

At dinner that night Letty was radiant. She had sent one of the slaves to her house for a change of clothing and the violet moire gown trimmed with pale, frothy lace proved a perfect foil for her glowing, lightly tanned complexion and elaborately coiffed, golden hair. Creamy, smooth shoulders rose enticingly above breasts bared nearly to pink aureoles just visible above the deep vee of her gown. Francis was entranced and spent the entire evening ogling the two perfect mounds.

"Tell me about father, Tony," Letty asked when the meal was nearly concluded. "His letter instructs me to sell the plantation and lands and join him in England."

"He bought a townhouse in London and seems quite content. In fact," revealed Tony, slightly embarrassed, "he is seeing a wealthy widow and I wouldn't be surprised if a wedding isn't in the offing."

"He hinted as much in his letter," said Letty sourly. "Well, he needn't think I'll come running to England when he obviously has no need of me."

"He misses you, Letty," reminded Tony. "But he leaves it up to you. The plantation is yours to do with what you will. I promised him I'd keep an eye on you if you decide to stay."

"Then it's settled," crowed Letty delightedly. "I'm staying, as long as you hold to your promise."

"I'll help all I can, you know that, Letty. And with Francis here assisting me I should be able to keep tabs on your plantation as well as my own."

Letty turned to Francis, giving him the full benefit of wide, guileless eyes. "Do you intend on settling in South Carolina?" she asked brightly.

"I'm seriously considering it," admitted Francis. "I'm learning a lot under Tony's able guidance but still have a long way to go before I consider myself qualified to run an operation such as this."

"Then you intend on remaining at River's Edge?"

"It suits my purposes as long as Tony doesn't throw me out," laughed Francis.

"You are welcome to stay for as long as you care to," tendered Tony graciously. "My home is certainly large enough to accommodate you."

Shortly after dinner, Letty, slanting a meaningful glance at Tony, excused herself and went to bed, none of which was lost on Francis. How he envied his friend, he thought grudgingly. Two gorgeous women at his beck and call! He wasn't sure at the moment which his own choice would be but it was evident who Tony intended to share his bed with this night.

Cory had been assigned to attend Letty and the nervous slave had already helped her into a frothy lace nightgown of pure white held at the shoulders by two narrow ties and was now brushing her waist length, golden tresses.

"Careful, you slut," warned Letty crossly when Cory encountered an unexpected tangle. But her mind wasn't really on her hair. It was on Tony and how long it had been since she had been with him. In desperation she had allowed Ben into her bed, only because she could not live without sex. But no one could make her feel like Tony did. When he took her, the savagery he unleashed in her was like nothing she had ever experienced before. She needed that special feeling, could not live without it, had missed it dreadfully and chaffed impatiently to drink deeply of its drugging cup once more.

Irrationally Letty's thoughts leaped to Francis. He had seemed inordinately taken with her and she briefly considered how she could use his infatuation to her own advantage. Letty was still uncertain where Amanda stood in Tony's affection. Or how far their relationship had progressed since he had returned. With the right inducement perhaps Francis could be persuaded to become her ally in ousting Amanda from Tony's life permanently. It certainly was worth considering.

Letty's thoughts were interrupted by the sound of a door clicking shut as Tony prepared to retire for the night, and she curtly dismissed Cory, who scooted out, relieved to be shed of so demanding a mistress. Letty waited exactly fifteen minutes after she heard Lionel leave Tony's room before she slipped silently from her own room and padded on bare feet across the hall. Quietly entering Tony's chamber, she poised dramatically in an errant patch of moonlight allowing Tony the full benefit of her glowing nudity clearly visible through her sheer nightgown.

Tony gasped, his breath a hard knot in his throat. "My God, Letty!" he rasped huskily, "it's been such a long time I forgot how lovely you are."

"Too long," Letty sighed, posing seductively before his hungry eyes.

And then she was in his arms pressing against his rising ardor. Tony wore only a robe, and that encumbrance left his body in moments as did Letty's nightgown as he deftly untied the bows at her shoulders and, eyes akindle with greedy anticipation, watched it slither sensuously down the length of her shapely body to lay in a shimmering pool around her feet. Reverently he touched a finger to a nipple, smiling as it leaped to life beneath his touch, pulsating, immediately erect.

As if with one mind they moved to the bed where Tony began a passionate assault upon her eager flesh. Long fingers found every raw nerve ending, lips discovered gently rising hills and deep valleys, tongue licked, teased, taunted, until Letty was crying out, begging, demanding, her body nothing but one throbbing sensation. Though Tony's loins were afire, his need so urgent he ached, he was fully aware of the fact that the writhing, moaning creature beneath him was not an auburn haired beauty with eyes as green as spring leaves whose small, supple body pleased him as no other ever had.

"What are you waiting for?" Letty groaned, sensing Tony's momentary distraction. "Do it now, lover! Do it now!"

Concentrating once more on Letty's heated flesh, Tony slammed into her with a savage thrust more punishing than passionate. Crying out, Letty welcomed and met his violent onslaught in a tornado of motion, grinding her pelvis into his each time they met. So frenzied were Tony's movements that he nearly beat her to the gate but in the end she caught up and surpassed him as she reached her zenith moments before Tony shuddered to a thunderous climax.

In the next room Amanda lay huddled in bed, hands covering her ears, tears streaming down her cheeks. If it wasn't for Tony's stupid pride she would be the recipient of his passion, not Letty. She could be the one crying out in ecstasy. How could she endure the long night listening to the sounds of love coming from the other side of the wall? Only too well she knew Tony's capabilities as a lover. Had she not experienced his brand of love many times over? He was a tireless, consummate lover, ever anxious to please, ever eager to carry her to new heights of passion. Her tears became sobs of frustration as she pictured vividly the two perspiring bodies entwined in Tony's bed, slaking their lust upon one another.

It was inevitable that the baby asleep in his cradle next to Amanda's bed should be awakened by his mother's heart-rending sobs. Dashing the tears from her eyes, Amanda arose, lit the candle, and went to her son, his little face screwed up, tiny arms flailing as he gave vent to his displeasure. Finding him wet, Amanda changed him, but even that did little toward quelling his screams of rage at being so rudely awakened. Though Jon had nursed his fill only two hours before it became increasingly evident that nothing less than another meal would satisfy him now. Sighing wearily, Amanda sat on the edge of the bed, drew aside her prim nightgown and offered him a plump breast. Gurgling contentedly the lusty little fellow immediately closed a rose-bud mouth onto an elongated, pink nipple, sucking greedily as small fists kneaded the warm flesh that was giving him so much pleasure.

Content and sated Letty lay dozing in Tony's arms. He had just made love to her a second time and her exhausted body glowed wetly in the flickering candlelight. At first the crying came to her as if in a dream. But as the sounds continued unabated she recognized them for what they were. . . a baby's angry wail. Tony stirred as Letty sat bolt upright in bed. Surely she wasn't ready to make love again? he blinked sleepily. He opened his eyes when she arose and was startled to discover her slipping into her nightgown.

"Leaving so soon?" came Tony's languid drawl.

"I'm going to find out where that crying is coming from."

Tony was up like a shot. The unmistakable cries of a baby drifted through the walls. "Damn! he cursed, hastily pulling on his pants and stepping out into the hall only a few steps behind Letty.

Easily locating the source of the disturbance Letty flung open the door to Amanda's room. Neither Tony nor Letty were prepared for the sight that met their eyes. Amanda sat on the bed cuddling her son, one pearly shoulder and breast fully exposed as the sleeping child's lax mouth still clung wetly to a rosy nipple. His small face was not visible but Letty could see his burnished hair glowing dully in the candlelight.

The tender, loving expression on Amanda's face as she gazed down at her son cut Tony to the quick. Like a Madonna and child he had once seen in a museum in Paris. A pang of jealousy twisted his gut. That opalescent, rose-tipped globe once belonged to him alone. Why should someone else's child have what he could not? he asked himself irrationally. Letty's enraged voice broke into his jealous musings and caused a startled Amanda to look up, her face a pale oval in the dimness of the room. Mindless of her partial nudity Amanda hugged the baby closer to her breast, determined that Letty should not recognize the telltale features that his own father chose to ignore.

"Calm down, Letty," Tony said. "Amanda and her child have nothing to do with you."

"But has much to do with you, I'll warrant," bit back Letty. "Is that your child, Tony? Yours and Amanda's?"

"The baby was born in November, Letty. Amanda arrived here in April. You figure it out."

Jubilation turned Letty's face radiant. "I was right all along only you refused to believe me," she crowed. "Amanda is a prostitute as well as a thief, just like I said."

"I am well aware of what Amanda was. . . or is," Letty," Tony ground out curtly. "Now that you've satisfied your curiosity I suggest we leave before we awaken the baby again. I have no desire to be serenaded the rest of the night by a squalling brat."

Red dots of rage burst behind Amanda's eyes. How dare he! How dare Tony speak of her precious Jon in such a derogatory manner! Once more her temper and wayward tongue caused her to speak injudiciously, forgetting that she had no right to direct her anger at her master who could punish her in any way he saw fit.

"How dare you burst into this room," she lashed out, swinging blazing green eyes from Tony to his mistress, "and call my son names. Jon is my son! Mine, do you hear! I wll not have him maligned by a pair of rutting pigs who care for nothing or no one but their own selfish pleasure."

"My God, Amanda, you go too far!" Tony was livid. To be spoken to in such a manner by someone no better than a slave, especially before Letty, was the last straw.

Letty was livid. Tony had to bodily restrain her to keep her from leaping at Amanda. Even though Amanda deserved to be punished, her innocent child was another matter, he told himself.

"Tony, if you don't do something about your mouthy whore, I swear I will," threatened Letty, wearing her righteous indignation like a suit of armor.

"You're right, Letty," Tony admitted grudgingly. "Amanda has gone too far this time. But I brought her here to be my housekeeper and she shall continue to function in that capacity. After all, she has a child to care for now and I won't allow an innocent child to suffer for its mother's transgressions. One thing is obvious, Amanda can no longer occupy this room. Tomorrow she and her child will be moved to the attic room which is more in keeping with her position in this household." Turning to Amanda, gray eyes stern and uncompromising, he asked, "Is that clear, Amanda?"

Nodding mutely Amanda deliberately turned her back to the couple. Letty could not help but slant a malevolent glare at Amanda's shapely back before departing but Tony, angered that the sight of Amanda's drooping shoulders and lowered head should cause him such feelings of guilt and remorse, stormed out without a backward glance. Immediately Letty headed for Tony's room.

"Go to your own room, Letty," Tony said wearily. "I'm tired and am in the mood for nothing but sleep right now."

"Darling, there's hours left before dawn," pouted Letty, disappointed. "You've been gone for so long and I'm starved for you." Her hands worked furiously at the fastenings of his pants.

"No more tonight, Letty. I'm home for good and there's no reason to deny ourselves in the future. There will be other nights, plenty of them," he said, flushing darkly as he thought of the woman in the other room.

Somewhat mollified Letty allowed Tony to see her to her room, kissing him passionately before she closed the door. Nothing stood in her way now, she exalted. Amanda had another man's child and was out of Tony's life. If only there was some way to remove her permanently from Tony's sight, for as long as she remained at River's Edge the temptation would still be there. Frowning, Letty wished she had gotten a closer look at the baby. But hadn't Tony as much as admitted the child could not be his? Still, a nagging suspicion continued to plague her. Deep in her heart she knew she would never rest until Amanda's beautiful face and enticing figure were placed out of Tony's reach.

Down the hall Francis quietly closed his door. Loud voices had awakened him and he heard nearly everything that had transpired between Tony and the two women. He could not help but feel compassion for Amanda even though he realized she must have committed some grievous wrong for Tony to turn away from her so completely and dramatically.

Amanda was barely up and dressed the next

morning before Tess and Cory appeared to help move her belongings to the third floor. The room assigned to her had been closed up and emitted a damp, dank odor the moment the door was opened. The first thing Amanda did was to throw open the single casement window and fling back the bedcovers to air out the narrow cot. The meanly furnished room was a far cry from the beautifully appointed bed chamber she had occupied for over a year. With little Jon's cradle at the end of her narrow bed there was barely enough room to turn around in. The only other piece of furniture was a large chest of drawers on which sat a chipped pitcher and bowl. Nails pounded in a board along one side of the wall provided hanging space for her meager wardrobe. The room held no comforts, not even a mirror or a rocker or padded chair. But it was neither better nor worse than she expected when she first arrived at River's Edge.

Amanda's biggest worry was the weather. With the onset of June came the promise of summer. Days and nights of torturous heat and humidity in which her room would become an oven. She did not even have the option of seeking cooler shelter in the quarters as did the other household servants. Amanda knew she and Jon would suffer dreadfully during the long summer, but somehow they would endure. If only Nathan could find some legal way to whisk her and her baby away to a safer haven. If Tony hated her as much as he professed, why did he stubbornly refuse to sell her indenture papers? she questioned dismally. Did he obtain some sort of perverse pleasure in making her and Jon suffer? There seemed to be little hope of convincing Tony that Jon was his child, and cruel as it might be, her baby was destined to be ignored and neglected by his own father. Why hadn't she listened to Jemma and told Tony that she was pregnant before he left for England? But hindsight could not help her now. Even if she survived the summer, could winter be far behind? Even more distressing was the fact that Letty was determined to make Amanda suffer for some imagined wrong, striking, no doubt, when she least expected it.

After that day Letty became a permanent fixture at River's Edge. On the nights she didn't spend with Tony in his bed, he could be found at Tidewater. Amanda's one consolation was the fact that she could no longer hear the erotic sounds of lovemaking coming from Tony's room. Letty now occupied Amanda's old room whenever she was in residence, imperiously ordering the servants about and driving them mercilessly with her endless list of needs and complaints. It was not unusual for Letty to slap one of the maids for their lazy ways and insolent behavior towards her. Amanda was powerless to intervene. She dare not approach Tony in their behalf for fear Letty would find out and inflict her own brand of punishment upon them.

Jon spent most of his days with Jemma in the big, friendly kitchen, the center of attention and loving every minute of it. But at night he slept poorly in their tiny, airless room. And the mosquitoes were becoming an even bigger menace. There was no screen on the single window in her room and the mosquito netting she found had been mended many times and worn too thin in some spots to mend. Jon's little face was already peppered with angry welts where the pesky insects had gotten through the netting and bitten him.

If the opportunity ever presented itself Amanda intended to ask Tony for a new mosquito netting for herself and her baby. Tony had suddenly begun issuing his orders through Jemma who would in turn voice them to Amanda. Amanda was certain Tony was unaware of her existence, or wondered if he even cared how she and Jon fared in the oven-like prison to which they had been banished.

But Amanda was totally mistaken in thinking Tony was ignorant of her existence. No matter how often or how passionately he partook of Letty's abundant charms or was the recipient of her practiced caresses, thoughts of Amanda seemed always to intrude upon their most intimate times. In moments of coupling, when his lust should have driven everything else from his mind he would experience an intense longing for Amanda's supple sweetness. The lush, burnished thickness of her hair, the soft curves of her slender form, the silky feel of her flesh next to his. And a sadness would clutch at his heart along with a deep fear that he would never hold her again.

Love and lust are so far removed, he thought. Sated lust is nothing but sated hunger, once satisfied, is done with. . . but love. . . love is so powerful you are forever in its grip, never free from its splendor. And then he remembered the sleeping child at Amanda's breast. . . another man's spawn. . . and his pride and anger drove him back into Letty's waiting arms.

June passed, each blazing day and heated night only a prelude to July's torrid onslaught. And Amanda still had August to contend with, normally the hottest month of the year. She became wan and hollow-eyed, harried and depressed, working tirelessly to please Tony and Letty, sleeping little, if at all. Pounds melted away until Jemma worried constantly about her health. Jon, now crawling and sporting two front teeth, suffered severely though not nearly so much as Amanda herself.

Amanda had not spoken to Tony in almost a month and was surprised when he called her into his office one morning. Without looking her in the eye he began speaking. "Amanda, Letty and I are to be married at Christmas." Amanda kept her face purposefully expressionless, striving gallantly to suppress her shock and hurt. "As a wedding gift she asked that I sign over your indenture papers to her."

Amanda blanched. Her entire body shook with a fear she could not put into words. She swayed dangerously from side to side, her sudden pallor alarming Tony who hadn't really looked at her closely for weeks. "You wouldn't! she choked out. "You can't! If you give me to her you are condemning me to death!"

Studying her upturned face, Tony was shocked. The faintest of lavender shadows marred the translucent flesh beneath her eyes. The pale, transparent skin was pulled taut across prominent cheekbones, every sharp plane and angle outlined dramatically. How could she change so drastically in one short month? he wondered uneasily. He hadn't laid a hand on her or harmed her in any way.

Only the day before Letty had confronted him, demanding that he come to a decision concerning their marriage. Concurring that Letty had a valid argument, that he had selfishly taken up three years of her life, he reluctantly agreed to a Christmas wedding at River's Edge. Then she had broached the subject of Amanda, stating emphatically that Tony owed it to her to let her dispose of Amanda's indenture papers as she saw fit. Shifting uncomfortably, Tony fought a losing battle. Once Letty had her mind set on a certain course she refused to waver. In the end Tony had agreed only if Letty promised not to separate mother and child or to sell her to a whorehouse. Smiling slyly, Letty gave her word, refusing out of hand Tony's suggestion that she allow Nathan to have Amanda. Now, listening to Amanda's pitious pleas and seeing her terror-stricken face he began to have second thoughts.

Tony cleared his throat, feeling it fill up again almost immediately. "You are imagining things, Amanda. Letty is no monster. She will see that you and your child have a good home once we are married."

"You don't know her, Tony!" Amanda's voice was a strangled cry for help. "She hates me! She'd see me dead before she'd allow me a moment's happiness!"

"Amanda, I think you are exaggerating."

Near hysteria, Amanda fell to her knees before Tony, determined to humble herself in any manner to save her son. "I beg you, Tony. Don't do this terrible thing. It is your own son you are condemning. If you care nothing about me, think of him."

Amanda sounded so sincere that Tony could almost believe her. Almost, but not quite. He knew a woman would do or say anything when she was desperate. Still, watching her grovelling before him was not pleasant. Secretly he had always admired her strength of will, her passionate spirit, her spunk. Why then did he have this terrible urge to break her to his will when she defied him?

Feeling Tony soften, Amanda's wan face grew hopeful. "Tony," she pleaded, "I'll do anything, be anything you want, only don't give me to Letty. I will even leave here peacefully if you find a new master for me instead of Letty. You know Nathan wants to marry me. He loves me and your... my son. Let him have me."

At the mention of Nathan's name Tony's gray eyes went murky. Never would he allow Nathan to have Amanda, he vowed irrationally. Even though he had suggested otherwise to Letty he could not bear the thought of Amanda with another man. His mouth was a straight slash across his face, his jaw a rock as he pictured Amanda's slim body being possessed by any other but him. Cold dots of sweat broke out on his brow at that disturbing thought. If Tony was certain of only one thing in this world it was the knowledge that a new master would bed her before the ink on her papers was dry!

Reaching down, he gently lifted Amanda to her feet, feeling the fragility of her bones beneath his fingers. For the first time that he could remember he was about to break a promise. But Letty be damned! She would have his name, his house, and bear his children. Moreover, if the violent reaction of his body to Amanda's closeness was any indication, he wanted her still. Why not satisfy his yearning? he asked himself with typical male conceit. At least until his marriage. Besides, hadn't Amanda just said she'd do anything necessary to keep Letty from owning her? He had three months to get Amanda out of his system and he fully intended to give his lust free reign. What Letty didn't know wouldn't hurt her, he concluded deviously.

Instinctively Tony's arms tightened about Amanda's slender form. "You win, Amanda," he shrugged, smiling. "I'll inform Letty I have changed my mind."

Tears of gratitude transformed Amanda's green eyes into shimmering emeralds, transfixing Tony. "Thank you, Tony." Her bottom lip trembled and Tony thought she had never looked more desirable.

"It's not so easy as that, Amanda," he said, shattering her happiness.

"What. . . what do you mean?"

"My meaning is clear. I want something from you in return."

"But. . . I have nothing. . . own nothing."

"Think again, Amanda." His eyes smoldered, their smoky depths opaque.

Amanda looked at him questioningly, delicate brows arched. Surely he did not mean what she thought he meant. Wasn't Letty enough for him? What manner of man was he?

Seeing comprehension dawn, Tony said, "Until my marriage you will be my mistress."

Stepping backward, Amanda gasped. "Tony, no! You can't mean that!"

"Oh, but I do. I find myself hungry again to taste your delights."

"But, Letty. . ."

"Need never know," he finished. "This is between you and me." At her horrified look he smiled sardonically. "Come now, weren't you begging at my feet only moments before, promising to do anything, be anything? It's no more than you offered Nathan, or any one of your other lovers."

"There's never been anyone but you, Tony," Amanda stressed tearfully.

"Then prove it, Amanda. Come to me willingly and I'll not let Letty have you."

"At this moment I hate you more than I ever hated another human," Amanda hissed, suddenly finding her courage. "You know perfectly well that I have no choice. Very well, Tony, you've won. I'll do anything for my son."

"I want you now," Tony demanded, afire with a need he hadn't known since the last time he had made love to her so long ago.

Abruptly, Amanda turned and ran to the door, but was impeded by her long dress wrapping about her legs. Tony easily caught her before she reached it. His mouth smashed down on hers and his rough hands forced her against his muscular frame, now grown rock hard with desire. Then his arms fell away and he said, "You are free to leave." Amanda slanted him a wary glance, knowing full well that he was not finished with her. "But if you do Letty will own you before nightfall. Should you choose to accommodate me, I suggest you undress immediately."

Amanda was stunned by his cold, calculating manner. Was there no limit to this man's cruelty? Did he enjoy tormenting her knowing that she loved him? she wondered resentfully. But even as her mind rebelled, her fingers worked on the buttons of her dress. Her pulsing body betrayed her.

Tony stared fixedly as piece by piece Amanda's clothing dropped to the floor. When she stood before him radiant in nothing but the cloak of her nudity he moved forward slowly, reaching with stiff fingers to release the neat bun at the back of her head. A pulse pounded erratically in his throat as her hair fell down in a soft cloud to caress gleaming hips.

Stonily Amanda glanced downward to the arrogant masculinity of him as he slowly edged her backward toward a low couch conveniently placed against one wall. When the backs of her legs came into contact with the smooth surface she fell heavily, followed by Tony's uncompromising hardness.

"I love you this way," he chuckled mirthlessly, "soft and yielding beneath me, naked to my touch, open and willing."

"Willing only under duress," Amanda countered angrily. She would not admit that she was also shaken by his close proximity. "I will never. . ." Her words were cut off as his mouth closed down, hungrily, possessively, angrily. There were times in their past relationship when Amanda was afraid of him, and now, with his lips bruising her was one of them.

Then, imperceptibly at first, his mouth softened, confusing her with long drugging kisses, tender, yet seductive. Splayed fingers played cat-soft upon flushed cheeks, neck, shoulders, finally finding an erect nipple. Tony laughed softly, pleased by her response despite her claims of being forced.

His mouth followed the contour of her breast, strangely moved by a drop of milk at the tip of one nipple. Hesitantly, he licked, finding the taste not unpleasant. The stimulation brought forth another drop and Tony did not hesitate this time to partake fully of the unexpected feast. Amanda's cries grew frantic as Tony's mouth continued to plunder what rightfully belonged to her son.

"Tony no! My baby!" she tried to explain.

Belatedly, Tony understood what she was trying to tell him and reluctantly directed his mouth toward other pursuits. Taut stomach, slim waist, rounded hips, soft inner thighs, not an inch of flesh was ignored as Tony's passion grew by leaps and bounds. Though Amanda stiffened with resolve she could not control the betrayal of her own body. She had not known a man's touch in nearly a year and no matter how hard she tried to deny it her love for Tony was like a burning candle whose flame still burned brightly and she thrilled to his caresses.

Aware of each tactile sensation her body took on a will of its own as she shyly ventured caresses of her own, urging him on with soft cries of encouragement. His questing lips found a spot more vulnerable than any other and this intimacy left her gasping as she grasped his head, arching into his warm, wet mouth.

"Oh God, Tony, what are you doing to me?" she ground out raggedly.

"Loving you, my love," laughed Tony, suddenly looming above her, his manhood jutting out like a weapon. His entry was smooth, effortless, her softness taking all of him, arms and legs wrapped around his driving body as if trying to absorb him into every pore. Pleasure consumed them like a roaring tide, and then, almost too soon, ecstasy shattered in a blaze of passion.

Amanda lay in a quiet eddy of contentment until she heard a self-satisfied chuckle rumbling low in Tony's chest. She froze, cheeks aflame, suddenly aware of her total abandonment to his lovemaking. "I'd say it's been some time since you've partaken of the delights of sex. Was Nathan too busy to accommodate you as often as you wished?" Tony drawled, cocking a well-shaped eyebrow.

"You arrogant, conceited. . ."

"Careful, my love," warned Tony dangerously, an underlying thread of iron in his voice.

Undaunted, Amanda jumped up and began throwing on her clothes, fumbling nervously at the buttons under Tony's hungry gaze.

"Tonight," he drawled lazily. "In my room."

"My baby. . ."

"After he is asleep. I'll wait. I want you again. Soon."

Raging inwardly Amanda slammed from the room.

At that moment Amanda didn't know which emotion ruled her heart, love or hate. How could Tony treat her so badly, she silently fumed, when they had shared so much together? Over and over she berated herself for responding to his lust, for what they did together certainly couldn't be construed as love in any sense of the word. He had made her want him when she knew he was using her as a vessel for his lust. That was what really hurt.

God, how she hated Letty! That despicable woman had finally succeeded in turning Tony away from her and back into Letty's waiting arms. In December Letty and Tony were to marry and Amanda knew her life would never be the same after that day. Not even if she and Nathan were eventually to marry. Nathan was a dear man but he was not Tony.

On that sad note Amanda went about her duties, every fiber in her body vitally aware that in a few short hours she would be in Tony's arms once again.

Usually their loving was wild, uninhibited, and all of Amanda's resolve to resist Tony's ardor dissolved at his first caress. The moment his lips swooped hungrily down on hers she was lost in a whirl of sensual delight from which there was no escape.

13

Amanda was grateful she was not obliged to be present when Tony informed Letty of his decision to deny her the nuptial gift she had demanded. It was enough that she could hear their loud bickering all the way from the dining room into the kitchen where the house servants were gathered for their own meal.

"Lordy, that woman shore is mad," Jemma chuckled. "But it do my heart good to know she ain't gonna git her way for once." Amanda had related to Jemma most of what happened in Tony's office earlier that day. She omitted details of their frantic coupling and his proposition that would keep her tied to his bed. As far as Jemma knew Tony had changed his mind because Amanda had finally convinced him that Letty was up to no good.

"I wonder if she gonna spend the night?" grimaced Cory.

"Most likely will," nodded Tess sagely.

"She shore do have a heavy hand," sighed Cory, remembering how Letty had slapped her for no apparent reason the last time she was an overnight guest at River's Edge.

Privately, Amanda hoped Letty would stay. At least it would free her for one night from this new form of degradation Tony had initiated. Sexual slavery was the appropriate word for it. Even more galling was the way her body responded to his touch. His passionate assault upon her senses left her drained of all will, unable to resist the sensual lure of fingers and mouth playing upon her heated flesh. Tony would settle for nothing less than her total response and active participation in their sexual encounters. . . she refused to call it lovemaking.

Suddenly all conversation halted as Letty's voice rose in anger. "What is it with you and your little whore, Tony? I always thought you were a man of your word."

"I have said all I am going to say on the subject, Letty. I can only add that I would feel responsible if Amanda and her child ended up with some depraved man who would take unfair advantage of her. When you and I marry I will be the one to find a suitable place for Amanda."

"How could anyone take advantage of a slut?" snorted Letty derisively.

After that outburst the voices grew too low to understand, but Amanda had heard enough to know that Tony had kept his word to her. Surely, she told herself as hope dawned in her breast, Tony must feel something for her to deliberately disregard his future bride's wishes.

Suddenly the voices were audible once more as Letty said, "Must you go to the fields again this afternoon? I thought we could go riding. I've brought a change of clothes so I could spend the night."

Tony flushed, looking down at his plate thoughtfully. "I don't think that's a good idea, Letty. For the next few weeks I'll be occupied night and day. The rice seedlings are ready to be transplanted and I won't have a minute to spare."

"But, darling," Letty cajoled, "surely tonight. . ."

Tony cut her off in mid-sentence. "By the time I get in tonight I'll be too tired to do more than eat and fall in bed." The lie came easily to his lips. "I'm afraid you would be bored with my company."

"I've never known you to be 'too' tired," she reposted, slanting him a meaningful glance, embarrassing Francis by her broadfaced hint.

"I had an excellent overseer before," reminded Tony. "I know you have seedlings to plant also. Why don't you go home and I'll contact you the moment I'm free to devote some time to you."

"Well, if you put it that way," sulked Letty.

Soon afterward she departed, leaving Tony and Francis alone.

"What are you up to, old chap?" Francis asked suspiciously.

"I don't know what you mean," answered Tony blandly.

"Come now, Tony. This is Francis, remember?" You know as well as I that you aren't all that busy. Are you having second thoughts about your marriage?"

"Certainly not!" protested Tony a little too vehemently. I suddenly find myself in need of a little breathing space, that's all."

"Pardon me for being blunt, Tony, but do you love Letty?"

Tony scowled darkly. Love? Oddly he had never thought of Letty in terms of love. "I'm fond of her and we suit one another. That should suffice. Besides, it is time River's Edge had a mistress and I had an heir."

"What about Amanda?" Francis made bold to ask.

"What about her?" demanded Tony impatiently.

"What happened to those plans you told me about? When we left England you were determined to make Amanda your wife. What caused you to change so suddenly?"

"Things were not the same when I returned," contended Tony glumly. "You saw the child. What was I to do?"

"Is the child yours?"

"Ha!" laughed Tony harshly. "Amanda claims he is but I know better. Amanda is and always has been a slut. A fact I deliberately chose to ignore at one time. It's amazing how love can distort the truth."

Francis remained silent. How much did he really know about Amanda? She had sold her services once and evidently Tony had good reason to believe she had betrayed him. But everything he had learned about Amanda since coming to River's Edge contradicted his memory of her as a young prostitute he and his friends procured for Tony.

To Francis she seemed innocent, loving, and totally devoted to her child. Could Tony's harsh judgment be wrong? he wondered. It was obvious to him that Tony did not love Letty, that he wanted Amanda no matter what she had done. Well aware of Tony's pride, Francis agonized over the mistake Tony was making in abandoning Amanda and proposing to Letty. Any fool could see little Jon was the miniature of his father. Was Tony blind?

That night Amanda began her first of many visits to Tony's room, all of them at Tony's express command. Some visits were later than others for the August heat was stifling and poor Jon fretted for hours before finally going to sleep, his little body drenched with sweat.

As always, she found Tony pacing his room impatiently as she slipped through his door. Most times he took her immediately, before he even drew off her gown, sometimes roughly. Then he usually took her a second time, taking his time, eliciting a response she fought desperately to withhold; but in the end his practiced caresses, soft seeking lips and tender touch turned her body into a yielding mass of sensation. Afterwards she would return to her room to toss and turn in the few short hours left till dawn.

Because Tony saw her only through filtered moonlight he remained ignorant of the terrible toll his excessive demands had upon her frail body. The faint violet shadows he first noticed beneath her eyes were now purple smudges, her cheekbones more pronounced. But more importantly, her milk began to dry and Jon, a husky lad with a healthy appetite, was forced to subsist on a kind of gruel Jemma prepared for him. It was lucky that he was of an age to be given small amounts of cow's milk with no ill effects. But Amanda grew resentful of Tony because his selfishness taxed her strength and deprived her son, hating him even more for reducing her to nothing more than a sexual convenience. She never once considered that he could have turned to Letty for what he forced from Amanda, but preferred not to.

Two weeks had elasped without a night's respite from Tony's incessant demands. Amanda was amazed that he could make love every night at least once, more often twice, and still work a full day in the fields. It was later than usual when she slipped into his room that night. She was exhausted and irritable. Jon had a nasty heat rash and whined constantly, or so it seemed to Amanda. As was his custom Tony was naked, waiting impatiently for her arrival.

"You're late," he accused, sounding much like a deprived child.

"Aren't you ever sated?" lashed out Amanda angrily.

"My, my, we have a temper tonight. Would you rather return to your room immediately?"

Hopefully. "Yes, Tony, I would."

"We have a bargain, my love," reminded Tony sardonically. "I will keep my part if you hold to yours."

"Do you enjoy baiting me?"

"What I enjoy most is making love to you. Don't my actions prove it? Over and over, night after night?"

Before she could reply he claimed her mouth with practiced ease in a soul-destroying kiss, his lips hard and unyielding, forcing her mouth open to accept his stabbing tongue. And then she was in bed, his body pressing her down, down into the mattress. She felt his lips leave her mouth and fasten hungrily on a breast. It never ceased to amaze Amanda that Tony seemed to savor the droplets of milk he painstakingly extracted from her breasts as much as Jon. But tonight his patient manipulation gained him naught but pleasure as he shifted from one erect nipple to the other, sucking, tasting, waiting for the flow to fill his mouth. But the life-giving drops that nourished his soul refused to come. Puzzled, Tony lifted his head and looked at Amanda quizzically.

"It's. . . drying up," explained Amanda, immediately divining his unasked question.

"Surely it's not because I. . ."

"Perhaps, but I don't think that's the entire reason."

"But what will your baby do?" Suddenly he was suffused with guilt for taking his own pleasure at the expense of her innocent child.

"He's nearly six-months old. Hopefully he can be weaned soon."

His mind at ease, Tony returned to a more pleasant pasttime and soon neither could think beyond the sensations turning their blood to molten lava, erupting with volcanic force, shattering them in a million tiny fragments.

Amanda remained in Tony's bed till nearly dawn; mainly because she was too exhausted to climb the stairs to her own room. Tony awakened when she quietly slid from his bed.

"Amanda, I nearly forgot. We need every available hand in the rice paddies for the next few days. That means you as well as Tess and Cory. Only Jemma and Linus are exempt because of their age."

Amanda could not believe Tony meant to work

her in the fields along with the slaves as well as use her nightly for his own gratification. Instinctively she knew she was in no shape to toil under such conditions and told Tony as much.

"It's only for a few days," he reasoned testily. "If you're worried about your son, Jemma will gladly watch him. Now go back to your room, there is still an hour or two left before dawn."

Amanda bristled. What kind of monster was he? Did he expect her to labor both day and night? "Surely one pair of hands can't make that much difference, Tony," she declared hotly. "You don't seem to realize that. . ."

"I need you, Amanda," he stated, not ungently. "I promise it will only be for a day or two."

Defeated, Amanda walked from the room, knowing in her heart she could not hope to survive the backbreaking work in the fields for more than a few hours. But what choice did she have?

Amanda was up at dawn, haggard and weary after a sleepless night but determined to do her part in the fields even if it killed her. She carried the still sleeping Jon to the kitchen, settled him on a small cot, picked up a lunch prepared by Jemma and trudged the not inconsiderable distance to the rice paddies. Tony, Francis and every slave on the plantation was already toiling in calf-high water, bent at the waist as they carefully placed seedlings in the flooded beds. Following the example of the other women Amanda removed her shoes and stockings, hiked her dress up to her knees and waded in, unaware of dozens of pairs of eyes directed at her, including Tony's. Someone handed her an armload of green seedlings and she began the tedious task of placing them one-by-one in the ground. Concentrating on the task at hand she did not hear Francis voice his protest to Tony.

"My God, Tony, what is Amanda doing out here? You've gone too far this time. She is a nursing mother. Have you no conscience?"

"It's only for a few days, Francis. Amanda is not some hothouse lily. She is used to hard work." Tony's excuses sounded lame even in his own ears.

"Take a good look at her."

As if seeing her for the first time Tony suddenly realized that Francis was right. Amanda was in no condition to toil beneath the blazing sun, especially while engaged in such backbreaking work. She hadn't even the sense to wear a hat to protect her from the sun. But he wasn't about to let Francis know that he already regretted his decision to send Amanda into the fields. He would let her finish out the day, he decided, and then find some excuse to keep her confined to the house tomorrow, even if he had to invent some fictitious duty for her to perform.

Giving Tony a quelling look, Francis continued with his own work, determined to keep a watchful eye on Amanda.

At noon, while the workers rested and ate their lunches, Tony approached Amanda as she sat on the ground picking disinterestedly at her food. Pulling off the scarf he wore around his neck to soak up sweat, he tossed it carelessly at her. "You should know better than to work out in this sun without a proper headcovering. Wear my scarf for protection."

Wordless, Amanda reached for the scarf and began wrapping it around her bright head while Tony watched through a narrowed lids, the barest hint of compassion flitting across his tanned features. Amanda's face, he noticed, was already reddened from the sun and a sprinkling of freckles were visible along the bridge of her nose. Her eyes were effectively shaded by long, feathery lashes but the deep violet shadows beneath caused him a moment of intense discomfort. What was it about this particular woman to inspire such emotion? he wondered idly, surprising himself by the depth of his feelings. And suddenly he knew. No matter that she had lied to him, no matter what she was, or is, he loved her still!

Avoiding Tony's gaze Amanda wearily hoisted herself to her feet and began her trek back to the paddies to join the other workers. Tony put a restraining hand on her arm with every intention of ordering her back to the house. But she pulled from his grasp and waded out into the water without a backward glance. Shrugging, Tony decided to allow her to remain the rest of the day rather than create a scene in front of his slaves, thus undermining his authority over them. Surely another half-day would do her no great harm, he temporized.

Amanda worked tirelessly for two more hours before her diminishing strength began to fail altogether. Her cheeks were burning, head swimming. Brilliant, wavering lines danced before her eyes. Groping in the air for non-existent support, she sank to her knees in the muck. But before she toppled forward, Francis, who had been watching her closely, had her in his arms. His cry of alarm alerted Tony who reacted instantly the moment he realized what was happening.

"You insensitive oaf!" ground out Francis, struggling out of the water with Amanda's limp form. "I told you this would happen if you drove her too far. Amanda is no slave, nor is she strong enough to toil in the fields! Where has your mind been these past few weeks?"

Smarting under his friend's rebuke, Tony mounted his horse which was tethered nearby and motioned to Francis to hand Amanda over to him. Reluctantly, Francis yielded up his feather-light burden and watched with accusing eyes as Tony raced toward the house with Amanda draped across his lap.

He strode into the house taking the stairs two at a time, calling frantically for Jemma. By the time the panting slave waddled through the door, Tony had Amanda stretched out on the bed in the same bedroom she first occupied when she arrived at River's Edge and was working furiously on the buttons of her dress, his nerveless fingers gone suddenly numb.

"Massa Tony," cried Jemma, stricken. "What you done to that chile?" Amanda's ashen face and shallow breathing motivated Jemma into immediate action. "Don't jest stand there," she rounded on Tony, "help me git her dress off so's I kin bathe her with cool water. See how flushed she is?"

Springing to Jemma's aid, Tony wordlessly assisted in removing Amanda's dress and petticoat, leaving her clad in nothing but a thin chemise. Unconsciously his hand moved to brush back wispy strands of hair clinging to her damp face.

He flushed guiltily at the direction on his thoughts as he gazed longingly at the slender body clearly outlined beneath the thin shift. Jemma's harsh voice brought him quickly back to reality. "I needs a clean nightgown, Massa Tony."

"Where. . . where will I find it?"

"Up in Amanda's room, I 'spects," came Jemma's exasperated reply.

Moving with alacrity Tony hastened up the stairs to the third floor. When he reached the landing a blast of hot air nearly bowled him over, leaving him gasping for breath. He was shocked! But more than that he was angry with himself for subjecting Amanda and her son to such cruel treatment . . . and all because of his damned pride. He was amazed that Amanda could even survive in such an atmosphere. He immediately noted that the open window did nothing to alleviate the unrelenting heat. If anything, it added to the discomfort by allowing flies and mosquitoes into the closet-like cubicle. No wonder Amanda was so ill! Never would he forgive himself for allowing his jealousy full reign, needlessly punishing Amanda and her innocent babe!

Scanning the room for the nightgown he was sent to fetch, Tony noted that the narrow cot was not covered by a mosquito netting and afforded no protection against flying insects, and he loudly cursed his own stupidity and blindness that allowed him to act so heartlessly toward someone so totally dependent on him.

Moving to the battered dresser he found what he was looking for in a drawer, noticing for the first time Amanda's meager wardrobe hanging from hooks without even the benefit of a covering to keep the dust from them. Without a backward glance he left the room he considered no better than a hovel, vowing that Amanda and her son would soon occupy much better.

When Tony returned with Amanda's nightgown, Jemma had already stripped her of her chemise and turned her on her stomach, her lower body covered modestly with a sheet. She appeared to be still unconscious as Jemma worked over her.

"Hold up her hair, Massa Tony, so's I kin run this wet cloth over her pore back." Instantly Tony obeyed, gently raising the waist length mass of coppery curls, savoring the silky feel against his roughened palms.

The sight that met his eyes set him back on his heels and left him reeling from shock. "Jemma, what in the hell are those marks on Amanda's back?" Her entire back from shoulders to waist were criss-crossed with white lines. They no longer were angry welts, but to Tony's sharp eyes were unmistakable in their origin. "It looks like she's been flogged!" Tony was accustomed to seeing Amanda only in his darkened room, her long hair effectively hiding those telltale scars on those passionate nights she shared his bed.

"That's jest what happened, Massa Tony. Amanda done had the whip laid on her." Jemma had waited a long time to inform Tony about this terrible thing his mistress had done to Amanda, and there was no stopping her now that the vile deed had finally come to light. Tony's loud gasp of outrage spurred her on.

"Miz Letty done it! Came here right after you left for England and had her overseer beat my pore child. And her pregnant, too. Me and Linus tried to help but what kin we do? We jest slaves," she added, the expression in her eyes unreadable.

"I can't believe Letty would go to such lengths," protested Tony weakly, knowing in his heart it was so.

"Look at Amanda's back and tell me that," snorted Jemma derisively. "Miz Letty said

Amanda done embarrassed her for the last time and needed to be punished. Said you were too easy on her."

Tony realized Jemma would not lie about such a thing but he found it difficult to believe Letty could have perpetrated such a vile deed behind his back. Then he remembered that he had begun to suspect her true nature even before he left for England. But his misguided anger at Amanda had caused him to overlook Letty's faults.

Having gained Tony's ear, Jemma recounted the details of Amanda's punishment while Tony listened, mouth agape. "That pore chile took four lashes on her back afore Massa Nathan arrived, and jest in time to stop Miz Letty from marking up Amanda's beautiful face. My man Linus nearly done himself in running to fetch Massa Nathan from the fields," she boasted, straightening herself with pride.

"Why wasn't I told before this?" demanded Tony. "How dare you and Amanda keep something so important from me!"

Amanda wouldn't 'low it. Said you wouldn't believe us. I 'spects she was probably right. When you gits a bee in your bonnet there jest ain't no talking to you."

I haven't been very pleasant lately," admitted Tony sheepishly. "I'm sorry, Jemma. It's just that things weren't the same when I returned from England. There was Amanda with a baby and. . ."

"You's talking about 'yore' baby, Massa Tony," emphasized Jemma, shaking her head in exasperation. "You ever take a good look at that boy? Up close, I mean. If you ain't, yore in for a big surprise. Ask Massa Nathan, or even Massa Francis. They know what's been in front of yore face all along."

"But Jon was born. . ."

"I ain't saying nothing more," shrugged Jemma stubbornly. "You jest have to judge for yoreself. Now help me git this here nightgown on Amanda."

Tony worked in silence beside Jemma, all the while mulling over the slave's words. Surely Jemma wouldn't lie to him, would she? No wonder Nathan was angry enough to leave River's Edge! My God! he thought, startled. I have a son! A son I've barely looked at in three months. Amanda was right, he concurred, wholeheartedly, I am a fool as well as a pompass ass!

"Will Amanda be alright?" asked Tony anxiously as Amanda moaned and tossed her head restlessly from side to side.

"Don't fret none. I'll take care of her. She's done wore out. Cain't work both day and night without proper rest. She don't have the strength no more to nurse her baby." Jemma glared accusingly at Tony letting him know without words her exact sentiments of his nightly demands upon Amanda.

"I want Amanda to have the best care possible, Jemma," Tony declared. "And. . . and, Jon, too. Find him a wet nurse and turn one of the guest rooms into a nursery. I don't want Amanda to have to care for him while she's recuperating."

"Kinda late in coming but you knows I'll do my best, Massa Tony," grumbled Jemma.

For the next three days Tony was in the house only long enough to eat and sleep. No matter how badly he wanted to see Amanda he held himself back. He had no idea how she would react to him. Would she resent him? Be bitter? Hate him? Through Jemma he learned that she was recovering apace and would probably be up and about in another day or two.

Jemma told him Amanda had been surprised to learn that a wet nurse had been found for her son and that the child seemed to be thriving. He spent a good part of each day with his mother under the watchful eye of Flora, his new nurse. the arrangement seemed to agree with Amanda as well as Jon. What no one knew, except perhaps for Flora, was that each night Tony tiptoed into the nursery to gaze wonderingly down at his small son. At first he could do no more than stand and stare at the burnished head. But before long he grew bold enough to stroke one finger along a downy cheek. One thing followed another and soon he was cuddling his son in the crook of his arm as if he was born to fatherhood. Once, Jon opened large blue-gray eyes and gurgled delightedly at his father, capturing Tony's heart completely and forever.

Finally the seedlings were in the ground and both Tony and Francis looked forward to a respite from their arduous labors. Tony realized he had to make amends with Amanda before another day went by. Of course they would marry. There was no longer any doubt in his mind. His son would have his name. When he confided as much to Francis, he was reminded that he was already engaged to be married to Letty in December.

"My God, Letty!" Tony groaned, slapping his forehead. "Well, there's no help for it. As soon as I talk with Amanda I'll tell Letty our engagement is off. Amanda has to marry me. She has a child to think of and I won't have my son branded a bastard."

"Isn't that just what you called him, Tony?" asked Francis, showing him no mercy.

"I deserve that," flushed Tony. "But I swear things will change if only Amanda will give me a second chance. In fact, I intend to burn her indenture papers as proof of my feelings. She is free to do what she wants. I can only hope that what she wants somehow includes me."

It didn't, or so Amanda informed him when Tony finally found the nerve to face her. He had dressed carefully for his visit in tight, black trousers, gleaming black boots and spotless white shirt beneath a buff suede jacket. He felt as nervous as a bridegroom, as awkward as an untried youth.

"I suppose I should be grateful for all this," were Amanda's first words as she gestured broadly around the large, beautiful room she had come to think of as her own.

"I don't want your gratitude, Amanda, only your forgiveness."

"It's a little late for that, isn't it? I could have died out there in your precious rice paddies. Then who would have raised your son, Letty?" she asked scathingly. Jemma had informed her that Tony did a complete about face in his attitude toward Jon.

"I know. I don't deserve you or Jon. He. . . He's a wonderful child, Amanda."

"Those weren't your words a few weeks ago. Shall I repeat them to you?"

"Forget what I said. I was angry, disillusioned, and too proud to admit that I loved you. Perhaps I always knew Jon was my son." Silence. "Who did you name him after?"

"My father," said Amanda grudgingly, not wanting to give him even that much.

"I want to make it up to you, darling. Marry me. I. . . I love you, Amanda. I always have."

More silence.

"Please answer me, darling. Did you hear me? I love you."

"I heard you, but I don't know, Tony. So much has happened between us. I need time to think. Besides, aren't you forgetting Letty?"

"Damn Letty to hell!" he thundered. "I saw with my own eyes what she did to you. Did you think I would take that lightly? Even if you refuse to marry me, Letty and I are finished."

Amanda's heart beat wildly in her breast. Even if she did eventually decide to marry Tony she wasn't about to salve his conscience by giving in to him so easily. She decided to let him stew awhile in recompense for all the heartache he had caused her.

"I. . . I don't know, Tony," she temporized. "I need some time to consider your proposal." Then, a sudden thought to terrible to contemplate came unbidden to her mind. What if she refused in the end to marry Tony? Would he sell her papers to just anyone out of anger and frustration? Worse yet, would he give her to Letty? "Tony," she asked hesitantly, "what will happen to me if. . . if. . ."

"Rest easy, my love," soothed Tony. "I have already decided to burn your papers no matter what your decision. But you must realize that I will never allow you to take my son from me. And I promise I will never force you again. From this day forward you are a free woman."

Amanda could hardly credit his words. "Tony, do you really mean that? Am I truly free? No matter what I decide?"

"As free as a bird, darling. Only I hope you don't sprout wings and fly away from me." With her lovely face tilted up to him Amanda had never looked more appealing or desirable.

"Tony, you've made me so happy!"

She looked so adorable that Tony could not help but gather her slight form in his strong arms. Then it seemed only natural that he should kiss her with all the love and longing he felt in his heart. But he released her immediately when he felt her stiffen in his embrace.

Amanda was determined that no one but herself should control her life from now on. No longer would she be forced to become a plaything or a possession. Her ultimate decision would be her own, without Tony's soul-shattering kisses or devastating lovemaking confusing her mind and enslaving her body. Actually, she had no doubt that she would marry Tony one day, but there was still Letty to deal with. She was not about to devote the rest of her young life to a man who was so easily beguiled by a woman like Letty. She had to be certain Letty was no longer a threat to her before giving herself to Tony. In the meantime she was free! Free!

Sensing Amanda's resistance, Tony reluctantly moved away and said, "Will you join Francis and me for dinner tomorrow evening if you are up to it?"

"Yes, if you wish," she acquiesced, lowering her lashes to conceal the pleasure in her eyes.

"Thank you, darling," he replied, a wide grin splitting his tanned face. "I'll leave you now and visit with my son." His words brought tears of joy to Amanda's eyes. How she had longed to hear Tony call Jon "son." "Oh, by the way," he added, turning back to Amanda from the doorway, "Francis would like to see you. Are you up to another visitor?"

"I'm fine," smiled Amanda. "Send him in, I'd like to see him." Tony departed in a better mood than he had been in for months. Though Amanda had not accepted his proposal of marriage immediately, neither had she rejected him out of hand. His mood seemed suddenly bouyant and his footsteps light as he retreated down the stairs.

Francis perched gingerly on a chair at Amanda's bedside. He found it difficult to believe she was the same girl who had collapsed in the rice paddy three days before. She looked rested and much happier now than at any time since his arrival at River's Edge.

"I'm happy to see you looking so well, Amanda," he smiled crookedly. "Is Tony treating you well? Because if he isn't I'll. . ."

"He's been wonderful, Sir Francis. He's going to burn my indenture papers! You don't know how happy that makes me!" Her enthusiasm was catching.

"Please, call me Francis. And you deserve to be happy, Amanda." Francis appeared to be staring into space before he spoke again. Clearing his throat, he began cautiously. "I may not have the right to ask this, but how did you happen to. . . to. . . end up in prison? The last time I saw you my friends had just purchased your er. . . services on Tony's behalf that night before he sailed from England."

"You and your friends made a terrible mistake, Francis," informed Amanda quietly. "Let me tell you about a young, frightened girl, barely sixteen years old and still a virgin, lost in a fog on a dark night."

She told her story, leaving out nothing. At first Francis was spellbound, then speechless, finally, guilt-ridden. "My God, Amanda!" he cried when she stopped to catch her breath, "what can I say?

I'm sorry seems so. . . so. . . mild an apology in this case. No wonder Tony never said a word about this to me. He was too ashamed."

"You will probably find this impossible to believe but Tony has no idea I am the same girl he deflowered in that inn."

"He must be blind, or stupid!" gasped Francis, astounded.

"He was," giggled Amanda, surprised that she could laugh about it now, "blind drunk."

"Too drunk to know he took a helpless virgin?"

"Yes, I believe so."

"After all this time why haven't you told him?"

"Initially, I thought only of revenge. I blamed Tony for everything bad that happened to me after he destroyed my virginity. But later, I came to love him, and I. . . I believed he loved me in return."

"He does love you, Amanda," offered Francis, who was ever an astute observer. "He never stopped."

"How could you say that after living here three months?"

"Take my word for it, I know."

"He accused me of terrible things when he returned from England," Amanda contended sourly.

"He truly believed he had good cause."

"What did you think, Francis?"

"You must remember, Amanda, that I knew you only as a very young prostitute. But when I finally came to know you it taxed my imagination to think of you in those terms. I knew nothing about you except what Tony chose to tell me, and the unorthodox way you came to be in America did not fit the mold of a woman Tony could fall in love with. When I finally came to know you I found it difficult to believe you had been a felon and. . . and prostitute."

"Thank you, Francis," Amanda murmured gratefully. "I'm glad I confided in you. I feel ever so much better."

"I am aware that Jon is Tony's son even if he is not," Francis contended, stunning Amanda by his calm pronouncement. "It amazes me just how obtuse Tony can be at times."

"He knows now," smiled Amanda happily. "I think he realized it all along but was too stubborn to admit it. He. . . he asked me to marry him."

"I know," responded Francis. "Did you accept?"

Amanda's lovely brow furrowed. "No, I. . . I didn't accept, not right away, but neither did I reject his proposal."

Francis laughed heartily. "Teaching Tony a lesson?" he teased. "It serves the devil right."

"Perhaps," admitted Amanda, grinning mischievously. "He certainly deserves it."

"Definitely," agreed Francis. Suddenly Amanda turned serious. "What is it, Amanda?" Francis asked, noticing her sudden change of mood.

"Letty. No one knows better than I what she is capable of when crossed."

"Leave the witch to Tony, my dear. I'm certain he will know how to handle her. Just concentrate on recovering your strength."

14

Amanda was astonished the next day when she appeared downstairs to find Tony sitting in the parlor with a giggling Jon balanced on his knee, happily bouncing up and down. She could not suppress the smile that came unbidden to her lips at the sight of father and son totally engrossed in one another. Deciding to leave well enough alone, she silently backed out of the room and wandered out to the kitchen to talk to Jemma.

Meanwhile, Flora came to collect her charge in order to feed him and settle him down for a nap leaving Tony feeling oddly alone and abandoned. Remembering he still had a promise to Amanda to fulfill, he went directly to his office and began rummaging around in his desk drawers, finally extracting a long envelope. Glancing inside to assure himself of the contents, he walked with it to the fireplace intending to destroy all evidence of Amanda's submission to him. But before he could accomplish that act the door was flung open and Letty barged in without knocking. Tony stared at her as if she were the last person in the world he wanted to see.

"Letty!"

"Is that all you can say? It's been two weeks since I've seen or heard from you. Is that any way to treat your future wife?" As usual, Letty was beautifully garbed and coiffed, looking cool and unruffled despite her obvious displeasure.

"I'm glad you're here, Letty. I was going to come and see you in any case," Tony said, steeling himself for one of Letty's tantrums when he broke the news about his decision to call off their marriage.

"I knew you'd miss me, darling," crowed Letty delightedly. "I'll show you just how much I missed you tonight." Her blue eyes sparkled with promise.

"Letty, a lot has happened in two weeks. First of all I've learned what a despicable thing you did to Amanda while I was in England. You had no right to come to my plantation and abuse one of my servants."

"But that happened long ago," she protested weakly. "Why would she wait till now to tell you?"

"It's unimportant why or how I learned about your brutal act. What matters now is that I cannot marry you because I love Amanda. I intend to marry her if she will have me. Immediately."

"No!" sputtered Letty, disbelief contorting her face. "I won't let her have you! You belong to me!"

"I never belonged to you. Not from the moment Amanda entered my life. Probably not before that, either. You may as well know that I was about to destroy Amanda's Articles of Indenture when you so rudely burst in here," he informed her coldly, holding out the offending document before her eyes. "As long as you are here you might as well watch me."

Selecting a sulfer-tipped splint from a box on his desk, Tony made to draw it through a sand-paper coated with phosphrous when loud voices outside the door distracted him. Within seconds Nathan flung open the door, startling the two occupants.

"Nathan! What the. . ." The look on Nathan's face stopped him in mid-sentence.

"This is no time for lengthy explanations, Tony," Nathan informed him. "I came to warn you."

"Warn me? What about?"

"Indians!"

Letty's loud gasp brought a look of disgust from Nathan before he turned back to Tony.

"The Cherokees have raided several plantations in this area during the past week. Mostly they steal horses and food. Ned Collins, he owns that small farm down river, and his wife and child were killed. I didn't know if you had been warned so I came out as soon as I heard."

"That's really good of you, Nathan, con-sidering. . ."

"Tony, let's forget our differences for now. I came to offer my help. I know this plantation as well as you do. We need to alert all your people to the danger."

"You're right," flushed Tony, duly chastized. "Let's go."

"What about me?" Letty's anguished plea effectively halted both men.

Tony frowned at her as if he wished she could

drop off the face of the earth. "You'll have to stay here, Letty, there's no help for it," he finally said. "But once the danger is over you'll have to leave. Just keep in mind what we discussed." Then he was gone, hard on the heels of Nathan who had already disappeared through the door.

Letty was livid. So Tony thought to dump her, she silently fumed. Well, she wasn't that easily discarded. All she had to do was find a way to get rid of Amanda and Tony would come running back to her. And it seemed that fate had been kind to her. The Cherokee activity in the area would give her just the excuse she needed to remain at River's Edge for a few days. Long enough to take care of Amanda once and for all!

Then Letty's eyes fell upon the envelope Tony had been holding when Nathan interrupted his little burning ceremony. It was laying conspicuously on the desk where Tony dropped it in his haste to leave. Picking it up, Letty drew out the single sheet of parchment. Hastily skimming over it, she slipped it inside the bodice of her dress, replaced it with a blank sheet she found laying nearby, and placed the envelope exactly where she found it, a satanic smile curving her sensuous lips.

Later that day when Tony returned to his study, he accomplished what he had set out to do before Nathan's arrival. The ashes lay in the grate without Tony ever having opened the envelope to verify its contents.

"It's done," he said aloud, heaving a sigh of relief. Tony felt lighter than he had in months.

Before dinner that evening Tony found time to speak privately to Nathan, telling him of his desire to marry Amanda. Though Nathan wasn't exactly happy with the news he accepted it with good grace. The one thing that convinced Nathan that Tony meant what he said was the growing love and affection Tony displayed toward his son. It was late in coming but obviously sincere, Nathan decided as he watched Tony playing with the baby before dinner that evening. Nathan had been told about Amanda's illness by Tony who did nothing to conceal or diminish the part he played in her collapse. At first Nathan was livid with rage, but when Tony revealed that he had burned Amanda's indenture papers he became somewhat mollified. He was anxious to see Amanda for himself before he allowed his anger to cool completely.

Francis and Letty would also be present at dinner that night and Nathan found himself wondering what kind of mischief Letty would concoct for he did not believe for one minute that she would give up Tony so easily. Being stranded at River's Edge for a few days seemed too good a chance for her to pass up. Tony could not in all conscience send her home with her father away and Indians in the area. She would definitely bear watching, Nathan rightly surmised. He was certain he would enjoy dinner that night knowing that Letty was finally aware she no longer had a place in Tony's life.

Only when Amanda remembered that she was no longer a servant did she relax and begin to enjoy her meal. It was wonderful seeing Nathan again and she experienced a surge of happiness when she noted Tony's obvious jealousy as she devoted her full attention to her would-be suitor.

Tony had visited Amanda earlier to inform her of the threat of an Indian raid and also that Letty would be a guest in the house for a few days, carefully stressing that Letty was well aware that it was Amanda he loved and intended to marry. Told that Tony had burned her indenture papers, Amanda could not suppress the tears of gratitude welling in her green eyes.

Tony could not turn his warm gaze from Amanda as she reacted to his disclosure. Ill clad in a threadbare dress that seemed too large for her thin frame, her beauty remained pure and undiminished. Tess had been appointed her personal maid and took great pleasure in brushing Amanda's burnished curls till they gleamed with reddish lights and then arranging them becomingly around her heart-shaped face.

Even Letty grudgingly gave Amanda her due, for she knew she could not hope to compete with the younger girl in Tony's affection. . . as long as Amanda was alive, that is.

Nathan was kept busy during dinner answering questions about the Cherokee and their raiding parties. "They travel in small groups," Nathan explained, "no more than four or five in a party. They hit fast and hard, steal whatever they can lay their hands on, particularly horses and slaves, leaving death and destruction in their wake."

Ignoring Letty and Amanda for a short time the mens' conversation was devoted to the various measures they had taken to protect the plantation.

Suddenly, a muffled cry intruded upon their conversation. All talk halted as five pairs of ears strained toward the sound. Nothing. Talk resumed only to be interrupted again by Lionel, Tony's valet, who staggered into the room nearly on the point of collapse, his face bloody from a gash across his forehead.

"My God, Lionel, what has happened?" exclaimed Tony, jumping up to assist the injured slave.

"Indians!" panted Lionel. "They in the quarters now, Massa Tony. They heading for the stables."

"How many?"

"It's hard to tell but from what I saw there cain't be too many of them."

"Get the guns, Nathan! You know where they are. Hurry man!" shouted Tony. "Francis, stay here with the women."

"No, Tony," protested Amanda bravely. "The Indians won't dare invade the house. Take Francis with you. You need him more than we do."

"No! Don't pay any attention to her, Tony!" screamed Letty. "Leave Francis here to protect us."

"Just leave a gun, Tony," Amanda said, completely ignoring Letty's hysterical outburst. "Please hurry. You must protect the slaves."

Tony realized the truth of Amanda's unselfish words. The Indians would steal a few of his horses and slaves and make a run for it, he reasoned. So small a raiding party would not come near the house. Francis would be much more useful in helping repel the raiders than remaining with the women.

"You're right, darling," Tony concurred reluctantly. "I'll leave a gun with you just in case, but please see to the house slaves and lock all the doors and windows. Even the ones on the second floor."

"Be careful, Tony," she urged softly, aware of Letty's narrowed gaze upon her.

"Take care of my son," he whispered in her ear as he kissed her briefly on the lips.

Letty was so consumed with jealousy that it was all she could do to keep from grabbing the gun Nathan had placed on the table and shooting Amanda then and there. But that would be like cutting her own throat, she realized. Amanda's demise had to be much more subtle.

Amanda's authoritative voice roused Letty from her devious thoughts. "You heard Tony. I'll begin down here latching all the windows while you take the second floor." Without waiting for Letty's reply Amanda hurried to the kitchen to bring Jemma, Linus, Tess and Cory to the main part of the house.

Letty moved away from the window in Tony's room, immobilized by fear. When she set the latch she spied two shadowy figures creeping stealthily toward the house. Had Amanda had time to secure all the windows and doors on the first floor? she wondered. She debated whether to go downstairs and warn the others or remain on the second floor in relative safety.

Unbidden her thoughts flew to the gun lying on the dining room table, galvanizing her into immediate action. If she had the gun she could defend herself. Lionel had said the raiding party was small and she had seen only two figures approaching the house.

Rushing downstairs Letty found Amanda alone in the dining room. "Jemma and the maids are latching the windows in the parlor," Amanda said when she saw Letty. Are you finished upstairs?"

"Of course," Letty answered tartly. "Do you take me for an imbecile?"

"Never an imbecile," sighed Amanda wearily. Suddenly she became aware of the strange expression freezing Letty's features. A flicker of apprehension coursed through her. "What is it Letty? What do you see?" she asked in alarm, whirling to peer out the long dining room windows that seemed to hold such terror for Letty.

In that instant Letty knew what she had to do. Never would the opportunity be as great as it was at that moment. They were alone in the room with no witnesses to question or doubt her. "I. . . I just saw Jemma outside," Letty finally said, horror straining her voice.

"Impossible," scoffed Amanda. "She was here only a few minutes ago."

"It was her, I tell you," insisted Letty doggedly. "How could anyone mistake her figure?"

"Oh, no!" cried Amanda, her face drained of all color. "Linus wasn't in the house when I went to the kitchen earlier. Jemma was worried about him. She must have gone out to look for him."

"That must be it," agreed Letty readily, suppressing a gleeful smile.

"I've got to do something. Nathan said the indians are looking for slaves and horses."

"But what can you do?" asked Letty, goading her on. "Wait! I just saw her rounding the house." One shapely hand gestured broadly into the encompassing darkness.

"I must go after her," Amanda declared irrationally. "I don't think those savages are anywhere near the house but I can't take that chance. Lock the door after me, Letty, and stand close by so you can let me in the instant I signal."

"Yes, yes I will, Amanda. Hurry."

"Wait!" Amanda cried. "The gun, give me the gun!"

"Would you leave your son unprotected," scolded Letty sternly. "If the gun was left with me

I could at least protect him should the indians break through the windows."

Worry about Jemma as well as her son made Amanda incautious and unthinking. Of course Letty should keep the gun, she rationalized. No one was more important to her than Tony's baby.

Letty closed the door firmly behind Amanda's departing figure and leaned against it grinning evily at her own cleverness. She did not notice Cory who had entered the hallway just as Amanda slipped through the door and stood rooted to the spot, her eyes white and frightened in her dark face. She could not believe her eyes. Stealthily she melted back into the shadows, waiting and watching. She was only a slave, she decided. Better to remain a hidden observer until she discovered what Letty was about.

Amanda circled the house unaware of the moccasined feet gliding noiselessly from tree to tree, following her trim figure. She was nearly to the front door when warning spasms of alarm erupted inside her. Abruptly she turned, fear turning to panic. And then she saw them. For a whole minute she remained motionless, struck dumb by the sight of the two broad forms materializing from the darkness like harbingers of death. Panic born of shock released her feet and she rushed toward the front door and safety.

Panting from sheer terror, Amanda reached the door only moments ahead of the indians. There would have been enough time to save herself had Letty thrown open the door the instant Amanda signalled. But Letty chose to ignore Amanda's desperate pleas for entrance. Letty smiled sardonically, thinking that Amanda's knuckles must be bloodied by now, and somehow that thought comforted her.

Cory, still concealed within the shadows of the hallway was shocked by Letty's cruel disregard for Amanda's safety. Why had Letty deliberately ignored Amanda's frantic cries for help, choosing instead to abandon her to the indians? Cory asked herself, horror-stricken.

Finally, unable to stand helplessly by while Amanda fought for her life, Cory rushed forward. "Let her in, Miz Letty!" she cried, flinging herself at the door. "You jest gotta let Amanda in!"

"What!" Letty's furious gaze fell malevolently upon Cory's small form as she hurtled herself forward. "How long have you been here?"

"Don't matter, Miz Letty. You cain't let them savages have Amanda, you jest cain't!"

"Silence!" ordered Letty, grasping Cory's forearm and forcing her away from the door with considerable strength. "You saw and heard nothing, do you understand? Nothing, I say!"

"But, Miz Letty. . ."

"I could just as easily push you out the door to join that slut. Surely you've heard what indians do to women? One by one they rape her until she is witless. The whole tribe, until she wishes for death. Is that what you want, Cory? To spread your legs for dozens of dirty savages?"

"But, Miz Letty," Cory repeated helplessly, "I jest got to do something."

"Get out of here," Letty ordered harshly. "If you ever speak of this to anyone I'll have your tongue cut out. It won't be long before I'm mistress here and you can rest assured you'll be severely punished. Now go!" After giving Cory a rough shove, Letty focused her attention once again to the closed door, suddenly aware of the ominous silence on the other side.

Cradling her bruised arm, Cory slunk away,

devastated by the thought of Amanda at the mercy of savages. And all because of Letty's jealousy. Cory was well aware that Amanda faced ravishment, enslavement, torture, and perhaps death. But even death would be preferable to an uncertain future as a slave to the Indians.

Tony, Francis and Nathan arrived back at the house at dawn, tired, dirty, and blurry-eyed. The indians had stolen four horses, but luckily the raiding party had been small, four or so, and the three armed men had proven formidable foes. No slaves had been taken. A final count had satisfied Tony that the Cherokees had been unsuccessful in capturing any of his people. He had patrolled the quarters all night in case the savages returned, giving up his vigil only after Nathan scoured the surrounding woods and assured him that the indians had melted into the night and in all probability would not return. They had what they came for.

The moment Letty opened the door to him, Tony knew something was terribly, desperately wrong. Jemma, Linus, and the two maids stood huddled in the center of the hall.

"What is it?" exclaimed Tony, immediately noting Amanda's absence, but assuming her to be upstairs with the baby.

"Amanda is gone, Tony," Letty announced abruptly.

"Gone! Are you crazy! If this is any of your doing, Letty, I'll kill you with my bare hands. Now, tell me exactly what you are talking about."

"I had nothing to do with it," sniffed Letty in an aggrieved tone. "I could not stop her. She thought she saw Jemma wandering around outside and insisted on leaving the house to bring her back. I waited at the door to let her in but she never returned. The. . . the indians must have been closer to the house than we thought. I. . . I think they have her, Tony.''

Nathan's shocked cry and Francis' strangled gasp delighted Letty immensely, but she managed to keep her face expressionless. But she was totally unprepared for Tony's violent reaction as she found herself the receipient of ten steely fingers digging painfully into the soft flesh of her upper arms.

"I don't believe you, Letty," Tony shouted, unrelenting in his rage. "You would stop at nothing to gain your own end. There's more to this than you've told me and I want the truth!"

"I'm telling the truth, Tony," Letty stuttered from between clenched teeth. "You're hurting me!"

"That's not all I'll do to you if I find you're responsible for this night's work. Do you have any idea what those savages will do to her?"

"I. . . I think so." She began to cry.

Defeated, Tony released Letty, turning instead to the weeping slaves. "Jemma, what do you know about this? Were you outside?"

"Lordy, Lordy, Massa Tony," wailed Jemma, her grief uncontrollable. "I wasn't outside. Amanda knowed that. I was latching the windows just like she tole me. I don't know why she left the house. It jest don't make sense." Unable to continue, Jemma broke down completely and Tony turned his attention to Linus.

"I was in the spring house, Massa Tony, but hightailed it back to the house soon's I heard all the commotion. I found Jemma and we was together all the time."

Tess gave nearly the same version, moaning and crying until Tony could stand it no longer and ordered Jemma to take her from the room. Cory could not seem to find her voice. She was riddled with guilt, overcome by indicision and frightened out of her wits. Only her eyes gave her away as they darted restlessly from Tony to Letty.

"She knows something!" insisted Nathan as Tony questioned the terror-stricken girl.

"Cory," Tony began gently, "no one is going to harm you. Just tell us what you know."

"Oh stop it, Tony," cut in Letty worriedly. "Can't you see the girl is frightened. She knows nothing. Let her go." Her icy eyes impaled Cory, causing the poor girl to cringe and stutter with fear.

"Cory," Tony continued, ignoring Letty's outburst, "I repeat, you belong to me. No one can harm you."

Cory's black eyes slid to Letty but she had already made her decision. No matter what happened to her she could not allow Letty to go unpunished for the terrible thing she did to Amanda.

Gulping back her fear, Cory pointed an accusing finger at Letty who blanched as she knew a moment of panic. "She did it, Massa Tony. Don't know why Amanda went out that door but I do know that Miz Letty jest stood by and laughed when Amanda begged to be let back inside. Finally it was too late. The indians done carried Amanda away. I tried to help but Miz Letty, she tole me she'd throw me out to those savages if I said anything." By now, Cory was sobbing uncontrollably.

"It's all right, Cory, I don't blame you," Tony managed, anger and grief robbing him of his voice. "You can go now."

Only by exerting the most stringest control was Tony able to contain his rage until Cory and Linus had departed to join Jemma and Tess. Then he whirled on Letty, all his anger, all his frustration, clearly visible on his granite-like features and in his cold, unrelenting eyes.

Sucking in her breath sharply, Letty took a step backward, fearful of Tony's rage, and with good reason.

"You she-devil!" he bit out from between clenched teeth. "Somehow you'll pay for this! Do you know what will happen to Amanda? What probably already has?" With a will of their own his hands shot forward to encircle her slim throat.

"Tony, I didn't," gasped Letty, struggling for breath. "Are you going to believe a frightened slave?"

"Cory had no reason to lie. She told the truth, Letty. Now you're going to die! I'm only sorry your death will be relatively painless compared to what Amanda is suffering." Then he began to squeeze until Letty slumped forward. Still he was not satisfied as he increased his cruel pressure.

Francis was the first to act, leaping forward to grasp Tony's arm. Nathan was not far behind. Together they managed to pry Tony's hands from around Letty's bruised throat. Immediately she fell to her knees gasping for breath.

"My God, you could have killed her, Tony!" said Francis.

"That was my intention," replied Tony, remorseless.

"Let her go. She's not worth it," urged Nathan. "Amanda is our first concern. If we start immediately we have a good chance of catching up with the raiding party. You want her back, don't you?"

"I need her, Nathan," came Tony's anguished reply. "My son needs her. I'll do whatever is necessary to get her back."

"Then pull yourself together," Francis chided gently. "There are still several good horses left in the stable. We can be on our way within an hour."

Nathan and Francis left immediately to prepare for their dangerous journey but Tony remained behind a few minutes, turning cold eyes back to Letty who was slowly recovering from his attack.

"I want you gone before I leave here, Letty," he spat out the words contemptuously. His gray eyes darkened like thunderclouds as he thought of how Letty had cold-bloodedly abandoned Amanda to the indians. "And I never want to see your face again. Is that clear?"

"Perfectly," croaked Letty hoarsely. "But you've not heard the last from me. Do you really think you'll find your precious Amanda? And even if you do she'll not be the same. Surely you can't still want her after all those savages have. . . have. . ." she shrugged eloquently, her gesture saying it all.

"Get out, damn you!" Tony ground out, "before I change my mind and kill you anyway. I'll find Amanda if she is still alive. And I'd never abandon her no matter what has been done to her. If you are smart you'll join your father in England. No one wants you here."

Letty glared at his retreating back, hating him for the way he had humiliated her. No one could treat her like Tony just did and get away with it. "No, Tony Brandt," Letty vowed with quiet, desperate determination as she massaged her aching throat, "you'll pay one day. And so will your mistress, if you should have the misfortune of finding her alive."

15

From the time she began pounding on the front door pleading for help until the very moment the two indians seized her, Amanda did not believe that Letty would actually abandon her to a fate worse than death. Then, comprehension dawned in a blinding flash that sent her reeling backwards in shock. Letty had cold-bloodedly planned such a fate for her all along! Suddenly a calloused hand stifled her cries and bruised the tender skin of her lips, the pressure of teeth against flesh bringing the taste of blood to her mouth. Amanda fought, but her waning strength was no match against the heavily muscled, superbly conditioned savage. One heavy-handed clout along side her head and she slumped forward, unconscious. Grunting in satisfaction the man slung her slight weight unceremoniously over his shoulder and melted cat-like into the woods.

Consciousness came back slowly, between brief spans of darkness and intense discomfort.

She was being bounced and joggled in an unfamiliar manner, her arms and feet tightly bound. Amanda could tell by the heat upon her back that it was daylight and she had obviously been unconscious all night long. Risking a terrified glance from under lowered lids she saw that her first impression had been correct. Someone had thrown her across the withers of a horse, face downward and bound arms and legs together around its stomach. An Indian rode behind her. She could feel his sturdy legs pressing against her body. Her head ached, her limbs were numb, her flesh bruised and battered. Thirst raged within her. She had no idea where they were but she heard the river nearby and assumed it be the Santee.

Suddenly Amanda became aware that the horses had halted and panic welled sharply upward inside her, routing her from her apathy. Roughly the bonds securing her to the horse were cut and she fell heavily to the ground in a rubbery heap. Derisive laughter filled her ears and she cringed inwardly as four sets of sturdy, brown legs surrounded her. In her heart she knew what was coming next but dare not dwell on it. She closed her eyes and prayed that her captors would kill her, for if these four savages raped her she would find some way to do it herself. Having known Tony's love she could not bear to live with herself after being ravished by savages.

She was dragged roughly to her feet by one of the braves and shoved toward the bank of the river where she was pushed face downward into the water. Then the pressure on the back of her head was relaxed and Amanda realized they meant only for her to drink and did not intend to drown her.

Gratefully, she slurped up the cool, reviving liquid, considerably easing the pain in her parched throat. When she had drunk her fill she sat back on her haunches, uncertain what to do next as she surreptitiously studied her four captors who were kneeling beside her slaking their own thirst.

They were very young, of medium height with heavily muscled legs, massive chests and slim waists. Streaks of yellow and white paint decorated their not unhandsome hawkish faces making them appear even more fierce and war-like. The one braid at the nape of their neck appeared to be greased or oiled. They were clad only in leggings with loincloths covering their genitals.

Their thirst appeased, the Indians turned bright obsidian eyes on Amanda who immediately divined their salacious intent and jumped to her feet, eyes darting furtively from side to side searching for some means of escape. The brave closest to her seized her by the hair, speaking in some unintelligible tongue as he pointed and gestured, obviously delighted by its color and texture. Before long each man was fingering her matted curls until finally their hands became bolder, moving downward over breasts and hips with growing excitement.

"No!" Amanda pleaded, twisting desperately to elude their grasping hands. "Please! Please leave me alone!"

Ignoring her pleas as if she had never uttered them, one of the Indians grasped the neckline of her dress and jerked downward while the other three laughed uproariously at her reddened cheeks. Then all four fell upon her ripping and

273

tearing until she was entirely nude except for her shoes and stockings tied at her thighs with delicate bows. Never had Amanda felt so helpless, so degraded, so completely at the mercy of another human being. Hands were all over her shrinking flesh, hard, hurting, punishing, and she screamed a long, loud wail of despair. One of the braves struck her and she fell to the ground, stunned, her head spinning, mouth bleeding. Then she felt herself being dragged toward the nearest tree, her back scraped raw by twigs and dead brush along the path.

Before she knew what was happening, her stockings were stripped from her thrashing legs and used to bind her arms above her head, then fastened together around the tree trunk. Two of the indians grasped her ankles and spread her legs wide apart until she thought she would split in half. For a moment all was quiet while the savages admired the coppery thatch at the juncture of her thighs, testing its silky texture with cruel fingers. Amanda opened her mouth to scream again but a warning grunt from the brave who appeared to be the leader effectively cut it off before it was born, though it did not stop her from glaring at him defiantly from blazing, green eyes.

Motioning for his companions to hold her still, the leader pulled aside his loincloth baring a swollen manhood, purple and pulsating with lust. The rest of the Indians made appropriate sounds of admiration low in their throat as their leader brandished his proud weapon before the helpless girl pinioned to the ground. Dropping to his knees between Amanda's outstretched legs, he plunged ruthlessly into her, the force of his thrust pushing her sharply backward until her head struck the tree to which she was bound. Pain exploded like an erupting volcano in her lower body as well as in her head as the Indian continued to tear into her dry, unprepared flesh. Everyone knew that the Indians used rape as a form of degradation and subjection and Amanda could well understand why some women did not survive the assault. In her own mind she was certain she would be dead long before the fourth Indian finished with her. Her last thoughts were of a quick death as she slid into darkness.

The Indian pounding into her was taking his time, savoring the fear and horror he knew the white woman beneath him was experiencing. Brave Fox had taken many female captives but raping this proud red-haired woman gave him more pleasure than most. Despite the fact that she was terror-stricken, the defiant tilt of her chin and the contempt for him clearly visible in her wide, green eyes told him that she would not take the yoke easily. Until her spirit was defeated she would be unacceptable to the tribe. A slave with pride was unheard of. Repeated rape was the only way to conquer and subjugate a woman such as Copper Hair, he thought ruefully, giving Amanda a name that would be applied to her during her captivity. In addition to his companions each man in his tribe would have a turn on her. Soon she would be tractable enough for the women to train. Then all conscious thought left Brave Fox as all the rage directed at her race and sex exploded in a boiling rush into her unresisting body, his high, keening wail echoing through the trees. But Amanda was beyond feeling or hearing. The shock, the punishment, the violation of her body had been too much for her to bare. She had passed into blessed oblivion the moment Brave Fox had first thrust into her.

Amanda never knew that she had been saved from further acts of rape and brutality by an unexpected interruption. One of the other braves, White Feather, had already taken his place between her legs when a frantic gesture from Brave Fox warned him away. Obeying instantly, albeit reluctantly, White Feather moved away from Amanda's prone form.

"Riders," explained Brave Fox in hushed tones. "Listen."

Cocking keen ears in the direction of Brave Fox's pointing finger, White Feather nodded.

"We are still too close to the white man's settlement," grunted Brave Fox. "The woman will wait until we bring the horses safely back to our camp, my companions. I promise you that you shall be the first to take her."

Grumbling, yet too young and untried to openly defy Brave Fox, White Feather and his companions released Amanda, tossed her nude, limp body across Brave Fox's horse and leaped upon their own stolen mounts as the approaching hoofbeats grew louder.

They rode steadily, stopping only to relieve themselves, allowing Amanda to do the same, when they remembered her at all, as long as she performed her duty within eyesight. Burning with humiliation, Amanda had no choice but to see to her private needs in full sight of all four leering braves.

Once she regained consciousness Amanda wrongly assumed that she had been raped by each member of the raiding party. Her aching, bruised body felt as if she had been abused repeatedly, and she cursed the Gods that had seen fit to keep her alive to endure further torture and degradation. Silently she vowed to find a way to kill herself before having to submit to the rest of the tribe.

Amanda sought desperately for something with which to cover her nakedness but aside from small pouches dangling from their waists the Indians carried nothing, neither blankets, clothing or cooking utensils. They ate riding, munching on jerky and parched corn stored in their pouches. They offered no food to Amanda, nor did she ask for any, preferring to suffer in silence rather than beg and grovel before her captors. At least they had let her ride upright once she had come to her senses. She was held firmly in place by the leader, his hard, sinewy legs pressed intimately against her own bare thighs which were chafed raw and still throbbing with pain from her recent ravishment. Periodically she would stiffen and ease her body away from her captor's hard flesh but it was impossible to keep her balance without his support.

The Indians appeared immune to exhaustion as they kept up their steady pace throughout the long night. Amanda dozed fitfully, shivering uncontrollably once she was deprived of the sun's warming rays. Unconsciously she sought the warmth of Brave Fox's body.

Amanda was rudely awakened from a pleasant dream of Jon nursing at her breast. He was playfully nipping at a nipple like he sometimes did when he was sated. Suddenly his playfulness turned vicious and she cried out, only to find herself laying on the ground, the Indian leader straddling her, perversely pinching her nipples to awaken her, much to the amusement of the other braves. Amanda's eyes flamed as she rolled quickly to her feet.

"She is not sufficiently subdued," said White Feather in a language Amanda did not understand. "You have tasted her pale flesh, let me punish her with my mighty weapon until the fire in her leaf-colored eyes grows dim."

Brave Fox mulled over White Feather's words. Under tribal law female captives were usually raped first by those responsible for her capture, and all four in the raiding party had the right to her body. Only the fear of being discovered had saved this particular woman from such a fate. If riders hadn't been hard on their heels each one of his companions would have had ample time to slake their lust upon her until they grew weary of the task. But the knowledge that they were still far from their own main group and only four strong decided Brave Fox against allowing his followers to take their pleasure from the captive's body. Once back in camp there would be a big ceremony and he, White Feather and the others would have great honors heaped upon them for returning with horses as well as a white captive. The white woman would be led to the center of a great circle and there would be raped by each member of the tribe once her captors were finished with her.

Nodding decisively Brave Fox informed White Feather of his final judgment. Much more honor would come to them, he told his companions, if they waited to take the woman after purification rites and in front of the rest of the tribe. White Feather and the other young braves argued otherwise while Amanda lay motionless, aware that some controversy was being waged, with her as the prize. There was no doubt in her mind that each man was ready to fall upon her at a moment's notice. After some minutes the leader appeared to have won and the braves sullenly mounted their horses, their eyes glazed with salacious intent.

Grasping a handful of bright hair Brave Fox yanked Amanda roughly to her feet, her cry of pain bringing a cruel twist to his lips. Eyes wide and frightened she watched as the Indian reached in his pouch and extracted her stockings that had been used the day before to bind her to the tree while she was being raped. Brave Fox quickly tied both stockings together to form a long rope, tested it for strength and looped one end of it around her slim neck, pulling it taut but not tight enough to strangle her. The other end was secured to his wrist. Then he mounted his horse, jerking the makeshift rope to indicate to Amanda his desire that she should follow on foot. Unbeknowst to her this was the accepted method used on all captives, leading them into camp nude, raped and degraded if they were women and tortured and nude if they were men, the rope a symbol of their complete subjection.

For two hours Amanda stumbled behind Brave Fox's horse, sometimes dragging her bleeding feet, other times falling to her knees only to be painfully jerked upright again by the cruel tether about her neck. Time had no meaning. Her stomach was so empty it touched her backbone, intense hunger causing her to hallucinate. All manner of wild imaginings flashed before her eyes in a red haze of bright hurts, each one more excruciating than the last, until nothing or no one in this world could make her continue. But there was no need for Amanda to continue. The Cherokee village lay stretched out before her feverish eyes.

But Amanda's ordeal had only begun. When Brave Fox proudly led her into camp at the end of the rope her tender flesh was prodded, probed, poked, pulled and plundered. No part of her anatomy was left inviolate. For the most part her violators were women. The female members of the tribe took it upon themselves to torment and torture her while the men stood aside laughing at her humiliation. The louder Amanda screamed the more the indians seemed to enjoy themselves. Even the children joined in the sport by jabbing pointed sticks into the pale flesh of her buttocks and back.

Intuitively Amanda sensed that the more fear she displayed the more prolonged her torment. Squaring her small shoulders, willing her exhausted, pain-ridden body to move, she turned her mind to the mundane task of setting one foot in front of the other without flinching or screaming. To some extent Amanda was successful in blocking out the agony and humiliation being inflicted upon her by the women and children for they soon began to lose interest in her and drifted away toward more rewarding pursuits. Everyone knew that before long the pitiful, skinny slave would become the camp prostitute and was deserving of nothing but their contempt and revilement.

Stumbling along at the end of her cruel tether, Amanda was jerked to a sudden halt. Brave Fox dismounted and bodily dragged her to a sturdy post placed at the center of the camp. The open area she found herself in appeared almost like a parade ground to Amanda's pain-glazed eyes, with tents forming a large circle around it. Securing the end of her tether to the post, Brave Fox maliciously kicked her legs from beneath her and left her laying in the dust without a backward glance. Raising painfully to a sitting position, Amanda finally gave in to her despair. She realized she was going to die and prayed for it to be soon and quick. The most difficult part was the realization that she would never see her son again. Or Tony. If only she had told him she loved him before Letty had betrayed her.

In a way, Amanda pondered, everything bad that had ever happened to her had been the result of her association with Tony, beginning the night he had stolen her virginity to two days ago when his ex-mistress had carefully orchestrated her capture. What had Letty told Tony? she wondered miserably. How long would he mourn her before turning to Letty for consolation? Knowing Tony and his appetites, it wouldn't be long before he found himself in Letty's bed, she wagered. But the burning question in Amanda's mind was whether Letty could influence Tony enough to turn him away from his own son. "Oh Jon," she sobbed, hugging her arms around her bare breasts, "I will never see you grow to manhood. Will you be tall and handsome like your father?"

Turning a bruised and dirty face to the post Amanda allowed herself the luxury of bitter tears until her exhausted, abused body was beyond feeling and she fell asleep. She was unaware of the stealthy, moccasined figure creeping close and dropping a rough blanket over her nude body before melting back into the shadows.

The sun was stabbing relentlessly at Amanda's swollen eyelids and she groaned, instinctively shielding her eyes with grimy hands. An angry growl brought her to full wakefulness and she jerked upright, crying out when her tether cut cruelly into her slender neck. Her captor, Brave Fox, stood above her, legs apart, a black scowl darkening his fierce features. Screaming words she did not understand, he angrily pulled the blanket from her body and flung it out of her reach, aiming a vicious kick at her ribs as punishment for something she knew nothing about. In fact, she had been as surprised as he to find that some unknown benefactor had taken pity on her.

Amanda's thirst was so great that her throat was nearly closed. If they did not bring her water and food soon she knew she would not live long enough to suffer the vile torture the savages planned for her. Suddenly the thought of expiring from hunger and thirst seemed eminently desirable.

Amanda's fair skin had begun to redden and blister, particularly her face, back and tender, white breasts. Her burnished hair was a dirty, stringy mass of tangled curls. Green eyes blinked dully in a grimy face devoid of all hope. She was exactly the way the indians wanted her, a witless creature, degraded and submissive. A female slave worthy of only the meanest chores who would meekly accept the role of camp prostitute. The final breaking point, the ultimate degradation would take place the following night when she would be raped by every member of the tribe. She would be reviled, spat upon and beaten regularly by the women who would have complete charge of her life during the day. At night she would be confined to a tent set apart from the main camp, a whore to be used at will by the male tribe members. Of course, as yet Amanda had no inkling of her fate.

Amanda knew she was dying. Her mouth was like cotton, her feverish body already burning in the fires of hell. Hunger was a knife twisting in her empty gut. The sun was at its zenith. By nightfall her corpse would be rotting in the dust. But the indians were not about to allow so valuable a slave to die. When they deemed her sufficiently demoralized they would act to keep her alive for their own vile purposes.

Amanda barely roused from her stupor at the approach of footsteps. But when a gourd of cool water was held to her lips she drank so greedily she had to be restrained lest she become sick.

"Easy, Princess," warned an oddly familiar voice from out of her past. "Don't drink too fast."

It took a few minutes for Amanda's fuzzy brain to register the fact that the woman squatting beside her spoke English.

"Who. . . who are you?" she asked through cracked, bleeding lips.

"Later," warned the woman casting a furtive glance around.

Amanda found it difficult to focus her blurry eyes on the figure and was unable to identify her before she turned to leave. But she had left the gourd of water and Amanda eagerly grabbed it up again and drank her fill.

During the long afternoon Amanda was completely ignored by the indians, men and women alike. Occasionally a group of children would stop their play to gape and jeer at her. Once a small, grubby child had bravely toddled closeby and dropped a piece of some kind of flat bread which Amanda had eagerly snatched up from the dirt and popped into her mouth like a starving animal.

At dusk tantalizing odors of food cooking over

open fires wafted to Amanda on the breeze. Hunger was a palpable, clawing ache that never left her. Resting her head on her knees, eyes closed, she dreamed of the delicious dinner Jemma would be preparing about now. A sob of abject misery escaped her bruised lips.

"I've brought some food for you, Princess."

That voice again! Amanda raised her head and looked into sky blue eyes set in a perky face covered with freckles. Brassy hair had been braided and toned down with some kind of grease but there was no mistaking the quick smile of Peony, the convict who had accompanied her to South Carolina aboard the prison ship.

"Peony, is that you? I can't believe it. What are you doing here with these savages?" Amazement followed disbelief across Amanda's sunburned face.

"I. . . I can't talk now but I'll tell you everything when I come back for you later."

"Come back for me? Where am I going?"

A strange look settled on Peony's features. Compassion? Pity? A tingle of apprehension prickled Amanda's spine. "Tell me, Peony, what have these savages planned for me?"

"I can't right now, Princess, believe me. I'm leaving some hot food for you. You'll have to eat with your fingers but the food is good and nourishing. Please eat it all, you. . . you'll need your strength to get you through the next hours." Then cat-like she was gone.

Amanda didn't take the time to analyze Peony's ominous words. If she had she would have been unable to swallow one bite of the delicious stew thick with vegetables and meat she tentatively identified as rabbit. As it was she bolted the entire bowl down so fast that she came close to losing it just as quickly. After breathing deeply and swallowing several times, the lump in her throat dissolved and thankfully the ache in her gut somewhat diminished. There was still a bit of water left in the gourd and she sipped at it sparingly, uncertain when she would be given more.

Still exhausted from her ardous trek through the woods and abusive treatment, Amanda fell asleep before Peony returned later that evening. She awoke with a jolt to find herself being prodded in the ribs by a moccasined toe. Brave Fox stood over her, Peony slightly behind. With a jerk Brave Fox untied her from the tree and brought her swiftly to her feet, leading her like a dog on a leash past the main cluster of dwellings to a single tent set apart from the others. Brave Fox motioned her inside and wordlessly she obeyed, followed meekly by Peony. To Amanda's surprise Brave Fox took a post just outside the flap, hunkered down on his haunches and prepared to wait for Amanda knew not what.

Peony motioned toward a bearskin pallet and Amanda sat down warily, her questioning eyes speaking more eloquently than words. A fire burned in a firepit at the center of the tent providing just enough light to make out Peony's features. Her face purposefully expressionless, Peony knelt before Amanda and removed the makeshift rope from around her neck, clucking loudly at the raw burns marring her tender flesh.

"Peony, please tell me what's going on," pleaded Amanda. "What will happen to me?"

"First things first, Princess," Peony hedged, deliberately avoiding Amanda's question. With Brave Fox just outside the door she knew she could not put off for long what she must eventually tell Amanda.

From the corner of the tent Peony uncovered a water jar and with a soft piece of deer hide began gently to wash Amanda's bruised body, wincing as each black and blue mark brought back painful memories of her own ordeal before she was adopted into the tribe. If only Amanda was as lucky as she had been, Peony sighed, her heart heavy with pity for the proud spirited girl now brought so low. It was because of that same pride that Amanda had been dubbed Princess so long ago and Peony remembered how she had once used it derisively. But somehow the name fit admirably. The will to survive burned brightly in Amanda's green eyes and Peony wondered if Amanda would feel the same tomorrow. Somehow she doubted it.

After Amanda had been washed and the tangles combed from her hair with a bone comb Peony produced from a pouch at her waist, Peony knew she could no longer delay informing Brave Fox's captive what her fate was to be. Sensing Peony's uneasiness, Amanda sat back on the bearskin and waited nervously, more frightened than she had ever been in her life.

"Amanda," began Peony hesitantly, "I. . . that is, Brave Fox is waiting outside for me to explain what will happen to you later tonight."

"Brave Fox?"

"The brave who captured you. His name is Brave Fox. He. . . he is the one who raped you first. It is the way of the Cherokee. Female captives are almost always raped immediately."

Amanda flushed painfully, remembering the horror of Brave Fox's assault. "Were you raped, also?"

286

"Yes," nodded Peony solemnly. "There were six in the raiding party that captured me. The preacher and his wife were on their way to visit friends upcountry when the indians attacked us. They killed everyone but me. But before they brought me here all six of them raped me."

"Oh, Peony," commiserated Amanda, "how terrible for you."

"Ha!" laughed Peony scornfully. "Not any worse nor any better than having to submit to that animal who called himself a preacher. He was the worst, Princess, and believe me, in my profession I seen them all."

Amanda's face turned a bright pink. "I'm sorry you had such a bad time of it, Peony. If it wasn't for Tony your fate would have been mine."

"Better me, Princess. You weren't made for that kind of life. Me, I just took it in stride, but I wasn't sorry to see the last of that hypocrite and his mean-tempered shrew of a wife."

A loud grunt from outside the tent alerted Peony to the fact that she was taking too much time and Brave Fox was becoming impatient. She did not look forward to his brand of punishment so she hurried on.

"Listen, Princess," she said softly, "I'd rather do anything than be the one to tell you this but I'm the only one what can speak good enough English to explain."

Amanda froze, every nerve ending in her body tingling in fear. "Explain what?"

"Very soon you'll hear the drums. The men will perform a purification ceremony that usually takes place after all the raiding parties have returned. There will be dancing and chanting and a potent drink will be consumed in large quantities." Peony paused dramatically.

"Then what, Peony? My God, tell me! If you have any pity, tell me!"

"I do have pity, that's why it's difficult for me to put it into words." Amanda waited, her face a study of hopelessness and despair.

"Did you happen to notice that this tent is set apart from the others?" Amanda nodded mutely. "This tent is to be yours. It is also a place set aside for the village whore."

"Village whore!" gasped Amanda in total shock. "Do you mean that I... that I..."

"Exactly," Peony grimaced. "After the ceremony tonight each man in the tribe, beginning with the four who captured you, will rape you in full view of the entire tribe."

"No! Oh God, no!" gasped out Amanda, her face a white oval in the dim light. "Don't let it be so!" Her eyes grew wild, her breath a hard lump in her chest.

Brave Fox chose that moment to burst into the tent, grinning evily. He barked out a few curt words to Peony who immediately backed out of the door after slanting a piteous look at Amanda.

"What does he want?" cried out Amanda, her eyes pleading as Peony disappeared from sight. But Peony's words came back to her through the tent flap.

"He was just waiting for me to tell you about... about tonight. When you cried out he knew I had done what he asked. He thinks you are still too proud and defiant and... and intends to... further demoralize you before the ceremony takes place. Female slaves are supposed to be submissive and meek. They believe that too much spirit renders a slave useless for their purposes."

"Oh dear God," sobbed Amanda, completely destroyed when she realized that what had happened to her on the trail would happen again.

Brave Fox turned beady eyes on Amanda's cringing form and dropped to the bearskin beside her, pushing her rudely onto her back. Amanda fought back bravely when he drew aside his loincloth and taunted her. But he did not enter her. Instead, he deliberately pinched her tender nipples, grunting in satisfaction when they grew erect despite Amanda's fear and pain. She screamed when he bit into her white flesh, and he smiled maliciously when she fainted. Then he left, satisfied that she was sufficiently cowed.

When she came to Peony was bending over her, compassion flooding her pixie face.

"Did. . . did the same thing happen to you?" Amanda choked out. "How did you live through it?"

"No, Princess. Something happened that saved me from your fate. Don't ask me how or why it happened, but it did."

Suddenly the sound of drums reverberated through the night and Amanda drew in her breath sharply. "Can't you help me, Peony? Isn't there something you can do?"

Peony shook her head sadly. "Believe me, I would help if I could but there is nothing I can do. There are too many and I am only one woman."

Amanda seemed to shrink into herself, her small shoulders quivering. "What happened to save you?" she asked, still hoping for some miracle.

"The brave who captured me, Deer Stalker, decided he wanted me for his second wife. I was not raped again after that first time but was kept tied to the post for several days while the chief decided if I should be adopted into the tribe and given to Deer Stalker. I. . . I have a baby," she said shyly. "I never thought I could be happy, but I am. In his own way, Deer Stalker is kind to me and seems fond of the baby."

"What if one of the braves wants me? Will I be given to him?"

"I'm afraid not. Only the man who captures you has the right to ask for you. If he doesn't want you then you will become the camp drudge and. . . whore."

"Oh God," sobbed Amanda as a fresh torrent of tears coursed down her cheeks. "Then Brave Fox. . ."

"Didn't want you," finished Peony lamely. "He believes you incapable of becoming a meek wife to him and it is his wish that you should be given over to the tribe."

"No!" asserted Amanda in a sudden spurt of grim determination, her small, pointed chin thrust outward. "I will not become whore for a tribe of savages! I will kill myself first!"

"Princess," contended Peony sadly, "how do you propose to do that?"

"You can help me, Peony. There is no way they can blame you if I kill myself. I once vowed to end my life if ever I was faced with such a situation. I'll do it without your help, Peony, but you can make it easier for me. Bring me a knife. Please!" Her anguished plea tore at Peony's heart.

"I don't know," said Peony skeptically, pausing several minutes to ponder Amanda's request. In her heart she knew Amanda spoke the truth. A girl such as Amanda could not be expected to submit willingly or to take lightly her role as whore to a tribe of indians. As for herself, she was happy in her new life. Deer Stalker treated her well, especially after she bore him a son. She was no longer mistreated by the women of the tribe and enjoyed full freedom. Even if she were to be returned to civilization what would she have to look forward to? More years of slavery, perhaps. Then back to her old life of prostitution. She would probably die young of disease. No, she'd take her chances with the indians, Peony decided.

Sensing Peony's indicision Amanda's pleas grew more fervent, "Please, Peony, bring me a knife before those savages finish their ceremony and come for me."

Amanda's eyes, wide and horror-stricken, were what finally decided Peony. "You win, Princess. I'll help you if you promise to wait until the last possible minute before... before doing... it. Perhaps I can persuade Brave Fox to change his mind."

"I promise," Amanda readily agreed. "Only hurry, please." She did not add that she was not sure she would want to live even if Brave Fox wanted her for himself. Not after having known Tony's love. Aloud she said, "I don't think I would want to be wife to a red savage."

"It's not so bad, Princess," confessed Peony shyly. "I have my son. And I'm even fond of Deer Slayer. I'm accepted now and wouldn't go back even if I could. Being Deer Slayer's woman is far better than spreading my legs for all the rough seamen in Charles Town and eventually dying of the pox."

"I don't mean to criticize, Peony, because you did what you thought was right for you. I am doing what I feel is right given my circumstances. Don't deny me the choice to die my own hand rather than be violated by a hundred savages and end up dying anyway."

"No, Princess, I told you I'd help you, but I still want your promise to wait until there is no hope left. The drums will be your signal. When they stop you'll have a few minutes to. . . do what you have to do."

"Is there any hope at all for escape? You haven't mentioned that possibility."

"I haven't mentioned it because it is virtually impossible. Even now there is a guard outside. If you did manage somehow to get away how far would you go naked and barefoot, without food and water? If you are determined to die it's best to do so quickly."

"Thank you, Peony. I never thought we would one day become friends or that I would be begging you for help. I do promise to wait at least until the drums stop."

"You could still be saved at the last minute. Stranger things have been known to happen," shrugged Peony doubtfully. "But no matter what, I'll never forget you. You'll have your knife. Goodby, Princess, may you find the courage to do what's necessary." Then she slipped wraith-like from the tent leaving Amanda alone to ponder her short life and those few months of happiness she had shared with Tony.

The drums continued for what seemed like hours as Amanda waited for Peony to return. Each blood-curdling yell renting the stillness caused her to cringe inwardly. "Peony, where are you?" she whimpered into the darkness.

Amanda offered up a silent prayer of thanks

when Peony finally appeared in the doorway. Mutely, Peony placed a gourd of water and a bowl of food at her feet. As she straightened up she pulled a thin, sharp blade used for skinning deer from her long sleeve and placed it in Amanda's hand. Then she was gone.

Amanda had no appetite. Nor was she thirsty. With the moment of death at hand she spent what she thought were her last minutes on earth bidding a silent goodby to her son. And to Tony. How happy life could have been for the three of them. She knew that Jemma would care for Jon and hoped they wouldn't let him forget her. Suddenly Amanda was aware of the sound of absolute silence. The drums had ceased! Resolutely, she grasped the handle of the knife in her sweat drenched hands and raised it directly above her heart.

16

Exhausted, hollow-eyed and frantic with worry, Tony watched the Cherokee village under cover of a copse of trees approximately one hundred yards distant. Nathan and Francis, equally weary and desperate, flanked him on either side. They could see that some sort of ceremony was in progress but knowing little of Indian lore or tradition had no idea what was taking place. The men of the tribe were the main participants and as they danced around a huge fire to the tattoo of drums they drank freely from gourds filled with some kind of liquid that appeared to increase their wild contortions and piercing cries. Every now and again one of the braves would stop and gesture obscenely toward a tent set apart from the others. It was to that tent that Tony now trained his bloodshot eyes.

As far as he could tell he and his companions could not be more than two days behind the raiding party that had taken Amanda. Twice they had become lost and only Nathan's tracking skills had put them on the right trail again. A terrible moment had come when they stumbled upon the remnants of Amanda's torn and blood-spattered clothing, pieces of rope and ominous signs of a struggle in the tall grass. Each man stared grimly at the indisputible evidence, fully cognizant of the fact that Amanda had probably been ravished by the Indians at that very spot and might even now be dead, or worse yet, driven mad by the horrifying experience.

Tony fell to his knees, striking the ground in impotent fury. How could a young and gentle girl like Amanda hope to survive vicious rape by savages? he raged inwardly. What had she ever done to deserve such unjust and cruel punishment? She had to be alive, he fervently prayed. If she survived, somehow, someway, he would get her back, and never let her go again. He vowed to protect, cherish and love her for the rest of her days. And if her terrifying abuse at the hands of savages left her unable to bear the physical side of marriage, well, he would cross that bridge when he came to it. For it was entirely likely that Amanda would never want a man to touch her again. He prayed his love would be enough to overcome whatever fears Amanda might retain as a result of being raped.

Tony, Nathan and Francis had pressed on tirelessly, eating in the saddle, sleeping little, determined to find Amanda, yet fearful that she might already be dead. No one spoke, there was nothing to say. When Nathan lost the trail causing them to wander aimlessly for several hours, Tony nearly went out of his mind. When they suddenly and unexpectedly came upon the Cherokee village,

his relief and exhilaration was so great that he had
to be forcibly restrained from rushing headlong
into the hostile camp.

It was nearly dark when they reached the
village and shortly afterwards the celebration
began. Of Amanda there was no sign.

"Do. . . do you think she is still alive?" Tony
asked in a hushed voice. "With all she's had to
endure it might be preferable if she. . ." His words
trailed off but his meaning was all too clear.

"Don't say it, Tony," reprimanded Nathan
sternly. "Don't even think it. Amanda is strong and
resourceful. Look at what she's already endured
and survived."

"My God, Nathan, you know as well as I what
they've done to her! Put yourself in her place.
She. . . she told me once she would kill herself
before submitting to rape. You know yourself that
more than one. . ." He choked back a sob. "I'm
afraid she may already be. . ." Tony could not go
on. The thought of Amanda's slim, white body
being brutalized by scores of savages fired his
blood until only the restraining hands of his
companions kept him from losing his head and
stalking openly into the camp.

"Tony," Francis warned in a strained voice.
"Keep your head, man. You will do Amanda no
good if you rush in there and get yourself killed in
the process."

After that they played the waiting game. Upon
closer observation they unaminously agreed that
someone of importance was being confined to that
lone tent set apart and guarded. They remained
watchful, eyes focused on the tent in hopes that
their intuition proved correct. Their vigil was
rewarded when they saw a small figure, obviously

a woman, enter the tent and leave again, all within a few minutes.

"That does it," announced Tony, exultant. "I believe Amanda is being held in that tent. Look," he pointed excitedly. "See how those savages keep gesturing toward it? I'm right, I know it!"

"You may have something there," agreed Francis with alacrity.

Nathan nodded, flushing darkly. "A friend of mine who visited a Cherokee village once told me about a custom of theirs. Women captives were confined and used as whores by the whole tribe."

"Amanda would kill herself first," muttered Tony with grim conviction. "If what you say is true, Nathan, then Amanda is already dead."

"Not necessarily," countered Francis thoughtfully. "Perhaps she hasn't been forced to submit yet. It's a distinct possibility that Amanda is in that tent waiting for the braves to finish their ceremony before they. . . they. . ." God, Tony, don't make me spell it out."

"If only I could believe that," answered Tony fervently, unwilling to believe a woman as vital as Amanda could be dead.

"Let me go to her," insisted Nathan. "If Amanda is in there and she's alive I'll get her out or die trying."

"No!" grated out Tony. "If anyone goes for Amanda it will be me. So far the indians are unaware of our presence. While they are still carrying on around the campfire I'll make my way around to the back of the tent and attempt to enter from the rear. Thank God there is no moon tonight and the shadows are deep enough to conceal my movements."

He paused for a moment, his mind working

furiously. "Francis, bring the horses around through the woods and wait for me to appear with Amanda. Nathan, you can help by creating a diversion and scattering the indians' ponies. They may have left a guard so be careful. By the looks of it their ceremony should keep them occupied for a while yet. Keep one of the horses for yourself and ride like hell. We'll rendezvous in the woods near Saddle Creek as soon as I have Amanda safely away."

"What if Amanda isn't in that tent?" Nathan asked fearfully.

"That's a chance I'll take," answered Tony, undaunted. Then, drawing a deep, steadying breath, he briefly clasped each man on the shoulder and said, "Let's move!"

Dropping to his stomach Tony noiselessly crawled, inch by painful inch, around the perimeter of the village until he was some yards behind the rear of the tent that he believed held Amanda captive. Scarcely daring to breathe he wormed forward, acutely conscious of every sound, the rustle of leaves beneath him, a snapped twig, all of which sounded like thunder in his ears. But he needn't have worried. The drums all but drowned out every other sound for miles around. Even the camp dogs, sated from their feast of leftovers from the banquet, paid him no mind.

It seemed like hours but was in reality only minutes before Tony reached his destination and crouched on all fours, listening intently. When no sound was forthcoming he drew out his knife with shaking hands and carefully made a long slit in the taut canvas. Silently he slipped through the opening. What he saw turned his insides to jelly and caused great beads of sweat to break out on his forehead.

Her nude body turned to a pale gold statue, Amanda knelt before the dying embers of a fire, both hands upraised, the razor-sharp point of a dagger aimed directly at her heart. As if hypnotized, Tony stared numbly as the blade unerringly descended toward a delicately curved breast, her hand steady, her features set. Focusing on her face Tony could see that Amanda's lips were pressed tightly together so that no sound could burst forth.

Suddenly the night was filled with the sound of absolute silence and Tony instinctively realized he must act swiftly or it would be too late for Amanda as well as for himself.

"Amanda, no!" he called out softly, leaping forward at the same time in an effort to deflect the downward thrust of the dagger.

Amanda froze the moment she heard Tony's voice, but was powerless to halt the momentum of the deadly weapon meant to end her life. If Tony hadn't knocked her hand aside the blade would have found its mark. As it was the point only grazed her shoulder in a superficial wound. But Amanda felt no pain. The miraculous appearance of Tony in time to prevent her death had been too much for her. She was unconscious long before Tony snatched up her slight form and exited through the same opening he had made earlier.

Crouching low, he reached the line of trees some yards from the Cherokee camp in record time. He breathed a sigh of thanks when he saw Francis waiting for him with their horses. He spared but a moment to wrap a blanket hastily extracted from his saddlebag around Amanda; leaping on his horse he settled her in front of him.

Then all hell broke loose in the Indian camp.

Brave Fox's howl of rage was enough to curdle the blood, causing Tony to spur his mount ruthlessly, anxious to put as much distance as possible between himself and the Cherokee village.

Within minutes they encountered Nathan who had successfully managed to scatter the indians' hoard of stolen horses. It wasn't too difficult to outdistance their pursuers since the indians were on foot and slightly inebriated besides, but Tony wasn't taking any chances by slowing their pace. Soon darkness and the dense forest closed around them as the war cries behind them grew dimmer and dimmer. Still they rode on without respite, finally stopping when fingers of dawn lit the sky, and then only out of concern for Amanda.

Sometime during the long night Tony felt Amanda stir in his arms but she did not speak. She seemed quite content to lean against his hard frame, her face turned into his chest. Automatically his arms tightened around her slim form. What was she thinking? he wondered worriedly. Did she still wish for death? What had they done to her? Would she be grateful to him for rescuing her? Or angry because he foiled her suicide attempt? God, how he loved her! If only his love was strong enough to make her forget what had happened, he prayed.

When they finally halted beside a stream, Francis and Nathan immediately took themselves off to hunt for food leaving Tony and Amanda alone. Tenderly he lifted her from his mount and sat her down on the soft ground with her back resting against a sturdy tree trunk. She remained silent while he carefully washed and bandaged her knife wound. He tried to make light of her injury, assuring her that in time the scar would be hardly noticeable. All the while her long, dark lashes fanned her pale cheeks, deliberately hiding her thoughts from him.

"Amanda, look at me," Tony urged gently, putting a finger under her chin to tilt it upward. The lashes quivered but did not raise. "Open your eyes, darling. I love you. Nothing can change that."

Slowly Amanda raised her eyes. Unintentionally Tony flinched at the naked pain visible in their fathomless green depths. Mistaking his reaction for revulsion she thought he must be feeling for her, Amanda allowed two fat tears to slide from beneath lowered lids.

"Don't hide from me, Amanda," Tony commanded. "I don't care what those savages did to you. Don't you understand? It doesn't matter, Nothing matters because I love you."

Finally Amanda found the courage to speak, but her voice was flat and emotionless. "You. . . you know what they did to me? All four of them. I fought, but. . . I was too weak, too exhausted to prevent what happened. After the first one I passed out. I don't even know how many times I was raped. When I came to my senses hours later, it was all over. How could you still love and want me knowing I have been defiled by savages?"

"Haven't you been listening to a word I've said?" Tony chided gently. "It doesn't matter to me. You're still the same woman I love and still want for a wife."

"But. . . Tony. . . Indians!" Savages! How can I hold up my head again? I'll take my son and leave. You deserve better."

"Damn it, Amanda! Stop feeling sorry for yourself. Where is that high spirited girl I fell in love with?"

Tony would do or say anything to shock her out of her apathy even if it took deliberate cruelty on his part. "Do you think I'd let you take my son away from me? he taunted mercilessly. "No, Amanda. Even if you leave me my son stays. I've already made up a will naming Jon my heir. River's Edge belongs to him and there he'll stay."

Sadness dimmed Amanda's green eyes and Tony's heart constricted painfully. "You would take my son from me, Tony?" she asked, her voice trembling.

"It's not what I want, darling. I want you both. Jon needs his mother and I need you, too. You are a part of me. You pull all the pieces of my life together and give it meaning. Don't forsake us Amanda."

Amanda searched Tony's face and saw nothing but love and tenderness. "Do you really mean that, Tony? After what those savages did to me?"

Tony's harsh voice grated in her ears, temporarily stilling her protests. "From this moment forward neither of us will ever mention this incident in your life. It will be as if it never happened. Do you understand, darling? What could four indians do to change you from the warm, loving woman I love? Of course, if you don't love me enough. . ."

Then, without knowing how, she was in his arms, weeping, laughing, his kisses healing her spirit, feeding her soul. Until his caresses became too ardent and she stiffened, drawing back, fear freezing her mobile features.

"What is it, my love? What have I done?"

Blushing, Amanda managed, "It's not you, Tony. "It's. . . it's me. I'm not sure I have anything to give anymore. I feel so dead inside. After those savages I . . . I am not able to respond to you. Are you willing to have me, only half a woman?"

Elated, Tony smiled broadly, his mouth a wide slash in his tanned face. "Contrary to your beliefs I can be a patient man when need be, my love. But for now just knowing that we love each other and that you forgive me for all the pain I've caused you is enough for me."

Tenderly, Tony helped Amanda into the dress Jemma had thoughtfully provided before he left River's Edge, exclaiming angrily over every· hurt and bruise on her battered body. What caused him the most anguish were the rope burns around her slender neck and teeth marks on her breasts. If Letty had been anywhere near he would have strangled her without a moment's regret. But he purposefully masked any sympathy he might have felt lest Amanda think pity was all he felt for her.

When Nathan and Francis returned with two rabbits they were greeted by a woman completely different from the apathetic creature they had left in Tony's care just a short time before. Though a hint of overlaying sadness lingered about her violet-smudged eyes, Amanda, shyly at first, then with growing warmth, joined into their conversation. She ate heartily of the roasted rabbit, washing it down with cool water, then promptly fell asleep.

While Amanda slept Tony revealed some of what she had related to him concerning her·ordeal as a captive of Brave Fox and his raiding party.

Nathan cried shamelessly when Tony confided that she had been repeatedly raped and mistreated by the indians. But the telling of Amanda's suffering proved too much for Nathan. Abruptly he rose and stalked off by himself until he was able to control his emotions.

"He loves her, you know," Francis said, nodding his head toward the departing Nathan. "This has been as hard on him as it is on you."

"I know," admitted Tony wearily. "And it pains me to think how I almost lost her. How could I have been so stupid, Francis? Even though Letty is to blame I feel responsible for Amanda's suffering. I shudder to think how close I came to marrying that blonde witch."

Francis stared hard at Tony, trying to resolve something in his own mind. Finally, coming to a decision, he asked, "What do you know of Amanda's life in England? Before she came to Carolina on the prison ship?"

"Only what she told me," replied Tony, puzzled. "Why?"

"Then she never told you she met you before coming here?"

"What are you talking about? I've never met Amanda before that day I first saw her aboard the prison ship. Although," he mused thoughtfully, "from the first I've had the strangest feeling that I've known her from somewhere in the past. But that's ridiculous."

"Not as ridiculous as you think, Tony. You did know Amanda. As intimately as any man knows a woman."

"You're crazy, Francis!" exploded Tony indignantly. "I assure you I can remember the women I've bedded and Amanda isn't one of them.

Why, she couldn't have been more than a child then. Barely sixteen at the most. Give me some credit."

"That was her exact age, Tony, when you deflowered her." At Tony's scandalized expression and fervent denials, Francis added quickly, "But you weren't entirely to blame." Then he went on to relate all he knew about that night in England so long ago when he and his comrades mistook Amanda for a young prostitute.

When he finished Tony was thoroughly shaken. He cursed himself for a fool, blaming himself for everything that Amanda had endured, beginning with the time he had callously stolen her virginity, until now.

"Why didn't she tell me?" asked Tony, baffled.

"You'll have to ask her that one yourself, my friend," Francis answered cryptically. "But if I were to venture a guess I'd say her pride is as strong as yours. I'm not even certain I should be telling you this for if Amanda wanted you to know she would have told you herself."

"Thank you for telling me, Francis. I'm sure that one day Amanda will come to trust me enough to confide in me completely. And I promise to make it all up to her somehow. I want her for my wife. Nothing would make me happier than to spend the rest of my life with her."

Shortly after that conversation Nathan returned and Tony awakened Amanda. Soon they were back on the trail traveling at an easy pace to accommodate Amanda. They did not halt again until nightfall, eating what was left of the rabbit. Afterwards Francis disappeared to take the first watch and Nathan tactfully withdrew to sleep some distance away behind a tuft of brush.

Wordlessly Tony made up a bed for himself and Amanda amidst the tall grass that grew along the riverbank.

At first Amanda lay stiffly beside Tony, hardly daring to move, but once she realized he only meant to hold her close she relaxed and fell asleep. Not so Tony. It was torture feeling Amanda's softness curling so trustingly in the crook of his arm without making love to her. But he was determined to do nothing to destroy that thin line of trust, still so fragile that an overt move on his part could send her fleeing from him.

At first light the four riders were once again on the trail. Amanda felt well enough to ride by herself and they made much better time. Her shoulder wound caused her little or no pain. Some of the purple smudges had disappeared from beneath her eyes and the worry lines etched across Tony's forehead were miraculously eased. Francis hummed a tuneless ditty and even Nathan was considerably more cheerful now that Amanda was back with them safe and sound. Even if Amanda could never be his, Nathan contended, at least she was alive and well and in fairly good spirits considering her harrowing experience. It didn't seem possible that only days ago they had started out on a seemingly hopeless rescue mission, for if the truth be known, not one of them expected to find Amanda alive.

Because of their slow pace they were forced to spend another night on the trail, choosing a small clearing for their camp. But it worried Tony little for he doubted the indians would trail them so far from the village. Once again Nathan and Francis hunted while Tony built a fire to cook their catch of rabbits. They had not built a fire the night before in the remote chance that they may have been followed, but as the day passed Tony was so confident that they were out of danger he saw no need to post a watch. Nathan and Francis agreed and they took their horses with them into the woods where they bedded down even a greater distance from Amanda and Tony than they had the night before.

As he had done the previous night Tony spread his blanket down and he and Amanda lay side by side, barely touching at first. But as the night grew colder Amanda curled her body into Tony's warmth and automatically his hand sought the tender curve of her breast. He felt the nipple peak beneath his palm and he could not stop himself from slipping his fingers into her bodice to test the warmth of her flesh. Half asleep, Amanda murmured a protest which Tony promptly ignored, needing her desperately as he did. He was so encouraged by Amanda's apparent willingness that he ran a hand beneath her dress, along a sweetly fashioned thigh to rest lovingly on her silky mound.

When he eagerly parted the lush forest of curling hair to massage the tiny peak situated directly above pouting lips, Amanda came fully awake, crying out in such distress that Tony immediately desisted.

"I won't hurt you, my love," he whispered gently. "I want to make love to you. I need you."

"No, Tony," Amanda quivered. "I can't be touched like that. Not now, not yet. Please don't force me."

"I am not a monster, Amanda. I love you. And I promise one day soon you will want me. Until then I will do nothing further to frighten or harm you." Entirely unconvinced that Tony could still want her despite the fact that she had been sullied by the indians, Amanda finally fell asleep. But it was a long time before Tony followed her to slumberland.

Neither Tony, Nathan or Francis had any idea that Brave Fox would pursue them with such single-minded tenacity. Along with White Feather and another brave named Running Bear, they managed to catch three of the ponies set loose by Nathan, and after arming themselves began immediately to track their hapless prey, hoping to catch them unawares. Brave Fox, proud, defiant, arrogant, would never live down the shame of allowing a female captive to be stolen from under his nose. He had promised the men of his tribe a whore and he would not go back on his word.

Brave Fox and his companions easily found the small stream where Tony had tended to Amanda's injury and they paused briefly to drink and water their horses. Smiling maliciously, Brave Fox knew he and his friends couldn't be more than a few hours behind their runaway captive and her rescuer, and he happily contemplated the many and varied tortures he would inflict upon the pair.

Because both Francis and Nathan had waited in the woods they had not been seen by the indians. Only Tony had been spotted by the wily Brave Fox carrying Amanda's limp body through the woods to where Francis awaited with their horses.

"We cannot be too far behind," Brave Fox remarked, screwing his mouth into an evil grimace.

"They travel slow to accommodate the

woman," White Feather said sullenly. "Because of you I have not had a taste of her white flesh. You should have allowed me to take her on the trail as I wanted to."

"You shall have your fill of the woman, I promise," boasted Brave Fox grimly. "As will every man in the tribe." White Feather grunted, mollified for the time being.

At nightfall encroaching darkness prevented them from continuing and they huddled in a circle munching parched corn and hardtack, refusing to light a fire so as not to alert the fleeing couple. At first light they were off again, knowing that by nightfall they would not only have their whore back but a white man as well to torture at will.

The remnants of Tony's campfire drew Brave Fox and his companions like a beacon, causing White Feather to remark scornfully, "Did they think we would give up so easily? Or do they believe we are children unskilled in the art of tracking?"

"I will kill them while they sleep," Running Bear announced grandly, brandishing his tomahawk.

"No!" growled Brave Fox, exercising his right as leader. "We will take them alive. The man will suffer greatly for what he has done. The woman will be put to better use." If the truth be known Brave Fox had thoroughly enjoyed raping Amanda and had not yet had his fill of her.

Because Nathan and Francis had moved far into the woods with their horses to spend the night, the braves saw only Amanda and Tony asleep beside the dying fire with their mounts grazing nearby. They had purposely left their own ponies some distance away and crept on their stomachs to the edge of the small clearing, crouching behind a fallen log as they awaited a signal from Brave Fox.

A curt nod from Brave Fox and they slithered noiselessly into the clearing, not even a snapped twig alerting the sleeping couple. Raising his tomahawk menacingly, Brave Fox expertly brought the blunt edge against Amanda's temple with just enough force to render her unconscious. A soft sigh was all there was to alert Tony of their danger. But it was too late. He heard the escapage of breath and felt Amanda's body shudder and go still, and instinctively he reached for his pistol.

White Feather had anticipated Tony's reflexive move and forestalled it effectively by whacking Tony's head with the side of his tomahawk, employing twice the force Brave Fox used on Amanda.

Still working stealthily, they were too close to civilization to relax their vigilance; the three tied Amanda and Tony face down over the backs of their horses, arms and legs bound beneath the horses' stomach much as Amanda had been bound and transported the first time she had been captured. Satisfied with their night's work, they began the long trek back to their village.

It was hours before Amanda opened her eyes to the light of day. Her head hurt so badly she thought at first she had been scalped and somehow survived. But as her mind began to clear she realized how foolish her assumption. Almost at the same time the haze before her eyes dissipated and she could see that she once again hung ignominiously across the back of a horse, helplessly tied hand and foot.

Indians! The thought was a scream in her

brain. Somehow the savages had tracked their small party and come upon them while they lay sleeping! "Oh, God, no!" Amanda cried out in anguish.

Her only reply was a whack upon her tender backside and an unintelligible grunt from one of her captors, causing her to cry out again, this time in pain.

Twisting her head about with difficulty, Amanda saw that Tony was trussed up and immobilized in the same manner as she was. Not only that but she could see the trickle of blood seeping from a gash on his forehead. "Tony, you're hurt!" she cried when she saw his eyes blink open.

"Not badly, Amanda," he managed to gasp out. "Please save your strength, my love. Before this is over with you'll need it."

White Feather, who had been leading Tony's horse, turned around and shouted a guttural oath which Tony took as a warning. Fearing that Amanda would suffer needlessly if they continued their conversation, he immediately became silent, his expressive silver eyes telling her of his sorrow.

White Feather spurred his pony, taking Tony's mount along with him, effectively preventing further contact between Tony and Amanda.

Suddenly Amanda thought of Francis and Nathan, and her spirits rose, until the horrible thought entered her mind that White Feather had killed the two brave men who had accompanied Tony on his rescue mission. Otherwise they would be in the same desperate situation in which she and Tony found themselves, Amanda reflected dismally. But there was still a chance, albeit a slim one, that the indians had not discovered Francis and Nathan asleep in the woods, that help could still arrive in time to save her and Tony.

Throughout the long day the Indians did not bother to release Tony and Amanda from their uncomfortable positions. Nor were they offered food or water although their own thirst was quenched at several of the numerous streams in the vicinity and their hunger appeased by munching on parched corn and jerky. Amanda, still weak from her previous ordeal, passed in and out of consciousness. In one of her more lucid moments she wondered how Tony was faring and decided if she had to die at least it would be with the man she loved.

Amanda awoke to find herself jerked roughly from her horse. Her stomach hurt dreadfully, her thighs and breasts were chaffed raw and she was nauseous. She collapsed in a heap on the ground and when she turned her head saw that Tony was being treated in much the same way. The moment Tony was released he attempted to go to Amanda but a well-aimed kick from Brave Fox quickly disabused him of that notion.

For the first time Amanda saw the face of her captors as Brave Fox grinned down evily at her. He laughed harshly as she quailed before him, recalling vividly what had taken place the last time he had looked upon her with lust in his dark eyes. Would they rape her with Tony looking on? she groaned, her anguish twisting Tony's gut into knots.

It seemed as if Amanda's worst nightmare was about to be realized as Brave Fox fell upon her, tearing viciously at her clothes. "Take her like a dog, Brave Fox," laughed Running Bear, his loin-cloth insufficient to hide his own rising desire for Copper Hair, as Amanda had come to be known.

Brave Fox seemed to like the idea as he barked, "On your knees, whore!"

Amanda only looked at him stupidly. He pinched her breast cruelly and flipped her on her stomach, raising her knees until her buttocks rose temptingly in the air. When he shoved aside his loincloth baring his engorged manhood, Tony howled with outrage and not even White Feather's restraining hands or barked warning could keep him from reaching Amanda.

Determined that he would save Amanda from being raped again even if it cost him his life as well as the life of the woman he loved, which would probably be best in the long run, Tony threw himself at Brave Fox, struggling for the tomahawk the warrior carried in his waistband. He would kill Amanda himself, Tony vowed, before he would allow her to be abused and tortured again by these savages.

But Tony was only one man, unarmed and weak from being restrained in one position for hours on end. Though his strength and resolve was considerable it was nothing compared to three armed savages bent on rape. He was easily subdued by White Feather and Running Bear and rendered unconscious with the flat of a tomahawk wielded gleefully by Brave Fox. All this happened so fast that Amanda had no time to gain her wits and run, not that it would have done her any good.

"Tie the white-eyes to the tree," Brave Fox ordered brusquely, turning his attention back to Amanda to take up where he left off before Tony's untimely as well as short-lived intervention.

Still on her knees, terror released Amanda's wits as she began to scramble to her feet. Almost instantly her face was shoved into the dirt and her knees lifted while White Feather and Running Bear, just returned from securing Tony's unconscious form to a tree, laughed raucously, blatantly exposing themselves before Amanda's shocked eyes.

"Hurry, Brave Fox," White Feather urged excitedly. "By rights I should have her first for you denied me before."

"I will have Copper Hair first," Brave Fox proclaimed, effectively curbing further protest. Then he casually flipped up Amanda's skirt exposing her bare flesh while White Feather placed a moccasined foot on her neck in order to hold her still for his friend's assault. "You, White Feather, may have Copper Hair next," Brave Fox announced, appreciative of his companions help in subduing his captive. "Running Bear will be last. The night is young. Perhaps we will have her many times before the sun rises."

Grasping her buttocks hurtfully with both hands, Brave Fox prepared to enter Amanda's cringing flesh. Suddenly a loud scream rent the air. "Aieee!" Immediately Amanda felt the pressure on her neck lift and painfully swiveled her head to encounter Brave Fox's horrified expression.

All three braves seemed to be staring at Amanda's pale thighs but she hadn't a clue as to what made them treat her as if she were an object of scorn. But whatever it was she was grateful she had been spared the terrible indignity of being raped again and again by the three savages staring at her with repugnance. She could only hope that her reprieve was a permanent one.

"Do not touch her," spat Brave Fox, disgustedly. "She is unclean. You know the tabu against taking a woman whose time is upon her as well as I. To touch her now would bring disaster as well as contaminate us."

"Shall we kill her?" offered Running Bear, ready to do his worst when he realized his lust was to go unappeased.

"No," replied White Feather cunningly. "Do we kill our women when their moon time is upon them? In a few days she will be able to accommodate us. There is a stream nearby where she can purify herself when her time has run its course." Nothing was going to prevent him from tasting the white flesh of Copper Hair, he thought slyly.

"White Feather speaks the truth," declared Brave Fox. "Copper Hair will not be taken back to the village while she is unclean. She will remain here until after the purification rites which will cleanse her body. Once we have our fill of her she can take her place as village whore."

Amanda realized the three savages were talking about her but she still had no inkling as to what turned them away from her at the last minute. As they began backing away, she moved to put herself to rights, pulling her skirts down to cover her legs. She gasped aloud, suddenly aware of what had caused the savages to view her with disgust and saved her from rape. Running down her legs was a thin stream of blood and Amanda realized that her time of the month had come upon her.

Although unaware of the strict tribal tabu prohibiting sexual relations with a woman who was bleeding, Amanda realized with a start that she was only safe for a few days, that no doubt she would be raped when her menses ceased. The most she could hope for was three or four days. Perhaps she and Tony could come up with an effective plan for escape during that time, she thought hopefully.

The three braves appeared to be arguing about something among themselves when Amanda noticed that Tony was beginning to regain consciousness, and she cautiously crawled along the ground until she reached his side. Brave Fox watched her through slitted eyes but made no move to stop her. While she dabbed at the cut on Tony's forehead with a piece of her chemise, the warriors had come to a decision. Copper Hair would be taken off into the woods where a crude hut would be built to shield her from their eyes until the time of her purification ceremony.

White Feather and Running Bear set off to build the isolation hut out of sticks and leafy branches while Brave Fox remained behind. Meanwhile Amanda and Tony spoke in low tones. "I'm sorry, Amanda," Tony choked despairingly. "I tried to save you. Did. . . did they hurt you badly?"

"They didn't touch me, Tony," she quickly assured him.

Tony was astounded, thinking his befuddled brain was playing tricks on him. "But. . . I saw. . . I mean. . ."

"Something happened, Tony," Amanda explained when words failed him. "I didn't know it at the time but. . . but my woman's time began and they saw and refused to touch me after that."

"Thank God," breathed Tony, nearly collapsing with relief. He went on to explain about the tabu concerning women and how they were considered untouchable at the time of their menses.

"I'm surprised they allowed you to remain in sight," he told her, puzzled. "I have been told that Indian women have a separate tent apart from the others that they go to at that time so their men will not be offended by their unclean bodies. Other women bring them their meals and they do not emerge until their purification after they have stopped. . ."

Tony's words faltered and died as he saw White Feather and Running Bear, their task completed, join Brave Fox and start toward them. He had no idea what they were up to but tied up as he was he could offer no resistance.

Brave Fox, never quite meeting her eyes, made a few guttural sounds that Amanda ignored. When she failed to respond he became angry and quite animated, pointing and gesturing with violent motions.

"He seems to want you to move deeper into the woods, my love," Tony said fearfully.

"No, Tony," Amanda shook her head. "I won't go! I won't leave you!"

Brave Fox seemed to understand Amanda's negative response for he picked up a long stick and prodded her cruelly with the sharp end while his friends herded her without touching her toward the isolation hut they had just fashioned out of sticks and branches and vines.

His body trembling with impotent rage, Tony had no choice but to watch helplessly as Amanda was being prodded and pushed deeper into the woods, probably to be killed, for all he knew. As they were swallowed up by the dense growth, Tony struggled and strained against his bonds, but to no avail. He listened intently for a sound, any sound that would tell him that Amanda still lived.

Nothing but an ominous silence greeted his ears.

For the first time since he and Amanda had been captured, Tony had time to think about their desperate situation as well their chances of being rescued. His thoughts flew to Francis and Nathan and he quickly realized their only hope for escape lay with his two friends who might well have been slain while they slept by Brave Fox and his youthful companions.

The sudden appearance of Amanda's monthly time had been a Godsend. To Tony's way of thinking the braves wouldn't kill her but simply isolate her until her time was past and then take them back to their village where Tony would be slowly tortured and killed, while Amanda's fate, though no less painful, would not include death but a lifetime of bondage and sexual abuse. Tony began to pray fervently that Nathan and Francis had been overlooked by their captors and spared death, that they were even now seeking a way to aid them.

With trepidation, Amanda, goaded on by her tormentors, approached the rude dwelling hastily erected for her by her captors. It was crudely built of leafy branches and sticks held together by vines, and Amanda was forced to her hands and knees in order to enter. She saw that there was room to sit or lay but not enough to stand upright. Peeking through the chinks between the branches Amanda was disheartened to observe that two of the braves departed but left their companion to stand guard.

Sighing heavily, Amanda set about tearing strips of soft cloth from her petticoat to take care of her needs then sat down on the damp ground to ponder the deplorable situation in which she and

Tony found themselves. Shortly after dark a large leaf containing dried jerky and berries was pushed in to her with the end of a long stick as well as Tony's canteen filled with water. At least they weren't going to let her starve, Amanda thought dully as she gnawed hungrily on her meager fare. She could only hope Tony was being fed also.

Shortly afterwards exhaustion claimed her and she fell asleep. But not before she first checked to ascertain if her guard still stood sentinel. He did. Only this time White Feather had been appointed her keeper.

Nathan awoke first the morning that Tony and Amanda had been taken by the Indians, surprised to find that he had slept so long. Nearby, Francis still slept soundly and Nathan wondered if Tony and Amanda had also overslept. Hesitating lest he intrude upon the couple, Nathan awoke Francis first and together they tramped the short distance through the woods to the spot where they had left Tony and Amanda to make their bed for the night. The blanket they had shared still lay upon the ground, but of Tony and Amanda there was no visible sign.

When Francis discovered the two horses missing, he panicked, a premonition of dread prickling his spine. Nathan was the one to discover drops of blood splattered on the blanket and signs that indicated two bodies had been dragged the short distance through the underbrush to where their horses were tethered.

"Dear God," groaned Nathan, anguish twisting his features. "We were followed. Those damn savages have Tony and Amanda."

Francis looked confused. "Why weren't we killed or taken prisoner along with them? It doesn't make sense for them to leave us behind unharmed."

"They probably had no idea we were here," Nathan said thoughtfully. "We must have gone into the woods to make our beds before they came upon us and naturally assumed Tony and Amanda were alone."

"Do. . . do you think those bloody beasts have already. . . killed them?" Francis asked fearfully.

"No!" came Nathan's decisive answer. "Tony will be taken back and slowly tortured, while Amanda. . . well. . . we both know what they want her for."

His imagination working overtime, Francis could indeed picture what the indians had in mind for Amanda. What they probably had already done to her while poor Tony looked on, helpless to intervene. "We must go for help, Nathan," he insisted. "Those savages have had several hours head start and no doubt will reach their village before we can catch up with them. There are only two of us and we have no idea how many there were in the party that took Tony and Amanda."

Before he answered Nathan closely examined the surrounding area for footprints. Long minutes dragged by before he seemed satisfied with his findings. "As close as I can judge there were no more than four, possibly fewer even. They won't expect to be tracked so we have the advantage. I suggest we go after them rather than kill precious time by returning to River's Edge for help. Surprise will be on our side this time."

"But what if they reach their village before we can overtake them?" asked Francis, the consequence to Tony and Amanda if they should fail, too gruesome to contemplate.

"Don't even think it, Francis," Nathan frowned darkly, reading Francis' thoughts. "We can't fail."

They left immediately, traveling tirelessly throughout the long day. They had no idea that the culprits were not as far ahead of them as they had supposed, for in their haste to rape Amanda, they had stopped long before dark.

Nathan and Francis did not make camp at dark, being quite familiar by now with the trail leading to the Indian village. It was close to midnight when they suddenly and quite unexpectedly came upon the kidnapers' camp. They heard the murmur of low voices echoing through the stillness of the night long before they saw the dim glow of dying embers.

"Do you think they might be the indians who took Tony and Amanda?" Francis whispered, his face bright with hope.

"I'm not sure," answered Nathan quietly. "We'd better leave the horses behind and travel the rest of the way on foot. Don't speak or make any noise," he warned, "for those savages have the ears of a deer. And we'd better keep upwind of them, too, for their noses can smell a white man a mile away."

With a courage born of desperation Nathan and Francis crept cat-like through the darkened woods toward the beckoning campfire. When they came to a low ridge rising above the Indian camp they hunkered down in order to observe and acquaint themselves with the surroundings before making a foray into enemy territory.

Tony had been untied briefly, taken to the

stream to drink and relieve himself; fed just enough to leave his stomach growling. Now he was tightly rebound and expected to spend an uncomfortable night in the cramped position. He saw White Feather take water and a meal of sorts through the trees to Amanda and again thanked God she had not been killed.

During the early part of the night Brave Fox and Running Bear eased their boredom by taunting Tony, using the point of a sharpened stick to prod and goad him into impotent rage, laughing raucously as he strained ineffectively at his bonds. When they grew tired of their sport they settled around the dying fire speaking in low voices until their heads began to nod and they dozed.

From the ridge, Nathan and Francis watched, both puzzled by Amanda's absence. "Nathan," Francis whispered urgently, "you don't think they. . . they have already killed Amanda, do you?"

"I don't know what to make of it, Francis. But I aim to find out. Wait here while I have a look around."

Before Francis could protest, Nathan melted into the darkness. He made a complete circle of the camp and was nearly back to the place where Francis waited when he bumped into the small lean-to where Amanda was being kept. Scarcely daring to breathe, Nathan peered into the crude structure through the cracks, but darkness prevented him from identifying the body stretched out on the dirt floor. He prayed with a fervency he hadn't experienced in years that it was Amanda who occupied the hut and that she was alive and unharmed.

Just then Amanda sighed and turned in her

sleep, alarming White Feather who was hunched against a nearby tree. Nathan was surprised when the tall, menacing form uncoiled itself, and warily approached the small opening that served as a door to the hut, and stared into the dark interior. When no other sound was forthcoming he grunted and returned to his former position beneath the tree. Thankful that the brave had revealed himself, Nathan spent a few minutes planning his strategy.

Employing extreme caution Nathan crept further into the woods, angling his way behind the tree where White Feather rested. Though his eyes were shut Nathan could tell the brave had not relaxed his guard. Drawing his knife Nathan moved along stealthily until he lay directly behind White Feather. He knew he dare not allow the Indian time to cry out and give warning so he chose a spot on White Feather's throat, striking with the swiftness of a cobra. The actual killing took only a few seconds with nothing but the rushing and gurgling of blood breaking the silence.

Amanda awoke the moment the strong hand covered her mouth, stifling her cry of alarm. "It's Nathan, Amanda, don't be afraid," Nathan murmured into her ear. Immediately Amanda relaxed, relief and joy flooding her frail body.

Helping her rise, Nathan grasped her hand and led her from the hut, moving slowly through the forest to the ridge where Francis waited. Francis was so astounded to see Amanda that he could do nothing more than stare at her. "Close your mouth, Francis," Nathan chided gently. "As you can see Amanda is safe. Now let's get Tony out of this mess."

"Oh, yes, please," begged Amanda, finally

finding her voice. "There are only two savages left now, Brave Fox and another."

Francis gave Amanda a quick squeeze and said, "Wait here, Amanda. Nathan and I will free Tony and take care of those two savages. Have you been harmed?"

"I'm fine," she assured Francis. "Or I will be once Tony is free."

Things moved swiftly after that. Nathan and Francis inched their way toward Tony from behind, their luck holding as Brave Fox and Running Bear continued to doze beside the fire. Even Tony seemed to be sleeping as Nathan carefully cut through the thongs that bound his wrists to the tree. But that's all it took to alert him that his friends were alive and had caught up with them. When his hands were free he felt the blade slap against his palm and closed his hand around the handle. Making certain that the sleeping indians still had their backs to him, Tony freed his legs, stretching them to flex his screaming muscles.

Nodding in silent communication the three men crept along the ground toward the hunched figures of the two sleeping men. But luck deserted them as Tony's hand, cramped and numb from being bound for hours scraped over a dry twig, snapping it with a crisp report that immediately alerted their foe.

The fight that ensued was fierce for all that the Indians were slightly outnumbered. Before Brave Fox and Running Bear lay dead, Nathan had sustained a superficial knife wound in the thigh and Francis had a lump on his head the size of an egg.

From her perch behind the ridge, Amanda

watched until the Indians had been struck down and then she left her concealment, flew into Tony's arms, laughing and crying at the same time. Now that there was no longer a need for silence, their reunion became boisterous, with everyone speaking at the same time. After disposing of the three dead bodies, they rested until dawn and once again began their long trek home to River's Edge.

Though the remainder of their journey proved uneventful, they did not let down their guard again, not even when they crossed the river onto Tony's property.

The closer they came to River's Edge the more anxious and excited Amanda grew. When had she last seen Jon? So much had happened in those few days that it seemed a lifetime had passed. Had he missed her? she brooded. Or had Jemma and the others already taken her place in his affections?

Determination and a steady pace brought them to River's Edge just as late afternoon shadows lengthened. It was obvious from the swiftness with which Jemma came rushing from the house that she had been waiting and watching for their approach. Despite the slave's generous girth it looked to Amanda like the woman had lost twenty pounds in her absence.

"Lordy, Lordy, you's back! My chile done come back! I knowed Massa Tony wouldn't let them savages have you. Thank the Lord!" she loudly praised.

Her cries of jubilation and praise soon brought out every house servant within hearing. But Amanda's anxious eyes glossed over all but that which she sought. Uttering a cry of gladness she flung herself from her mount and flew to greet her son. Exclaiming loudly, laughing, crying, she snatched her baby from Flora's arms and hugged him to her breast. Never had anyone witnessed a more tender scene.

Amanda spent the next several days recuperating from her harrowing experience as well as becoming reacquainted with her son. The baby was the healing catalyst in Amanda's recovery. Tony had issued orders forbidding anyone to speak about or question Amanda concerning her ordeal at the hands of the Cherokees, and so her days passed in peace, filled with love and tender care.

Nathan was dispatched to Charles Town for supplies and a large selection of materials suitable for a whole new wardrobe for Amanda; plus a selection of shoes, underthings, gloves, cloaks, and a fur-lined cape for the coming winter. Nor was baby Jon forgotten. Nathan was provided with a lengthy list of items for the little fellow. Tony would have gone himself but couldn't bear to leave Amanda at a time when she was still hurting and vulnerable. She seemed to take great comfort from his presence.

Francis hied himself off with Nathan, insisting he had already overstayed his welcome. "I think I have learned enough about running a plantation," he contended when Tony would have him stay longer, "to look around for a place of my own. Since I've decided to settle in South Carolina it's about time I started searching for something suitable. I now feel confidant enough, thanks to you, Tony, to manage a large plantation."

What Francis did not say was that he thought it wise to leave Tony and Amanda to themselves to work out their problems. They needed time together to come to grips with their differences and feelings for one another. Francis was aware that Tony wanted Amanda to marry him but as yet she hadn't given him an answer. It wasn't difficult for Francis to surmise the fears and inadequacies nagging at Amanda and he sagely chose to disappear from their lives for the time being.

The first few nights after Amanda's return to River's Edge Tony was content just to have her near. Each night he gallantly saw her to her room, kissed her chastely on the cheek, then spent a sleepless night in his own lonely bed plagued by memories of the way her silken body felt in his arms and the special magic that was theirs alone when he made love to her. Would he ever again experience the exquisite pleasure of burying himself deep within her velvet softness? he wondered achingly, his loins afire as he paced his empty room. But he knew the time was not yet ripe to resume their relationship or speak of marriage again. But soon. . . soon. . . .

Unfortunately Tony's good intentions and resolve went for naught. Being human as well as a healthy, virile male, he found it increasingly difficult, to maintain iron control over his emotions. He wanted Amanda, needed her as a man needs the woman he loves. But how could he make her want him as badly as he wanted her? he pondered. Loving her as he did he did not moralize on his motives. He only knew he could not live without her in his arms and in his bed and he intended to have her there no matter what it took to convince her.

Having made his decision, Tony acted swiftly, not being one to postpone anything of such monumental importance in his life. That night he followed his usual routine of leaving Amanda at her door and continuing on to his own room. Only this time, after undressing and donning a robe he returned to Amanda's bedroom, hesitated a moment before the closed door, then slipped inside without knocking.

Amanda had just slid one of her new nightgowns over her coppery curls and settled the filmy material about her slim hips when she was startled to see Tony hovering nearby, his handsome face suffused with love and longing.

Completely entranced by the vision of loveliness standing before him, Tony could do nothing but stand and stare. The transparency of Amanda's nightgown hid nothing from his hot appraisal. The full curve of a breast, slender roundness of hips, burnished triangle nestled enticingly at the juncture of slim, white thighs. Each treasure revealed drove home his need for her as his body reacted violently and dramatically.

"Tony! I. . . I didn't expect you," Amanda stammered, flustered by his unexpected appearance in her bedroom. "Is there something you want?"

"Amanda," Tony answered firmly, "I think it's time we had a talk." Amanda nodded warily, instinctively reaching for a robe. Tony stayed her hand. "No, don't. There is nothing you can hide from me. I'm going to be your husband, remember? Many times I've seen you in much less."

Amanda flushed and lowered her long lashes but remained immobile before Tony's warm regard. "I want us to marry soon, darling. It's torture seeing you every day and not being able to love you like I want to. Like you deserve."

"I told you what to expect, Tony," Amanda reminded him sadly. "I love you and. . . and want to marry you. But I need a little more time to master my revulsion."

"You've had a month, my love. Have I given you any reason to mistrust me in all that time?" Amanda shook her head. "Then let's try it my way. It will be different with me, for I love you."

Panickstricken by Tony's words and their implication, Amanda paled. "Tony, no! I'm not ready yet to resume. . ."

"Did I say I would force you?" he chided gently, cutting her off in mid-sentence. "Or demand what you cannot give? I gave my word and I mean to keep it no matter how painful."

"Then, what. . . ."

"Just let me spend the night with you. No," he amended quickly, "not just one night, but every night. I only mean to hold you, to be near you. How can you expect to conquer your fears if you hold yourself aloof from me? You can't withdraw from life, Amanda. Let me remind you how it once was between us. Have you forgotten so soon the excitement, the ecstasy you felt in my arms when I made love to you? If. . . if after tonight you don't want me to return I will respect your wishes."

Amanda tried desperately to quell her involuntary reactions to that gentle, loving look of his. She shrugged to hide her confusion as she intently searched his face. During the past weeks he had shown her the extent of his devotion in a thousand different ways. Yet, something inside of her held her in a kind of limbo where all decisions and actions were impossible. It wasn't that she was unaware of Tony as a man. There were times of late when she found his nearness disturbing and exciting. Her brain was in a constant turmoil. At night in her lonely bed she relived over and over again the moment Brave Fox tore into her helpless body, thrusting, punishing, penetrating more than her flesh with his vile weapon. More than anything the thought of Tony bedding her and discovering for herself that she was no longer capable of responding to him, or to any man, held her back.

Suddenly Amanda paused in her mental roamings to question her own motives for denying Tony that which he so ardently desired. Why shouldn't she allow him to discover for himself the full extend of her anquish, both mental and physical? Why not make him aware of what being ravished by savages had cost her in terms of self-respect? Why not allow him into her bed if only to prove to him that she had nothing left to give? she asked herself irrationally.

With a start Amanda realized that Tony was still waiting for her answer. Her stomach was clenched into a tight ball when she finally spoke, but her voice was clear and firm. "I don't believe I am capable of being a whole woman again, Tony, but if you'd like to stay. . ."

"Darling," grinned Tony happily, "just trust me." Amanda managed a weak smile in return.

Amanda watched in consternation as Tony boldly walked to the bed and pulled back the counterpane. "Get in, my love," he invited breezily, lifting up a corner of the sheet.

Amanda complied instantly, then settled back, holding her body stiff and unyielding. Her eyes widened as Tony loosened the belt to his robe and casually shrugged until it fell at his feet. "I always sleep in the raw," he announced, grinning impishly.

With a will of their own Amanda's wayward eyes were drawn to the thick, jutting shaft springing proudly from the dark juncture of long, heavily muscled legs. She gasped at the shock of hard, heated flesh sliding confidently against her own cool skin as he slid into bed beside her.

"Don't fret, love," Tony whispered when she made to draw away. "I gave you my promise. You tell me when to stop."

His lips were gentle, almost soothing, and Amanda's tense body soon began to relax under his tender ministrations. His hands found her breasts and he gently massaged her nipples between thumb and forefinger. But when his questing hands finally settled on the softness between her legs, his fingers seeking a more vulnerable spot, Amanda cried out in sudden panic. Somehow those exploring fingers teasing her flesh and that probing manhood nudging her legs apart belonged to a dark, squat savage who wanted only to hurt and humiliate her in the vilest manner possible.

"Oh God! No! No! Amanda fought desperately as Tony sought to quell her rising terror. She began to shudder as fearful images built in her mind.

"Amanda, it's Tony. Please, darling. I won't hurt you. I love you."

After a while his soothing words and gentle tone must have gotten through to her because she ceased her struggling, sobbing quietly against his chest.

"Go to sleep, my love. It's all right. I'll just lay beside you and hold you."

Drawing a steadying breath, Amanda whispered raggedly, "I'm sorry, Tony. Truly, I am."

Deeply disturbed by Amanda's violent reaction to his attempts at lovemaking, Tony lay a long time while sleep eluded him. Suppose Amanda was right, he pondered grimly. How could he be expected to exist in a state of perpetual frustration? There was no way, he concluded decisively that he could live in harmony beside a woman he loved; a woman he desperately wanted yet could not make love to. Somehow, some way, he had to find out how to rekindle that spark he believed still dwelt deep within her waiting for the right moment to burst into flame.

Doggedly Tony continued to seek Amanda's bed each night, heartened when she did nothing to discourage him. In fact, he would have been jubilant had he known just how much his presence comforted her. She allowed Tony to kiss and caress her until he nearly reached the point of no return, and then only his steely control prevented him from taking his own pleasure. At those times Amanda loved him more than ever. But whether she realized it or not she was beginning to weaken under Tony's constant barrage of sexual stimulation and tender words. Usually he was able to contain himself before actual penetration took place but he knew it could not go on much longer. His continual state of tension and arousal was taking its toll. Even Jemma was aware of the suffering and deprivation plaguing Tony.

"When you gonna put that pore man out of his misery, chile?" Jemma asked one day when she and Amanda were alone in the kitchen. "It jest ain't natural what you doing to him."

"I can't help it, Jemma," Amanda responded unhappily. "I don't like it anymore than he does. I told you what happened to me. And I wouldn't blame Tony if he. . . he. . . found himself someone who could respond to him in bed as he deserves."

"I'm 'shamed of you!" reproved Jemma. "You jest feeling sorry for yoreself. Yore the woman he wants. Why don't you act like one 'stead of a hurt chile? You ain't gonna git no better iffen you don't try."

All that day Amanda thought on Jemma's words, knowing in her heart that the slave was right. But was she willing to put herself to the ultimate test?

Amanda stepped out of the tin bathtub, her body flushed from the heated water, damp skin satiny in the flickering firelight. Nights were turning chilly now and the crackling fire warmed her rapidly cooling flesh.

Shivering, she reached for the towel Tess had left by the fire for her use and was startled to find Tony standing behind her. He had quietly entered while she was bathing and stood watching her with hungry eyes, unable to break the spell she cast upon his senses. When she stepped from the tub all soft and glowing, droplets of water shimmering from the rosy crests of her breasts and from the burnished triangle at the juncture of her thighs, a burst of white hot lava scorched his loins. Instantly he was hard and throbbing.

"Let me dry you, my love," Tony offered gallantly, the timbre of his voice seductively low.

Amanda felt the roughness of the towel caressing the smoothness of her damp skin and was immediately aware of a tingling sensation along her entire body creating a heated response she found disconcerting. The towel, guided by Tony, touched her everywhere, her breasts, taut stomach, curving hips, between smooth thighs. The sensation he created was not unwelcome.

It took several minutes for Amanda to realize that strong, firm hands and questing lips had long since replaced the towel. Tony sought and found her mouth, easily parting her lips with probing tongue, tasting, teasing, devouring, until Amanda was gasping for breath and weak with excitement. Tenderly his mouth lingered at the corner of her lips, sliding along a cheekbone, touching the vulnerable hollow at the base of her neck with flicking tongue.

Amanda was powerless to resist, her legs a mass of quivering jelly as she clung to Tony for support. In one graceful motion he lifted her slight weight and carried her the short distance to the bed. It took but a moment to shed his robe and take his place beside her, his body half covering hers as he began the slow art of arousal at which he was so adept.

Not an inch of Amanda's trembling, eager flesh was inviolate. Her nipples fell into his mouth like ripe cherries as his tongue hotly caressed the tender fruits, fully erect and pulsating with need.

"You are so beautiful, darling. So desirable," Tony croaked, his voice hoarse with passion.

Effortlessly his hands found the core of her womanhood as his fingers probed the tiny, throbbing bud of her femininity; his excitement mounting with each ecstatic whimper and moan wrung from her parted lips.

"You're all woman, my sweet," Tony groaned. "How could you ever doubt it? Tell me! Tell me you want me!"

Amanda was beyond coherent speech, but she managed to gasp out, "Yes, yes, Tony, darling, I want you! Oh God, how I want you!"

Jubilant, Tony slid smoothly down Amanda's writhing body, his mouth poised above her. "I'm going to make you happy, sweet. I want to do this for you."

Then, before she could protest, his hot, questing lips and tongue located her most tender spot. At his first shocking touch Amanda drew her breath in sharply, arching her back, but there was no escape from that relentless mouth. Giving in to the sensation singing through her veins, her hands sought his thick, black hair in an attempt to draw him closer as his stabbing tongue drove her higher and higher until her passion erupted in a surge of ecstasy, once, twice, and again, so violent she thought she would break into a million parts.

"I can wait no longer, my love," Tony panted raggedly as he positioned himself for his long awaited entry. At his first thrust, Amanda stiffened, her legs automatically drawing together. "Darling, I've waited too long for this moment to stop now." Amanda's body relaxed as she breathed deeply. 'That's right," Tony urged, "relax. Open your legs. Let me share your joy. Let me love you."

Automatically Amanda obeyed and Tony thrust deeply, feeling himself sheathed completely by velvet, throbbing flesh. "That's where I belong, my love," he sighed as he began to move slowly within her; then more vigorously when he felt the beginnings of her first tentative response. He was harder and stronger than he had ever been in his life and suddenly all of Amanda's fears were forgotten as she matched him stroke for stroke, breasts, hips and loins pressed together. Miraculously she felt it building again, the intense pleasure she could not hold back even if she wanted to. When she felt Tony stiffen and his body shudder, she was right there with him, her joy every bit as dramatic, her cries mingling with his harsh groans of fulfillment.

Amanda slept. Not so Tony. After a brief interval of renewal he awakened her with a hot burst of passion that surprised even him. When Amanda gently teased him, calling him greedy, Tony laughingly informed her that she had put him on a starvation diet these past weeks and she was lucky if he allowed her any rest at all this night. She could almost believe it as once again he began a sensual assault upon her willing flesh.

When Tony woke Amanda for the third time she protested mildly but in the end his demanding lips and seeking hands reduced her to a mindless, witless creature as desirous of release as he was.

Just before dawn Tony arose and donned his robe. But when he bent to kiss Amanda's forehead, she opened her eyes and smiled tiredly. "Where are you going?" she asked dreamily. "It's not yet light."

"I forgot to tell you in my excitement last night that I am leaving for Charles Town today."

"Charles Town! Why?"

"I'm going to fetch a preacher, darling. It's time we got married. I refuse to wait another day. Do you think it's fair to Jon that we continue to live in sin?" he smiled roguishly. "Certainly you don't expect me to live like a monk after last night, do you?"

Amanda suppressed a grin. "Hurry back, Tony. I'll miss you," she yawned sleepily. "How long will you be gone?" she called after him.

"Three or four days at the most. I'll bring back Francis, too. He and Nathan can be our witnesses. Now go back to sleep, love. I'm afraid I wore you out last night."

During the next four days Amanda sewed furiously on her wedding dress. She had saved a particularly beautiful piece of off-white chintz printed with pale gold flowers and realized she must have intended it for this very purpose all along. Yards of material flowed in tiny pleats from a deep point at the center of a tightly fitted bodice. The deep, square neckline accentuated her long, slender neck and creamy shoulders. She even fashioned new clothes for Jon. But at the end of four days Tony failed to return. When a week passed with no word of any kind, Amanda grew frantic with worry. And with good cause.

17

Letty was livid with rage when she heard that Tony had been successful in his quest to rescue Amanda from the Indians. Her anger and frustration was awesome to behold and no one escaped her violent temper unscathed. Her house slaves were beaten for no apparent reason; field hands flogged at the slightest provocation. The hate she harbored for Amanda spilled over to Tony until the passionate love she once held for him became a forgotten memory. Vengeance twisted like a serpent in her gut and endless days and nights were spent devising various ways to dispose of both Tony and Amanda, each one more vile and devious than the other.

When Ben her overseer, returned from Charles Town on one of his trips for supplies he informed Letty that he had encountered Francis who told him Tony and Amanda were planning to marry very soon. Letty's fury knew no bounds. No one could humiliate her as Tony had done and get away with it, she seethed, her mind working furiously. She silently vowed to spend the rest of her life, if need be, making certain that Tony and his whore paid dearly for the affront to her pride. Her twisted mind could not accept the fact that Tony had never loved her, that he preferred Amanda. Letty's whole world became centered upon revenge against Tony for spurning her love for a woman who had been his indentured servant.

Then, with the swiftness of a summer storm an idea was born in Letty's fertile mind. An idea so devious, so vile, that the devil himself would have been proud of her. That it meant the untimely death of a man she once professed to love bothered her not at all.

Enlisting the aid of her overseer, Letty put her plan for revenge into immediate action. Ben was dispatched forthwith to Charles Town to engage the services of the most disreputable pair of thugs he could find along the waterfront. Men who would be willing to disappear once their job was completed to Letty's satisfaction. The sum agreed upon was so generous that Ben had no problem finding exactly the type of men willing to do anything for a price.

When Ben returned to Tidewater he was accompanied by two rough and unkempt backwoodsmen sporting a veritable arsenal of guns, knives and axes in their belts. Both had long, matted hair, yellow, rotted teeth and were dressed in buckskins coated with grime. Even Letty appeared a little intimidated by their size as well as their stench. But as long as they did the job they were being paid to do she could care less how ferocious they looked or how badly they smelled.

After kissing a sleepy Amanda goodby, Tony

left River's Edge that fateful morning in a light-hearted mood, unaware that two pair of beady eyes noted his departure with uncommon interest. The two thugs hired by Letty had kept a vigil night and day waiting for just such an opportunity. They could barely contain their glee when they realized Tony was not headed for the fields as was his usual custom but instead turned his mount in the direction of Charles Town. As they followed a respectable distance behind they were already counting the windfall that would enable them to resume their long postponed trapping expedition into the high country.

Unsuspecting, Tony rode into the glorious morning, his thoughts full of Amanda and their love-filled, ecstatic night together. By rights, he grinned foolishly, he should be exhausted, but all he felt was intense joy and exhilaration. He felt more alive and vital than he had at any time in his entire life. What was it about Amanda that inspired such emotion? he wondered.

Certainly she was a beautiful woman, he acknowledged. And proud, and faithful, tender-hearted, a good mother, an exciting lover. He could go on forever. He had probably loved her long ago in England when he thought he had bedded a young prostitute.

Still engrossed in his pleasurable musings, Tony halted beside the river to rest his horse and quench his thirst. Dismounting, he slipped to his knees intending to drink deeply of the cool, clear water. Suddenly he felt the hair raise at the nape of his neck, noting at the same time a shadow rising above him, blocking out the sun. But by that time it was already too late to act. The blunt edge of an axe slammed into his skull and he toppled forward into the water where he floated on the surface a few minutes before slowly sinking from sight. It appeared that Letty had planned her revenge well for not even a ripple remained to mark Tony's passing. Unfortunately for Amanda, Letty's revenge did not stop with Tony's death.

"Should we wait around to see if he resurfaces, Elmer?" asked the man who had struck Tony.

"Naw, Clem, he's done for," Elmer answered, scanning the river with squinted eyes staring from a face wrinkled from too many years of living with the elements.

"Do you think Miz Letty will want proof that we done our job before she pays us?"

"Jest show her the bloody ax, that aughta satisfy the bloodthirsty bitch," jested Elmer crudely.

"Do you think there's anything of value in his saddlebags?" asked Clem when he noticed Tony's horse standing nearby.

"Cain't hurt to take a look," grinned Elmer, cautiously edging toward the skitterish animal.

Recognizing danger, Tony's horse snorted, pawing the ground as the two men gingerly approached. But before they had a chance to grab the reins the animal turned abruptly and crashed through the woods. Clem made to follow but Elmer called out, "Forget the damn horse, Clem, we got more important things on our mind. Let's collect our money so's we can get the hell out of here. I think that poor bastard we jest done in is someone important and afore long this here woods is gonna be jumping with searchers. I want to be long gone afore then."

Letty paced anxiously back and forth waiting

to hear from the two men Ben had hired to take care of Tony. They had been watching River's Edge for several days now, surely they've had sufficient time to do what they're being paid for, she reasoned. They looked pretty stupid to Letty and she hoped they hadn't been caught snooping around the plantation and questioned by Tony. They probably were the kind who would tell all they knew the first time any kind of force was employed. But Ben had assured her the men were reliable and could be depended upon to get the job done.

It was just after dark when Ben approached Letty's house with Clem and Elmer in tow. They had waited until darkness fell, Ben explained, so they wouldn't be seen by any of the slaves. "Is it done?" Letty asked curtly. Their stench was so offensive that Letty could barely stomach being in the same room with them, and she held a scented handkerchief to her delicate nose.

"He ain't nothing but fish bait, Miz Letty," snickered Clem, showing an expanse of rotted teeth.

"You're sure he's dead?" asked Letty. Both Clem and Elmer nodded vigorously.

"You got no reason to doubt us, Miz Letty," whined Elmer, disgruntled. "We said we done killed the man. Are you calling us liars? He's floating on the bottom of the river right now."

A loud hiss escaped from between Letty's clenched teeth as she exhaled loudly. A travesty of a smile curved her full lips and her eyes were like chunks of granite, making Clem and Elmer glad that her vengenance wasn't directed at them. Abruptly she turned, walked to a small desk and withdrew a weighted bag.

343

"Here's your pay," she sneered, tossing the bag in the air. "Now get out of here."

Clem grabbed at the bag, snatching it in midair. Eagerly he undid the drawstring and peered inside, grunting in satisfaction at what he saw.

"It's all there," proclaimed Letty haughtily. "In gold, just like you asked. "I don't want to see your faces again. If you're smart you will stay out of Charles Town for a good long time."

The moment the two hired killers left, Letty broke out in raucous laughter, shocking even Ben who had remained behind. "At last!" she gasped, wiping her eyes with the back of her hand. "At last that bastard is finally dead! He has humiliated me for the last time; him and that slut he wanted to make his wife. My God! I offered him everything and he turned me down in favor of a convict who had nothing to offer but herself."

Letty's eyes sparkled viciously as she thought about Amanda and what she had planned for her. With Tony out of the way Amanda would be hers to punish at will. Finally her brittle gaze fell on Ben who until now had remained silent, waiting. He knew exactly how Letty's mind worked.

Just thinking of what she would do to Amanda set Letty afire. To her, cruelty and sex made compatible bed fellows, and her lustful intent was clearly understood by Ben who knew Letty well enough to recognize desire when she saw it.

Without preliminary Letty began tearing off her clothes, inviting Ben with raised eyebrows to do the same. Her husky voice promised ecstasy and Ben needed no further urging as his own clothes melted away and the two writhing bodies fell to the floor, coupling like two animals in heat.

The time for Tony's return came and went, and when he did not appear Amanda became mildly concerned. At the end of the week when Tony still did not materalize, Amanda grew frantic. Nathan did his best to allay her worst fears but Amanda was positive something dreadful had happened to her beloved. It was as if he had become a part of her and the premonition of disaster she felt in her bones was very real. At the end of ten days she was beyond consolation. By then, even Nathan suspected that something dire had occurred to prevent Tony from returning to River's Edge.

"I hate to leave you alone but I think it imperative I find out just what is keeping Tony in Charles Town," Nathan informed Amanda before he left.

"Don't worry about me, Nathan," Amanda replied anxiously. "Just find Tony. I'm so afraid. I couldn't bear it if something happened to him."

Nathan left almost immediately. He was back within a week, tired and haggard, deep worry lines etched across his brow. Francis was with him looking even more woebegone.

"What is it?" cried Amanda the moment they entered the house. Where is Tony? Did you find him?"

"Amanda, I..." Nathan began hesitantly, glancing at Francis for help.

"Amanda, dear," Francis took up where Nathan left off, "Tony never reached Charles Town."

"Never reached... No! What does it mean? There must be some logical explanation."

"Amanda," Francis explained gently, "Nathan and I scoured the city and no one has seen or heard from Tony in months. He never contacted the preacher."

"Oh God, Francis, what can we do?" choked Amanda, tears clogging her throat.

"We'll find him, Amanda, don't panic," Francis soothed. "We'll organize the slaves and search the countryside from here to Charles Town if necessary."

"Please find him," Amanda begged, looking helplessly from one to the other.

The search party was gone a week. . . and came back leading Tony's riderless horse, found wandering aimlessly in the wood several miles from River's Edge. They made a thorough search of the vicinity and discovered what they thought were blood stains in the grass growing at the edge of the river bank. Further investigation had revealed Tony's hat caught in the brush along the shoreline. The evidence had been irrefutable. Nathan and Francis had come to the identical conclusion that Tony was dead, probably set upon by thieves, robbed and slain, his body consigned to the bottom of the river. He had never reached Charles Town.

"It's not true!" protested Amanda, refusing to believe that evidence. "I would know if Tony was dead, wouldn't I?" And then she broke down completely, trembling, crying, shaking from head to toe. In the end Jemma had to put her to bed and dose her with laudanum.

The next few days were among the worst Amanda had ever experienced.

Even her ordeal with the Indians paled in comparison to what she felt when faced with the fact of Tony's demise. Only Jon's presence seemed to alleviate the pain tearing her apart. Tony's son was her consolation and her salvation. Francis remained at River's Edge to lend what help he could but nothing or no one could take Tony's place in Amanda's heart. Yet, somehow she survived, living one moment at a time, forever conscious of the void in her life.

Two weeks after Nathan and Francis returned with proof of Tony's untimely death, Letty appeared at River's Edge accompanied by the constable and two deputies from Charles Town. It was Francis who opened the door to them.

"Good afternoon, Francis," Letty smiled blandly. "This is Constable Frazer. He and his deputies are here to lend me assistance."

Francis nodded curiously, certain that Letty's appearance at this time spelled trouble. "Good afternoon, Letty, Constable. What can I do for you?"

Letty slanted a sly look at the constable who cleared his throat and said, "I understand Sir Tony is dead. I have investigated his disappearance and have concluded that foul play has been involved."

"We have no real proof," argued Francis, unwilling to divulge anything to Letty that might be used for her own vile purposes. "It's true that we have neither seen nor heard from him in weeks but we have no real evidence of his death."

Letty smiled sweetly, deceptively. "That's a long time to be gone with no word of his whereabouts."

Francis flushed darkly. "Yes," he admitted grudgingly. He'd be damned if he'd satisfy that bitch's morbid curiosity. "Would you please state your business? Things are a bit hectic right now and I'm very busy seeing to Tony's affairs in his

347

absence."

"Our business is with the indentured servant, Amanda Prescott," stated the constable. "Please summon her."

Just then Amanda walked into the hallway. When the constable spoke her name she came forward. "Does someone want me, Francis?" she asked, failing to see Letty standing slightly behind the constable and his men. When she finally stepped forward, Amanda stared directly into vibrant blue eyes, catching a glimpse of hell. Instinctively she recoiled, one slim hand clutching her throat.

"Are you Amanda Prescott?" asked the constable, not unkindly.

"Yes," whispered Amanda faintly, green eyes wide and frightened. "What. . . what do you want with me?"

Letty chose to answer Amanda's question. "I have come to claim my property."

"What property?" challenged Francis.

Smiling smugly, Letty pulled a document from her reticule and handed it to Constable Frazer who nervously cleared his throat once again before speaking. "I have in my hand the Articles of Indenture of one Amanda Prescott, convict. I also an in possession of a bill of sale executed by Sir Tony Brandt relinquishing all rights to said servant to Mistress Letty Carter. As you can see the bill of sale was witnessed and duly signed by Sir Tony. It appears all legal and binding. Amanda Prescott is now the property of Mistress Carter until the convict's sentence has been fulfilled."

Amanda staggered backward and would have fallen but for Francis who put a steadying arm about her quaking shoulders. "You lie!" she gasped. "Tony would never do such a thing to me. He loved me! We were going to be married!"

"May I examine the papers?" asked Francis calmly. Inwardly he was as shaken as Amanda. He supposed there was some mistake that could easily be rectified. Tony would never willingly sell Amanda, especially not to Letty. He would stake his life on it.

Constable Frazer handed both documents to Francis who studied them intently for several minutes. When he finally turned to face Amanda he looked as if he wanted to cry. The Articles of Indenture was the original document, sporting the king's own seal! Even the bill of sale signed by Tony appeared to be authentic. Francis had seen Tony's signature often enough to recognize it.

"I don't know what to say, Amanda. In my heart I know some trick has been perpetrated but everything appears to be legal and binding. These are indeed your indenture papers and according to the law you now belong to Letty."

"Do you think I would lie?" huffed Letty indignantly. "If you'll look at the date on the bill of sale you'll see that Tony stopped by my plantation the same morning he left for Charles Town." Francis glanced briefly at the date then looked pityingly at Amanda who was white as a ghost and on the verge of collapse.

"It can't be true," repeated Amanda, sounding much like a hurt little girl. "I don't care what you say. I know Tony loved me."

"He grew tired of you," Letty taunted cruelly. "He got what he wanted from you. That's why he was anxious to be rid of you. He told me he was on his way to Charles Town to arrange passage to

England."

"Letty, I don't know how you managed all this but you won't get away with it. There is no way I will allow you to take Amanda from River's Edge," Francis asserted firmly, fully cognizant of the fact that Letty had the law on her side but was unwilling to admit it.

Letty smirked and looked to Constable Frazer who was fidgeting nervously. He wasn't happy with what he had to do but he was sworn to uphold the King's law. "Get your things together, young woman," he ordered brusquely, nodding at Amanda authoritatively. "You are obliged to go with Mistress Carter."

"My baby!" remembered Amanda suddenly. "What about my baby?"

"Baby?" puzzled the constable. "I know nothing about a baby. But if it belongs to you it will have to go with you."

"You are wrong in that respect," cut in Francis. "In Tony's safe is a document recognizing Jon as his son and heir. If Tony is dead, which hasn't actually be proven yet, River's Edge belongs to his son and I am named the child's legal guardian until he comes of age."

"I don't want the brat anyway," shrugged Letty. "Just bring the wench along. Never mind her clothes. She won't need a thing. I'll provide her with everything she needs."

"What's going on here?" All eyes turned to Nathan who had just entered the hall through the connecting breezeway. The moment Jemma's sharp eyes spied Letty approaching River's Edge she immediately sent for Nathan.

"Tony sold my papers to Letty!" cried Amanda, frantically clutching at Nathan's arm as if he were her saviour.

"Impossible!" scoffed Nathan. "Tony isn't capable of such deceit. He was on his way to Charles Town for the preacher when he disappeared. He and Amanda were to be married upon his return."

"Well, he changed his mind," snapped Letty tartly. "He had you all fooled. In all likelihood he faked his own death and skipped to England on the first available ship."

"You seem to know a lot about Tony's affairs," said Nathan suspiciously.

"Tony and I have been friends. . . a long time," Letty replied slyly. "Is it so surprising that he should confide in me?"

"After what you did to Amanda? Admit it, Letty. Tony hated you," Nathan retorted derisively.

"If he hated me so much why did he sell Amanda to me? Fortunately I hold her indenture papers as proof."

At the mention of the offending documents, Francis silently offered them to Nathan. As Nathan scanned the paper as well as the bill of sale his face grew red with rage. Somehow Letty had stolen the document Tony had supposedly destroyed. Unfortunately Tony was not present to either affirm or deny Letty's claim to ownership. With the constable backing up Letty, Nathan's hands were tied. Whether or not trickery was employed somewhere along the line made little difference to the final outcome. Amanda was obliged to go with Letty. Nathan could only thank God that little Jon was safe from Letty's vengeance for he was positive her lust for revenge was what brought this all about in the first place. Fortunately Letty hadn't known about Tony's will acknowledging Jon. Feeling impotent and useless

Nathan could only stand aside and watch helplessly as Amanda was led off like a sacrificial lamb.

When Amanda made to hang back Letty was quick to proclaim, "Do your duty, Constable, take the girl."

"I'm sorry," shrugged the constable, authorizing his deputies to seize Amanda and drag her off. "The law is specific and justice must be done. Take the girl, lads, and let's be off."

Panicstricken, Amanda looked helplessly from Francis to Nathan, her eyes bleak with despair. "Please, give me a moment with my baby," she begged, turning pleading eyes on the constable.

"I have no time for a sentimental leavetaking," Letty announced heartlessly. "Perform your duty, Constable." Without another word she spun around and strode purposefully away, icy eyes implacable.

Amanda fought for control, determined to conceal her grief and deny Letty the satisfaction of seeing her grovel for favors. When the deputies grasped her arms to hasten her forward she pulled away and, with head held high, small chin thrust forward, walked stiffly to the wagon Letty had driven from Tidewater. Francis and Nathan followed helplessly, both seething in impotent fury.

If you attempt to harm Amanda in any way I'll find the means to finish what Tony started," Nathan called out as they rode away."Just remember, Letty, word travels and I'll know if you've hurt her."

Nathan's angry threats still rang in Letty's ears when she reached Tidewater. Instinctively she knew the powerful man did not make idle threats and she knew she had to tread carefully for the time being. Amanda must not be allowed to die or disappear too soon, she decided, but there were better means than flogging to punish and degrade the woman Tony had unwisely chosen over Letty. And once vengeance was served Amanda would be sold to the lowest brothel on the waterfront.

After the constable and deputies departed Tidewater, Letty turned hate-filled eyes on Amanda. "Come with me," she snapped, leading the way to the slave quarters. Halfway to their destination they were met by Ben.

"Where are you taking her, Mistress Letty?" Ben asked, licking his lips wolfishly as his eyes roamed insultingly over Amanda's lithe curves.

"She needs to be tamed," Letty offered spitefully. "A few days in solitary confinement will soon break her spirit. If not, what I have in mind for her most certainly will."

"I can gentle her real good for you, Mistress Letty. Give her to me." Ben's small eyes gleamed with salacious intent but Letty only laughed.

"No, Ben, not you. She's not good enough for a white man. Especially one I've bedded. Don't you know she's served as whore to the Indians? No," she reaffirmed, "you'll not have her."

Letty didn't really care all that much for Ben but at the moment he was all she had. Just the knowledge that he wanted Amanda sent jealous rage coursing through her veins.

Letty's words did little to dispel Amanda's gloom but she was grateful she wouldn't be ravished by Ben whose repulsive gaze made her flesh crawl. It wasn't difficult for Amanda to imagine the type of punishment Letty had in store for her, and she instinctively knew she would not be allowed the luxury of a quick death.

Ben was careful to keep the disappointment from his face. He wanted Amanda but not enough to risk his own skin. He was well aware of the cruel bent in Letty's nature but he was determined to have Amanda on his own terms, in his own good time.

Letty halted before a small cabin, opened the door and rudely shoved Amanda inside. Both she and Ben were close on Amanda's heels. The room Amanda found herself in was small and dingy, sporting a single window high up on one wall. On the floor in one corner lay a cornhusk pallet covered with a dirty, torn blanket of sorts. A chamber pot sat nearby. Other than that the room was devoid of all furnishings. It appeared she would not even be allowed the comfort of a fire for although there was a fireplace there wasn't a stick of wood in sight. Amanda was later to learn that the cabin was used as a jail for unruly slaves.

Amanda shivered convulsively. She had left without a wrap and the chill seeped into her bones. Letty's sharp voice roused her from her stupor.

"Take off your clothes!" Amanda could only stare, mouth agape. "You heard me, slut, remove your clothes!" When Amanda remained a frozen statue, Letty said maliciously, "Would you prefer to have Ben do it for you? You've been without a man for a long time, perhaps you would enjoy his attentions."

Moistening his lips expectantly, Ben stepped forward. "No!" cried Amanda, slowly backing against the wall. "I'll do it myself."

Her face a bright crimson Amanda began disrobing, fearful of what was to come next. When she was completely nude Letty stood back critically appraising the woman who had surplanted her in Tony's affections. High, rose-tipped breasts quivered under Letty's minute scrutiny but Letty's ruthless gaze did not waver from the perfect form, taking special note of the unblemished, alabaster skin, narrowed waist and rounded hips tapering to a fiery vee at the juncture of long, slim legs. The girl was younger, Letty conceded grudgingly, her flesh a shade more supple, perhaps, but certainly no more beautiful and desirable than she was herself. It was far easier for Letty to believe that Amanda was a temptress, a witch who wove a spell around Tony's heart. What other choice did Letty have than to rid herself of both Tony and Amanda? Turning abruptly she gathered up Amanda's discarded clothing and headed for the door. Ben lingered, feasting his eyes on Amanda's lush form until Letty grew impatient and ordered him from the cabin. The clanking of metal told Amanda that she had been locked in.

Alone with her thoughts, cold and miserable, Amanda sank to the pallet and hugged the single blanket mummy-like about her quaking body. "Oh Tony," she sobbed morosely, "how could you do this to me?" She had been so happy the night before he left on that fateful journey to Charles Town. Loving each other again had seemed so right, their pleasure in one another more intense than any they had ever known. Hadn't Tony told her over and over how much he loved her? He had been so patient, so understanding of her fear to resume their physical relationship. Was it possible that once he had bedded her he found her lacking in some way? Or had he lied and could he not bear the thought of her being used by the Indians.

"No!" denied Amanda aloud. "I'll never believe that!" But what other explanation was there? Tony was well aware of Letty's hatred for her and knew that she would stop at nothing to hurt and humiliate her. How else could Letty gain possession of her indenture papers if Tony hadn't sold them to her? Amanda puzzled, her emotions all ajumble. Had she been betrayed? Betrayed by the man she loved? He was probably on a ship bound for England this very minute just as Letty said, for no matter what Tony had done Amanda refused to believe him dead. At first death seemed the logical explanation but his body was never found. It had to be as Letty claimed. He was probably somewhere on the high seas laughing at her child-like trust as he sailed away to a new life.

Amanda's befuddled brain failed to register the fact that Tony loved his home and would never leave River's Edge willingly.

No one came near the small cabin the rest of that day. No food or drink was forthcoming. The next morning, after a sleepless night spent huddled beneath the threadbare blanket, the rattle of the lock awakened her from her light doze. The door to her prison opened, admitting Ben who approached ·boldly, set down a jug of water and a few crusts of bread before her, stared intently at the places where her flesh shown through the ragged blanket, then left. The same thing happened that night except the meal was an unsavory cornmeal mush.

For the next two days the routine never

varied. The odiferous chamber pot became so offensive that she began vomiting upon awakening each morning. She begged Ben to empty it but her pleas fell on deaf ears. Even her requests for soap and water were studiously ignored. When she wasn't being humiliated she was ridiculed for her appalling state. It was fortunate she had little appetite for the unpalatable food only made her ill.

By the third day Amanda's weight loss was noticeable to Ben's discerning eyes. Deep purple smudges marred the pale skin beneath her eyes which seemed to have grown more luminous with each passing day. But no matter that she looked haggard and tired, or that her hair was matted, face grimy, Ben still wanted her, his lust growing daily until it ate into his gut like a swarm of maggots.

After a week of confinement Amanda became listless and disoriented. Lightheaded from lack of food she struggled to maintain a clear head, knowing that at any time Letty could appear to mete out her own brand of punishment. But no matter what, Amanda was determined to survive; if only for her son who needed a mother more than ever now that he had no father. When she believed she was about to be ravished by Indians she had welcomed death. But she was not about to be defeated by Letty. Amanda was well aware of the pleasure Letty took in seeing her debased and demoralized and she was determined to retain her pride no matter what the cost. Letty did not dare kill her outright for fear of reprisal from either Nathan or Francis. She was certain her two friends were working tirelessly on her behalf. She had to perservere for as long as it took Nathan and

Francis to set her free.

One day, nearly two weeks after she had been imprisoned, Ben entered the cabin at his usual time early that morning. His face wore a strange light and Amanda immediately became watchful. His desire for her had grown daily until he could no longer slake his passion on one of the hapless slave girls unlucky enough to catch his attention. Only his fear of Letty's vile temper had thus far prevented him from venting his lust upon Amanda. He knew that Letty planned on moving Amanda to another location very soon so time was drawing short. If he wanted her he had to act quickly.

"You smell like a stable," insulted Ben, wrinkling his nose in distaste. Amanda shrank within herself as Ben's beady eyes pierced her like a well-honed blade.

"Whose fault is that?" shot back Amanda with more spunk than she had displayed in days.

"Don't get uppity with me, girl. You're no better than a slave. Now get up, you're going to have a bath."

"Is this Letty's idea?" Amanda found it difficult to believe Letty was actually relenting to the extent of thinking of her comfort.

"What Letty don't know won't hurt her," grinned Ben lasciviously. "Hurry, girl. I haven't got all day."

Amanda thought to refuse but she wanted a bath too badly to balk. Perhaps Ben felt sorry for her and meant to help her, she contended. Deciding a bath sounded too delicious to refuse Amanda rose unsteadily to her feet and followed the overseer into the bright sunshine, blinking as the unaccustomed glare assaulted her eyes. She tottered after him some distance until they came to a secluded section of river. Handing Amanda a piece of soap and whipping the blanket from around her naked body, Ben shoved her rudely into the water. Neither his rough handling nor the icy water could dampen Amanda's spirits as she used he soap to good advantage, first scrubbing her skin until it glowed, then washing her hair. Ben paced impatiently along the riverbank while Amanda splashed happily in the water, already beginning to feel human again.

"Come on out, girl," called Ben, eagerness causing him to lose all patience. "You've been in there long enough. If you keep that up you're going to rub all that luscious flesh off your bones until there ain't none left for me."

His words and intent more chilling than the water, Amanda reluctantly started back toward shore, reaching for the blanket the moment she attained dry ground. Ben chuckled evilly but did nothing to stop her. Docily she allowed him to lead her back to her reeking prison. Only when Ben followed her inside and firmly closed the door behind him did Amanda divine his salacious intent.

"Shuck down, girl," ordered Ben crudely. "Letty says you're nothing but a whore so I'll treat you like one. Drop that blanket and spread yourself!"

"You're disgusting," spat Amanda, clutching the blanket convulsively about her slender body as if for protection.

"Hurry up, girl, I ain't got all day." With those words he pulled the edges of the blanket from Amanda's shaking hands and tore it from her shrinking body. While he spread it on the cornhusk mattress Amanda whirled about and made a wild dash for the door.

"Oh no, you don't," snarled the wiry Ben spinning on his heel and catching a handful of hair before she could make good her escape. Ignoring her cries of pain, Ben pulled her roughly to the pallet and fell on her like a demented savage. He tried to capture her mouth but she fought him bravely, tossing her head from side to side in a wild attempt to avoid his wet lips.

"Slut!" Ben taunted angrily. "If you had any idea what Letty has planned for you you'd beg for my attentions."

"I doubt that," panted Amanda, her exertions beginning to take a toll upon her meager strength.

Enraged by Amanda's resistance and unexpected display of courage, Ben grasped her flailing arms with one hand, pinioning them over her head and slapping her repeatedly with the other. Red dots of pain exploded behind Amanda's eyes, stunning her for a few brief moments. Those moments provided Ben with just enough time to unfasten his breeches and roughly nudge Amanda's legs apart with his bony knees.

"Now you'll feel what it's like to have a real man between your legs, girl," Ben rasped hoarsely.

"I think not, Ben," came a cool voice from behind. Amanda felt Ben's huge erection wilt against her thigh and for the first time ever felt something akin to gratitude toward Letty.

"Mistress Letty," stammered Ben, confused, "I was. . . was. . . just. . ."

"I am well aware of what you were doing, Ben. If it wasn't that I still had need of your services I'd fire you. Now get out of here!"

Amanda breathed a sigh of relief as Ben shifted his weight from her slim body, hastily adjusting his clothing before sidling past Letty and out the door. Letty watched narrowly until he was out of sight before turning icy blue eyes on Amanda still crouched warily on the pallet rubbing her wrists.

"Put this on," Letty ordered curtly, tossing Amanda a shapeless garment made of some kind of drab, rough material obviously meant for a field worker.

Amanda slid the garment over her head, happy to have anything at all with which to cover her nakedness. Letty's cold gaze roamed freely over Amanda's slimness, apparently satisfied with what she saw. Although Amanda was noticeably thinner she did not look as bad as Letty expected considering the near starvation diet forced upon her. Nathan had sent word that he was coming to Tidewater today demanding to see for himself that Amanda was well and unharmed.

"One of your lovers is coming to check up on you today," said Letty sarcastically as she motioned Amanda through the door.

Amanda looked startled. "My. . . my lover?"

"Of course. Do you think I'm stupid. I'm sure Nathan misses your. . . er. . . companionship. No doubt Francis does too. Both seem exceptionally taken with you."

"Nathan is coming here?" repeated Amanda numbly, hope illuminating her fragile features.

"Yes, and when he arrives you are to do exactly as I say."

"And if I don't?" shot back Amanda defiantly.

"Nathan will never return to River's Edge alive."

Amanda gasped. "You wouldn't dare harm Nathan!" But in her heart she knew Letty capable of any evil.

"I would and I will," Letty assured her calmly. "Are you ready to listen now? Dumbly Amanda nodded. "If you want Nathan to live you will tell him that you are well and decently treated. Whatever else you tell him is up to you as long as he is made to understand you are not being mistreated."

Amanda flushed angrily but in the end had no choice but to agree to Letty's demands. In all good conscious she could not sacrifice Nathan's life, she was much too fond of him to put Letty's threat to the test.

Letty led Amanda into the kitchen where a tall, rawboned slave stood by the stove stirring a furiously boiling pot. The woman was rendered speechless by the sight of the beautiful white girl dressed no better than a field hand.

"Lottie, this is Amanda, your new scullery. I've ordered your other helpers into the fields," Letty informed the gaping woman. "Amanda is to perform all the most difficult chores, scouring, scrubbing, emptying chamber pots, nothing is too menial for her. She is to be at her tasks by dawn. Ben will see that she gets back to her quarters at night when all her work is completed for the day. I expect to see her on her feet toiling every minute, without respite or letup. If she isn't, I will personally hold you responsible. Is that clear?"

"Yas'm, Miz Letty, I understands. I shorely do," replied Lottie, rolling huge, black eyes in Amanda's direction. "But 'lessen you wants to kill her off quick-like you better let me feed her. She's as skinny as a rail and looks near to starving."

"She'll eat what the field hands eat, Lottie. She is to be given no special treatment. She is a thief and a whore and far beneath any slave on this plantation. If I find she is shirking her duties or that you are deliberately coddling her you will both be flogged. Do you understand?"

"Oh, yas'm, Miz Letty. You be the boss. This here girl gonna work her tail off. You jest leave her to me."

"Good," nodded Letty, satisfied. Then she was gone, unaware of the hatred blazing from the depths of Lottie's inky eyes.

Hesitantly, Lottie approached Amanda. "Are all them things Miz Letty says about you true?" she asked shyly. "You don't look like no. . . no. . . whore."

"I am not a whore!" reputed Amanda hotly, "It's true I was deported and indentured for stealing a loaf of bread and I guess that makes me a thief. But that was a long time ago and I'm paying my debt to society."

"Don't get so all-fired touchy," grinned Lottie. "I never for a minute believed Miz Letty. But she shore do hold a powerful hate for you, chile. Now sit down and put some hot food in yore belly. You looks like you ain't had a good meal in weeks."

"It has been a long time since I've tasted any-thing remotely appetizing," admitted Amanda wryly. "But you heard Letty. I'm to be allowed no favors. I have no desire to see you punished on my account."

"That witch ain't gonna be back here for awhile. How she gonna know what I feeds you? We jest has to be careful, that's all. I ain't gonna 'low no nice white gal like you to starve in my kitchen," she huffed indignantly.

Amanda watched hungrily as Lottie placed several dishes of food in front of her. Before she finished she had devoured a large serving of fried ham, two huge slices of fresh bread dripping with butter and a fruit tart, washing it all down with cool cider. She felt better than she had in days; weeks actually. More importantly, for the first time in days Amanda was able to keep her nourishing food in her stomach.

Later that day when Nathan arrived for his expected visit he found Amanda bent over a huge tub of steaming water industriously scouring crusted pots and pans. Letty accompanied him, much to Nathan's chagrin, for he hoped to be able to speak to Amanda alone without any interference.

"There she is," pointed out Letty. "I told you she was unharmed. Maybe now you will believe me."

The smile he had prepared in greeting quickly disappeared from his face the first moment Nathan saw Amanda bending over the tub, pounds thinner, her face haggard and flushed from the hot, steaming water.

"My God! What have you done to her?" he exclaimed in impotent rage.

"Nothing's wrong with her, ask her yourself," replied Letty smugly.

Nathan needed no further urging as he rushed to Amanda's side and drew her fragile body into his arms, aware of every protruding bone. There was a transparency in the pale skin stretched across her taut cheekbones that frightened him.

"Amanda," he whispered in a voice too low for Letty's ears. "What has she done to you? Have you been ill? Has Letty hurt you, dear?"

Oh, how good it felt to be enfolded in Nathan's protective embrace. How she yearned to tell him the full extent of Letty's cruelty. But heeding Letty's words Amanda remained mute. She was well aware of Letty's cruel nature. Hadn't she been the brunt of that cruelty often enough?

"I. . . I have been ill, Nathan," lied Amanda lowering transparent lids over revealing eyes. "But I'm fine now. Today is the first day I've been allowed. . . out of bed to take up my duties. Mistress Letty has done me no harm," she insisted loudly enough for Letty's ears.

Despite Amanda's fervent words, Nathan was not fooled by them. "You can tell me the truth, dear. I'll do whatever I can to help you. Francis is in Charles Town this very moment pleading your case before the Magistrate. It won't be long before we'll have you back at River's Edge with your son."

"I told you," persisted Amanda, "I am fine. Just tell me about Jon, please. Does he miss me? Is he well?"

Nathan spent the next several minutes expounding on Jon's exploits while Amanda sobbed softly, aching with the need to feel her son's warm body held tightly in her arms.

Letty's shrill voice interrupted. "You're upsetting my servant, Nathan. I must insist you leave. As you can see Amanda is well and unharmed. You have no further business here."

"You win, Letty," Nathan sighed heavily, reluctantly. "But I'll be back, and when I return I expect to find Amanda looking healthier than she is now. For the time being I'll accept her word that she's been ill."

"I agreed that you should visit my servant this

one time, Nathan, but you won't be allowed that privilege again. The law is on my side. At one time you saw fit to drive me from River's Edge and I intend to repay your insult in kind. You are never to set foot on Tidewater again."

"By God, Letty, if you think. . ."

"Nathan, please," interrupted Amanda, "you'll only make things more difficult for me if you don't leave."

"I'll leave," agreed Nathan reluctantly, "but neither Francis nor I have given up by a long shot. One day soon you'll be back with us at River's Edge where you belong."

"Do you miss your mistress so much, Nathan?" taunted Letty slyly. "I would think any one of the other slaves would do just as well."

"By God, Letty, you go too far," warned Nathan. "One of these days you'll pay. . . and dearly."

"Leave my property, Nathan. And if you or that weak-livered Francis show up here again I'll have my overseer treat you like any other trespasser."

Ignoring Letty's ominous threat, Nathan turned back to Amanda. "Don't give up, Amanda. Letty hasn't won yet." Then he was gone, the harsh sound of Letty's derisive laughter thundering in his ears.

Amanda worked until she was on the verge of collapse. She realized now that Letty did not intend to beat her into submission but meant to punish her in more subtle ways. She wished she knew what was in store for her next for she had no doubt that Letty was far from finished with her.

The last of the pots and pans had been scoured and put away for the night and the floors scrubbed spotless when Letty and Ben appeared in the kitchen.

"Until now I've been lenient with you," Letty informed Amanda coldly. "But your day of reckoning has finally arrived. After tonight you will be fit for nothing but the lowest cribs along the waterfront, if they'll have you. I have a little surprise in store for you. Who knows," she shrugged eloquently, "you might even enjoy it. But by morning no decent man will want you again."

Shuddering, Amanda took an involuntary step backwards, the strange, wild gleam in Letty's eyes frightening her as nothing had before. But Amanda was allowed no time to dwell on her fate. Obeying a nod from Letty, Ben grasped Amanda firmly by the upper arm and pulled her unceremoniously out the door, steering her toward the slave quarters. Letty followed, smirking triumphantly.

For one hopeful minute Amanda thought she was being taken back to her cabin prison, but soon learned she was mistaken when she was hustled past that odious place and led directly to another cabin, larger and neater than any of the others. Letty rapped twice then flung open the door without waiting for a reply. Ben shoved Amanda inside the open door, the thoughts of what was about to take place causing his loins to contract painfully.

Amanda stifled a scream as a huge giant emerged from the shadows dwarfing the confines of the small room. The man was nearly seven feet tall, if she was any judge, clad only in a pair of ragged trousers ending at his knees and held in place by a rope knotted around his enormous girth. His legs were like tree trunks, his biceps thick and roapy, hands like two huge hams. His body glistened in the firelight like well-oiled mahogany. But most frightening was the man's face, criss-crossed by jagged, white lines. Long ago in Africa those welts adorning his face were a thing of pride, distinguishing him as a fierce warrior whose valor had been tested and not found wanting. They had been carefully and deliberately carved then rubbed with a white powder while the wounds were still raw. It was obvious the giant wore them proudly.

When the slave saw the trio burst into his cabin he scowled darkly, making his features even more forbidding. His black eyes widened as Ben pushed a scrawny, ill-clad white girl forward.

"I have a surprise for you, Buck," Letty gloated, slanting Amanda a smug smile. Buck looked confused. He knew his mistress to be a cruel, vindictive woman and wondered what the poor white girl had done to incur her wrath. It was obvious to Buck that the girl was somehow meant to be punished and he was to be the instrument of that punishment.

"A surprise, Miz Letty? For me?" intoned Buck dully, playing along at Letty's vile game.

"This is Amanda," Letty informed him, pushing the terrified girl at the huge slave. "I am giving her to you." At Buck's horrified expression, Letty smiled, then continued breezily. "After her chores are completed for the day she is yours to bed and use in any manner you see fit." Then she dropped the bombshell that left Amanda reeling with shock and Buck gasping in disbelief. "You have two months to get her pregnant. If she isn't breeding by that time I will have you castrated and give her to another, more capable than yourself."

"You wants me to put a sucker in this white gal's belly?" Buck asked scandalized.

"Exactly," nodded Letty complacently. "Two months, Buck. Live up to your name and you will be rewarded. If not. . . you know what it means to be castrated, don't you?"

"Oh Gawd, Miz Letty. I shorely do. You gonna cut off my balls iffen I don't put a sucker in that gal's belly."

"We understand each other perfectly."

"But, Miz Letty," Buck protested weakly, "iffen I tries to pleasure that little gal I shorely gonna bust her in two. She too small to take all of me."

"You'd better try damn hard, Buck, or you will never put it in anyone again," warned Letty ominously.

"Oh Lordy, Lordy," moaned Buck softly, only the whites of his eyes visible.

"Mistress Letty, I think Buck is right," interjected Ben. "Amanda isn't built to accommodate someone like Buck. Why not let me. . ."

"No! I won't be satisfied until I see a black bastard swelling her belly. And I want it done now! I want to watch it happen!"

Amanda could neither speak nor move. Like a marble statue, cold and remote, she appeared to have retreated from reality. She once thought being raped by the Indians to be the worse kind of degradation. But she was mistaken. Letty had just devised a far more evil form of humiliation. Never would she be able to fight off the giant, as she came to think of Buck. Letty was determined to force a black man's spawn on her unwilling body. She knew she was capable of conceiving for she had quickly borne Tony a child. Letty had won after all, she shuddered, refusing to acknowledge or understand what she had just heard.

"Do you comprehend what I am saying, Amanda?" Letty demanded harshly. "Buck is going to bed you here and now. While Ben and I watch."

"Why you want me to spread this white gal, Miz Letty?" Buck dared to ask, still confused by all that was happening.

"Amanda is my slave to do with as I please, just as you are. And it pleases me to see you bed her. That's all you need to know. Now get on with it, I don't have all night. Or would you rather Ben cut you? He's good with the knife."

"Oh Lordy, I gonna spread her, I shorely am, Miz Letty. Jest don't let that overseer near me with his knife." Then he turned to Amanda. "You heard Miz Letty, gal, shuck down." Amanda stared, nearly catatonic from shock and disgust.

Buck was a prince, a warrior, a man unlucky enough to be captured by an enemy tribe in Africa and sold to slavers plying the ivory coast. Among his people his valor and daring had never been questioned. When his father departed from the earth he was to become the chief of one of the bravest tribes in Africa. But an enemy raid had changed all that overnight.

After a nighttime attack in which his mother and father had been killed and his sisters raped and taken captive, he had been severely wounded, chained, and led off, only to be sold a few days later to slavers. His journey to America had been a nightmare but he lived despite his grave injuries which had healed during the long voyage to America.

If there was one thing Buck learned during that

harrowing journey while chained to his fellow man it was compassion for those smaller and weaker than himself. Though he gave the impression of ferocity, inside he harbored a protectiveness toward the weak and the oppressed. What he saw in Amanda was not a member of the race who enslaved him, nor a white girl whose mistress gave him the right to bed her, but a small, defenseless creature too helpless to protect herself. Fortunately, Buck was smart enough to conceal his true nature from Letty, fearing that the vindictive woman would carry out her threat to have him castrated. He had no choice but to carry out Letty's terse orders—up to a point, that is.

Buck reached out with huge paws, grasped the neckline of Amanda's sacklike dress and yanked. The worn material tore easily and fell at her feet in two neat halves. "Lay down, gal, and spread yoreself," Buck ordered, scowling fiercely.

When Amanda refused to move Buck picked her up and dropped her roughly onto the makeshift bed of cornhusks and pine boughs covered with clean but threadbare blankets. Glancing casually over his shoulder to make sure Letty and Ben watched from a respectable distance, Buck fell heavily atop Amanda, his huge frame rendering her completely invisible to the two other occupants of the room. He fumbled for a few moments with his rope belt all the while whispering frantically into Amanda's ear in an effort to break through her barrier of shock.

"When I say scream, gal, you scream. Scream like you ain't never screamed before. Just like I'm killing you," Buck whispered urgently.

From across the room Letty and Ben were

unable to make out Buck's mumbled words, thinking he was instructing Amanda on how best to position herself in order to take his huge erection. Buck raised his rump in the air as if poising for entry. "Now, gal! Iffen you value your life and mine, scream!"

Amanda needed no further urging. Even if Buck's mumbled instructions hadn't penetrated her dazed brain, she knew she was about to be ravished and hurt in a way she never thought possible. With Buck's downward thrust, a long, agonized wail issued forth from Amanda's open mouth. On and on the cries continued as Buck pumped furiously, beads of perspiration glistening like dewy pearls on his dark skin. It was some minutes before Amanda realized that Buck hadn't actually penetrated, that he was only simulating copulation for Letty's benefit. But for some reason she could not stop her insane screaming.

"My God, Letty, that black bastard is killing her!" Ben mouthed, awestricken by the sight of ivory and ebony so intimately entwined.

"She'll live," declared Letty, taking great pleasure in Amanda's agony.

By now the sight of Amanda being raped was thoroughly arousing Letty. She was sweating profusely, her entire body flushed, her loins afire as she fastened lust-glazed eyes on the glistening black buttocks and straining torso. Wetness flooded her soft woman places and she clutched Ben's arm convulsively.

Buck worked himself to the point of ejaculation, knowing full well he could not fake that moment for Letty was far too knowledgeable to be fooled so easily. Finally, he could hold back no longer and, howling like a banshee, spilled his seed harmlessly into the mattress and over Amanda's outstretched thighs. But Amanda was oblivious to that final act. She had obligingly passed out.

As the last shudder left his huge body, Buck rose unsteadily to his feet, his breath still ragged, rib-cage heaving. "How's that, Miz Letty?" he asked innocently. "I spread that little gal jest like you said. Don't know iffen she'll live through it, but I done it. You ain't gonna cas. . . castrate me now, are you?"

Letty's passion-glazed eyes stared pointedly at Buck's flaccid manhood, larger than any she had ever seen despite his recent sexual encounter with Amanda. Slowly her gaze traveled upward until she reached his scarred face, almost handsome in its ugliness. Licking her lips wetly, she said, "You did just fine, Buck. And as a reward you will have Amanda in your bed every night for the next two months. Spread her at least twice each night. More, if you are able. But I expect her to be breeding soon."

"You jest leave her to me, Miz Letty. I kin pleasure her all night long and still be in the fields at dawn," assured Buck proudly.

Letty's eyes shifted to Amanda's limp form and then back to Buck's huge manhood, almost envious of the prostrate servant on the receiving end of Buck's passion when all Letty had to satisfy her lust was Ben with his less than impressive tool.

Sighing wistfully, she said, "I'm sure you can, Buck, I'm sure you can."

18

Amanda awakened in fits and starts, as if coming out of a bad dream. It was still dark outside but the glowing embers in the fireplace cast dancing shadows on the rough walls. Amanda saw that someone had covered her with a blanket and instinctively pulled it up around her neck. Gingerly she moved her leg and came in contact with a hard, immovable object. Then memory came flooding back like a raging tide. The giant! She was still in Buck's cabin! In fact, she was in his bed!

Amanda screamed. She could not help herself. Buck reared up, a deep frown creasing his scarred brow. "What you hollering about, gal?" he asked, annoyed. "Ain't you caused me enough trouble for one night? Cain't you see I ain't gonna hurt you?"

In a jumble of fragmented thoughts, Amanda remembered that Buck had only pretended to rape her for Letty's benefit. But why? she wondered anxiously. Why would he deliberately disobey his mistress when he had so much to lose by doing so?

Gathering her courage she asked him that same question.

"Don't want no white gal," Buck shrugged sheepishly. " 'Sides, I already got me a woman. A real woman. Tildy wouldn't take kindly to me spreading a white gal."

"I thank you, Buck, truly I do," said Amanda sincerely, losing some of her fear for the black giant. "But what's going to happen to you when your mistress finds out what you did? You heard her, she expects me to become pregnant within two months. What then?"

"I purely don't know, gal," replied Buck, scratching his wooly head. "I'll think of something when that time comes." To Buck two months was a long time in which to find a solution, but to Amanda it loomed just around the corner.

Amanda's woebegone expression brought an outpouring of sympathy from the huge man whose fierce visage and gigantic proportions belied his gentle nature. "Don't worry, Amanda, gal, ole Buck will think of something. And iffen he don't his Tildy will. She's some woman, my Tildy," he grinned proudly. "She's all the woman I wants or needs. You and me might be forced to share this cabin, but I ain't gonna hurt you. You kin rest easy. You jest keep Miz Letty thinking I'm spreading you and everything's gonna work out. Now go back to sleep."

Thanking God and the fates that had delivered her up to someone as kind and gentle as Buck, Amanda went back to sleep, the trying day having taken a heavy toll on her emotions.

Arising at dawn Amanda hurried to the big house clutching the torn edges of her dress together. While Lottie repaired the ripped garment Amanda revealed to her all that had transpired the night before. She knew she could trust the kindly cook, for all the slaves at Tidewater hated Letty nearly as much as Amanda did.

"What's gonna happen when Miz Letty discovers you ain't breeding?" asked Lottie, worried. "That woman shore do hold a powerful hate for you, honey. I shudder to think what she gonna do to you and Buck."

"I know, Lottie," admitted Amanda unhappily, "it scares me, too. I can only pray that Nathan and Francis will find a way to help me before then."

The rest of that day Amanda had little time to ponder her plight. She toiled long and hard but thanks to Lottie was not being starved. Letty showed up only once to assure herself that Amanda had survived Buck's attack. Mostly she wanted to satisfy her own curiosity.

"Well," said Letty, eyeing Amanda's slight form speculatively, "you look none the worse for wear. I should have known sluts like you enjoy being ridden by brutes like Buck. Tell me, what was it like? Did you faint from pleasure or pain?"

Amanda whirled to face Letty, her features mobile with rage. It took every ounce of self-control to keep from spitting in Letty's beautiful face, or tearing her blond hair out by the roots. Except for Letty's faulty judgment of Buck's gentle nature Amanda might have been cruelly raped and already impregnated. Thank God that she had been given to Buck and not to one of the other slaves who would have been only too happy to comply with Letty's wishes.

She realized that she dare not give the slightest inkling that Buck was not bedding her.

Far better to play along at Letty's foul game, Amanda sagely decided, deliberately allowing the anger to drain from her face and assuming an expression of pain, degradation and resentment in order to create the impression that she was being used by Buck against her will.

"What kind of woman are you to order that brute to rape me and then have the nerve to ask how it felt?" challenged Amanda angrily. It wasn't too difficult to pretend the resentment and rage she felt for Letty. "Have you no conscience? No mercy? Please don't send me back to him again. I. . . I can barely stand it when he. . . when he. . . . Oh, God, the humiliation! Haven't I suffered enough?"

"Not nearly enough," laughed Letty, Amanda's obvious pain and humiliation giving her immense pleasure. Amanda's fervent pleas assured Letty that Buck was carrying out his orders with obvious enjoyment.

"I would prolong your suffering indefinitely if I could," Letty coldly informed Amanda. "Perhaps I will keep the result of Buck's endeavors right here on Tidewater as my own personal slave. But then again I might sell it. Light colored slaves are in big demand nowadays and command huge prices. As for yourself," Letty taunted, "once you are delivered you will be sold to the lowest brothel in Charles Town, or perhaps shipped to Cuba or South America where red-heads are highly prized. Doubtless you will suffer, Amanda. Just as I was made to suffer when you took from me the one person I wanted above all others."

Before Amanda could reply, Letty turned on her heel and was gone. Two months was to elapse before she saw or heard from Letty again. It fell to

Ben to escort Amanda to Buck's cabin each night, pushing her inside and watching intently as Buck undressed her and shoved her onto the bed before leaving the cabin to seek out his own pleasure with Letty or some nubile slave girl unlucky enough to catch his eye.

The moment Ben disappeared from sight, Buck, contrite over his rough handling, left Amanda alone in the cabin to allow her a measure of privacy to wash and undress for bed. Sometimes he shared the pallet with her, always careful to keep to his side. But more often than not Buck could be found in Tildy's quarters, remaining until nearly dawn. Amanda had met Tildy and liked her immediately. Tall, golden-skinned, proud and regal in bearing, Tildy was a perfect match for the massive but gentle Buck. It was obvious to Amanda that the two slaves were deeply in love. But Tildy had sadly informed her that Letty would ot allow them to jump the broom together—their equivalent to marriage. She planned to breed Tildy to a light-skinned male in order to produce pale hued offspring for larger profit. Buck, nearly ebony in color, did not suit Letty's purposes where Tildy was concerned.

The end of the alloted two months was approaching swiftly and neither Amanda nor Buck had come up with a probable solution to the dilemma facing them. If Amanda was not pregnant she would be passed on to another slave while Buck suffered a far worse fate. How could life be so cruel? Amanda bemoaned. In the ensuing months she had heard nothing from Nathan or Francis and she assumed they had found no way to help her.

If only Tony hadn't left her that morning

nearly three months ago, she agonized. Where are you Tony? Are you really dead? Or did you disappear in order to be rid of an unwanted hindrance just as Letty intimated. Were you playing some cruel trick on me? Why did you make me respond to you again after I thought I was dead inside? It made no sense. Nothing of what happened made sense. If it wasn't for Jon and her own indomitable spirits she would have given up long ago. Amanda had no idea how it all would end, and end it must the minute Letty discovered she wasn't carrying Buck's child. She might as well be dead; surely she would be better off dead.

One brisk morning in November, Letty made a special trip to the fields to confront Buck. The last of the indigo was being harvested and Buck was bent over the long rows, his powerful muscles rippling along his smooth, glistening back. Letty stood silently by a few moments admiring the play of massive sinews in the hard body before speaking.

"Do you know why I'm here, Buck?" she finally asked.

Buck immediately straigthened, then turned to face his mistress, his bulk dwarfing her. "Yas'm, I 'spects I do."

"You've had your plaything two months. Is she breeding?"

Buck made a big show of scratching his head, a lopsided grin creasing his ugly features. "Don't rightly know, Miz Letty, but iffen she ain't it cain't be 'cause I ain't tried. I spreads her every night jest like you says," he lied, bringing a nasty smile to Letty's lips.

Letty could not refrain from asking, "Does

she. . . like it? Or does she still fight and scream?"

The foolish grin grew wider. "She likes it jest fine, Miz Letty. Oh, at first she cried a lot, and hollered, too. But she takes to it well enough now. I gives it to her good, Miz Letty. She gots to have a sucker in her by now. Iffen she ain't, it shorely ain't no fault of mine."

Buck's words brought back vivid images of a huge, black body covering a slender, white form; of a firm, tight buttocks pumping, filling that resisting body beneath him with an enormous, purplish-black shaft. She began to perspire profusely despite the cool air and her body tingled and ached for those ham-like hands to take possession of her own heated flesh.

"So the slut likes bedding you, does she?" gloated Letty. "You must be right, Buck, if Amanda hasn't conceived it couldn't possibly be through any fault of yours. I can't bring myself to destroy any part of your magnificent body. But Amanda has proved fertile once, and given the time will conceive again. If she isn't breeding I'll give her to another. I have other plans for your special. . . talents."

Buck hung his head. Poor Amanda, he thought sadly. If there was only some way he could save her from being ravished by another slave who would either be too cowed to disobey his mistress or else desired a taste of forbidden white flesh.

"Uh, Buck," Letty said, interrupting his morbid thoughts, "I'd like you to show me some-time just what it is you do to Amanda that she likes so much."

Buck's black eyes bugged out and the cords in his neck tightened painfully. Letty's meaning was all too clear. But if his mistress wanted him to bed her then bed her he must, even though it cost him Tildy's love. "You come by any time, Miz Letty, and I be pleased to 'blige you," he intoned dryly.

"I have some unfinished business with your whore before I can think of my own pleasure," Letty sighed regretfully. "I've arranged for Auntie May to examine Amanda tonight after she returns from the kitchen. Auntie May is an experienced midwife and quite capable of detecting even the earliest stages of pregnancy.

Buck worried and fretted the rest of that day. He had no way of warning Amanda beforehand of Letty's plans for her. Once she proved barren, as she was certain to, she would be handed over to another slave who would no doubt take great pleasure from that small, white body. There were times when even he had been tempted to take her, had actually been aroused by that slender form curled next to him in bed. Only his own rigid control and his love for Tildy had saved her.

Amanda was more exhausted than usual at the end of the her long day. Or at least it seemed so to her. Vaguely she wondered why she tired so easily of late making the hours more difficult than usual to endure. Once Buck and Amanda performed their nightly charade for Ben's benefit, Amanda was asleep almost instantly, barely able to drag herself from the bed at dawn when her exhausting day began.

Amanda was completely unsuspecting when Ben returned her to Buck's cabin that evening. As usual he waited until Buck tore off Amanda's single garment and tumbled her as gently as possible onto his pallet. Only this time Ben didn't leave immediately as was his habit. He appeared to be waiting for something or someone. They learned what it was when Letty burst into the room followed by a small, shriveled black woman wearing a bright red kerchief over her snow white hair. Her age could be anywhere between fifty and one-hundred, for despite her wrinkles she seemed ageless. Amanda searched frantically for a blanket to cover her nakedness.

Letty looked searchingly from Amanda to Buck, smirking smugly as she noted the state of amanda's undess and the position of her nude body sprawled across the crude bed. A surge of excitement flooded her loins.

"I hate to spoil your pleasure," she jibed crudely, "but I warned you what to expect at the end of two months." Icy slivers focused on Amanda's taut stomach. "Has Buck put his bastard in you yet? Are you breeding?"

Amanda froze. What could she say? For days she had considered the possibility that she might be pregnant. Not with Buck's child, certainly, but with Tony's. Her menses had not come since Tony's death but she had laid it first to grief and later to shock. Could she already have been pregnant when Letty brought her to Tidewater?

Her next words came unbidden to her lips, as shocking to Buck as they were to her. But it was too late to call them back. "I. . . I think I might be pregnant. It's a little early, but, yes, I believe it to be true," she lied calmly, half believing her own brave declaration.

A radiant smile transfixed Letty's face. All those months spent planning the perfect revenge had finally come to fruition. Tony was dead and now his beloved mistress would bear the child of a disfigured, black brute. The mother of Tony's child would be degraded in a way that even he could not visualize were he alive. But Letty, untrusting as ever, had come prepared. Dragging the wizened midwife forward, she ordered curtly, "Examine her, you old hag. And if you lie to me I'll have your hide."

"Please, make the men leave," begged Amanda as Auntie May prepared to perform the embarrassing exam. Buck automatically dropped back, but Ben crowded closer in order to view as much of Amanda's open body as possible.

Auntie May frowned, her ancient face a mass of sagging wrinkles. She, along with all of the slaves on Tidewater were well aware of the malice Letty bore her white servant. In that instant she decided to help Amanda to the best of her ability.

"How you 'spects me to examine this gal with all these mens watching?" she stated brazenly. "I'll do my job jest as soon as they leave. You, too, Miz Letty. Any fool kin see this here gal is all tied up in knots inside. Cain't do nothing lessen you all waits outside."

Letty glared disgustedly at Auntie May, but the old slave was undaunted. Shrugging, she shooed a disappointed Ben from the room, then reluctantly followed. "Call me the moment you are finished," were her parting words. Proving Amanda pregnant was more important than quibbling over whether or not privacy was required for the exam.

The moment the door closed Auntie May fixed her penetrating gaze on Amanda, clucking sympathetically at her wild-eyed expression and tense body. "Relax, chile," she gentled, "I ain't gonna hurt you. But we both knows I gotta do this."

Numbly, Amanda nodded. The slave waited

until some of the stiffness left Amanda's body then began a thorough examination that left her burning with embarrassment. When the midwife finished she studied Amanda intently through wise, slightly myopic eyes.

"You breeding, chile, ain't no doubt about it."

Again Amanda nodded, the slave's findings almost anticlimactic. "I. . . I only began to suspect. . ."

"It ain't Buck's chile." It was not a question but rather a statement. Auntie May knew the exact day Amanda had arrived at Tidewater and it didn't match her findings.

"It. . . couldn't be," admitted Amanda candidly.

"Far as I can tell you more than two months along."

"That would be about right," agreed Amanda. "What. . . what are you going to tell Letty?"

"Why, the truth, honey," the old crone said innocently. "Ain't no doubt in my mind that you breeding. What else is there to say?"

"Thank you," said Amanda gratefully, hugging the old woman affectionately.

"Don't need no thanks, child. Jest being able to put one over on that witch is thanks enough for me."

A few minutes late Auntie May summoned Letty, her anxiety and state of excitement obvious.

"Well, old woman? Is she pregnant or not? You've had more than enough time to find out," she said impatiently.

"You got no cause to scold me, Miz Letty," whined the wily old slave. "I done what you asked."

"Out with it!" spat Letty, growing more irate

by the minute. "And don't lie to me!"

"Got no cause to lie," muttered the old woman darkly. "I knows what I knows and for sure this here gal is breeding."

Letty let out a wild shriek that brought both Ben and Buck rushing into the cabin. "You're great, Buck!" she shouted jubilantly at the truly astounded Buck. "Your whore is breeding. I've done it! My God, I've really done it! Revenge! How sweet the taste!"

When her excitement abated she turned to Buck, eyes shining. "You seem to enjoy your whore so as a reward you can keep her until she is ready to deliver," offered Letty magnaminously. "Just take care. I want to see her completely broken and demoralized when the get of a slave is placed at her breast. The same breast that nursed Tony's child." Her hysterical laughter carried as far as the big house, sending shivers along the spines of all who heard the demonic sounds.

Later, when they were alone, Buck asked Amanda the question that had been burning within him since Auntie May revealed her surprising findings. "What Miz Letty gonna do to Auntie May when she finds out she been lied to?"

"Auntie May didn't lie, not about that," smiled Amanda shyly. At Buck's puzzled frown she quickly explained. "I was pregnant before I arrived at Tidewater but wasn't aware of it. The baby belongs to Tony, the man I was going to marry."

Immediately Buck's face cleared and he grinned foolishly. "I 'spects we both owes Massa Tony our gratitude. Miz Letty could have gotten real mean iffen you wasn't breeding."

After Amanda's pregnancy had been firmly

established her work load had been somewhat lightened. Letty, obsessed with the idea of Amanda bearing a slave's child, wanted nothing to interrupt the normal course of her pregnancy. To Letty's thinking Amanda's degradation wouldn't be complete until that moment when the child was put to her white breast; a dark splash against pale ivory.

At first Letty was watchful, fearful that Amanda might attempt to do away with herself or deliberately abort the child. But as time passed it became increasingly evident that she would do neither. Letty was almost disappointed by Amanda's casual acceptance of her pregnancy by Buck.

Soon, the entire plantation was abuzz with the news that Amanda was breeding. But so far only Buck, Tildy, Auntie May and Lottie knew the truth, and the secret was well kept. Amanda wondered how Tony would feel about having another child, until she remembered that he was never likely to know because he was dead. And if he wasn't dead he was no doubt far away and could care less.

19

Tony stared morosely into the swirling, muddy water of the Santee River. Some yards behind him stood the small, neat cabin that had been his home for the past three months. Just outside the doorway two children played with a frisky, lap-eared black and white puppy. From the moment Tony regained full consciousness he had grown very fond of the family who had saved his life and cared for him so selflessly.

It was big, congenial Howard Morrison, a trapper by trade, who had found Tony floating amid debris in the middle of the river more dead than alive. Howard had been in his boat checking traps when he spotted what he thought was a corpse.

Pulling Tony's lifeless body into the boat, Howard detected a faint spark of life and immediately brought him to his cabin where his pretty wife Melissa instantly set about saving the stranger's life without a second thought of who or what he was.

For days it was touch and go and the couple expected the injured man to expire at any time from his grievous wounds. But to their surprise and delight he clung to the fragile threads of life with a tenacity that was awesome to behold. Tony's most serious wound was the gash in the side of his head where the axe butt had inflicted a near-fatal injury. It was a miracle that his body became wedged in floating debris that saved him from drowning. Even Tony could not venture a guess as to how long he had been in the water before Howard found him.

He had remained in a coma for nearly a month, nursed by the compassionate Melissa. When he finally opened his eyes to the light of day it was as if he had just been born. He remembered nothing of his past. Not his name, the location of his home or his marital status. Nothing the Morrisons could tell him helped, for they knew little except how he came to be in their cabin.

Tony recuperated slowly but steadily, but another month elapsed before he was strong enough to leave the bed that Howard and Melissa had unselfishly given up for him. When they showed Tony a pocket watch they found in his clothing he became excited because it bore the initials "T.B."

But sadly, it did nothing to jog his memory. After that Howard and Melissa took to calling him "Tom." No other identification had been found on him due to the fact that it was his custom to carry all his papers in his saddlebag, and his horse was not found.

If anything spurred Tony's recovery it was the Morrison children, Jason and Anne. Tony harbored a great fondness for the youngsters aged two and four. Anne, the four year old, blond and blue-eyed, was a miniature of her mother. Jason, a robust toddler of two seemed to spark an illusive memory somewhere in the compartments of Tony's brain. He often wondered if he had a child or children someplace waiting for his return. Or a wife pining for him. There were days he brooded until his head ached and he was forced to turn his mind to less distressing thoughts.

Howard had promised to take Tony to Charles Town the moment he was able to withstand the rigors of the trip in hopes someone there held a clue to his identity. In the following weeks Tony pushed himself relentlessly in an effort to regain his strength. His second sense told him that he was desperately needed somewhere, by someone he held dear. When he voiced those sentiments to the Morrisons they did not question him but allowed him to set his own pace on his arduous road to recovery. Finally, after months of being fed and cared for by his new-found friends he felt ready to begin the search for his lost identity.

The entire family would accompany Tony to Charles Town. Howard had furs to sell and Melissa hoped to purchase supplies for the coming winter. Early one morning they loaded furs and children into a dilapidated wagon, hitched two mules to it and started off with Tony riding the only decent mount Howard owned.

With the children along the trip took longer than normal and they camped two nights beside the trail. The closer they got to Charles Town the more anxious and excited Tony became. They were nearly within sight of the sprawling town when disaster struck. Tony, fighting to cope with visions and memories warring inside his brain did not see the small deer leap from the woods directly into his path. Consequently he was caught unprepared when his frightened mount shied, pawing frantically in the air with flailing front hooves. The stodgy mules, somewhat behind Tony, did not even bat an eye, but the skittish horse was another matter altogether.

Tony fought valiantly for control but he still hadn't regained his full strength from his previous brush with death. While Howard and Melissa looked on in frozen horror, Tony plunged backwards off the rearing animal, landing heavily on the ground, his head striking a large rock laying in the path.

"Is he dead, Howard?" Melissa asked fearfully as her husband bent over Tony's prone form.

"No," came Howard's terse reply. "Just unconscious. But it's best we get him to a doctor immediately. It's hard telling what further damage he's done to himself."

"Melissa sobbed softly while they wrestled Tony's limp body into the wagon bed, resting his head on a bale of furs. "It's not fair," the softhearted Melissa contended. "Just when he was recovering. The poor man."

"He's not dead, sweetheart," comforted Howard. "He'll be just fine once we get him to town and to a doctor. Now dry your eyes before your tears upset the children. They've grown mighty fond of him, you know."

Within the hour the wagon bearing Tony's unconscious form entered Charles Town. Asking directions, Howard easily located the doctor who reacted immediately when informed there was an injured patient in the wagon.

"Don't stand out there, man, bring him in,"

ordered the doctor, quickly dispatching one of his slaves to help Howard carry Tony into his office.

The doctor's back was turned when the two men placed Tony gently down on the examining table. Melissa and the children followed them inside.

When the doctor approached his injured patient, his gasp of shock startled everyone in the room. "I thought you told me this man's name was Tom?" he asked. "Anyone within miles could tell you that this man is Sir Tony Brandt, owner of River's Edge plantation. He's been missing for months and assumed dead."

While the doctor worked over Tony, Howard explained how he had found the severely injured man in the river more dead than alive, suffering from a head wound that caused a loss of memory. They had called him Tom for lack of a better name.

"How is he, doctor?" Melissa asked anxiously when the doctor finally lifted his head. "We've grown mighty fond of him during the time he's been with us."

"He appears to have a slight concussion but I can find no other injuries. We'll know more when he regains consciousness."

"Thank God," breathed Howard, vastly relieved.

The doctor studied the couple surreptitiously from beneath lowered lids, taking special note of their threadbare but meticulously clean and pressed garments. The children looked healthy and happy but it was obvious the family barely eked out a living.

"Sir Tony owes you two a great deal," he said thoughtfully. "I'm sure he will wish to reward you for your kindness to him."

"Sir Tony doesn't owe us a thing," Howard countered indignantly. "Me and Melissa would have done the same for anyone. We were just grateful to be there when he needed us. What will happen now? Especially since he can't remember a thing about his past."

"Luckily one of Tony's friends is in Charles Town staying at the Fenton Inn. I'll summon him immediately. Chances are good that in time Tony will fully regain his memory. Amnesia of this sort due to injury is often temporary. We can only hope once Tony is back in familiar surroundings he will recover rapidly."

"How long will he remain unconscious?" asked Melissa worriedly, her pretty features softening.

"It's difficult to judge," mused the doctor, stroking his stubbly chin. "An hour, a day? It's up to God."

When Tony finally opened his eyes some hours later, Francis, confused but jubilant, sat beside him. Howard and his family had reluctantly departed some time before to conduct their own business when Francis had showed up to take up the vigil at Tony's bedside.

For several minutes Tony did nothing more than stare at Francis. His head hurt so badly he could barely think without it causing him terrible pain. Francis also remained silent, watching his friend closely, waiting for some kind of reaction from him. He had been warned beforehand of Tony's amnesia and did not want to do or say anything to upset him for he realized that Tony probably would not recognize him.

Tony finally found his tongue. "Francis? Is that you?"

"My God, Tony!" Francis exalted. "You know me!"

"Of course I know you. What nonsense are you talking?" All of a sudden Tony became aware of his surroundings. "Where am I? What happened?"

"Do you remember anything at all?"

"Of course I do. I set out for Charles Town this morning to fetch a preacher so Amanda and I could be married. Why are you questioning me like this, Francis? Do you think I've suddenly lost my mind?"

Francis hesitated. The doctor had told him to do or say nothing to upset Tony, but he felt he had to say something to disabuse Tony of the idea that only one day had elapsed instead of three months since he left River's Edge.

"You haven't lost your wits, Tony, only your memory," Francis finally said. "You started out from River's Edge over three months ago."

"Three months!" gasped a thoroughly befuddled Tony, stifling a moan of pain as he tried to sit up. He did not resist when he was gently but firmly pushed back against the pillow. It was obvious to Francis that his friend was far from well.

"If you promise to listen quietly I'll tell you all I know," began Francis, alarmed by Tony's sudden pallor. Mutely, Tony nodded, grey eyes intent.

"Somewhere between River's Edge and Charles Town you were attacked and left for dead. Later your horse was found roaming the woods. We all thought you were dead."

"Amanda!" Tony interrupted, chilled by the thought of what his long, unexplained absence had done to Amanda.

"Tony, you promised to listen," chided

Francis. "The doctor said you musn't become exited or upset. When you are ready to listen I'll continue."

"I'm sorry, Francis. It is all so confusing."

Francis took up his story. "You were found by Howard Morrison. When you finally regained consciousness you had lost your memory." Francis paused as comprehension dawned in Tony's eyes.

"Howard and Melissa! Oh course!" Tony nodded slowly. In a rush it all came back to him, the unprovoked attack upon him, the shock of icy water closing around him, and finally awakening in the Morrison cabin.

"Do you know who attacked you, Tony?" Francis asked.

"I have no idea. It happened so quickly. One moment I was kneeling beside the river and the next thing I knew I was in the Morrison's cabin.

"But you must have seen or heard something," persisted Francis.

"I'm afraid not, Francis. Has it really been three months?"

"Yes, old boy, it has," Francis said grimly, thinking of Amanda. "Nathan and I were positive you were dead. As for Amanda. . .''

"Amanda! My God, Francis! Does Amanda believe I am dead, also?"

Francis flushed. He agonized over what to tell Tony. He seemed to be holding up well under the barrage of information he's had to assimilate so far, but what would happen when he found that Letty had taken Amanda? More importantly, was Letty's claim to Amanda valid? What would Tony remember about that transaction Letty insisted had taken place? Francis grew incensed when he thought back to that day when Amanda was dragged off by a gloating Letty. Nathan had seen Amanda but once after that, and since then had not been allowed back on Tidewater property. They had no idea if Amanda was dead or alive.

Francis' anger was such that when he dwelled on Amanda's fate he could not help but blurt out, "What you did to Amanda was unforgivable, Tony! How contemptible can you get? If you weren't ill I'd challenge you and be damned to friendship!"

Tony was truly astounded by his friend's wild outburst. What was he suggesting? he wondered, puzzled and hurt. "You're not making sense, Francis. What terrible thing did I do to Amanda? My last recollection was leaving River's Edge to bring back a preacher from Charles Town. We were to be married." Then he froze, his body numb with fear as the full implication of Francis' words finally penetrated his pounding brain.

"Francis! Has something happened to either Amanda or my son?"

While Francis hesitated, Tony attempted to rise from the cot. It took ever ounce of strength Francis possessed to restrain him.

"Jon is at River's Edge well and happy," Francis quickly assured him.

"And Amanda! What about Amanda?" Tony persisted.

"Tony, do you recall riding to Tidewater the morning you left for Charles Town? To see Letty?"

"Are you crazy, Francis? Why would I do that? You know how I felt about Letty."

"God, I want to believe you!" groaned Francis, shaking his head sadly.

"If you don't tell me what this is all about I'm going to ride to River's Edge immediately and see

Amanda for myself," threatened Tony.

"She's not there, Tony."

"Not. . . ! Where in the hell is she? Has she left?" Already Tony was on his feet, weaving back and forth in an effort to maintain his balance. Francis put out a steadying hand but Tony shrugged him off.

Francis realized there was no way to keep the truth from Tony. Either Tony truly did not remember what he had done or Letty was lying. Francis preferred to think the latter.

"You sold Amanda's Articles of Indenture to Letty. Don't you remember?" he accused hotly.

"No! Oh God, no!" moaned Tony as if in pain. "Don't tell me Letty has Amanda! Please don't tell me that!"

"It's true, Tony. Letty showed up with the constable shortly after you disappeared and there was nothing Nathan nor I could do to save her."

"And my son?"

"Luckily your will saved him from the same fate." What were you thinking of Tony, to bring Amanda to such a pass? I thought you loved her."

"Haven't you been listening, Francis? I thought you were my friend. How could you believe I would do such a thing to the woman I loved? I swear I haven't seen Letty since that day she let the Indians take Amanda and I ordered her from my house. Something is wrong. Terribly wrong."

"I saw Amanda's papers with my own eyes. There is no way they could be faked. Not only did Letty possess Amanda's Articles of Indenture but a bill of sale sporting your signature."

"I burned those damned papers months ago. I watched them go up in smoke myself."

"I want to believe you, Tony, but the facts speak for themselves. Nathan hounded Letty into letting him see Amanda, but that was weeks ago. Since then we have heard nothing. Nor are we allowed anywhere near Tidewater."

"She's in danger, Francis. I know Letty only too well." Tony lurched forward, fighting nausea and weakness.

"What are you doing?" asked Francis, alarmed. "You're not well enough to go anywhere."

"I've got to find her. Every minute she remains in Letty's possession may very well be her last."

"You're forgetting the papers! Legally you can do nothing," reminded Francis, always practical.

"I'll get to the bottom of that, too. Somehow Letty gained possession of Amanda's indenture papers and then forged a false bill of sale. There's no time to waste. After I find out what she's done with Amanda I probaby will kill her." said Tony with cool deliberation. "I love Amanda, Francis. I always have. She is the mother of my son."

If Francis had any doubts before, Tony's impassioned words convinced him of his friend's innocence in the matter. Letty deserved to die, Francis reasoned, but he could not in all conscience allow Tony to commit cold-blooded murder.

"Wait, Tony," he called as Tony started somewhat unsteadily for the door. "I'll go with you."

"No, my friend, this is something I have to do myself. If you want to help me, find the Morrisons and take them to River's Edge once their business in town is concluded. I can't let them go back home without thanking them properly for saving my life."

"Are you sure you want to go alone, Tony?" Francis asked doubtfully. "You are far from well."

"The longer you keep me here talking the longer it will take me to reach Amanda," Tony declared grumpily. "If you value our friendship, do as I say. I'll be fine. The dizziness has already left and my head feels less fuzzy."

Francis shrugged. Tony, always stubborn, would do whatever had to be done, and in his own way. "You win, Tony. Just try to keep in mind that murder is a hanging offense. Letty isn't worth dying for."

"I can't promise a thing, Francis. If Letty has harmed Amanda in any way I doubt I will be able to control my actions. Even if I find Amanda well and unharmed I'm uncertain whether I can keep my hands off Letty's lying neck."

Tony was already out the door when he suddenly halted and whirled to face Francis. "One other thing, bring the preacher to River's Edge when you bring the Morrisons. I intend for Amanda to become my wife the moment we return home." Then he was gone.

Mounted on Howard's horse, Tony left almost immediately, stopping only long enough to purchase a few articles he deemed necessary for his protection. If he were in better condition he would travel without respite until he reached Tidewater, but neither he nor his mount could take such a gruelling pace without collapsing. He needed a night's rest if he expected to arrive in any kind of shape to handle Letty and her wily overseer. To keep his sanity Tony refused to dwell on Amanda and all the horrible atrocities Letty was capable of. Nothing was too evil for a bitch like Letty. Amanda might well have been starved, or flogged, or sold, the list was endless.

Despite Tony's misgivings, the moment he rolled up in a blanket that night he was asleep. He did not awaken till pale streaks of mauve lent faint color to a lowering, gray sky. The wind was chilly and brisk and Tony shivered as a cold rain began to fall. He prayed it would not change to sleet as he donned the heavy jacket he had the foresight to purchase the day before.

Within minutes he was back on the trail, gnawing on a hunk of jerky as he rode. It was very late when he finally reached Tidewater. About midnight, he judged, eyeing the position of the moon in the overcast sky. Noiselessly he made his way around to the kitchen where he remembered from previous visits that the door was never latched. As a precautionary measure Tony removed from his coat the pistol he recently purchased and set it at half-cock.

Cat-like, Tony moved through the still, dark house; a house as familiar to him as his own River's Edge. Without a moment's hesitation he stealthily made his way up the staircase to Letty's room; a room in which he had passed many a pleasure-filled hour in the past. A pool of light showed beneath Letty's door and Tony could hear the low murmur of voices as well as an occasional moan. Under his steady hand the door opened noselessly, swinging inward on well-oiled hinges. A single candle left burning on the nightstand clearly illuminated the couple engaged in passionate pursuits on the same bed where Tony had often sought his own joy.

Letty's head was thrown back, her body

arched like a taut bow, hands clutching convulsively at the bedcovers while a man, his face buried between her outstretched thighs worked industriously to bring her to the peak of ecstasy. From the looks of Letty's heaving body and glazed face it appeared he was succeeding all too well in his endeavors.

Oblivious to Tony's presence, Letty cried out, her voice drugged with passion, "That's it, Ben! Oh, God, you do it so well. Don't stop, please don't stop!"

Just as letty twitched with the beginnings of her climax, Tony moved lightning-quick to grasp Ben by the hair and forcibly remove him from between Letty's trembling thighs.

"Noooo!" Letty wailed as her source of ecstasy was snatched away.

Ben found himself laying in a limp heap against the wall in a matter of seconds.

Letty fought desperately to control her harsh breathing as Tony picked up the candle and held it close to his face, revealing his identity. Letty's shocked gasp was like a pistol shot in the silent room. "You're dead," she whispered, more frightened than she had ever been in her life. "They... they swore they had killed..." She stopped, slapping a hand to her mouth as if suddenly aware of what she had unintentionally revealed. Terror flew through her slim body, jerking her upright.

"Who said I was dead, Letty? Tony asked coldly, his face a glowering mask of rage.

"No one, Tony. Truly. I heard it from Nathan. Or was it Francis?" she lied, realizing a shiver of panic.

The longer Letty talked and hedged, the more

clearly Tony understood the full extent of her involvement in the mysterious attack upon him. Knowing Letty, Tony rightly surmised that she had paid to have him killed.

He knew Letty to be cruel and vindictive but until that moment it was difficult for him to associate her with murder. Her plan might have succeeded if it hadn't been for the Morrisons and their persistence in keeping him alive.

"It's no use, Letty," Tony ground out from between clenched teeth. "You hired those men to kill me. Don't try to deny it. What I want to know is how you managed to steal Amanda's indenture papers."

"You've got it all wrong, Tony. I love you."

"Love! Bah! You don't know the meaning of the word. What I feel for Amanda and our son is love. Your heart is filled with hate and malice."

From the corner of his eye Tony detected a stealthy movement as Ben, under cover of Tony's rising anger, inched his way to where his discarded clothing lay. From his jacket he drew out a pistol and, priming it, aimed it directly at Tony. Divining his purpose, Tony reached for his own half-cocked weapon, whirled, dropped to the floor and fired. The guns went off simultaneously. Ben's bullet whizzed harmlessly over Tony's head and embedded itself in the wall behind him. Tony's bullet unerringly found its mark.

Letty screamed when she saw her lover on the floor breathing his last. Tony's aim was perfect, striking Ben in the middle of the forehead, killing him almost instantly.

"You fiend!" shouted Letty, unmindful of her own evil intentions. "You've killed him in cold blood!"

"The same way I'm going to kill you if I find you've hurt Amanda. Where is she?"

"She's not here."

"Don't play games with me, Letty," he warned darkly. "I'm not in the mood. Where is she?"

"Why?" mocked Letty, her mouth thinning in a strangle smile. "You won't want her when you do find her."

"By God, Letty, I've had enough of your nonsense."

Before Letty realized what was happening, Tony grabbed her by the hair and hauled her out of bed and onto her feet. "I'll have the truth from you, bitch, if I have to force it from you! How did you come by Amanda's papers? I burned them myself."

Despite the seriousness of her situation, Letty could not resist the temptation to taunt and goad Tony, if only to demonstrate her cleverness. "Just before you burned the packet you thought contained Amanda's papers I made use of your convenient absence from the room to remove them from the envelope. It was a simple matter to replace them with blank sheets of parchment. It wasn't until much later that I conceived the rest of the plan. After I found out you actually planned to marry your convict whore."

"The rest of the plan being?" prompted Tony.

"To kill you! There was no stopping Letty now. It was as if a dam had burst as the words spilled forth. "I hate you! No one has ever treated me as you did. I wanted you dead in order to get to Amanda.

"It was a shame I was forced to resort to such measures, Tony, because I did love you. But at the time it seemed like the only way I could get at

Amanda to punish her for causing me such misery. Even if you find, Amanda, Tony, it's too late," Letty gloated, throwing the words at him like stones. "Much too late."

Tony resisted the impulse to kill Letty immediately. He was much too concerned over Amanda to give in to his rage. "If you've harmed her in any way you may as well say your prayers," Tony spat as anger singed the corners of his control.

"I can truthfully say I haven't laid a hand on her," informed Letty smugly. "You will not find one mark on her white skin that wasn't there before."

Letty's calm pronouncement truly terrified Tony. If she hadn't physically hurt Amanda then she had surely devised a far worse punishment. He knew it was imperative that he find Amanda as quickly as possible. Listening to Letty's wild rantings was not doing him one bit of good.

"I'm going to count to three, Letty," Tony warned ominously, "and if you haven't told me where Amanda is by then I'm going to kill you without the slightest hesitation."

"Wait!" Letty cried before Tony could begin the count. "That slut isn't worth my life."

"Well?" came Tony's terse reply.

"You'll find Amanda in the quarters. The last cabin on the left."

"Amanda lives with the slaves?"

"You could say that," hinted Letty cryptically.

Although Tony's hands itched to tighten around Letty's slim neck, he reluctantly relaxed his grip which had been curled up into tight fists. "If she isn't where you say she is, I'll be back," he promised darkly. "And if you attempt to run away you can't run fast enough or far enough to escape me."

He was nearly out the door when Letty's insane laughter halted him in his tracks, every muscle in his body taut with dread. "The last laugh is mine, darling. Turn around," Letty commanded, "I want to see your face when I tell you what your little convict has become."

Instantly Tony whirled on his heel. "Go ahead, Letty. Tell me." Though his face was calm, inwardly he died a little.

"You remember Buck, don't you, darling? "That ugly, scarred giant father bought two years ago? Amanda is Buck's woman! His whore! I gave her to him. And I must admit he took to his job with vengeance, using her two and three times a night from what I'm told. And if Buck can be believed she enjoyed every minute of it. Oh, not at first, perhaps. I watched that first time and she certainly screamed loud enough before she passed out. But once Buck broke her in to accommodate his magnificent size, she took to it readily enough. Being the whore she is, she probably loved every minute of it."

Tony blanched. The shock, the horror, of Letty's words hitting him with the force of a sledgehammer. He was beyond movement as he stood very still, his eyes blank as disbelief siphoned the blood from his face. But Letty was far from finished with the man she once loved. She was determined to impart to Tony the one thing she believed would destroy him and turn him from the woman he loved. She wanted to hurt him in the same way she had been hurt.

"Amanda's pregnant," Letty said, smiling sweetly, a glimmer of triumph darkening her lustrous eyes. "She's a fertile bitch, I'll give her that much. It took Buck only two months to get her breeding. But like I said, Buck enjoyed his work so much he refused to let up until he had accomplished what he set out to do, at my orders, of course. As far as I know he is still enjoying his plaything because I saw no reason to remove her from his cabin. Oh, yes," Letty continued blithely, ignoring the storm clouds gathering in Tony's incredulous face, "her... condition has been confirmed by a midwife." She paused thoughtfully. "I'm truly glad you're alive, Tony, otherwise you would have missed out on the final chapter of Amanda's degradation. Revenge is much sweeter when there is someone to share it with.

"Picture in your mind, Tony," grinned Letty sardonically, "that brutish black beast defiling Amanda's innocent white body! Can you bear the thought of your own son's mother nursing a mulatto infant fathered by a slave? I love it! Wasn't I clever, darling?"

Tony exploded in a tornado of seething, violent outrage. In two long strides he was at Letty's side, grasping a handful of fair hair with one hand so as to steady her head while striking her again and again with the open palm of his other hand. Briefly he considered killing her, but when she slumped unconscious to the floor, he knew he could not. Francis was right, after all. She was not worth killing or dying for. Amanda needed him, now more than ever. He would not, could not, abandon her, no matter what she had been forced into. She was but an innocent pawn in Letty's cruel game. Without a backward glance at the two bodies decorating the floor, one dead and the other unconscious, Tony swiftly left the house.

20

Guided by feeble splinters of moonlight, jaws tightly clenched, his face a grim mask, Tony made his way unerringly toward Buck's darkened cabin. The night was cold, a freezing rain was falling and Buck had built up the fire to ward off the chill, filling the room with a suffused glow, clearly defining the two bodies pressed close together on the makeshift cot. In a fever of impatience Tony burst unceremoniously through the door, bellowing like an enraged bull and the moment he spied the two occupants of the cabin innocently sleeping side by side.

Buck was instantly awake, raising himself in bed, a confused frown wrinkling his scarred brow. The blanket protecting Buck against the cold fell away revealing a naked torso glistening like polished ebony in the warm glow from the dying fire. Amanda was slower in stirring, exhaustion from her day's labors and the burden of pregnancy claiming her frail strength. But when

Tony's anguished voice rent the air, she, too, roused from her stupor, dislodging her own covering. Ill-clad in a worn chemise, Amanda's thin, pale shoulders provided a startling contrast to Buck's massive, black torso. Even in the dim light Tony could clearly make out the pointed, pink tips of Amanda's breasts pushing against the thin material of her undergarment. Just the thought of that tatooed giant putting his huge hands on Amanda's tender flesh was enough to send Tony into a scorching, towering rage.

Vengeance uppermost in his mind, he flung his not inconsiderable strength at Buck, fists clenched, arms flailing wildly. At first Buck was too startled to do more than hold Tony at bay, his slow brain unable to comprehend the reasoning behind the white man's unprovoked attack.

But if Buck was startled and confused, Amanda was totally and completely astounded. Initially, the light had been insufficient to identfy their nocturnal visitor. But when Tony hurled himself forward, a spark of flame in the fireplace ignited a piece of wood illuminating his beloved features, and for a moment Amanda thought she was dreaming. All the color drained from her face and she trembled with an emotion she thought never to feel again.

"Tony!" she gasped as the shock of seeing him alive rendered her nearly mute. "You're alive!" Tony was too busy pounding at the hapless Buck to answer.

Regaining her senses, Amanda immediately sought to separate the two struggling men. "Tony! Please stop! You don't understand!"

What Amanda failed to notice was that Buck, now fully awake, was having little or no difficulty deflecting Tony's blows. As strong as Tony was, Buck was more powerful. Had he a mind to, Buck could have easily defeated Tony, for the slave surpassed him in both girth and height. But the moment Amanda called out Tony's name Buck realized the identity of his assailant and had no wish to harm Amanda's lover and future husband.

When it became apparent to Buck that Tony was too incensed for coherent thought, he did the only thing he could think of. Immediately Tony found himself ignominiously trapped and held captive by two massive arms, effectively putting a halt to the foray that had quickly become one-sided.

"Damn you!" Tony cursed loudly. "I'll kill you for what you've done to Amanda!"

The shock of seeing Tony's beloved face again, like a spectre from the grave, was nearly too much for Amanda, and the sudden vibrancy of his voice caught her off guard. Her green eyes were huge in her pale face, her color ashen. She swayed back and forth in an effort to control her rampaging emotions.

"Tony," she whispered, afraid to speak too loudly lest he disappear. "I can't believe you're alive. Everyone told me you were dead." One slim hand reached out to caress a stubbly cheek.

Tony's anguish was unbearable. With a strength far superior to his own, Buck had somehow rendered him helpless. Why hadn't he reloaded his gun before rushing recklessly into the cabin like an untried boy? he wondered wretchedly.

"As you can see I'm very much alive, darling," Tony gasped out, sliding her a tender look. "I'll explain everything to you later. I rushed here the

411

moment I found out what Letty had done." He paused to renew his struggles against Buck's punishing hold. "Has she... has he..." he eyed Buck malevolently, "hurt you badly?"

"Tony, if you promise to listen to me and do nothing hasty, Buck will release you," said Amanda. "You don't understand the situation at all."

"Letty told me in explicit language exactly what took place in this cabin, and it's all right, my love. Nothing was your fault. Letty is a depraved monster whose twisted sense of humor and quest for revenge forced you into this intolerable, deplorable..." He was too choked to continue.

"Tony, Buck has not harmed me," insisted Amanda. "He hasn't touched me, not in the way you think."

Openly skeptical, Tony's silver gaze slid from Buck to Amanda, then back to Buck. "Let me loose, you ugly giant," Tony demanded, slanting a loathsome look at Buck. "I'll listen to Amanda, but keep in mind that I'm far from finished with you."

Buck's arms fell away. "I wouldn't hurt you, Massa Tony," he grinned foolishly, "but you shore was powerful mad."

Amanda's breath left her chest in a long, ragged sigh as she collapsed weakly against the pillow. Her face shown nearly white in the dim light, alarming Tony. Tenderly he reached out and drew her trembling body into his arms.

"Rest easy, my love," he crooned. "I won't ever let anything bad happen to you again." Amanda buried her bright head into his chest feeling more at peace than she had in months.

The reunited lovers, engrossed in each other, totally, completely, were unaware when Buck slipped unobtrusively from the cabin in search of more congenial company. He instinctively knew he was neither wanted nor missed, that Amanda would somehow explain to Tony's satisfaction all that had transpired in the past two months, including the fact that he was found in the same bed with a white woman. At that moment Buck desired nothing more than the peace and quiet of Tildy's small cabin as well as the solace of her loving arms.

Hesitantly, almost shyly, Amanda raised the heavy lashes that shadowed her cheeks, searching Tony's gray eyes for the smoky quality she loved so well. She was not disappointed. His misty gaze swept over her with tenderness and compassion.

"You don't have to explain a thing, darling," he said softly, misinterpreting her shyness for shame. "You don't have to tell me anything you don't want to. I... I know you are pregnant." Startled, Amanda opened her mouth to speak but he quickly forestalled her. "Letty told me everything; how she ordered Buck to rape you until you conceived and that the midwife had already confirmed your condition. It's true, isn't it?" he asked, hoping against all odds that somehow Letty had been lying.

Amanda nodded wordlessly. Finally, she said. "It's true, Tony. I am pregnant, but..."

"Don't talk about it if you don't want to, darling. I know how painful it must be for you. I told you before it doesn't matter. I'll not abandon you. We'll be married as soon as Francis arrives at River's Edge with the minister."

Despite the gravity of the situation a small smile played about the corners of Amanda's mobile mouth. "You'd accept Buck's child?" she couldn't help but tease.

Tony's face turned a shade lighter but he nodded, never more serious in his life. He was determined to stand by Amanda no matter what. Once the baby was born was time enough to think about its future. After all, wasn't the child a part of Amanda? "I swear, darling, I'll take care of you both."

Hesitantly, Tony's lips captured hers, his kiss gentle, thorough, agonizingly tender. He remembered how skittish she was after her terrible experience with the Indians and was fearful of her reaction to him. But he needn't have worried. Amanda's small body arched upwards to meet his mouth, eagerly parting her lips beneath his gentle probing, allowing Tony free access. Her arms crept around his neck to pull him even closer. Tony was the first to break it off. "Thank God, Amanda," he breathed gratefully. "I was so afraid you would be repulsed by me after Buck. I couldn't help but think of the way you were after the Indians." He stopped in mid-sentence, unwilling to dredge up old, painful memories.

Hugging her slim body close it seemed impossible to Tony that she was expecting a child. He was struck by the fragility of her bones, the spareness of her flesh. That she had suffered at Letty's hands was all too apparent. It hurt him to think of the anguish and pain she must have endured when that brute Buck raped her time after time. Yet, those thoughts kept intruding upon his joy at finding her again.

"Why didn't you want me to fight with Buck, darling?" Tony asked suddenly, puzzled. "How could you stand the sight of him after what he did?"

"You might find this hard to believe, Tony, but Buck never touched me, not once."

"I. . . don't understand. Letty told me she watched while Buck raped you."

"Letty saw only what we wanted her to see. She stood across the room while Buck supposedly attacked me. What she didn't know was that it was all a charade to fool her and Ben."

"A charade?" Tony found it difficult to believe Amanda's far-fetched explanation. "Why should Buck pretend when Letty gave him permission to take you?"

"It's simple," said Amanda, blushing. Buck didn't want me. He has a woman whom he loves. Besides, he said I was too small for him." Tony could only stand there stupidly, his face a mask of utter disbelief. "Did you hear me, Tony? I did share Buck's cabin but nothing happened. It was all a pretense to keep Letty from harming either of us. She threatened Buck with castration if he failed to get me with child."

"Then I have much to thank Buck for," Tony replied, finally finding his voice. And he meant it. Surely Buck was one man in a million. Any other man, black or white, would not hesitate to ravish so delectable a creature as Amanda. Especially when given leave to do so. Suddenly a niggling thought joggled his dazed brain. Amanda was pregnant!

"Amanda!" he blurted out thoughtlessly, "how could you be pregnant if. . . My God!" he mouthed, comprehension dawning, "the baby is. . ." His discovery rendered him almost speechless.

"Yes, Tony. It must have happened that one night we spent together before you disappeared.

Are. . . are you sorry?'' she asked shyly.

Tony threw back his head and laughed with sheer joy. He had been utterly devastated when Letty told him what Buck had done to Amanda, but now he was suffused with a happiness so intense he thought his heart would burst of it. "Sorry!" he cried out. "Sorry to have another child by you? A brother or sister for Jon? I'm delighted! I'd like to tell the world!"

Belatedly he remembered Amanda and what she had suffered. "Are you sure you and the baby are well?" he asked worriedly. "Has Letty done you any harm?"

"It was pretty bad at first," admitted Amanda hesitantly. "Thoughts of Jon was all that kept me from losing my mind. I kept thinking how empty his life would be without father or mother to love and guide him. I had to live for him. But once Letty learned I was pregnant things went easier for me. In fact, she became watchful of me, fearful lest I miscarry and spoil her revenge. Later, she. . . she was going to sell me to a brothel. But enough of me. Where were you all this time, Tony? Why didn't you return to River's Edge, or at least get in touch with us? Letty said you sold her my papers because you grew tired of me and wanted to return to England. Nathan and Francis were certain you were dead.''

"Letty lied, darling. I told you I burned those damned papers and I genuinely believed I had. Letty stole them replacing them with blank paper, which I burned believing I had set you free. She also planned my death.''

Amanda stifled a gasp of outrage, her eyes round as saucers. Then Tony proceeded to tell her all he remembered of those months he lay near death. "And I owe my life to the Morrisons," he said when he had explained how his newfound friends had literally pulled him from the edge of death.

"I thank God they were there when you needed them. I wish I could thank them in person," said Amanda gratefully.

"You'll have your wish," smiled Tony. "Francis is bringing them to River's Edge when he returns with the preacher. I wanted them present at our wedding. Their children will be good company for our son."

"I'm glad," replied Amanda dreamily, already picturing herself as Tony's wife, raising his children, Mistress of River's Edge, the home she had grown to love.

Sometime during that time Tony had rekindled the fire, for the night had grown very cold. They continued talking for awhile until both of them knew all there was to know of their lives during the past three months. Realizing that it was much too late to take Amanda out into the chill air, Tony suggested they spend the remaining night in Buck's cabin, but was uncertain how Amanda felt about remaining at Tidewater a moment longer than necessary. Tony knew they had nothing more to fear from Letty, and it was obvious that Buck had found more hospitable quarters for the night with his woman.

"Would it upset you, darling, if we stayed here in Buck's cabin until morning?" asked Tony.

"Letty. . ." began Amanda fearfully.

"She'll not bother us."

"Then Ben, he's just as bad."

Tony hesitated a moment. "Ben won't be a threat to you or to anyone else ever again."

"You mean he is dead?" Did you. . . ?"

"I had no choice, darling. He fired the first shot. My aim was better. Do you think Buck will have any objections to our using his cabin?" he asked, abruptly changing the subject.

"He's probably with Tildy right now and isn't giving us a thought," smiled Amanda. "They want to marry but Letty won't let them. Can we do anything for them, Tony?"

Tony gazed at Amanda thoughtfully a few moments before answering. "After what Letty has done to you I'm sure she will agree to anything I suggest. I'll send Nathan to deal with her later."

Then as long as you are here with me I don't mind staying until morning. This cabin holds no unpleasant memories for me."

Actually, Tony was exhausted and a few hours sleep appealed immensely to him. He had had little sleep the night before in his anxiety to reach Tidewater and Amanda.

With a weary sigh he stretched out beside Amanda and took her in his arms, settling her comfortably in the curve of his body with every intention of going immediately to sleep. But for some reason sleep eluded him. He could tell by her breathing that Amanda was as wakeful as he was.

It had been so long since he held her in his arms that his wayward body reacted violently to her nearness. Nor could he stop his hands from discovering her full, sweetly curved breasts, his thumbs rubbing gently back and forth against upthrust nipples with startling results as the pulsating, pink buds swelled against his palms.

Amanda's soft sigh lent Tony courage as he buried his face in her fragrant curls, breathing in her special aroma. "It has been so long, my love," he whispered softly into her ear. "I want you."

Amanda turned in his arms, her eyes luminous. "I've missed you, Tony. And... and I want you, too," she revealed shyly. Their last time together seemed so far in the past that the shyness came naturally.

Her pliancy acted as a command to him. Tenderly he removed her ragged shift, then his own clothing, pausing to stare admiringly at her satiny skin glistening dully in the dim light and curved so enticingly in all the right places. Her breasts were fuller with her pregnancy, the nipples more prominent, tilting sharply upward as if begging for his attention. Never one to turn down a challenge, Tony immediately drew one erect bud into his mouth, his tongue touching the pink tip, tracing it in warm moist circles. Amanda's slender body arched, thrusting her breast even deeper into his mouth. She sighed softly as his lips left one breast to lavish the same tender attention on the other.

Tony's hands followed his mouth to her breasts as his lips found the pulse at the base of her throat, traveled the long column of her neck and pressed soft, feathery kisses to her eyelids before covering her mouth in a searing kiss that left her breathless. Her lips parted and his tongue eagerly sought the warmth of her honeyed mouth. He kissed her so hungrily, so thoroughly that burning waves of desire swept through her, clamoring for possession. But Tony was not about to let her off so easily despite his own rampaging ardor.

His lips left her mouth and moved slowly downward once more, pausing at her quivering breasts, nipples hardened as his tongue played a heated path from one to the other. As if by magic his lips were at her curving waist, worshipping at her slightly rounded stomach, the gentle swell of hips; but still he did not desist.

Amanda jumped when Tony's hands found the copper curls at the juncture of her smooth thighs, but she did not protest when he gently spread her legs. His long fingers teased and caressed until she was tense and throbbing, drawn as tight as a bowstring. She gasped aloud when he sought and found the velvety warmth of her innermost core. Her body jerked violently when he slid his big frame downward and she felt the hard, hot thrust of his tongue, probing, tasting, exciting her beyond belief.

"Oh God, Tony! No!" she cried out against his devastating intimacy. But the cry turned into a moan of pleasure as his tongue drove her higher and higher.

"Lie still, darling," came Tony's hoarse reply, "you are as beautiful there are you are anywhere. I want to fill myself with the taste and feel of you."

Abandoning herself to Tony's tender ministrations, Amanda writhed and groaned, driven by a terrible, grinding need, grasping his thick, black hair in order to pull him even closer. Within moments he felt the first spasm begin in the region where Tony's mouth, lips and tongue worked with diligent care and continued in wave after ecstatic wave until she thought she would break into a million jagged fragments. Tony did not stop until she was quiet and her breathing slowed to tiny, sucking gasps.

"I love to please you, my love," he whispered, smiling at her sigh of contentment. "Almost as much as I enjoy losing myself within your sweet flesh."

He lifted himself to rise above her and then lowered himself until he felt the magic of her enfold and enclose him within her. When he was completely sheathed inside her, he thrust smoothly, filling her as he never had before. His mouth played a tune of sweet pleasure on her mouth as their bodies touched, clung and molded together into one. His breath came in harsh, rasping gasps and hers was a responding breathlessness. Amanda thought she had already experienced the ultimate with her dramatic climax only moments before, but when Tony began moving, pulling his throbbing, engorged manhood nearly all the way out, then thrusting to the hilt, she felt as if her blood had turned to white hot lava and was astounded by her quick response.

Eagerly she paced herself to his speed, and when his movements increased, so did hers. Feeling the first tremor begin in her slender body, Tony allowed his own thundering passion to burst forth. Mouth to mouth, their breath mingled, their cries rose and fell; their passion was finally appeased. Afterwards, Tony could not bear to leave her body and, thoroughly exhausted, they fell asleep, connected to one another by a bond of everlasting love.

The sky turned a soft mauve that comes as the moon wanes and the sun rises low in the east when Tony next awoke. He doubted if they had slept more than two hours but he was anxious to return to River's Edge with Amanda. They had not seen their son in months and that thought spurred him to action. Gently he awoke Amanda, a surge of anger twisting his gut as he helped her into the shapeless slave garment Letty had forced her to wear. After wrapping Buck's blanket around her slim shoulders, they left the cabin.

Tony smiled when he saw Buck loping toward them leading Howard's horse, the same one he had ridden to Tidewater the day before.

"Thanks Buck," he grinned, accepting the reins from the huge slave. "I guess I owe you an apology. Amanda explained everything to me."

"Don't owe me no 'pology, Massa Tony," scoffed Buck. "Iffen I so much as touched yore woman my Tildy would have had my skin."

"Then perhaps I should thank her, too," Tony suggested wryly. "Have you been to the big house? Is your mistress around this morning?"

"The huge man scratched his wooly head. "That's what I was coming to tell you. Lottie tole me Miz Letty done gone. Lit out of here sometime last night jest like there was a tiger on her tail.

"There's a dead man in her bedroom, though. Don't 'spose you know anything 'bout that, do you, Massa Tony?" Buck questioned, grinning broadly. When Tony didn't answer, Buck continued. "Lottie had me and one of the hands bury the overseer in the cemetery. I don't think nobody gonna miss him nohow," he chuckled.

"He is no great loss, Buck," Tony heartily agreed, "and Lottie did the right thing. If Letty doesn't show up in a couple of days send someone over to River's Edge and I'll see what can be done. Stanley is still my friend despite the actions of his despicable daughter and I can't allow his plantation to fall into ruin. I'll write to him and see what he wants done here."

When Nathan looked out across the fields and saw a lone rider approaching with what appeared to be a bundle of rags in his arms, he immediately tensed, expecting trouble. No one at River's Edge had the slightest inkling that Tony was alive so when the rider was close enough to identify, Nathan blanched, the shock of seeing his friend and employer alive causing him to falter. Finally gaining his wits he sprinted forward, happiness lighting his mobile features.

"I knew it! I knew it!" he shouted jubilantly. "Against all odds I knew you couldn't be dead! But for God's sake, Tony, where have you been? Don't you know that Amanda. . ."

Just then the bundle in Tony's arms shifted revealing a wealth of coppery hair and a pair of dancing, green eyes peeping above a ragged blanket.

"Amanda! Thank God you've found her, Tony. And she's alive and well. You are well, aren't you?" Nathan asked anxiously, noticing for the first time the pale mauve shadows marring the delicate skin beneath her eyes.

"I'm fine, Nathan, just fine. Especially now," Amanda answered shyly, gazing raptly into Tony's smiling face. Their joy in having found one another again was so obvious that Nathan could not help but rejoice with them even though something akin to pain shot through his heart.

"Has Francis arrived with my guests?" Tony asked.

"No one is here except little Jon. The place is like a morgue without you and Amanda," Nathan answered, grinning foolishly.

"Jon!" cried Amanda anxiously. "How is my son?"

"Our son," reminded Tony gently.

Amanda flushed. "Our son."

"Well and happy, but he misses his parents. But don't worry. He lacks for nothing. Not with all those doting servants around to spoil him. I. . . I make a special effort to visit with him every day."

Soon Tony and Amanda were making their way towards a happy, boisterous homecoming. Jemma cried unrestrainedly, Tess and Cory wailed hysterically, and even staid, old Linus was more animated than he had ever been in his life. But more importantly, at least to Tony and Amanda, their son appeared just as Nathan described him, healthy, happy and content. When all the excitement died down Tony related to the wide-eyed listeners all that had transpired during the previous months to keep him from returning to River's Edge.

"I never saw who attacked me or if there was more than one person," Tony said. "I still had a few coins in my pocket so I knew robbery wasn't the motive."

"Your horse was found in the woods," Nathan revealed, "and all your possessions were intact. We didn't know what to make of it. We could only assume you were dead. Like a vulture waiting to pick the bones, Letty showed up here with the authorities waving Amanda's Articles of Indenture like a red flag."

"The bitch," spat Tony derisively. "She planned it all. She paid to have me killed then forged a bill of sale. I only wish there was some way I could prove what she did."

"But she had the papers in her hand, Tony," Nathan insisted, his tone tinged with disapproval. "You swore to me you burned them."

"It's the truth, Nathan. I did burn the envelope that I assumed held Amanda's Articles of Indenture, but Letty had taken them from the envelope and put in blank paper."

"Where are those papers now?" Nathan

asked. "Did you get them from Letty?"

Tony shook his head negatively. "I don't know what happened to those damned papers. If Letty still has them she won't dare use them now that I know what she did. Even Letty isn't that stupid."

Then the subject changed to the family who had. sheltered Tony during his convalescence. "What kind of people are the Morrisons?" Nathan asked curiously.

"The best," grinned Tony. "Howard and Melissa opened their hearts as well as well as their home to me. Melissa refused to let me die. Singlehandedly she pulled me from death's door. I literally owe them my life. That's why I want them here for our wedding," he explained, turning to Amanda.

"So you can see why I want the Morrisons treated kindly," Tony said when his narration ended. "They saved my life and I feel as if they are family. Nothing is too good for them."

"Don't you worry none, Massa Tony," Jemma sniffed, wiping her eyes with the corner of an immaculate apron. "We gonna take good care of yore friends." Then, in an authorative voice she quickly dispatched Tess and Cory to ready the two remaining guest rooms while Linus was sent to check the larder.

Finally, Amanda and Tony found themselves alone with their son. With tears of joy shimmering in her eyes, Amanda buried her face in his soft, sweet-smelling neck, kissed his downy cheek, and hugged his chubby body until he began protesting violently. Laughing, Tony took him from his mother's arms and together they mounted the stairs to the privacy of their own room where they continued playing with him until he grew sleepy.

Only then did they reluctantly relinquish him to a beaming Flora.

After taking turns bathing in a big, tin tub before a blazing fire, Amanda and Tony ate a delicious meal served in their room by Linus and went immediately to bed, sleeping the clock around.

Three days later Francis arrived with the Morrisons and Parson Johnson. Once again the reunion was spirited and boisterous. Amanda looked radiant after a good rest, wholesome food and proper clothing. Tony briefly glossed over the months Amanda had spent at Tidewater, mentioning nothing about Letty's vile plan to debase Amanda using Buck as her instrument of torture.

Amanda took to the Morrisons immediately. The little family was forthwith given two adjoining rooms and the children taken to the nursery to join little Jon and his nurse. Without too much argument they were persuaded to stay on at River's Edge for an extended visit. That evening a festive dinner, lovingly prepared by Jemma and served by the two giggling maids, was thoroughly enjoyed by the happy group.

After dinner was concluded Melissa and Amanda went upstairs together to put their children to bed and become better acquainted. At first Melissa was shy but soon the two young women were chatting and laughing over the antics of their children.

"Look how well Jason and Jon get along," Amanda smiled as the two sturdy toddlers tumbled about the floor of the nursery.

"And see how Anne acts the little mother," Melissa added fondly.

"They will make good companions," Amanda hinted. "Tony told me your home is quite remote. Do you ever get lonely?"

Melissa laughed softly. "My home, Amanda is a small hovel compared to Tony's grand house. You are a lucky woman."

"Did Tony tell you anything about me?"

"No, nothing," admitted Melissa shyly. "For months he didn't even remember his own name. When he finally came to his senses we had already left the doctor's office. Afterwards Francis came looking for us to tell us the good news. He said Tony had already left on an important errand and wished us to accompany Francis to River's Edge once our business was concluded."

"And Francis told you nothing about me?"

"Only that the preacher was coming along to marry you and Tony. "I. . . I didn't know you had a child together." These last words caused her to blush so profusely that Amanda could not suppress a grin.

"Are you shocked?"

"Of course not," stammered Melissa indignantly. Although, if the truth be known, Melissa was a trifle shocked. Why hadn't they married before the child was born? she wondered vaguely. But it didn't matter, she truly liked Amanda.

"My relationship with Tony has been. . . er. . . slightly irregular, to say the least. I am, or rather I was, until Tony set me free, an indentured servant. Tony purchased my papers and I became his housekeeper."

"Oh, Melissa mouthed, her eyes big and wide. "That means you were a. . ."

"Convict," supplied Amanda, the words bringing a frown to her smooth brow. "Unjustly imprisoned for stealing a loaf of bread to feed my dying mother."

"Oh, Amanda, how horrible for you," commiserated Melissa. "And how romantic that Tony should find you and fall in love."

Amanda smiled wryly, recalling how Tony had fought against his feelings for her but in the end their love for one another had prevailed.

"It was not easy for us, Melissa. Tony is the son of an earl and I, I am from a poor but respectable family. But against all odds we fell in love. Unforeseen circumstances prevented our marriage until now."

"All that will be rectified when you become Tony's bride tomorrow," beamed Melissa.

"I'm so glad you're here, Melissa," Amanda said, hugging the pretty woman. "I've never had a friend my own age before, except perhaps for Peony."

"Peony?" Melissa asked blankly.

"A girl from out of the past; a convict like myself who once tried to help me. I thank God I am here to tell about it. But enough talk of me." Amanda smiled cheerfully, putting the past behind her once and for all. "Let's see our children to bed and join the men."

Later, when Francis and Tony were alone, Francis imparted a bit of information that left Tony flabbergasted.

"I came across Letty in Charles Town just before I left," Francis announced blandly.

Tony scowled darkly. He had hoped never to hear that name again. Francis ignored Tony's apparent agitation as he continued blithely. "I am now the proud owner of Tidewater, lock, stock, and barrel."

"Tony was stunned. "What?" he cried. "Is this another of her tricks?"

"Not this time, old boy," Francis gaily informed him. "She is gone. Gone for good. Took the North Star out of Charles Town the day before I left. To join her father, or so she said. It looks as if we'll be neighbors."

Tony had only one request of Francis, one to which he readily agreed: To allow Buck and his woman, Tildy, to marry. Tony was pleased to know that Letty's slaves would fare much better under his friend's protection.

The parson Francis brought to River's Edge was a funny little man who seemed to have a perpetual smile pasted on his not unpleasant features. His wit appeared out of keeping with his profession.

"Are you prepared to perform a marriage ceremony, Parson?" Tony asked when they were all seated in the parlor enjoying coffee after dinner.

"That's what I am here for," beamed the little man.

"We will have a huge celebration with all our people on hand to participate. Amanda and I have more than a marriage to celebrate," he announced slyly, ignoring Amanda's gasp of outrage, for she knew exactly what Tony intended to divulge.

"Tony! No!" she protested, embarrassment coloring her features.

Slanting her an indulgent glance Tony blithely

continued. "Our marriage alone is cause enough for a celebration, but," here he paused, his mouth drawn up in a lopsided grin, "I have recently learned that I am to become a father for the second time. Our happiness is twofold."

The painted smile never left Parson Johnson's face but he unaccountably dropped his fork in his plate. Francis and Nathan were generous with their congratulations while the Morrisons, a little shocked and more reserved, nevertheless added their expressions of happiness to the beaming Tony and somewhat subdued Amanda. Amanda was more than a little put out that Tony had blurted out such delicate information before the parson and her new friends.

"I would say," began the parson, clearing his throat dramatically, "that I should have been summoned months ago." Everyone laughed uproariously but for the non-plussed parson and a furious Amanda.

The gay evening came to an end all too soon. Amanda had found a friend in sweet-faced Melissa who confided that she, too, was expecting another child. Amanda dreaded the thought of losing her only friend once their visit came to an end and she confided as much to Tony when they retired to their room later that night.

"I've decided to ask Howard to remain at River's Edge as overseer, darling," Tony informed her as he undressed for bed.

"It would be so nice to have Melissa here," she replied wistfully. "Did you know she is going to have a baby, too?" Suddenly Amanda's eyes widened as something Tony just said finally registered. "But we have an overseer. What about Nathan? You just can't let him go after he's been so faithful to you."

Tony went on to explain that Francis had just purchased Tidewater from Letty and ended by saying, "And he asked Nathan to act as overseer. Francis doesn't consider himself experienced enough to run so large a plantation without expert advice."

"I'm certainly not sorry to hear that Letty has gone to England," Amanda contended, "but I can't believe Nathan would desert you."

"Did you ever stop to think that Nathan loves you, darling?" Tony explained gently. "How do you suppose he feels seeing you day after day, knowing that you are another man's wife and he can never have you? Believe me, this way is for the best. Francis needs him, and he can still visit with us often. He's grown terribly fond of our son, considers himself an uncle."

Amanda paused thoughtfully as she sat brushing her lustrous hair before Tony's admiring eyes. "I suppose you are right," she sighed as she finished her task and settled comfortably in bed. "I'm very fond of Nathan myself and I'd be sad to think I couldn't see him again."

"Not too sad, I hope," teased Tony as he slipped into bed beside her.

"You don't ever have to worry about me, Tony. I'm yours forever."

"And I am yours," responded Tony pulling her into his arms. "Now go to sleep, my love. Tomorrow is your wedding day and I want you fresh and beautiful. You have our child to think of, too," he reminded her, patting her stomach fondly. Both were asleep within minutes.

At high noon the next day Amanda became

Tony's wife. The wedding took place in the parlor with Howard and Melissa acting as witnesses. Nathan was best man and Francis gave the bride away. Amanda was breathtakingly lovely when she appeared at the top of the curving staircase on Francis's arm. She wore the off-white dress she had fashioned expressly for that purpose months ago. The squared off neckline provided a tantalizing glimpse of the tops of creamy breasts while the tiny pleats falling from just below the bustline emphasized the shapely curve of hips and thighs. Tess had becomingly arranged her burnished hair atop her head in a regal mass of curls held in place by a white ribbon, allowing tiny ringlets to frame her radiant face.

Tony, too, was resplendent in a black broadcloth suit that hugged his powerful shoulders and outlined his muscular thighs. Spotless white stock and gleaming black boots lent a touch of elegance to his costume.

The house servants watched solemnly as the little parson pronounced them man and wife. Then they all crowded onto the wide veranda beyond which the entire population of River's Edge waited for the festivities to begin. Soon everyone was feasting from heavily laden tables set up in the yard, and later a huge bonfire was lit and kept burning throughout most of the night. Dancing began at dusk and Tony was loudly acclaimed when the following day was declared a holiday in honor of his marriage.

Shortly after dark Tony quietly led Amanda away from the celebration and into the house. When they reached the foot of the stairs he swept her off her feet and carried her in his strong arms the rest of the distance to their room. A fire burned in the grate, casting long shadows against the walls. Tony set her on her feet and kissed her hungrily while long, deft fingers disposed of the fastenings at the back of her gown. Within minutes she stood tremblingly nude, a pool of shimmering cloth billowing about her dainty feet.

Tony's throat thickened until he was sure he could not speak. But his low, constricted moan spoke louder than words. Reverently, his lips touched her eyelids, sliding along a smooth cheek, nibbling at the corner of her mouth, pausing at the wildly beating pulse at the base of her throat. The rasp of his palm against her nipple sent a jet of fire through her. Amanda burned everywhere he touched with the scorching pressure of lips and hands. She felt as though she was being seduced by a thunderstorm.

She cried out in deprival when he stepped away to remove his own clothing, but it was only seconds before he was with her again and gently easing her onto the bed, staring down on her with hot appraisal before he came down on his knees beside her. Amanda opened her arms and pulled him close, rolling until they lay side by side, flesh to flesh.

Tony lowered his head and Amanda felt her nipples rise to meet his warm mouth and hot, flicking tongue. Everything that had gone before, all the pain she had suffered at his hands disappeared in a surge of passion that ignited her senses and sent her blood rushing through her veins. The only reality was now, this room, this bed, her husband's naked flesh pressed urgently against hers. Tony lavished tender, loving care on every inch of her pulsating body until she felt like she harbored a bubbling inferno about to erupt.

Amanda's own hands roamed freely over Tony's muscular form, seeking all the sensitive places to give him the most pleasure. He gasped aloud when she found his hardness, stroking it gently with her small hands until he groaned in ecstasy.

"That's enough, my love," he whispered urgently, "or your wedding night will end before it begins." Grinning foolishly, Amanda relea_ d him instantly and lay back, allowing him free reign to all her secret places.

He touched her, caressed her, and held her, making love to her with a wild, frenzied ardor, filling her only to leave her hungry for more.

When he finally thrust into her she accepted him eagerly, wrapping her arms and legs around his pounding body. She was all feeling and passion, her entire being concentrating on that moment when her soul left her body.

Tony held himself in check by the most stringest effort of will, desiring only to give her the greatest pleasure possible. When he felt her slender form tremble with the first spasms, he captured her mouth, sensuously exploring it with his stabbing tongue in a rhythm to match his thrusting body. Her cries of completion filled his mouth. Only then did he allow his own mounting ardor to soar. Grasping her firm buttocks in both hands, Tony lifted her hips to meet his final surge of unleased passion. Then suddenly his whole body tensed, arched, and he spun dizzily into space amid shooting stars and blazing light.

Amanda swam through an eddy of quiet contentment while Tony, raised on one elbow, watched her through smoky eyes, lavishing loving caresses on the slight rise of her stomach.

"I think I've found the perfect way to tame and conquer your heart forever," Tony teased lightly.

"How is that, my love?" asked Amanda dreamily, arching a delicate brow.

"Make love to you ceaselessly and keep you pregnant,' he said, a wolfish grin lighting the lean angles of his face.

"You've already accomplished the one," Amanda sallied impishly, green eye aglitter. "Are you man enough to attempt the other? So soon?"

Laughing happily Tony proceeded to demonstrate to her just how manly he was as once more he began a tender assault upon her senses.

21

Final Judgment
1764

Never in her wildest dreams had Amanda expected to be so happy Certainly not when she boarded the prison ship bound for a strange new world and an unknown master that day over three years ago. At that time she had thought her life at an end. Now, she smiled happily. She was a married woman with a two year old son and a three month old daughter nursing at her breast.

Amanda gazed lovingly at her baby daughter whose tuft of blond fuzz at the top of her head and leaf-green eyes gave hint of the great beauty she would one day become. They named her Laura after no one in particular and Tony was so enraptured by the tiny infant that he was loathe to leave her sight for an instant.

Placing Laura tenderly in her crib and leaving her for Flora to look after, Amanda trailed downstairs in a state of euphoria. Given her frame of mind, nothing or no one could mar her happiness.

Unaccountably her thoughts flew to Tony and she headed for his office, a dreamy smile curving her full lips.

"Are you busy, Tony?" she asked, peering into the room.

"Never too busy for you, my love," he answered fondly. "Has my daughter drunk her fill already?"

"Yes," grinned Amanda. "She isn't nearly as greedy as Jon was at her age."

"Or as greedy as her father," leered Tony with a twinkle. "I never grow tired of feasting at your bountiful table."

"Tony, you're impossible," blushed Amanda.

"No, my love, just completely and totally enslaved by love."

How those words thrilled Amanda. She had waited so long to hear them that she never tired of them.

"But seriously, sweetheart," Tony added, "I was about to come looking for you." Puzzled, Amanda waited for him to continue. "We received an invitation today. To a party."

"A party! How wonderful!" exclaimed Amanda, clapping her hands. "Is Francis having a party! It's about time he met some eligible young women."

"I agree, my love, but Francis is not giving the party."

"Then who. . . ?"

"Our new neighbors," informed Tony. "They have finally arrived from England and moved into the new home they had built on the land adjoining ours."

"I was wondering when they would show up," mused Amanda, who had been curious about the owners of the newest and grandest plantation on the Santee River, ever since construction had begun several months ago. It was a grand manor, far grander even than River's Edge or Tidewater. She was dying to see the inside and meet the owners.

On one of his trips to Charles Town Tony had discovered that Henry Worthington, the Duke of Westhaven, had purchased the land adjoining his and that his agent in South Carolina was overseeing the building of the house according to the duke's specifications.

"The Duke and Dutches of Westhaven are extremely wealthy," imparted Tony, "and I heard the party is to be a lavish affair."

"I hope the Duchess is friendly and that we can become friends. But perhaps I am assuming too much," she quickly added. "I am certain the Duchess has little time for the likes of me."

Tony's anger erupted, and, slamming a fist against his desk with such force Amanda jumped, he said, "Have you forgotten you are the wife of an earl? No one dare look down on you, my love. I won't allow it."

Amanda flushed, loving Tony all the more for his loyalty. He might have forgotten she had once been a convict and dreadfully used by savages but she could not. She shuddered to think what people would say or do once they learned of her past. So far only Francis and Nathan knew all the details of her narrow escape from Brave Fox and his companions. Of course, Letty knew of her ordeal, but she was far away in England and posed no threat.

"I love you, Tony," Amanda said, planting a kiss on his forehead, "but I'm afraid you're prejudiced. In any event we'll soon find out just how friendly the Duchess intends to be."

"I hear the Duke is an old man, well into his sixties. No doubt the Duchess is a staid matron, prim and proper. I can't imagine what brings them to South Carolina."

"We'll know soon. When is the party?"

"In one week, my love, so get out your prettiest gown."

It just so happened that Amanda had recently made a new party gown with the help of Melissa. The two young women had become fast friends and though their growing families kept them busy they still found time to visit one another so that their children might play together. A week after Amanda gave birth Melissa was delivered of a healthy son she and Howard named William. Little Will was a blond cherub almost as fair as Laura.

Amanda was delighted when she learned Melissa and Howard had also been invited to the Duke's party. So were Francis and Nathan. For a week the conversation centered on the coming event and speculation was rife concerning the highborn pair who had chosen to build their home in a virtual wilderness.

The night of the party Howard and Melissa brought their children for Jemma and Flora to look after and the two couples set out together in the new carriage Tony had recently ordered for his growing family. Until now it had been used mainly for travel between Tidewater and River's Edge.

Amanda had caused a mild sensation when she appeared at the top of the stairs shortly after the Morrisons' arrival. Her gown of vibrant green

satin provided a perfect foil for her fiery mass of
hair artlessly coiffed and groomed atop her head
in a profusion of sausage-like curls and springy
wisps falling about her face. The gown left her
creamy shoulders bare, hugged a miniscule waist
and flared out dramatically over several stiffened
petticoats. Tony had never seen her dressed in
such finery and thought her the most magnificent
creature alive. Amanda blushed prettily when he
told her so.

Melissa's blond loveliness was no less stunning in a royal blue creation that made her eyes
appear almost violet. A tiny, doll-like woman, her
diminutive form was perfectly displayed by the
cut of her gown. It was obvious Howard agreed
when Tony said, "We certainly are lucky, Howard,
to be married to two of the most beautiful women
in South Carolina."

"In America, I believe," quipped Howard,
causing Melissa to blush profusely.

The duke's house took Amanda's breath away.
Situated atop a hill overlooking the Santee River,
the long circular driveway finally led to the three
story structure painted a sparkling white. Six
huge columns at the front rose majestically to
support a second floor balcony then continued
upward where a final balcony rested atop the
curved spirals. It was from the second floor that
strains of music drifted down to the new arrivals,
and when they approached the carved doors they
swung open immediately revealing a dignified
black man resplendent in black and red livery.

Amanda thought the inside of the house even
more magnificent than the outside, if that were
possible, with its crystal chandeliers, rich
brocades and satins and priceless works of art

441

decorating the walls. The statuary looked to be originals and Tony commented dryly that the duke's fortune must be considerable to be able to present such a lavish display. It surely had taken one whole ship just to transport all the furnishings from England to America. Melissa was too awed to even comment as her wide blue eyes soaked up every detail.

The small group proceeded up the grand staircase to the ballroom which occupied nearly the entire second floor and were announced by a majordomo dressed in the same gaudy livery as the butler. Immediately a balding, rotund man somewhere in his sixties broke away from a group of guests milling about and made his way to the newcomers.

"Sir Tony," the Duke beamed, "I am happy to meet you at last. And this must be your wife," he said, turning faded blue eyes on Amanda. "I envy you, Sir Tony, she is a beauty."

Murmuring a polite response, Amanda studied the Duke while Tony introduced him to the Morrisons, then said, "In America I am just plain Tony. I have given up my title for a new way of life."

"I doubt I will go so far," laughed the Duke, "but if I must call you Tony then certainly you must also use my first name."

"Thank you, Sir Henry," Tony smiled, taking an immediate liking to the friendly man. For Amanda's sake Tony hoped the Duchess would prove equally agreeable.

After engaging the Morrisons in conversation for a few minutes, the Duke said, "I hope in time I will come to look upon America as my home just as you have."

"It surprises me that you are here at all," said Tony candidly. "There is nothing here to compare to England. You must have an extraordinary wife to give up the rich social life she enjoys in England for the relative seclusion of country life."

"My wife is indeed an extraordinary woman, Tony," Sir Henry beamed fondly, his pride evident. "But she was born in South Carolina and was unhappy in England. I promised her if she married me I would build a grand mansion for her close to her old home which she was forced to sell. You see, this is my second marriage. My first wife died several years ago and I was lucky enough to find a woman whose beauty and virtue have captured my heart."

A shudder passed through Tony. It was almost as if someone had walked on his grave. He glanced at Amanda and saw that she was frowning in consternation, her body tense. Instinctively he grasped her hand and found it chilled, but not as icy as the hard knot forming in the middle of his chest.

The Duke appeared unconcerned as he warmed to the subject of his Duchess. "I am lucky to have so young and beautiful a wife. She is nearly the same age as my youngest daughter, Alice, who accompanied us to America. She has just recently been widowed. But listen to me," he chuckled, "talking as if you have never met my wife. I'm sure you know her well, Tony. Her name is. . ."

"Letty," whispered Tony dramatically. "Letty Carter." The name was bitter on his tongue.

"Yes," beamed Sir Henry. "I was sure you remembered her for she spoke many times of you."

"I'm sure she did," muttered Tony darkly. Amanda was so shocked she could do nothing more than cling to Tony's hand to keep from drowning in the tide of emotions threatening to engulf her.

Suddenly Letty was beside them, her smile vicious as she raked over Amanda's elegantly clad form. "Ah, there you are, my dear," greeted the Duke expansively. "I was just telling Tony why I chose to settle in South Carolina. I think he is somewhat shocked to find that I had made you my Duchess."

Letty's laughter was not a pleasant sound. "Did you think I had left for good, Tony?" she asked coyly. Letty's loud voice began to draw the unwanted attention of other guests and Amanda felt herself slide into a maelstrom of hate and suspense bubbling around her, stirred by Letty's malice.

At that moment Tony wished himself anyplace but in the Duke's home.

"Where you are concerned I never know what to expect," Tony replied evenly. For the old Duke's sake he fought to contain the rage threatening to burst forth.

Her voice raised so that nearly everyone in the room could hear, Letty loudly proclaimed, "I see you finally made your convict housekeeper your wife. But please be careful, Tony dear," she said sweetly. "Once a thief always a thief."

"My dear!" Sir Henry exclaimed, shocked by his wife's damaging words. "Where are your manners? Tony and his wife are our guests. They didn't come here to be insulted." His pleading eyes begged Tony's forgiveness for Letty's unpardonable breach of etiquette.

Letty pouted prettily as she continued to glare at Amanda. "But, Henry," she cajoled, her tone suggesting no wrong doing on her part. "It is common knowledge that Amanda is an indentured servant sent to America to work out her sentence. And of course everyone must know that she was once held captive by Indians. Why, there's not a person present who isn't aware of what Indians do to women captives. I think it is wonderful of Tony to burden himself with used goods."

"My God, Letty! You go too far!" Sir Henry exploded. "Apologize to Amanda immediately."

By now everyone in the room was deathly quiet as they listened to Letty's malicious gossip, which none of them had heard before. The low murmur of incredulous voices and insolent stares directed at Amanda nearly broke Tony's heart as he put a protective arm about her quaking shoulders.

"Oh, I'm sorry, Amanda," said Letty innocently. "I had no idea you wished to keep your past a secret. I assure you I will be most discreet in the future." Then she whirled in a froth of scarlet silk before Sir Henry had time to catch his breath.

"My dear Amanda," he said in a pained voice. "Please forgive my wife. Believe me, had I known I would have spoken to her beforehand. I had no knowledge of this."

Amanda's jaw went slack with horror. Never in her life had she been so humiliated. With a tiny, terrified sob, she dashed past Tony and out of the room. Tony was hard on her heels, stopping her headlong flight down the long flight of stairs with the touch of his hand.

"Don't run away, Amanda," he pleaded,

urging her back into the ballroom with gentle force. "It's not like you turn tail and run. Where is the spirit that led you through all adversity in the past?"

"I want to go home, Tony. I don't belong here." Amanda's bleak green eyes were nearly his undoing, but at the last moment his rage at Letty won out.

"No!" came Tony's forceful reply. "I'll not have you sneaking out of here like a whipped puppy. You are just as good as anyone here and I won't have you degraded in such a manner."

"Just look around you, Tony," insisted Amanda, unshed tears spiking her long lashes. "Everyone is looking at me as if I'm filth. I don't want to be an embarrassment to you."

"Do I look like I'm embarrassed, my love? I love you. You are my wife. Don't allow Letty to have her way. Stay and show her you're not afraid of her."

"Don't ask it of me, please," Amanda begged.

"I'll protect you, my love."

Just then Francis and Nathan appeared beside them, their faces grave. "We heard, Tony," Nathan said. "Letty is a predator, and like all predators feeds off the weak. I could kill the bitch!"

"Not if I get to her first," Francis interjected. "Are you all right, Amanda?"

"Amanda is fine," Tony insisted before she could answer for herself. "I'm trying to persuade her not to leave."

"Of course Amanda won't leave," Francis retorted. "She promised me a dance."

"And me," echoed Nathan.

Against her better judgment Amanda allowed herself to be led off to the dance floor by Francis while Tony and Nathan looked on. They saw little of Letty the remainder of the evening but Sir Henry couldn't have been more gracious, attempting to undo the wrong done by his wife. As for Sir Henry's other guests, for the most part they acted as if Amanda did not exist, taking their lead, no doubt, from the Duchess who made her feelings known from the beginning. It was obvious Charles Town's illustrious citizens considered Amanda beneath their notice.

Amanda had just finished dancing with Tony when Sir Henry claimed her for a dance. Finding himself at loose ends, Tony wandered over to the refreshment table, helped himself to a generous splash of the Duke's excellent brandy then stepped out on the balcony for a breath of fresh air. He knew Amanda wished to leave and he decided they would depart after her dance with Sir Henry, putting her agony at an end. He was proud of the way she had deported herself in the face of Letty's malicious and unprovoked attack. Tony wished he would have killed the bitch when he had the chance. Her death would be no great loss, he thought bitterly.

As if his thoughts had conjured up her image, Letty appeared at his side. "Why did you marry her, Tony?" she asked scornfully. "What did you do with her black bastard? Don't tell me you allowed her to keep it?"

Tony smiled gleefully. "If you saw my daughter Laura, you would know immediately she is no spawn of Buck's."

Letty stared uncomprehendingly at Tony. What could have gone wrong? she asked herself as her memory flew back to those months when Amanda was forced to become Buck's plaything.

Aloud, she asked, "Are you telling me that Amanda did not bear Buck's child?"

"Exactly," Tony gloated. "She was carrying my child when you took her." He paused to allow his words time to sink in before continuing. "It was all a hoax, Letty. A hoax in which you were allowed to believe what you wanted. Buck never touched Amanda."

"But I saw . . ."

"What you saw was some damn good play-acting."

Letty's face turned red then pure white. Play-acting! How could she have been duped by an ignorant slave? she silently fumed. It appeared that her vengeance had been foiled each step of the way. Was there no justice? Suddenly an evil thought came to her and she grinned.

Tony saw her mouth twist in a travasty of a grin and an involuntary shudder passed through him. "Why did you come back, Letty? Couldn't you be satisfied to remain in England and play the Duchess?"

"I had unfinished business in South Carolina, Tony."

"If your business concerns Amanda, forget it. I'll kill you before I let you hurt her again."

Letty laughed softly, the sound chilling Tony to the bone. The woman was mad, he decided as he instinctively moved to put space between them. "You are forgetting something, Tony," she informed him spitefully. "I have Amanda's Articles of Indenture and I may just decide to claim my property."

Red dots of rage exploded in Tony's brain as he grasped Letty's bare shoulders, bruising her white skin.

"You have no right to those papers! They were never rightfully yours in the first place. You stole them!"

"I have a bill of sale in my possession that says otherwise."

"You bitch! I'll expose you for what you are, Duchess or no."

"My husband is a powerful man, Tony, and he fairly dotes on me. The authorities were on my side before and I doubt if anything has changed. Reclaiming my property should pose no problem with a Duke to back me up."

"I have never known a more despicable woman, Letty, and I'll never allow you to take Amanda away from me. I'll fight you every step of the way."

"I want to be reasonable about this, Tony," Letty confided, confounding Tony with her sudden about face. "I suggest we meet somewhere and talk about it."

"Letty, I don't. . ."

"The way I see it you have no choice," Letty interrupted, forestalling his refusal. "My husband built a small hunting lodge a mile or so in the woods behind the house. It's quite secluded this time of the year and no one will bother us. Meet me there tomorrow at two o'clock."

"Are you crazy?" panicked Tony. "I'm a married man! What are you thinking of?"

"Meet me tomorrow and I'll tell you," she promised coyly. Before Tony could form an appropriate reply Letty turned on her heel and was gone.

A few minutes later Tony followed her inside, his heart pounding painfully in his breast. No matter what the cost he could not allow Letty to hurt Amanda again, he vowed, shaking his head in disbelief at the swiftness in which the promise of a good time had gone sour. He and Amanda had started out in the best of moods, fully intending to enjoy Sir Henry's gala affair tonight. And then Letty had come into their lives once more spreading her venom like a loathsome disease. There was nothing he wouldn't do to protect the woman he loved and he had already decided he would meet Letty the next day and attempt to foil whatever devious plans she had for Amanda. Spying the object of his affections across the room talking with the Morrisons he unerringly made his way to her side.

"Shall we leave, my love?" he asked, noticing for the first time the lines of pain and embarrassment etched across her smooth brow. "I think we've had enough of these narrow-minded hypocrites."

"Oh, yes, Tony, please. I don't think I could stand another tilted nose or insolent stare," Amanda replied, vastly relieved.

Just then Francis appeared with Sir Henry's daughter, Alice, on his arm. A dark-haired beauty with winning ways, Amanda liked her immediately. Apparently so did Francis, who seemed unable to take his eyes off the slender young woman with soft brown eyes.

Alice appeared unconcerned about the malicious gossip Letty so heartlessly spread and begged them to stay, but Tony was adamant. Amanda had had enough for one night.

After it was arranged that the Morrisons should stay for the late supper and ride home with Francis and Nathan, Tony and Amanda left the Duke's palatial home with little fanfare and no regrets.

Tony was so quiet and subdued during the ride home that Amanda was loathe to interrupt his reverie. She feared that he might be having second thoughts about their marriage now that her sordid past was common knowledge, thanks to Letty. Amanda realized that she had suddenly become an encumbrance to Tony and wished there was some way she could make amends. Knowing Tony and his fierce pride Amanda cringed when she recalled how Letty had shamed him before his peers.

Tony's strange distraction continued even as he climbed into bed, absently gathering Amanda into his arms and settling down without attempting to make love to her. "Tony, is. . . is something wrong?" Amanda hesitated.

"What could be wrong, my love?" Tony asked absently.

"I don't know. You seem so distant. I'm sorry if I am an embarrassment to you but. . ."

"My God, Amanda! Is that what you think?" Amanda nodded solemnly. "You could never become an embarrassment to me. I love you. You and our children are all that I live for."

Though he tried to convince her otherwise, Amanda knew Tony was lying. She had known him long enough to realize something was bothering him. It hurt to think he did not love her enough to tell her what it was. When he made no attempt to make love to her, all Amanda's old fears and insecurities chewed at her remorselessly.

Would she never be rid of Letty and the poison she spread in her wake? she wondered dismally. Duchess or no, the evil woman didn't deserve to live."

Amanda was aware when Tony left the house

the next day and was hurt when he did not bother to let her know where he was going or when he would be back. It took a great amount of restraint on her part to hold her tongue, but in the end she merely watched him ride away, her green eyes troubled.

Tony approached the hunting lodge warily. He saw that it was a small building rudely constructed of logs with a wide porch across the front. Nearby, a horse hitched to a tree limb grazed peacefully. He dismounted, tethered his own horse and had one foot planted on the stairs when the door swung open with a resounding bang.

"You're late," Letty said sharply. Had Tony cared to notice he would have seen that Letty was becomingly dressed in a black velvet riding habit that presented a vivid contrast to her pale loveliness. But Letty's appearance was the last thing Tony had on his mind.

The moment he was inside Letty slammed the door, turning to confront him, hands on hips.

"I'm here, Letty," Tony hurled sarcastically. "What more do you want? I'm willing to discuss your terms of relinquishing Amanda's indenture papers."

"My terms are simple, darling," Letty smiled boldly. "I want you. If you agree to meet me here in this lodge, to make love to me on my terms, whenever I wish, I promise to destroy Amanda's papers at the end of one year."

Letty had never forgotten Tony, not the way he made her feel or the magic of his lovemaking. Though she had good reason to despise him, she craved him still. Every fiber of her being cried out for the touch of his hands and lips upon her body.

There was a place inside her that no one but Tony could reach. Heaven knows she had tried to satisfy that itch with any number of men in England but no one could do for her what Tony did.

Tony gasped, astonishment following disbelief across his face. "You're insane! What makes you think I would make love to you? I could not affect a passion I do not feel."

"I have every faith in you, darling," she smiled brazenly.

"You have a husband, Letty," reminded Tony. "Isn't one man enough for you?"

"That fat toad? Bah! He has never been man enough to please me with his inept fumbling and limp tool. But you, Tony, are magnificent, every inch of you."

"How much do you want, Letty? I'll pay whatever is necessary to free my wife."

"Money? I could buy and sell you many times over."

"I'll go to your husband with my tale. He strikes me as a reasonable man."

"Except where I am concerned," gloated Letty. "Henry would do anything for me. I have him completely beguiled. Who do you think he would believe? Especially after I have the authorities to back up my story." Believe it or not, I still hold strong feelings for you, darling."

"I find that hard to believe, Letty. You tried to have me killed once. If you were truthful you'd admit that revenge is a far more powerful emotion in your heart than love."

Letty shrugged negligently. "Perhaps. . ."

Regretfully, Tony realized that Letty was calling the shots, that he had nothing with much to fight her. Even confronting Sir Henry offered little hope as long as Letty held Amanda's papers and refused to part with them. A shudder went through his body. Making love to Letty was the last thing on earth he felt like doing. Since long before his marriage to Amanda he had desired no other woman, nor would he ever.

Letty savored her triumph as she watched the play of emotion across Tony's face settle into grim determination. "You win, Letty," he ground out from between clenched teeth, "but I'm afraid my performance will be less than adequate."

"For both our sakes I hope not, darling," she warned as she hastily began discarding her clothing. When her garments lay in a pile at her feet she worked furiously at Tony's until they both were nude, facing one another in the center of the room.

Feeling nothing but revulsion, Tony took her in his arms, pressing her close, hating what she was forcing him to do. Given Tony's frame of mind, his attempts at ardor were useless. There was little or no response in his body ordinarily finely tuned to every nuance of sex. Letty appeared undaunted by Tony's lack of interest as she slid to her knees, using her hands and tongue to excite and arouse. The tip of her moist tongue flicked across his ribs for an instant before sliding in a sweeping arc along his taut stomach, finally settling greedily upon the object of her desire.

"You bitch!" Tony groaned, feeling his body jump to her mouthed commands, her lips opening, encircling him, tonguing him eagerly. Against his will Tony felt himself ready to burst as he wound his hands in Letty's hair, jerking her roughly to her feet.

"The bedroom, where is it?" he asked tersely.

Letty pointed to a closed door and Tony flung her over his shoulder, swung open the door and threw her on the bed so hard she bounced.

Without allowing her a moment to catch her breath, Tony drove into her immediately, finding her receptive and eager as her legs clenched tightly about his waist, her scream of pain soon turning to cries of ecstasy.

She insisted Tony repeat his performance once more before she allowed him to leave, extracting his promise to meet her again the next day at the same time when Sir Henry usually took a nap.

Tony returned to River's Edge in a foul mood. So great was his guilt he could barely face Amanda, and when it was time to retire he sent his hurt and puzzled wife to bed alone while he remained in his study with a bottle of brandy and a conscience that allowed him little respite.

He was gone from the house before Amanda arose the next morning. Gone to the fields, Linus told her. Though he had returned for lunch he disappeared again at mid-afternoon without a word, returning well after five o'clock. The pattern continued for several days. And in all that time Tony did not once attempt to make love to Amanda.

To Amanda's fertile imagination, Tony's strange behavior suggested only one thing: Tony had taken a mistress. But who? There was no plantation close enough for him to carry on an intense affair except for Tidewater and Hillcrest, Sir Henry's new manor. She knew Francis was courting Alice, Sir Henry's lovely daughter, so who did that leave except. . . Letty.

Had Letty finally succeeded in poisoning

Tony's mind against her? Amanda wondered dismally. Surely Tony didn't want the woman after she tried to kill him, did he? Tony's erratic behavior began the night of the party when Letty had shamed her before dozens of prominent people. It was obvious to Amanda that Tony was sorry he had married her and that he felt she was besmirching his good name.

Determined to learn the truth for herself Amanda finally confronted Tony in his study late one night after she had waited hours for him to come to bed. She slipped quietly into the room, the diffused ligh rendering her nightgown nearly transparent as it floated about her slender form. She was shocked to find her husband slumped over his desk, a half-empty bottle of brandy at his fingertips.

"Tony," she murmured in a low voice, the sound of his name jerking him upright. Seeing Amanda standing before him looking so innocent caused him to frown and speak more harshly than he had intended.

"What are you doing here, Amanda? It's late, go to bed."

"I miss you, darling," Amanda teased, hoping to lighten his mood. "Come with me. It's been weeks since. . . since we've been together."

"Only two weeks," Tony mocked ungallantly. "I never realized I've been remiss in my duties as a husband." God how I love her! Tony thought, watching her hurt change to anger. Anger he could handle, hurt he could not. He wanted her so badly it became a pain eating into his vitals, but he fought his desire for her, unwilling to defile her while Letty was still making demands upon him.

"What has happened to you, Tony? Why have

you changed?" Amanda demanded to know. "Is it something I've done? Do you no longer love me? Talk to me, Tony! For God's sake, tell me what's wrong!"

"What foolishness is this, Amanda?" Tony growled. "You are my wife but I owe you no explanations." What else could he say? Could he tell his beloved that he was bedding another woman? That he was doing so in order to keep his wife safe? Would it hurt any less to tell the truth? No, Tony decided sadly, Amanda was better off not knowing the truth.

"I thought you loved me," she challenged, her temper flaring.

"I do."

"You have a funny way of showing it. You haven't made love to me in two weeks."

"My God, if that's what you want I'll make love to you here and now. Take off your night-gown!"

"Tony, I didn't mean. . ."

"You heard me, take it off!" Suddenly, all the rage, all the frustration, all the pressure riding him for the past two weeks, combined with the liquor he had been consuming, brought his barely restrained passion to a peak as he ripped the wispy garment from Amanda's supple form.

At first Amanda was terrified, and then she became angrier than she had ever been in her life. From his words and actions it was obvious that Tony no longer loved her and her pride would not allow her to submit meekly to his outrageous demands. "Why are you doing this to me, Tony?" she spat angrily.

"I'm going to make love to my wife. Isn't that what you wanted?"

"Yes, but not like this. Not to be used as a vessel for your lust."

"You talk too much," Tony rasped, peeling off his own restrictive clothing. It was too late to stop now. Desire swept through him like a raging tide until even Letty ceased to exist in his mind.

"Tony, no!" Amanda wailed as Tony scooped her up and carried her effortlessly out of the office and up the stairs to their room where he fell with her upon the bed that she had lain in alone these past weeks.

"Oh, God, Amanda," Tony moaned. "I don't want it to be like this between us. If I could only tell you. . ."

What Tony meant to tell her was quickly forgotten as he captured her lips, forcing them apart as his tongue shot forward to savage the warm moist recesses of her mouth. "Amanda, Amanda," he rasped hoarsely, "I need you so."

His kisses were liquid fire, blazing a fiery trail along a smooth jaw, the swan-like column of her neck, coming to rest at that taut crest of one breast where his tongue teased and taunted relentlessly. Lavishing loving care from one pink nipple to the other, Tony's strong fingers found the small pleasure peak nestled amidst the downy forest at the base of her stomach and gently massaged, moving in a circular motion until tiny buds of sensation flooded Amanda's loins, spreading upward to where Tony's mouth and lips were bringing her untold ecstasy.

"You're mine, Amanda," he murmured against her mouth as he once again drank deeply of her nectar. "No one will take you from me, no one!"

His words were as fierce as his ardor and

Amanda felt herself responding with an answering passion as his manhood took her, bringing her from darkness to gasping ecstasy in a matter of seconds. Plunging, withdrawing, plunging again, her legs now draped about his shoulders. The tension building, each tactile sensation an agony of pain and pleasure until her body sang a tune of indescribably joy, and broke apart.

Tony was gone when Amanda awoke the next morning and she knew that nothing had changed despite their shared passion of the night before. Deep in the private compartment of her heart she realized something was terribly wrong. But as long as Tony chose not to confide in her she was powerless to correct it or to ease his troubled mind. So many unanswered questions flirted within her aching brain that Amanda felt miserable. Last night's encounter with Tony demonstrated more than words that he still wanted her even though he might not love her. No matter how long and hard Amanda debated within herself, the only plausible answer to Tony's strange behavior and harsh treatment spelled. . . Letty.

22

When Tony awoke with Amanda curled so trustingly in his arms he was sick with disgust. His drinking was becoming a problem, his behavior toward the woman he loved, harsh and inexcusable. His self-loathing was turning him against all he held dear. It couldn't go on, Tony determined. One way or another, Letty had to be stopped.

After a morning of soul-searching Amanda came to a decision. She had to know where she stood in Tony's affections, had to discover for herself if another woman was the recipient of his love. Determination lent her courage as she waited until Tony left on the mysterious errand that took him from the house nearly every day. The moment he mounted and rode out of sight, Amanda saddled her own horse and followed at a respectable distance, keeping to the woods as much as possible. Caught up in his own misery, Tony did not bother to glance over his shoulder, thus allowing Amanda to keep easy tabs on him.

Amanda hesitated when Tony turned from the road into the woods, but not for long when the realization came upon her that they were very close to Hillcrest manor. By the time Amanda stumbled upon the hunting lodge, Tony had already tethered his horse and disappeared inside. Leaving her own mount some distance away should his soft whicker alert the occupants, she crept close until she was able to peer through the window of the log cabin.

An excruciating pain as swift and deadly as a knife thrust into her heart sent Amanda reeling with shock. As if her eyes refused to believe the message from her brain, she could only stand in frozen horror and stare at her husband making love to a woman they both had good reason to hate.

Nude, sprawled on her back, legs flung wide, eyes glazed with lust, Letty writhed beneath Tony's naked loins, his buttocks pumping furiously. Watching his face, Amanda saw not love, not even lust, but some greater emotion that she could not even begin to understand. Unfortunately, her distraught state did not allow for analyzing. She did not wait for the dramatic climax but flung herself away from the window, an agonized sob caught in her throat. Somehow Amanda reached home, not remembering of her headlong flight through the woods or of the tears blinding her sight. Inside she was dead.

When Tess knocked on her bedroom door two hours later saying that Francis wished to see her, Amanda was still in a state of shock and nearly refused to see him. But in the end she roused herself from her stupor and descended the long staircase somewhat in a trance. Francis realized the moment he looked into her stricken green eyes that something was wrong.

"Amanda," he asked anxiously, taking her hand and finding it chilled, "I came to invite you to a wedding and find a pale wraith of a woman. What is wrong, my dear? And where is Tony when you obviously need him?"

At the first mention of Tony's name Amanda broke into a storm of fresh tears. "I. . . I'm sorry, Francis," she stammered wretchedly. "Pl. . . please tell me about your. . . your wedding. Alice is the lucky girl, I hope."

"Indeed she is," beamed Francis proudly. "Her father has given his blessing and we plan to marry soon. But not another word until you tell me what has upset you. Is it Tony? Surely it can't be all that serious."

"Tony has taken a mistress," Amanda confided in a haunted voice.

Francis wanted to laugh at such a preposterous assumption but at the sight of Amanda's woebegone expression prudence prevailed. "That's ridiculous, Amanda. I've never seen a man so in love with a woman as Tony is with you."

"I saw him, Francis. Not two hours ago. There is a cabin in the woods behind Hillcrest. He's been meeting her there since the night of Sir Henry's party."

"Meeting who, Amanda? For God's sake, none of this makes sense."

"Letty, that's who. Tony and Letty have been trysting at that cabin nearly every day for weeks. I know what I saw, Francis."

Astonishment glazed Francis' features. "You saw them?"

Amanda nodded bleakly. "I followed Tony when he left the house a few hours ago."

"But Tony hates Letty," Francis insisted. "She tried to have him killed. Why should he. . . he. . . I am so confused."

"No more than I am," Amanda admitted despairingly. "I can't go on like this, Francis. I feel I must take the children and leave."

"No Amanda, not yet. Let me get to the bottom of this before you do anything so drastic. Is it all right if I talk to Nathan about this? Perhaps together we can learn the truth."

Amanda nodded. She needed her friends now more than ever before. "Please don't take too long. I feel my life is in a shambles. And Francis, I am happy about your wedding plans. I really do like Alice. She is perfect for you."

Before Tony left the hunting lodge that afternoon he came to a decision that could destroy his life as he knew it. It was brought about by his inability to continue with the lies and deception he had lived with these past weeks. He missed the closeness he had with Amanda dreadfully and this vile degradation he was living with was ruining his marriage and his life. He had come to the inevitable conclusion that the only way Amanda could ever be truly free was with Letty's death.

It was much later than usual when Letty finally released Tony from her lustful embrace, nearly dusk. He was so consumed by his own dark thoughts that he did not notice the two men concealed in the woods. After Tony passed, they did not reveal themselves but waited for the other occupant of the cabin to emerge. Only when Letty rode toward Hillcrest did they materalize from their concealment.

"Even after seeing Tony and Letty together with my own eyes I don't believe it," Nathan ground out, his warm brown eyes kindling into flame. "What in the hell is the matter with him?"

"So help me I will kill that bloody bitch, Nathan," Francis vowed.

"Don't be surprised if I beat you to it, Francis," Nathan returned.

Pleading a headache Amanda contrived to keep to her room that night and the next morning, avoiding Tony as if he were poison. She watched from her window as he rode out that afternoon, unaware of the drama about to unfold in which all the people she held dear would become involved.

Francis reached the hunting lodge well before Tony made his appearance, or so he assumed. He knew Letty had already arrived for her horse stood nearby, calmly cropping grass. His spine stiffened with resolve, he rapped once on the door and walked in without waiting for a reply. He remained inside roughly ten minutes before rushing back through the open door and riding away as if the devil himself was on his tail.

Nathan was thankful Francis hadn't seen him when he sped by his hiding place. He had recognized his friend's horse and decided to remain concealed until Francis departed. He meant to face Letty alone and finish the deed that should have been resolved long ago. He had no idea what Francis and Letty were talking about but he did know that his friend possessed too gentle a nature to do more than confront the witch. And a witch she must be to beguile Tony to such a degree.

The door was open when Nathan reached it

and he walked boldly inside, heading straight for the bedroom when Letty was nowhere in sight. A short time later he departed as quietly as he had arrived, beating a hasty retreat toward Tidewater.

Tony approached the hunting lodge with a feeling of dread, as if his mind was detached from his body. He felt no remorse at what he was about to do, only a perverse elation. Whatever qualms he had about killing in cold-blood had been resolved long ago, buried beneath layers of hate and disgust slowly building within him until the very thought of Letty's death brought him only pleasure.

Vaguely, Tony noted the fact that the door was standing open, but his mind was too consumed with murder to question it, or the fact that Letty was nowhere in view. Idly he wondered what kind of fun and games she had planned to wile away the long afternoon and smiled at the thought of never having to touch her loathsome flesh again.

"Letty," he called softly as he proceeded through the bedroom door which also was flung wide. Nothing but silence greeted his ears even though he clearly saw her form stretched out on the bed, arms akimbo, legs opened obscenely. Her head was turned away from him and she appeared to be sleeping, but Tony knew better. Always eager for sex, Letty would not allow herself to fall asleep until after she had been thoroughly sated.

With the stealth a cat would envy, Tony crept toward the bed, wondering if he could actually go through with his plan. Twice before he had tried to kill Letty but at the last minute his damned conscience prevented it. Looming above the sleeping woman he put a hand on her shoulder, finding her flesh slightly chilled to his touch despite the warm, humid day. It was at that precise moment that Tony realized Letty no longer posed a threat to anyone.

At first Tony was stunned, wondering who could want Letty dead as badly as he did. Amanda was the only other person to benefit from her death and as far as he knew Amanda had no idea what was going on. Turning her head to face him, Tony gagged at the sight of her grotesquely swollen features and protruding tongue. The purplish hue to her face and deep violet marks on her throat left little doubt in Tony's mind as to the cause of death. Letty had been strangled.

Backing from the room, Tony poised on the threshold of indecision. Should he notify Sir Henry? If he did so how would he explain his presence at the hunting lodge to Letty's husband? To his own wife, for that matter? In the end Tony left the scene of the crime just as he had found it. After all, hadn't he planned on killing Letty himself and leaving her body to be found by hunters? But for some reason his mind was vague on that score. Somehow or other his plans never progressed past the actual killing.

On the way home Tony was consumed with confusing thoughts. Who could have killed Letty? The longer he pondered the more puzzled he became. In the final analysis only one answer was forthcoming. Somehow either Nathan or Francis had found out about him and Letty and had saved him the trouble of killing her himself. Nathan was the more logical choice, for Tony knew Nathan still loved Amanda and would stop at nothing to keep her from being hurt.

Remorse rode Tony relentlessly. Though he

had been perfectly willing and even content to kill Letty himself, driving one of his friends to murder was despicable of him, causing im far more guilt than if he had done the deed himself. Driven by self-reproach Tony's only thought at the moment was to lock himself in his study and get roaring drunk.

Amanda heard Tony enter his study and slam the door; choosing not to bother or question him lest she set off a repeat of their encounter the night before. When he did not appear for supper she went to bed, but in her heart she knew their marriage was at an end. If Francis did not discover the cause of Tony's sudden infatuation with Letty soon, Amanda feared she would be forced to leave, for she could not stand to live this way.

Following a sleepless night fraught with nightmares in which Tony sported shamelessly with Letty, Amanda approached the study door, hoping that Tony had finally emerged. But she was disappointed to find the door still firmly closed, and locked, she discovered when she tried the knob. Deciding to take matters into her own hands, she called out, "Tony, aren't you ever coming out of there?"

"Go away, Amanda," Tony muttered groggily. He had been drinking heavily all night in an abortive effort to drown his feelings of guilt over what he had done to Amanda and what he had done to his friends to cause them to commit an act he should have performed himself. Given his frame of mind Tony knew he wasn't ready to reappear, confess to Amanda or confront anyone as yet.

While Amanda was planted outside Tony's study pleading with him to come out a message arrived from Hillcrest which Linus put in her hand; shaking his woolly head sadly at the sight of the closed door and Amanda's troubled face. Tearing open the envelope Amanda read the brief message from Sir Henry, and leaned against the wall for support.

"Tony," she called weakly through the closed door, her face drained of all color. "A message just arrived from Sir Henry. It's . . . it's about Letty."

Within minutes the door flung wide and Tony appeared, blurry-eyed, disheveled, and sporting a blue-black stubble on his chin. With shaking fingers he grasped the sheet of paper Amanda held, scanned the abbreviated message and began laughing, his mirth in face of the tragedy terrifying Amanda.

"My God, Tony, how can you laugh? Letty's is dead. Thrown by her horse, and killed in a tragic accident. What kind of a man are you?"

Abruptly his laughter ceased and he turned serious. "I don't wish to discuss this now, Amanda, we'll talk later." Before Amanda could protest he whirled on his heel, retraced his steps back to his study and slammed the door rudely in her face.

Alone, Tony sank into a chair, reading Sir Henry's words again and again before they made any sense. Why would Sir Henry wish to conceal Letty's murder? he wondered, his mind spinning with confusion. Suddenly everything became clear as comprehension dawned. Sir Henry was a Duke and couldn't afford to have his name dragged through the mud if he let out that his recent bride had been murdered by a lover in their trysting place. In fact, a man with the Duke's standing in society would do all in his considerable power to keep all knowledge of Letty's sordid affair from public knowledge.

Thinking back on how he left her, Tony assumed that Sir Henry had gone looking for his wife when she failed to return home that afternoon. He knew how the man doted on his young bride and the only sorrow he felt was for the aging Duke. According to Sir Henry's message the private funeral was to be the next morning, which Tony planned to shun.

About the same time Sir Henry's message was delivered to River's Edge, a similar missive was dispatched to Tidewater. Francis showed no emotion when he read Sir Henry's words, nor did Nathan when Francis showed him the note.

"It's no more than she deserved," observed Nathan, shrugging carelessly as he eyed Francis through slitted lids. "Only we both know Letty didn't die in an accident, don't we, my friend?"

Francis stared at Nathan for so long Nathan began to shift uncomfortably beneath his scrutiny. "I never would have mentioned it if you hadn't brought it up," he finally said. "I don't hold it against you, Nathan. God knows I would have done it myself if you hadn't."

Pure astonishment galloped across Nathan's mobile features and his mouth gaped open. "I didn't kill Letty, Francis. I thought you did. I watched you leave the hunting lodge yesterday and when I went inside Letty was already dead."

"Me?" Francis managed to gasp out. "I thought you killed her. She was dead when I got there."

"If you didn't do it and I didn't do it, then who. . ."

"You don't suppose Amanda. . . ?"

"No! My God, Francis, don't even think it!" Nathan exclaimed, shocked.

"Then that leaves only Tony." Both men were silent a long time while they digested all they had just learned. Actually, it wasn't so far-fetched to think that Tony had killed Letty. What they failed to understand were Tony's reasons for making Letty his mistress in the first place. Sir Henry's deliberate omission, though, was perfectly clear. Above all else the Duke must preserve his reputation and conceal the fact that his wife had been unfaithful.

"Because of Alice I feel obliged to attend the funeral," Francis said thoughtfully.

"Thank God I don't," Nathan muttered, lifting his eyes heavenward.

"Nathan, we must go to Tony immediately," Francis suddenly decided. "I promised Amanda we would get to the bottom of Tony's strange behavior of late and I think Letty's death leaves too much unexplained. Amanda did nothing to deserve Tony's shabby treatment and for her sake we have to find out what happened to make Tony take up with Letty again. It's time Tony was made to face up to and acknowledge his errors." Nathan nodded agreement and they left immediately for River's Edge.

Amanda was with the children when Nathan and Francis arrived at River's Edge so was unaware that they had come to call. Linus showed them to Tony's study but shook his head in bewilderment when he pointed his finger at the closed and locked door. "Don't rightly know what's wrong, Massa Francis, but Massa Tony ain't been hisself lately. He done locked himself in that room and won't come out for nothing or nobody. Not even for Miz Amanda."

"Leave him to us, Linus," Francis said kindly. "Nathan and I can handle Tony." Linus shuffled away and Francis rapped crisply on the door. Silence. "Tony, I know you're in there," he called, "so you might as well let us in." More silence.

"We'll break the door down, Tony," Nathan warned, his voice stern. "I think it's time you faced up to your mistakes and tell us what's been going on with you and Letty."

Just when the two men thought they would be forced to carry out their threat, the door opened slowly and Tony, looking as if he hadn't slept for a week, stepped aside to allow them entry.

"My God, man, you look terrible!" Francis exclaimed. "What happened to you?"

"Nothing, Francis. Leave me alone. Can't you see that my guilt over this is more than I can bear? How did you find out about me and Letty?"

"This may come as a shock, old boy, but Amanda told me," Francis admitted sheepishly.

"Oh my God," Tony groaned, pain contorting his features. "I had no idea Amanda knew about this tawdry affair. How she must hate me! So many times I was on the verge of confiding in her but the hopelessness of the whole deplorable situation prevented my confession."

"Tony, both Francis and I fail to understand your actions. We thought you loved Amanda. How could you take up with Letty the moment she re-entered your life?" Nathan complained bitterly.

His voice, made hoarse from lack of sleep and too much alcohol, Tony began telling the two men about the conversation that had taken place between him and Letty the night of Sir Henry's party and what had occurred with regularlity at the hunting lodge, at Letty's insistence. It was a tale of blackmail, deception, hate and lust. A tale in which Amanda was caught in the middle and destined to lose the most should Tony fail to comply with Letty's demands. At the end of the evil story drawn painfully from Tony's parched throat, all three men were subdued, each possessing their own reasons for being glad Letty was dead, but none so great as Tony.

"The worst thing about this whole affair is that it involved innocent people and hurt Amanda," Tony imparted sadly. "I didn't mean for either of you to do what should have been my responsibility. And. . . and I don't care which one of you did it. I'm only sorry I didn't arrive first."

"What in the hell are you talking about, Tony?" demanded Nathan, thoroughly puzzled. "Neither Francis nor I killed Letty, although God knows we both set out to do it."

"We. . . we thought you did it, Tony," Francis said cautiously. "Are you telling us we were wrong?"

"I wish to God I did do it, Francis, but I didn't," confided Tony. "She was already dead when I arrived at the hunting lodge. I assumed one of you beat me to it." Then a thought so terrible entered his brain that it left him shaking. "Dear God, you don't suppose Amanda. . ."

"Amanda doesn't have it in her heart to commit murder, Tony," Nathan chided, refusing to believe the woman he loved capable of killing despite the fact that she had good cause.

"Well, if neither of you killed Letty, and I didn't, nor Amanda, who did?"

From the open doorway a voice intruded upon their privacy. "I did. I killed Letty."

The three occupants of the room swirled toward the door to face the interloper who had just confessed to murder. "Sir Henry!" Tony gasped, shocked. "How long have you been standing there?"

"Long enough," he shrugged eloquently.

Suddenly Sir Henry's words of moments before reached the inner recesses of Tony's brain. "You killed Letty? I don't understand."

"Letty was sadly mistaken if she thought I wasn't aware of her mysterious disappearances each afternoon. Where Letty was concerned I missed nothing. One day I followed her to the hunting lodge, ready to kill her lover. I was shocked when I learned you were the culprit, Tony. You don't know how close you came to losing your life."

"What stopped you?" Tony sked curiously.

"At first thoughts of Amanda and your two children stayed my hand. Then, as I crept closer I heard the two of you arguing and learned the whole ugly story."

"I'm sorry, Sir Henry, I never meant to hurt you."

"I don't blame you, Tony. Letty was evil. It was difficult for me to associate my wife with all those things she said to you and threatened you with, but in the end I was convinced of her malevolent instincts. She deserved to die, Tony, but I truly did not mean to kill her. I loved Letty, adored her, and she. . . she. . ."

Sir Henry was so close to collapse Francis jumped to help him to a chair. "Perhaps you'd better tell us what happened, Sir Henry," he urged, not unkindly.

Sir Henry nodded slowly, his eyes bleak with

despair. "Yesterday I followed Letty to the hunting lodge, thinking only to confront her with her evil ways and force her to cease her vile games. When I entered the cabin she was already naked and waiting for. . . for Tony." A sob tore through his throat and Tony quickly poured him a measure of brandy to bolster his courage.

"She. . . didn't even blink when I appeared, only laughed at me for playing the jealous husband. She called me a. . . fat toad who hadn't the vigor to please her with my. . . inept tool." The memory of Letty's cruel words brought so much anguish several minutes passed before he could continue. "I gave her everything! I left my beloved England for her. Built her a mansion worthy of a Queen. Nothing was too good for my beautiful young bride." Sir Henry paused, sucked in a deep draught of brandy, coughed, then looked pleadingly at Tony, his voice so low his words were barely audible.

"I didn't mean to kill her, just to stop her insane laughter. Her ridicule and derision drove me to the brink of madness and before I knew it Letty lay dead beneath my hands." He held his hands before his eyes, staring at them as if they belonged to another.

"I'm glad you're here, Francis," he said, as if aware of Francis and Nathan for the first time. "My Alice has chosen you for her husband and I am leaving Hillcrest to her as a dowry."

"I love Alice, she doesn't need a dowry," Francis said indignantly.

"Nevertheless, it's yours. I'm telling you this now because I plan on returning to England immediately after I see Alice properly wed. I want to die on my native soil. I. . . I only ask that you not tell Alice of her father's terrible deed."

"She'll never hear it from my lips," Francis pledged. Francis was shocked by Sir Henry's appearance. It seemed as if he had aged ten years before his eyes.

Sir Henry turned to Tony again, speaking specifically to him, "I'll understand if you wish to turn me in to the authorities, Tony. I'll even confess if. . . if you decide I should own up to the terrible crime I committed."

"No, Sir Henry," Tony argued, "I'll not send you to the gallows for a crime not one of us here wouldn't have committed had we gotten to Letty first. Lord knows I had plenty of reason to hate the woman. Right now my main concern is making things right with Amanda. I love her more than my life."

"Perhaps this will help," Sir Henry offered, placing two folded sheets of paper in Tony's hand. "I found these in Letty's things. From what I heard they belong to you."

Tony's face registered shock when he saw Amanda's indenture papers and the false bill of sale Letty had forged. "Thank you, Sir Henry," he said sincerely.

"I. . . hope I have been some help in reversing the terrible wrong Letty did you and your lovely wife."

Shortly afterwards Sir Henry left for Hillcrest accompanied by Francis who feared the old man might come to some harm if left to make his own way home in his distraught state. Besides, he had a sudden urge to see his sweet, uncomplicated Alice. Nathan left also, but not before imparting a few terse words of advice to Tony. "Tell Amanda the truth, Tony. She loves you and doesn't deserve the treatment she's been getting lately." Tony couldn't have agreed more.

Amanda sat quietly in the shadows of her room, her anguish too great to bear without the relief of tears. Her cheeks were damp with her sadness but she refused to break down completely. She thought of her two children sleeping peacefully in the nursery and how their father had neglected them in the past weeks. Of late his life was centered around Letty while all he once held dear was ignored. Judging from Tony's behavior since Letty's untimely death it was evident to Amanda that he cared deeply for the woman. He had been immersed in grief ever since he received word of Letty's demise.

Absently Amanda roamed about the room, falling victim to the restlessness that had been plaguing her since Tony's betrayal, touching all the objects she had come to love so well. She would hate to leave but she could never take second place in Tony's life. If his actions these past weeks were any indication, she doubted he would even miss her or their children.

Tony entered the room on silent feet, poising on the threshold as he watched Amanda's aimless fidgeting, feeling her pain and disillusionment as if it were his own. He had taken time to bathe, shave and change his clothes and his appearance was vastly improved from the way he looked a short time ago.

"Amanda, my love," he whispered so as not to frighten her.

Startled, Amanda whirled, surprised to see Tony looking so well-groomed in so short a time. "I'm sorry, Tony," she said, her thoughts still on Letty and Tony's feelings for her. "I... know how grieved you must be over Letty's death."

"Letty? Grieved?" Tony repeated stupidly. "I hated the woman. It's ludicrous to think I cared whether she lived or died."

"Tony!" Shock drained all color from her face. "I thought. . . that is. . . I assumed you loved Letty."

"Never! It's you I love."

"You have a strange way of showing it," she reminded him sharply.

Instead of launching into an explanation immediately Tony handed Amanda the sheaf of papers he held in his hand. "What are these?" she asked, annoyed.

"Read them."

Briefly she scanned the pages. "These are my indenture papers. Where did you get them?"

"Sir Henry brought them to me. He found them in Letty's possession and thought I should have them."

"I. . . I didn't think she still had them after all this time," Amanda mused.

"I knew she had them, my love," Tony said softly. "She has been using them against me ever since she returned to South Carolina."

Puzzled, Amanda asked "Used them against you? In what way?"

"Somewhere in her warped mind lurked the idea that she still wanted me, despite the fact that I wanted nothing more to do with her."

Slowly comprehension dawned as Amanda began to understand the workings of Letty's sick mind. "She. . . she forced you to. . . to. . ."

". . . Make love to her," supplied Tony bitterly.

"You didn't really love her?"

"Damn it, Amanda, haven't you heard a word

I've said? I hated her! I despised myself even more because of what I was doing to you."

"Why didn't you tell me?"

"Would it have hurt any less to know I was making love to Letty against my will? If I didn't do her bidding she would have used those papers to have you returned to her. I'd do anything to keep you safe. I couldn't bear to lose you."

"What would have happened if Letty hadn't been killed? Would you have gone on with this. . . this terrible deception forever?" Amanda asked reproachfully.

Tony had already decided to keep the real cause of Letty's death from Amanda. It would serve no useful purpose to tell her that Letty's death hadn't been an accident, that Sir Henry had snuffed out his wife's life before anyone else had a chance.

"I had already done some serious soul searching and decided to end my servitude to Letty. I would have found some. . . some way to free us from her evil grip."

"I know I shouldn't say this, Tony, but I'm glad she's dead."

"Can you forgive me, my love?" A nearly imperceptible clouding of Tony's features caused Amanda's heart to constrict painfully.

"Oh, Tony," she cried, flinging herself into his arms. "I was so afraid you no longer loved me. You had no way of knowing, but I saw you and Letty together in that cabin."

"I know, Francis told me. I would have done anything to spare you that. You have no idea how desperately I needed you during that time but deliberately kept myself aloof. I felt such shame that I lacked the nerve to face you, to come to you from Letty's arms and make love to you. I treated you harshly as a means to salve my own conscience but I have never stopped loving you. You and the children are my life. We can be happy again, my sweet, I promise. Nothing or no one will come between us ever again."

Moving with exaggerated slowness, he pulled her lissome body against the length of his. A tremulous smile answered his wildly beating heart. "I love you," Tony vowed, sealing his pledge with a kiss.

"I love you, Tony," Amanda said softly, molding her sweet body against his hard maleness. "Make love to me now."

And he did, ravenously, tenderly, savagely, throughout the long night and all the days to come.